The
SEEMINGLY
IMPOSSIBLE
LOVE LIFE *of*
AMANDA DEAN

The
SEEMINGLY
IMPOSSIBLE
LOVE LIFE *of*
AMANDA DEAN

ANN ROSE

Berkley Romance
New York

BERKLEY ROMANCE
Published by Berkley
An imprint of Penguin Random House LLC
penguinrandomhouse.com

Library of Congress Cataloging-in-Publication Data

Names: Rose, Ann (Ann M.), author.
Title: The seemingly impossible love life of Amanda Dean / Ann Rose.
Description: First edition. | New York: Berkley Romance, 2024.
Identifiers: LCCN 2024003013 (print) | LCCN 2024003014 (ebook) |
ISBN 9780593815953 (trade paperback) | ISBN 9780593815960 (ebook)
Subjects: LCGFT: Romance fiction. | Novels.
Classification: LCC PS3618.O782823 S44 2024 (print) |
LCC PS3618.O782823 (ebook) | DDC 813/.6—dc23/eng/20240220
LC record available at https://lccn.loc.gov/2024003013
LC ebook record available at https://lccn.loc.gov/2024003014

First Edition: September 2024

Printed in the United States of America
1st Printing

Book design by Daniel Brount

*For everyone who believes in the possibility of love
and all of love's possibilities*

The

SEEMINGLY
IMPOSSIBLE
LOVE LIFE *of*
AMANDA DEAN

CHAPTER ONE

April 2019

IT WAS TOTALLY NORMAL to be terrified the day of your own wedding, right?

Maybe *terrified* wasn't the right word. Mandy was nervous. Anxious.

Petrified.

Her stomach seemed to shimmy its way further and further into her chest as she sat alone in her private hotel suite, staring at the long gown hanging from the curtain rod. All Mandy had to do was slip into the first—and last—white dress she would ever wear. Well, that and do her makeup and get her hair done and about a million other things. But she hesitated. More specifically, she couldn't move even if she wanted to. Had she really been so lucky not only to find the love of her life, but also to be getting married?

This was a good thing. Something she'd always wanted.

And now, she was mere hours away from walking down an

aisle sprinkled with rose petals in various shades of pink—why couldn't she breathe?

No.

Today was going to be fine.

Better than fine.

She took a deep sip from the coffee mug death-gripped in her hand, the steam fogging her vision as she continued to stare at her dress. There wasn't anything particularly extraordinary about the garment hanging there. It was simple, understated—except for the small train. It was definitely not something Mandy was used to picking out. She had always been known for her affection for black—or shades of black—in all her clothing choices, but that day, as she stood on the little podium in front of the three-way mirrors and felt the buttery silk lining caressing her skin as she was zipped inside the cream-colored gown, she never wanted to take it off. Except now, putting it on seemed impossible.

Or maybe it was that *today* seemed impossible.

On the surface, it all seemed simple—small tasks she needed to complete to get to her moment of walking down that aisle—but there was nothing simple about getting married.

It wasn't that she thought she was making the wrong choice. No, that wasn't it at all. This was a day Mandy had dreamed about for years—even decades, if she thought hard enough about it. The lace dress hanging on its satin hanger. The pink and white peonies tied together with gold ribbon. The light blue Chuck Taylors with *I DO* written on the soles. They were all a part of this perfect vision she had for herself on this day, and they were all waiting for her.

Soon over two hundred people would be waiting for her too. But here—*now*—in this hotel room, it was Mandy alone with her thoughts. And this, being alone, stirred memories inside her belly like ice cubes in a blender, sending gooseflesh rippling all over her skin. She'd kill for a margarita right about now. The hotel minibar was looking quite tempting—even at fifty dollars a miniature bottle—not as small as the airplane ones, but also not full-size, completely overpriced, and a terrible choice this early in the day . . . even if it would dull the nerves raging inside her.

Mandy had been in love more times than she wanted to count. Her heart had been broken just as many. Would this wedding mark the last time she'd put her whole soul into someone? Or was this the inevitable beginning of the end, and she'd be left scooping up the shattered pieces of her heart yet again? Mandy both knew it was different this time and struggled with the sense of impending doom as if the other shoe—a black Chuck with *I DON'T* emblazoned on the bottom—was about to drop and crush all the dreams she'd been constructing for as long as she could remember.

These were *not* the kinds of thoughts someone should have on their wedding day, but they spun through her mind and stuck like melted marshmallow. A cobweb of white gooey uncertainty that she needed to clean away.

The Belgian waffle she special-ordered sat untouched in front of Mandy as she took another long drink of her coffee and watched the pulp in her orange juice drift to the bottom of her glass. Edmund hated fresh-squeezed orange juice, said juice should be sipped and never chewed, but Mandy loved to catch the little bulbs of fruit flesh between her teeth and bite down. Little explosions, like nature's Pop Rocks. But she couldn't bring herself to drink it today, or even take a bite. Instead, she alternated

between staring at her dress and staring at the uninspired artwork hanging on the wall. It was the basic bulk buy most hotels
did—some cheap reproduction they put in a gaudy frame in an
attempt to make it look expensive. Mandy could've painted
something better with her eyes closed.

Thankfully the bed was comfortable enough, and the coffee
was hot—unlike her shower. She tried to convince herself it
wasn't a sign of how things would go today. But the fact that she
had woken up late, and the icy water, and then room service
forgot the bacon with her order, well, things weren't off to a
great start. She sat in the hotel-issued bathrobe, towel wrapped
around her wet hair, trying to get warm—willing herself to believe all those things were not omens or harbingers of doom, and
that they, in fact, had nothing to do with each other. They were
all just flukes. One-offs. Not the universe's way of preparing her
for what was to come. She really should go down to the desk and
complain, but that would be one more thing to add to Mandy's
to-do list, and she couldn't move.

Why was there this great importance placed on weddings
anyway? One day in a relationship blown out of proportion compared to all the other days a couple proved their commitment
and love for each other. Why today and not last Tuesday? Not to
say that Mandy hadn't bought into the hype. Hell, she *was* the
hype. Teen Mandy could've looked at bridal magazines for hours.
Adult Mandy just had to have the ever-fashionable s'mores bar at
her reception complete with miniature chalkboard signs that
named each individual ingredient even though it was an addi-
tional charge. Add-on packages were Mandy's Achilles' heel.
They were literally made for her. She needed everything to be
perfect. But why? And for whom?

It was just a day, wasn't it?

Marriage was for a lifetime, right?

"The Imperial March" blasted from Mandy's cell, and she quickly swept it up. "Yes, I'm up, and I have food."

"Good," her mom said. "We don't want you passing out during your vows."

"That can't really happen, can it?" There was a reason Mom's ringtone was what it was. Mandy's mother was the queen of giving others just one more thing to worry about. If Mandy actually made it down the aisle without slipping on one of the rose petals, now there was a possibility she'd end up on the ground in a dead faint, embarrassing herself more than she had in the fifth-grade talent show, and *that* was beyond humiliating. How many people there would be repeat audience members? Isa would laugh her ass off. Aunt Mary would snap the world's worst candids that would haunt Mandy at every family event from now until the end of time.

"Not if you eat something." Mom tried to sound reassuring, but once the anxiety train got rolling down Mandy's track, there was little that could slow it. "Have you talked to Isa today?" It was like Mom knew exactly what Mandy needed. Her best friend. The person she'd been able to count on for anything and everything since kindergarten. Just hearing her name seemed to calm the swarming hornets in Mandy's stomach.

"I texted her, but she's probably not awake yet." Mandy used the side of her fork to slice off a piece of waffle, dipped it in the now-cold maple syrup, and shoved it into her mouth. She was not fainting today. No way. No how.

"Well, I'm sure you'll hear from her soon."

Mandy hoped. Isa was the only one who would be able to

convince Mandy she was just being silly with her thoughts of "signs from the universe." "You picked up the programs from the printer, right? And have the box of favors to give to the caterer? Oh, and did you get a chance to call—"

"Everything is taken care of. There's nothing you need to worry about right now except for making sure *you* get ready," Mom said. "Don't forget the hairstylist will be there within the hour, so you need to get a move on if you're going to be on time for pictures."

"Yes, Mom," Mandy said with a mouthful. Despite not being hungry, she thought the waffle was delicious—crisp on the outside, and soft, still a little warm in the middle.

"Now don't get angry," Mom said, and Mandy's heart started pounding. Nothing good ever came after those words. Like the time Mom took Mandy to get a perm. Or the time Mom threw out Mandy's entire seashell collection. "But I bought those shoes just in case you wanted to have them for the pictures."

Mandy shouldn't have told her mother about the baby-blue tennis shoes she purchased—but she had been so excited about them. Mom reacted exactly as expected. Creased brow. Puckered lips like she took a bite of expired yogurt. "I *have* shoes." Mandy attempted to keep her voice level, but she should've seen this coming. *This* was Mom's MO.

"I know. I know. And you can do what you want. But you really can't wear those shoes for a proper ceremony, and I think you'll really like these. They have blue soles and everything." Mom sounded much too cheery.

Mandy was getting a headache. She couldn't deal with this right now. "I'll look at them."

"That's all I'm asking," Mom said. "Now hurry up, and don't

forget *not* to wash your hair. The stylist said dirty hair is easier to work with."

Too late. Mandy hadn't forgotten, she just didn't want stinky hair on her wedding day. "I remember."

"And eat," Mom said.

Mandy shoved another bite in her mouth. "On it."

"Don't talk with your mouth full. You'll choke, honey."

Mandy *was* thinking about choking someone.

They said their goodbyes, and Mandy checked the clock. Somehow an hour had passed since she'd gotten out of the shower. Her stylist would be there any minute, and Mandy was supposed to have her makeup done before she arrived. This was not a sign. But the conversation with Mom about the shoes played over in the back of her mind. Who was she to tell Mandy what she could or couldn't wear to her own wedding? Or what was "proper" for her special day?

In less than five hours, she was set to marry the love of her life. Who saw her for who she was—flaws and all—she was sure of it. And it was going to be wonderful, and perfect, and there was nothing that was going to ruin this day.

She shoved waffle in her face like she'd been starved for a week—not even taking the time to enjoy her favorite breakfast food—and raced into the bathroom for her makeup.

CHAPTER TWO

August 1998

IT FELT MORE LIKE an October afternoon instead of an August one that day on Huntington Beach, but Mandy couldn't have cared less. Her parents had finally given her and Isa permission to walk down to the beach for an hour by themselves. With *no* adult supervision. And it was glorious.

It wasn't that Mandy didn't like her parents. Actually, she loved them very much. And if she was being completely honest, she—*occasionally*—liked spending time with them; not that she'd ever tell them that. But Mandy was in middle school now. She was practically an adult, so it was time for them to stop treating her like a baby. Today's excursion, with the salty breeze biting at her cheeks, felt like a step toward independence.

"What do you want to do now?" Isa pulled at Mandy's arm, imploring action with her whole body. Her best friend was a doer, not an overthinker like Mandy, which normally was a difference in personality that served them well.

Mandy wiggled her toes in the sand, digging them down to the cold layer underneath. "That's the best part." She let the sea air fill her lungs. "Anything we want."

Isa cocked a dark eyebrow at Mandy—raising just one—how did she do that? "Okay. Well, you have any ideas?" Isa spread her arms out, gesturing at the mostly deserted beach. Long stretches of sand and foamy surf lay in front of them, but all Mandy could see was possibilities.

A couple walked hand in hand along the shore. Every so often one of them would bend over and pick something up—collecting shells, most likely—and show it to the other. Mandy liked collecting shells—but she was particular about the ones she would bring home and display on her dresser. Plus, the water had to be freezing. Okay, not *freezing* freezing, but much too cold to swim in without a full wet suit, and even the idea of walking in it to look for shells sent shivers up Mandy's spine.

She glanced around, her gaze sweeping over the long pier that jutted out into the ocean not far from them—Mandy could almost smell the funnel cakes mingling in the salty air. She instead focused on what looked to be an abandoned bucket buried in the sand, likely left by a small child. Mandy was *not* a small child . . . but she did have an idea. "Let's build a snowman."

There went that eyebrow of Isa's again. Her tell that something Mandy said sounded ridiculous.

"Fine. A sandman then." Mandy made her way over to the purple bucket and dug it out, the sand burrowing under her fingernails in the process. A yellow shovel was attached to the handle, and it was completely intact, which was serendipitous. Like this was what they were meant to do.

Isa smiled and shook her head a little. Another one of her tells that she still thought the idea was silly, but she was more than willing to go along with it anyway. "Fine."

That's how their friendship had been ever since that fateful day Marisa Jiménez walked into Mandy's kindergarten class— the pair had been inseparable. Mandy and Isa just got each other. They had a way of communicating that didn't always require a lot of words—which was good, because Isa didn't talk much back then, and Mandy never learned how to stop talking. They were perfect for each other. Isa was the cheese to Mandy's macaroni. The peanut butter to her pickles. The salsa to her chips. Her best friend knew how to keep Mandy together when she felt like her world was falling apart. And even back in those kindergarten times, there were plenty of days where Mandy's world was shaken and cracked, and Isa was there to put it all back together.

Things had gotten much better since then. Her parents went to marriage counseling, and Mandy got a therapist of her own— Miss Heather—whom she still saw regularly.

But today, a day of independence from adult supervision, all was well in Mandy's world, and she was ready to enjoy the heck out of her afternoon with her best friend.

Even though Mandy had thought the water would be too cold to stroll in, they switched off subjecting their feet to the frigid water, turning their toes into ice cubes, filling buckets from the incoming tide to complete their project.

"Making a man of sand is a lot different than making one out of snow," Mandy babbled on. "For one thing snow is a lot colder, and you have to wear gloves. Maybe we should bring gloves with us next time we do this. And if the snow is too wet or too dry, it doesn't really work. And you can't just add water like we can here." She loved making a snowman with her parents almost every winter when they took trips to go skiing pretty much anywhere white stuff fell from the sky—Switzerland, Colorado, Canada, Italy, and of course Tahoe for quick weekend getaways. Isa nodded along like she knew what Mandy was saying even though Isa had never seen snow herself.

"Maybe your mom will let you come with us next week." Mandy patted down a clump of wet sand on their second mound and smoothed out the side. Not that there would be any snow this time of year, but there were other fun things to do in Lake Tahoe, and it would be cool to hang out with someone other than her parents while she was there.

Isa chewed her lip. "Maybe." That meant the likelihood was slim, but there could always be a chance. The truth was, Isa never liked to leave her mom and abuela for very long—this was something Mandy knew well. While she was like a bird ready to spread her wings and fly, Isa was more like a rabbit. She was curious about the world but never liked to stray too far from home. Mandy had slept over at Isa's at least a dozen times before Isa ever slept over at Mandy's. The first time she didn't even make it all the way through the night, Mandy waking to an empty bed and Mom telling her Isa had gone home but that she would be back for breakfast. The second time Isa got lost coming back from the bathroom—luckily Mandy got impatient and went looking for her. It of course got better with each visit, but it was clear Isa preferred her own casita—that's what Isa called it.

Mandy really liked spending time at Isa's too. At Mandy's house she always had to wear socks or slippers, otherwise her feet would get cold, but at Isa's it was always warm and cozy. Abuela always had something delicious cooking and ready for taste testing—which Mandy loved to do. It was a well-established fact that no one volunteered to taste test Mom's cooking. It was pretty bad—okay, it was awful. Nothing had any flavor. At least not the way Abuela's food did. It wasn't as if Mandy didn't like her own house; there was just something special about being at Isa's. Mom and Dad were always busy, and Abuela always had time to do things with them.

The wind along the shore started to pick up, blowing sand into Mandy's eyes. She pulled the sleeve of her hoodie over her hand to wipe her face, and when she glanced up, there he was. Brandon Martínez. He and Clay Anderson tossed a football back and forth not far from where Mandy and Isa were getting ready to put the head on their sandman. Brandon's dark brown hair and bronze skin seemed to shimmer in the late afternoon sun. Or, at least, he shimmered to Mandy. Brandon was the only boy in her class who had dimples—one in each cheek—and every time he smiled, they sucked in, in the most adorable way.

As though Isa already knew what Mandy was thinking, she said, "Ugh, please don't invite them over here."

"Come on, they aren't that bad," Mandy retorted. But they were. Most boys in the sixth grade were just . . . different. Like for some reason they needed to show off, and they thought being rude was funny, and when they ran around a lot, they smelled kind of peppery. But Brandon—even though that described him perfectly—had those amazing dimples.

Mandy had heard all about the "talk" Isa got about boys. It sounded embarrassing and awkward. Mandy was glad her parents never sat her down the way Isa's mom did. But ever since then, Isa had been way too cautious; and where was the fun in that?

"We don't have a lot of time before we have to get back. And we can't leave Sandman here without a face," Isa rationalized, but a rogue football toss had Brandon and Clay already heading their way. Isa huffed, but Mandy ignored it.

"Hey," she said as she scooped up the ball. She didn't throw it back though. Mandy had no idea how to throw a football, and she wasn't about to embarrass herself by trying for the first time in front of Brandon.

"Hey," Brandon said back, but Mandy heard, *Wow, it's so good to see you.* It was finally happening. The cute boy with the dimples was taking notice of her, Amanda Elizabeth Dean. This was one of those moments in the movies her mom watched, the meet-cute that indicated the two characters were meant to be. And it was happening to Mandy, on *today* of all days, her first day of independence.

Heat rose in Mandy's cheeks as she passed him the ball, swooped her ponytail over her shoulder, and ran her fingers through her wind-tangled blonde hair.

"Are you making a snowman out of sand?" Clay asked.

"Well, we can't make one out of snow." Isa didn't roll her eyes, but everything in her voice said she really wanted to.

"Cool." Clay seemed oblivious to Isa's annoyance. He didn't know her the way Mandy did.

"Yeah, great." Brandon nodded.

"I think I saw some driftwood back there you could use as arms." Clay pointed.

"We're supposed to be practicing." Brandon spun the ball on

his hand. Did pro football players do that? Mandy bet they did. It looked so cool.

"We have to leave soon anyway," Isa said.

"Then we should help you finish," Clay said as he scooped a handful of wet sand from near Isa's feet and added it to their creation. "I think that's, like, a rule of sand building."

That rule didn't exist—Mandy was sure of it—but Clay's braces-filled smile made her not want to argue. Clay wasn't like most of the sixth-grade boys. This was probably the most Mandy had ever heard him say at one time, actually. Isa looked like she'd eaten a rotten tomato.

Brandon grimaced. "Fine. I'll go get the stupid wood." He dropped the ball and turned to head down the beach.

"I'll help." Mandy caught up to him. This was her chance to hang out with *the* Brandon Martínez.

He kicked the sand and flipped his hair out of his face as they walked toward the water, with the salty air growing thick around them. Brandon always wore the newest Air Jordans, but today he was barefoot, and somehow his feet were flawless. Unlike Mandy, whose toenail polish was beyond chipped—a couple of toes didn't even have any polish left. What was Mandy thinking? Sure, she'd been paired up with kids she didn't really know all that well for class projects, but this was *Brandon Martínez*, and there were no grades at stake, no instructions to discuss or tasks to distribute. What was she supposed to say? How was she supposed to act? How did the characters move on from the meet-cute in the movies?

That's when she noticed his T-shirt.

"I can't believe they traded Piazza." Given the amount of time Dad had spent bemoaning the trade, it felt like a pretty safe thing to kick off an actual conversation with.

Brandon's head pivoted in her direction. "*You* like the Dodgers?"

She wouldn't say she *hated* the Dodgers, but technically she wasn't exactly a fan. If she was being truthful, she didn't care one way or the other about baseball or about going to the ballpark with Dad. She loved the snacks and the people watching, but she didn't pay much attention to the actual game. "My dad's company has a box, so we go all the time." To Mandy's ears this sounded like the dumbest thing to say, but from the way those dimples in Brandon's cheeks made an appearance, it must've been good. Mandy's heart fluttered.

"Really? Do you ever get to take people with you?" Brandon asked.

Mandy shrugged. Isa didn't really like baseball either, so on the rare occasion Mandy was allowed to bring someone, she would drag Isa along with the promise of popcorn—even though it was better at the movie theater. But Mandy supposed that Dad wouldn't mind someone new, especially if they were actually into the sport; then maybe he wouldn't be so annoyed that she didn't watch much of the game. "Yeah, sometimes."

Those dimples seemed to grow a little deeper, and Brandon's smile got a little bigger. "Awesome." The way he was looking at her *was* awesome—very, very awesome. "Did you see the way Adrián Beltré—"

"Oh, look." Mandy pointed at the driftwood floating in the surf just ahead of them. She would have to ask Dad for more details about the Dodgers before she could have a conversation with Brandon about baseball. Dad would be elated, but Mandy wasn't sure she'd done the right thing. Now that she thought about it, learning about baseball sounded more like homework than something fun to do.

"I got it." Brandon ran out into the tide, splashing water all the way up to his athletic shorts, and grabbed what would become the arms of their sandman.

As the pair walked back to the others, they didn't talk about baseball, but Brandon did seem to be a lot more interested in their current sandman-building project. And right before they got into earshot of their friends, Brandon turned to Mandy and said, "You know, you're pretty cool." He handed Mandy the wood they'd just collected. "Here."

Wow.

Did *the* Brandon Martínez just tell Mandy she was cool?

Mandy had to be dreaming. But no, Brandon and Clay worked on getting one of the pieces of wood just right for Sandman's arm, and Isa had that eyebrow cocked at Mandy, so she moved toward her with the other piece.

It wasn't much longer before they were finished with what had to be the best sandman Huntington Beach had ever had on its shores. Too bad they didn't build it farther back so the tide wouldn't wash it away. But nevertheless, it had been fun.

As they all said their goodbyes and went their separate ways, Mandy got one last display of those dimples.

"I don't know," Isa said as they used the showers at the edge of the parking lot to wash the sand from their feet before putting their flip-flops back on.

"He's nice," Mandy said. "And he's cute."

Isa pinched her lips together.

"I think Clay likes you." Mandy raised her brows—both of them, because she couldn't do that one-brow thing Isa could.

Isa frowned. "No thanks."

Mandy shook her head. "Okay, but we could totally double-date. It would be sweet." Mandy pictured them all together hanging out, and those dimples. Oh, they were just so amazing.

"I'll think about it." Isa dropped her shoes to the ground with a slap and slipped them back on. "I almost forgot." She handed Mandy a fully intact sand dollar.

"Oh my god, it's beautiful. I know just where I'll put it." Mandy hooked her arm with Isa's, and they headed back toward Mandy's house.

Isa would eventually come around and understand what Mandy saw in Brandon. He wasn't so much like all the other boys the way she'd thought before. Plus, he didn't make a single fart joke like he always did at school—that had to mean something, right?

Clay was nice too. Isa was just being cautious, as always. Mandy was sure it would all work out. She was just sure of it.

CHAPTER THREE

January 2015

THE LOS ANGELES ART scene was always something to get excited about. There were differences in the talent that came from the West Coast versus the East Coast. Not that one was better than the other. They just each had their own unique personality. It was the air, or people's attitudes that lived on one coast as opposed to the other that perhaps had an effect on their work. Mandy was never sure. But in her heart of hearts, she was a West Coast girl through and through.

"This is fucking unbelievable." Sophie's British accent really seem to punctuate those words even harder in Mandy's head and her palms started to sweat.

"You don't think I should've brought the smaller canvas instead of this one?" Mandy took stock of all her work hanging on the walls in the small off-the-beaten-path gallery that Friday evening. Was her work distinctive enough? Did her point of view come through clearly? Or were all these paintings just plain bad? Impostor syndrome was a powerful force.

"No. It's bloody perfect just the way it is. For fuck's sake, stop second-guessing yourself." Sophie sounded so confident. So sure. But that's how Sophie was—her entire persona had always been that of *don't-fuck-with-me-I-am-who-I-am*. It was one of the things Mandy found most endearing about her.

"If only it were that easy." Mandy had been working for years—years upon years, if she was being really honest—waiting for this moment. An art show, her first ever. There had been a couple of times she had a piece of hers on display here or there, but tonight it was all Amanda Dean originals. Even the way she ended up here was a fluke. One of those serendipitous moments when Mandy had been in the right place at the right time. So questions of *Did I deserve this?* swirled through her head as destructively as a hurricane.

Mandy had been standing in this very gallery one month ago when it happened. Sophie had flown into town for a quick layover, and the pair made a wrong turn looking for the Thai restaurant they'd decided to try out. One of those hole-in-the-wall places you needed to know someone who knew someone to find out about. After a few blocks, they found themselves not lost, but not where they had hoped to be. They stood in front of Beyond the White Wall instead of Aroy Thai.

"Ugh. What is wrong with this stupid app?" Mandy groaned. She'd spent the morning working on a new project and completely forgot to eat—which wasn't a terrible thing since she was about to gorge herself on Thai food. "This isn't where we're supposed to be."

"Or is it?" Sophie gave Mandy a knowing glance, and instead of turning around to figure out where the scent of garlic and spices was coming from, pushed through the door of Beyond the White Wall.

Even though Mandy was starving, she followed her friend inside. The space was much larger than it had appeared from the outside—deeper than it was wide. It looked as though it was still set up from a showing with some rather . . . interesting pieces on display. But aside from that, the space was chic and pristine—the walls all a shade of eggshell white without a single scuff or mark.

"What even is this?" Sophie tilted her head to one side and then to the other. The wall text next to the piece read *The Eye of the Beeholder*. Mandy got the bee reference with what was possibly honey dripping into a strategically placed container on the floor and a plastic honeycomb attached to a canvas that looked like a preschooler's finger painting project gone wrong. "Think they were spiffed when they made this?" Sophie asked.

The artist likely had done more than just smoke a little weed, but that wasn't important. "Do you think it's supposed to be some sort of discourse about the commercialization of honeybees?" It was a reach for sure, but Mandy didn't know what else to say about it.

"No. I think they were just spiffed."

"It didn't even get close to covering the overhead!" a voice rang out from the back room. "It was a catastrophe to the highest degree!"

Mandy glanced back at the door they entered through. "Maybe we should—"

"And miss the drama? No way." Sophie took a casual step closer in the direction of the voice while trying to make herself look interested in the work on display.

The yelling continued. Mandy attempted to busy herself by studying a headshot of the gallery owner posted on the wall— Aziz Bakshi—and according to the biography below, he had quite the extensive background as an art dealer. Although her eyes followed along with the words in front of her, she couldn't help but wonder what all the yelling was about. The finer details of what was being discussed weren't clear—there was a lot of swearing—but when the owner stormed out and found Sophie and Mandy standing in the middle of his gallery, he couldn't quite turn his frown around quick enough and ended up with more shock than smile.

They totally shouldn't be there.

"I'm so sorry. I didn't realize anyone was here. I'm Aziz, pronouns he/him. Welcome to my gallery." And there he was—the man from the photograph—even more stunning in person. Aziz actually was the most fabulous man Mandy had ever laid eyes on, and she had seen some fabulous men over the years. He wore a fitted black turtleneck and a floor-length skirt that wasn't metallic, but it looked like liquid metal the way it shimmered when he moved across the room in his four-inch stilettos. And he smelled like the air after a summer's rain—that was the only way Mandy could describe the fresh air effervescing off him.

"I'm Sophia Esme Zepeda, she/her, and this is my friend, Amanda Dean, also she/her." Sophie spoke like this was the most natural way of introducing oneself, and maybe it was in the elite artist circle Aziz lived inside—a circle Mandy could only dream of being a part of since she had no connections.

"Amanda Dean," Aziz said. "You're an artist too, aren't you?"

Mandy sucked in a breath. How could he tell? But then it dawned on her that there was paint still stuck to her nails and spots on her shoes. She was dressed for Thai food, not for going to a gallery, and definitely not for speaking to an *actual* gallery owner. Her stomach tightened.

But before Mandy could reply with something like, *Well, I hope to be someday*, Sophie stepped forward. "The most amazing artist. And better than this." She gestured around to the . . . *paintings* wasn't really the right word for what hung on the walls.

Mandy's heart stopped beating. What was Sophie thinking? For all either of them knew, this was Aziz's brother's show and she had just insulted him. Mandy was a nobody in the art world, and at this rate, she'd be staying that way.

Aziz threw back his head, his ink-black hair falling behind him like a dark shimmering waterfall, and laughed. "He is shit, isn't he?" He tucked his hair behind his ear. "That's what happens when you do your cousin's friend a favor. Never again. But that also means I'm left scrambling to find someone to fill the spot next month. You wouldn't know anyone with a collection ready to go, would you?" He laughed as though he knew what he said was absurd. Even the most talented artists needed months upon months to prepare for a showing. No one could possibly pull a collection together that quickly.

"Mandy can do it," Sophie said, pulling her phone from her back pocket. "Look at this." Before anyone could say anything, Sophie had shoved her cell into Aziz's hands and began flipping through the photos she had of Mandy's work.

Mandy's face was hotter than the depths of hell. "He doesn't want to—"

"You *are* exceptionally talented, Amanda Dean." Aziz said the words with surprise. Which was fair. He'd probably heard that line from friends and family many times and was then forced to look at work that wouldn't even pass for a first-year art student's. Mandy wasn't anyone important, and she had been privy to that same ritual—her mom sending her work to review from a friend at the gym or whatever, saying, if you could just look at this and let me know what you think—so she had had some incredibly *interesting* work to critique even with her limited experience.

Mandy wanted to say, *I'm sure Aziz is just being polite.* But the thing was, people like him—gallery owners—weren't ever polite to people like Mandy. To artists with name recognition, sure; to buyers with money to spare, of course. But not a lowly artist whose friend just shoved a bunch of terrible cell phone pictures in their faces—no. So Mandy didn't rebuff his compliment. Praise from people like Aziz did *not* come often or freely. Mandy's insides grew as warm as her face. She hoped her cheeks wouldn't give her euphoria away. Because even though compliments weren't given often, no one needed to know this was the very first one Mandy had gotten from someone who wasn't a mentor, professor, or one of her friends. She needed Aziz to think she had those kinds of things said about her all the time.

She also needed to remind herself to breathe.

Aziz broke into a long speech about what he needed, and what would work in the space and wouldn't, and what the house commission rate was and how that could change depending on if Mandy needed him to cover all of the marketing and opening night catering or not. Numbers swam inside Mandy's head, crashing against one another like bumper cars as she tried to keep up with everything that came out of his mouth. And then it was quiet.

Too quiet.

Shit. What did Mandy miss?

"She'll do it," Sophie answered for her.

"Amanda Dean. I'm gonna make you a star." Aziz spun with a swish of his skirt. "Let me just draw up the papers."

That moment four weeks ago had seemed like a dream. Or a nightmare, depending on Mandy's mood. But as she stood in the gallery that night surrounded by her work on pristine white walls, where caterers dressed all in black hustled around her, it seemed surreal.

"You are the fucking star tonight." Sophie squeezed Mandy's hands and brought her back to the present. "I've gotta jet, but anytime you start losing your nerve, I want you to say that to yourself. You got me?"

"I'm the fucking star tonight." Mandy's words didn't quite hold the same conviction that Sophie's did.

"Damn right you are." Sophie's dark curls with a pop of purple brushed against Mandy's face as Sophie kissed each of Mandy's cheeks.

"I wish you could stay," Mandy said. It was a low blow— Sophie absolutely would stay if possible, but it had been lucky she could be there to see this even if it was before the event truly started.

"You don't need me. You've got this. What was that again?"

"I'm the fucking star tonight."

Sophie winked and then she was gone—off to catch her flight and take the world by storm.

Tonight, Mandy's parents and friends said they would be there. And Edmund would of course show up as soon as his meeting wrapped. But until then Mandy was on her own.

CHAPTER FOUR

October 2002

NO DOUBT BLASTED FROM the CD player on Mandy's dresser, shaking the special collection of shells and sand dollars she kept displayed there, and the pile of M&M's that Isa and she had been snacking on—that they were always snacking on. Isa crawled on her hands and knees, threading her fingers through the plush carpet, searching for the earring she had dropped.

"Not again," Mandy moaned, joining her. "Maybe this is the universe's way of saying to skip the earrings." Mandy had told Isa she was not a fan of the rhinestone monstrosities. They were dangly with a mixture of white and light blue crystals that dripped down like a leaking faucet and didn't particularly go with the simple silk dress Isa's mom had made her. They were so heavy they kept falling out of Isa's ears and burying themselves in the deep textured carpet—like they knew they needed to die and not be worn for such an important event. Tonight was homecoming, and Mandy wanted everything to be perfect. And that included wanting everything to be perfect for Isa as well.

"I like them." Isa had told Mandy her dress was too plain and wanted something to sparkle up her look, so she had picked the earrings out from the clearance bin the weekend before when they had been shopping for all their last-minute odds and ends. Mandy refrained from saying that they were in the clearance bin for a reason, but maybe she should've.

"I'm just saying you don't *need* them. You look amazing already." Mandy handed the earring to Isa, who smiled in return.

Mandy had been prepping for the homecoming dance for weeks. Together, she and Isa flipped through magazines, cutting out their favorite looks, and went shopping almost nonstop. Mandy's date had been secured since her summer romance transitioned to the fall, so when Justin Reyes asked Isa to go, Mandy was extra excited to be double-dating.

And because Mandy was excited—this being their sophomore homecoming and their first with dates—her mother paid for the girls to get their hair done for the special event in exchange for pictures. There would be lots and lots of pictures taken, but it was totally worth it. Mom had also offered to have their makeup done, but Mandy insisted on doing it herself.

Isa stood in front of the mirror in her sapphire silk dress that kissed the tops of her knees. Her dark brown hair was wrapped in an elegant French twist with a few ringlets that hung down and framed her face. She looked absolutely stunning.

"Justin is going to die when he sees you," Mandy said as she sat down to lace up her new Vans. She had decided she would *not* be subjected to uncomfortably standing in heels all night. She did that for Dad's work parties—per Mom's request—and she was not about to have her feet crammed into wedges, her toes all pinched together, and then have to deal with the inevitable blisters that followed. So tonight, she was going to do things *her* way—even if her mother didn't approve. Sure, she'd probably look extra short next to Isa with her tall frame and high heels, but Mandy didn't care. She wanted to be comfortable. Even her dress—a two-piece that showed her midsection—was made of a soft jersey material, in a shade of green that complemented Mandy's pale peach skin tone.

Isa blushed. "He's okay, I guess."

"You're just nervous." Mandy reached over and turned the music up louder. "Come on, let's dance it out." She grabbed Isa's hands and started pulling her arms back and forth until they were both in the middle of Mandy's bedroom, spinning around and throwing their arms in the air.

This had always been their thing. When times got tough, when one of them was upset about this or that, or when they argued over something ridiculous, they would stop and dance like no one was watching. Sometimes they'd even create routines to their favorite songs. Tonight though, with Gwen Stefani's vocals rattling through Mandy's speakers, they just shook it all loose.

"We're going to have so much fun tonight, no matter what," Mandy yelled over the thumping rhythm.

Mandy had crushed on a number of people, but Isa had never really been interested in anyone—except for a comment about a celebrity here or there, but that didn't count. "Focused on more important things," Isa's mom called it. "A late bloomer," was what Mandy's mom had said. So the simple fact Isa agreed to this date in the first place was a step toward finding her true love; Mandy was sure of it. Or at least it was a way for Isa to not be a third wheel whenever Mandy and V went out. Not that

Mandy minded, but she was afraid that Isa might. And no matter whom Mandy dated, they had to know she was a package deal with her best friend. She may have been in love, but she loved her best friend just as much, so no way would she ever leave Isa behind.

When the song ended and the next one came on, Mandy turned the music down, flopping back onto her bed breathless, and Isa collapsed next to her.

There was a knock, and the bedroom door cracked open with Mom's petite frame sliding into view. "Girls, pictures downstairs in five." She waved her special digital camera with the fancy lens at them and was dressed for the occasion even though she wasn't going to the dance—but when wasn't Mom camera ready? Her blonde hair was swept up away from her face, and her pencil skirt and blouse were perfectly pressed. It was rare her mother ever dressed down. Mandy didn't think she even owned a pair of jeans.

Mandy pushed herself up on her elbows. "We're almost ready."

"Are you sure you don't want me to whip you girls up a snack before you head out?" Mom asked. "I have those little bagel pizza things." Mandy's mom wasn't exactly known for her culinary skills, although they would probably be safe with something that came from the freezer as long as she set a timer—and actually listened for it.

Mandy and Isa exchanged a glance, having a conversation with just their eyes. Their group of friends wanted to meet up for food before the dance, but Isa felt weird about the whole thing. Mandy agreed, so they had picked up something at the mall when they got their hair done earlier and were just going to meet up with all their friends at the dance. Afterward if they were hungry, they would grab something from a drive-thru. "No, we're good."

Mom stood for a moment and really seemed to be studying Mandy. "That doesn't look like the same dress you showed me before." She was right, it wasn't the same dress, because Mandy knew her mom wouldn't approve, so she had showed her something similar—the same color and length but not jersey, and definitely not two pieces.

"Well, it is." Mandy shrugged.

Mom narrowed her eyes. "I guess those shoes you wore to Dad's holiday party last year will work."

"Nope. I'm all good." Luckily, she was on the far end of the bed with her feet on the ground, so Mom couldn't see she had already put her shoes on. Mandy had been kind of hoping Mom wouldn't notice them at all, but that was wishful thinking. Mom always noticed everything.

"I don't want to know what that means, do I?" Mom asked.

"Probably not." Mandy shook her head.

Mom looked at Isa.

"She's wearing tennis shoes." Isa was never able to keep a secret from any parental figure—Mandy was surprised she lasted as long as she had. Probably because the topic had never come up.

"Oh, Amanda." Disappointment dripped from Mom's voice—a sound Mandy was extremely used to.

"Mom, you said this was *my* event and I could do whatever I wanted." Those were the exact words Mom had used.

"'Within reason.' Tennis shoes are *not* reasonable. And I still don't think *that* is the same dress."

"Well, it is, and I do. And it's *my* event."

With a glance at Isa, Mom tried once more. "Help me out here."

"I tried to tell her." Which was true, and likely another reason Isa picked out those hideous earrings, since Mandy ignored her opinion about her footwear.

"Perhaps you can put on those holiday party shoes for pictures," Mom reasoned. "I'm sure Isa's mom would appreciate it too." Mom would be sending all the pictures to Isa's mom since she had to work and couldn't be there.

"I'll think about it." Which meant she absolutely would not be thinking about it at all.

Mom huffed—most likely realizing she wasn't winning this one—then closed the door.

Mandy jumped up, grabbing a tube of Viciously Vamp lipstick from her makeup table, and applying another coat. It was Mandy's night, and she was *not* going to let her mother ruin it.

"Oh, good idea." Isa reached over, pulling a tube of sparkly lip gloss from her clutch.

"Lip gloss makes kissing really sticky." Mandy had purposely not used it when she applied Isa's makeup, instead opting for a soft pink that complemented her skin tone, but Isa loved her lip gloss. Especially the kind that smelled and tasted like bubble gum.

Isa scrunched her nose. "I don't even know if I want to kiss Justin."

"Ugh. Come on, Isa. You've got to get your first kiss over with at some point."

"I told you, I'm not sure I'm into Justin, you know?"

"Does it matter?" For Mandy it mattered—totally and completely. She couldn't kiss just anyone, because anyone she did kiss would also be the recipient of her heart. But maybe it would be different for Isa. They had talked about it only in the hypothetical sense before, and tonight it could be a reality for Isa.

"It matters."

Mandy shrugged. "Fine. But if you do think you want to kiss him, trust me and wipe the lip gloss off first."

Isa turned back to the mirror, applied another thick coat of the shiny gloss, and made a loud smack as she puckered her lips.

Mandy handed her lipstick to Isa.

Isa tipped her head to the side. "You could just carry your own purse."

"Or you could hold this for me, so I don't have to." Mandy batted her eyelashes.

Isa let out a huff and took the tube, making a show of dropping it into her clutch.

Mandy kissed the air in response—knowing Isa didn't really care about carrying Mandy's things, she was just annoyed with her about all the kissing talk.

As soon as Isa buckled up the straps on her heels, they each took one last look in Mandy's mirrored closet doors and went downstairs for pictures. Usually, Mom would have them pose in front of the fireplace, but this time, she immediately ushered them out to the backyard—where she'd had the gardeners plant fresh seasonal flowers just for the occasion. She also had the lawn mowed and the hedges trimmed, and did she have the fountain bleached? It looked brighter than the last time Mandy had been back there. Granted, it had been a while. The yard was more for aesthetics than it was for anything else. Just like inside Mandy's house, the outside always had to look picture-perfect, or magazine-ready, as her mother called it. As a designer, Mom couldn't ever be off her game. Mandy hated how everything always had to look immaculate.

The yard—just like the house—was too stuffy for Mandy. As stuffy as the outdoors could be, she supposed. The new flowers were pretty and had Mandy itching to go back inside to get her paints instead of going to a dance. But they would probably be just as inspirational tomorrow after she woke up.

Mom had the camera strapped around her neck and held it off to the side in one hand. "So this is the look, huh? No other shoes? Not even for pictures?"

Mandy was not going to let Mom bully her into those shoes even for one second on *her* special night. "You said . . ."

"Fine." Mom's lips puckered like she was holding in all the words she wanted to say, but then her face relaxed. "You're right. It's your night and you both look beautiful," she said. "Let's get you to stand by the begonias." Mom ushered them across the yard, positioned them each just so, and took a step back.

"You're cutting our feet out, aren't you?" Mandy asked.

"I'm getting some close-ups," Mom said, and the camera clicked a few times. She turned the camera this way and that while Mandy and Isa changed positions—facing each other with hands on hips, arms over each other's shoulders, leaning in for air-kisses. The whole time her mom never took a step back or changed her position in order to get their full bodies. She was being ridiculous. Mandy loved her outfit, and that included her shoes. Why did Mom have to be so stubborn?

"Now if you two could switch places, we'll do that all on the other side," Mom directed.

Mandy hiked up her skirt and held her foot up at her waist. "What about this? That way you can get all of me."

"Amanda!" Mom looked scandalized, like Mandy was showing off her underthings to the entire world, not an empty backyard. "Pull your dress down. It's a good thing Isa's abuela isn't here to see this." Mom's head pivoted as though she was making sure no one else was watching even though they were the only ones there. "I was getting to it, jeez."

Abuela would probably laugh and tell Mom she was being too prudish, but Abuela had an appointment she couldn't reschedule, which was why Mom was in charge of all the pictures.

Isa didn't copy Mandy, but she did say, "I'm sure my mom and abuela won't mind, Mrs. Dean."

"See." Mandy dropped her foot and leaned in and kissed Isa on the cheek.

Click.

"Fine." Mom took a few steps back, and this time, as Mandy and Isa posed, Mom surely got their whole bodies in the frame.

"You are really glowing tonight, Isa," Mom said. "Excited about the first big date?"

Isa glanced at Mandy, that single eyebrow of hers threatening to perk up in a *please save me* kind of way.

"It's not that big a deal, Mom," Mandy answered for her.

"Our little flower is finally ready to bloom," Mom said, either ignoring Mandy or not listening to what she just said. "I always knew if we gave you time . . ."

Isa's cheeks flared, and she reached over to squeeze Mandy's hand.

"Let's get some over there." Mandy gestured toward the corner of the yard, where a giant tree that kept them supplied practically year-round with lemons grew.

"Let's hide behind it," Isa said, "and we can pop out of each side and look at each other."

"Oh yes, that would be adorable," Mom agreed.

Mandy avoided stepping on a few lemons that had dropped to the ground since the gardeners had been there, and braced herself against the trunk. This tree had always been a favorite of hers. When she was little, she loved to climb it and get the lemons that were near the top. Per Mom's request, Dad would stand below Mandy, ready to catch her in case she fell—she never did though. But when she got high enough to see over the stone wall into the Browns' yard, their dog would bark and bark and bark. Then Mr. Brown would come out and say, "Shut up, you dumb mutt," and then Mrs. Brown would get mad at Mr. Brown, which made the dog bark even louder, and Mandy would laugh and laugh and laugh. The Browns didn't live there for long once the divorce papers were filed.

"Let's get you over by the fountain," Mom said, pulling Mandy from her thoughts.

She and Isa sat on the edge, legs crossed with their hands folded over their knees.

Mom clicked a few photos. "Lean back just a little bit."

Mandy did as she was asked, but Isa must've taken the direction to heart, as she screeched and grabbed on to Mandy, pulling her down toward the water. Mandy's elbow hit the side and luckily kept them both from toppling into the fountain. After a moment, Mandy glanced at Mom, who was still taking pictures, and then at Isa, and they both burst out laughing.

"Did you get the shot, Mom?" They both could've ended up going swimming, and Mom hadn't even budged from her spot.

"I would've helped if you fell in," she told them. "You're going to love these."

And that sent her and Isa into an even bigger fit of giggles.

It was then that V and Justin arrived. Mandy jumped up to greet her date, throwing her arms around V. Isa calmly rose and smoothed down her dress before welcoming Justin.

"Wow. You look beautiful," Justin said as he slipped a white rose corsage onto Isa's wrist. He wore a gray suit with a blue tie that almost matched Isa's dress. Isa never mentioned it, but they had to have planned it, which was what Mandy and V had done.

"My girl is gorgeous." V pressed her cheek to each of Mandy's cheeks. Since they both were wearing lipstick and they still had pictures to take, kissing would have to come later. And Mandy was already ready for some kissing with the way V looked. Her dress had cap sleeves and a princess-type skirt—it didn't match Mandy's, but the colors were complementary, and V also wore a new pair of Vans—not that you could see them under that skirt, but she and Mandy had picked them out together. Her dark hair was wrapped up in a bunch of small buns all over her head, and her dark skin glimmered with glitter from her peony-scented body lotion.

"That's a lovely dress." Mom gave V a hug. "Very classy." She quickly glanced at Mandy.

Mandy rolled her eyes.

"Are you kids hungry? I could whip up something really quick," Mom asked as she snapped pictures. Mom loved to try to feed people when they came over—the hostess inside of her was never satisfied until someone put something in their mouth. But tonight they had more important things to do than eat.

Justin unbuttoned and buttoned his suit jacket. "My mom made pho tonight, so I'm all set, Mrs. Dean."

"I'm good," V said.

"Mom, we're fine." Mandy looked at her friends and rolled her eyes.

"Well, let me grab a few pictures real quick before you all head out. You all look absolutely stunning." Mom never dropped the camera from her eye, continuing to snap photo after photo. At this rate there would be hundreds of pictures—probably thousands.

After a few group shots, Dad showed up in the doorway to the backyard. His normal work uniform of a suit and tie had been traded in for khakis and a polo—his casual weekend look. "We have a little issue with the cars out front." He sounded stern, but stern was his default tone. Dad had always been a man of few words, so the ones he did say held a certain amount of urgency that wouldn't register if someone else had said them.

Justin didn't have any experience with the tall man with thick white hair and a gruff expression, so his normally warm-toned skin paled. "Why did I park on the street?" he mumbled to himself.

Mandy caught the way Dad's lip curled up on one side just for a moment. He was up to something. And that, combined with the way V's fingers tightened around Mandy's, made her feel as though someone poured milk over a bowl of Rice Krispies inside her stomach—a tickly snap-crackle-pop rising up through her whole body. She pulled V through the house, threw open the oversized front door, and squealed.

A shiny black limousine sat parked in their roundabout

driveway with a tuxedo-clad driver—complete with top hat and white gloves—waiting by the open back car door.

"Thought my princess needed a carriage to take her and her friends to the ball." Dad lumbered up and squeezed Mandy into his side. Although she was taller than Mom, she was still much shorter than Dad, bringing the top of her head close to his armpit.

"You're the best, Daddy." It wasn't often Mandy called him that, but it made him happy, reminding him that she was and would always be his little girl—at least that's what he had told her.

He kissed the top of her head before Mandy pulled V toward the car.

CHAPTER FIVE

April 2019

AS EXPECTED, MANDY WAS not ready when her hairstylist, Ashley, knocked on her hotel room door. The breakfast plates were still out, coffee had not been adequately drunk, and Mandy hadn't even finished one eye. Almost every palette of eye shadow she owned was strewn all over the bed, because she had somehow forgotten to pack the one she needed most. She contemplated driving all the way home to get it, but she had no idea where it could be if it wasn't with all her other makeup supplies. Plus, she was already running behind.

This was an omen of things to come.

The thought sprang quickly and entirely unwanted into Mandy's head and brewed there like kombucha, fermenting until it turned sour.

How could she believe that this day was even possible? Only people in books or movies got to marry their one true love— princesses in fairy tales were guaranteed their happily ever after, not Amanda Dean. And despite Dad's insistence on calling

Mandy *princess*, she couldn't have been further from one if she tried.

Sure, she had more luxuries in life than most—this was something that never escaped Mandy's consciousness. She was privileged. But not when it came to relationships. And when it came to love, Mandy had always been downright cursed.

"Getting excited?" Ashley asked as she emptied her large metal case full of supplies. She had already plugged in a flat iron and a curling iron—although those two things seemed counterintuitive together—and unloaded at least half a dozen products onto the table in the hotel's kitchenette. Ashley had always rocked the casual comfort look. It was one of the things that Mandy liked most about her. She had an air of calmness about her, like nothing in the world was worth getting upset about. Ashley was the poster girl for *go-with-the-flow*. Today was no different: her red hair swept up into an effortless messy bun, her glowing porcelain skin—like did she even have pores?—and her yoga pants and tank had Mandy feeling a little jealous since she was such a wreck.

"Excited?" Mandy asked more to herself than to answer Ashley. *Nervous. Anxious. Completely terrified.* All better descriptors of what Mandy was feeling.

"Butterflies, huh?" Ashley opened a bag full of brightly colored rollers. "Everything's going to be fine. I've done this a thousand times, and I have no horror stories to tell." The look on Ashley's face said she wanted to add the word *unfortunately* to that statement. Would Mandy be Ashley's first horror story? Would she be the bride Ashley told all her future clients about? A warning to them about what not to do?

This last wedding I did, let me tell you, was doomed before I even walked into the hotel room, Ashley would say as she brushed out her future client's hair. *A garden wedding. In April. Enough said. Am I right?*

Mandy glanced out the sliding glass door at the gray sky. They paid the "sunshine tax" living in Southern California, but that wasn't paying off today. It was as if May haze had come early. Of course there was a plan B if it rained, but then it wouldn't be her perfect springtime garden wedding anymore, would it?

"Let's make you a mimosa or two and get you ready." Ashley held up a bottle of champagne that had been delivered earlier that morning, and water from the melted ice dripped back into the bucket. "What do you say?"

Mandy couldn't argue. If today was going to end in disaster anyway, at least she could be drunk when it happened, right? "Is it too early for a margarita?"

"Now that's my kind of girl." Ashley walked over to the hotel phone and ordered them each a margarita and some chips and salsa—because could you really drink margaritas without them? The answer was always no.

Mandy gestured to her face. "I should probably finish—"

"Yeah, go. We have plenty of time." Ashley plopped down into one of the overstuffed chairs in the main room as Mandy retreated to the bathroom.

It was quiet in there—aside from the gentle hum of the fan—but the sound soothed Mandy more than it annoyed her. How many times had she stood in front of a bathroom mirror questioning if what she was about to do would really turn out the way she wanted?

And how many of those times did things go her way?

Not as many as Mandy wanted to admit. But didn't that mean she was due? That now was her time, and the universe would find a way to start to balance it out for her? As she smudged a shimmering peach powder on her eyelid, Mandy could almost feel her spirits rise. If today was meant to be awful and terrible, at least she would look fabulous while it happened. Except, crap. Had she used a different color on her other eye? She had been so focused she didn't even realize what color combinations she'd used on each eye until it was done, and what a look that was. She got a makeup wipe out of its little bag, carefully removed the offending color, and started over.

"Margaritas are here," Ashley yelled from the other room.

Mandy stared at herself in the mirror. "We should've ordered a pitcher."

"Oh, come on, girl. You got this. I've seen the things you can do with an eyeliner pencil. You'll be done in no time, and everything is going to be okay."

How could she be so sure? "You're not married, are you?"

"Oh god, no. But that doesn't mean I don't know true love when I see it. You know I'd tell you if I thought this was a mistake."

It was true, Ashley never lied to Mandy, not even the time she toned Mandy's hair and it turned an awful ashy blue; Ashley straight-up said it looked like shit and that she would fix it. And she did.

"I'm gonna finish getting set up in here, and you just take your time." Ashley ducked out of the doorway and left Mandy alone with her thoughts.

"All brides are stressed on their wedding day," Ashley shouted from the other room like she was reading Mandy's mind. "This is all totally normal."

Hearing that allowed Mandy to calm down just enough to get into a groove with her makeup. And just like Ashley said, in no time at all it was finished.

She quickly cleaned up all her palettes, grabbed her cell, and headed toward the main room. But before she could even clear the doorway, her cell rang, and when she checked the screen, dread sank into Mandy's stomach.

There could be only one reason her wedding planner was calling right now, so before Mandy even pressed the phone to her ear, she braced herself for bad news.

"Candy?" Mandy tentatively answered.

"I don't want you to stress out"—*too late*—"but there is a little issue with the catering. It seems the boat that goes out each morning to catch fish for the day hasn't come back—"

"What do you mean the boat didn't come back? Where did it go?" Mandy tried to keep her voice level as her hand gripped her cell phone tighter and she began to pace.

"Listen, Mandy. There's no need to panic," Candy reasoned. "I've already reached out to my contacts, and I'm on track to get the freshest halibut you've ever eaten. No one will miss the golden trout. I promise." She sounded so sensible, so relaxed.

Mandy wanted to shake her.

"I don't think I can handle it if anything else goes wrong today." Mandy's chest was heavy. "Candy, promise me there won't be anything else."

Candy giggled. "Girl. Do. Not. Stress. This is what you pay

me the big bucks for. Let me do the worrying, and you just finish getting ready. I'll take care of everything."

Tell that to the fishermen who were now lost somewhere in the ocean. What was the name of the boat? The *Titanic*?

"I'm going to take your silence to mean you're good with the change and we're moving forward," Candy said.

No, the silence was because Mandy couldn't breathe, let alone talk about fish options.

"Go drink a mimosa. I got this. Candy out." And with that she disconnected.

Mandy walked past Ashley—who sat patiently on the couch—to the ice bucket holding the champagne, and chugged straight from the bottle.

"Easy now," Ashley said. "Let's order some sandwiches or something." Before Mandy could answer, Ashley was already on the phone with room service again.

It was silly to get this upset over fish, but to Mandy it was just another thing to go wrong. Cold shower, missing bacon, Mom and her stupid shoes, forgetting her eye shadow palette, gray skies, now a missing boat, then what? Maybe there'd be a monsoon? Or an earthquake that would open up a huge hole in the earth and she'd fall inside, never to be seen again.

"Get me a blueberry muffin, please," Mandy said. Candy would handle this. Everything would be okay. Trout was basic anyway. Mandy repeated these things over and over in her head.

Ashley took the phone away from her mouth. "They say breakfast is ov—"

"Blueberry muffin!" Mandy yelled. Then in a much calmer voice added, "Please."

"We don't care how much it costs," Ashley said to whomever she was talking to.

At that moment Mandy *didn't* care. She needed something to go right—to feel like things were back on track. To feel like she was in control.

But she wasn't, and the more time ticked on, the more it felt like she never would be again.

CHAPTER SIX

——————

December 1998

MANDY SAT ON THE floor in her bedroom, legs stretched out to her sides as far as they could go with her tape, scissors, and the special wrapping paper she picked out for one particular gift in a pile in front of her. The paper featured Santa with a soccer ball, playing with his reindeer—it wasn't baseball, but it was the thought that counted, right? After several attempts that ended with torn and crumpled balls scattered around her, she steadied her hands and tried again. It had to be just right. If it wasn't, how would Brandon know how much she liked him? She checked and double-checked before she cut and only used small pieces of tape. The bandage between her fingers from an early paper cut made it a little more difficult, but she couldn't get blood on it like her last failed attempt—that was just gross. Mandy folded and creased and tucked the corners in, and finally she had done it. Satisfied, she finished by sticking a big red bow right in the center.

Perfect.

Brandon was going to freak out when he saw the personalized jersey Mandy bought for him. She couldn't wait to see the look on his face. He was, after all, her first *real* boyfriend, and they had been dating for almost three whole months.

She kept a shoebox full of all the notes they'd exchanged, folded into little heart shapes. Brandon wasn't much of a writer, usually responding in a couple of sentences to Mandy's paragraphs, but she didn't mind.

Mandy's warm cheeks hurt from smiling so big looking down at his gift. Ever since Brandon started going to the ballpark with Mandy, she actually enjoyed herself—even if Brandon spent most of the time watching the game. It wasn't like she could get mad at him since Dad was the same way with football at home. Dad's time at the baseball game was spent between watching the field and "networking," which Mandy decided at the time was just a fancy way to say talking to other adults.

In other words, boring.

But watching Brandon get so excited when the Dodgers scored made it all worth it. Just like giving this gift would be worth emptying her piggy bank—all her saved birthday and tooth fairy money from years ago combined. Mom wasn't happy about Mandy's choice. Miss Heather—Mandy's therapist—suggested she might want to offer a smaller token. But Mandy had already drawn him more pictures than she could count. She imagined he had them all hanging on the wall in his bedroom—maybe one day he would invite her over so she could see for herself—so this had to be something extra special. It had to be the perfect gift.

"Mandy, we have to go," Mom called from downstairs. "We're going to be late."

"Coming," Mandy yelled back as she struggled to push the present under her bed. It was already pretty full with the ones for Mom, Dad, Isa, and Miss Heather. She would have to clean up the rest of the mess later before her mom saw it.

"Mandy!" Mom bellowed again. "Come on."

They were just going to her school's winter festival event, which meant they didn't have to be there at any certain time, but Mandy wasn't going to bring this up.

She ran to the stairs and slid down the banister so fast Mom didn't have time to yell at her not to.

"Amanda Elizabeth Dean. What have I told you about that?" Mom's hands were perched on her hips and her lips were pursed, but Mandy was pretty sure she was fighting not to laugh.

Dad chuckled. "I did it all the time when I was her age, and I turned out okay."

Mom gave Dad the look. "Not helping." Mom turned to grab her purse, and Dad winked at Mandy.

Mandy skipped along the driveway and hopped into the back seat of Mom's car as her parents got into the front. The Winter Carnival at GAT—more formally known as the School for the Gifted and Talented—was the most important fundraiser of the year, and everyone who went to school there, and a bunch of alumni that were still in the area, attended. Between the field and the parking lot there was enough room to set up rides and games where you could win prizes, and they even had cotton candy, fried Oreos, and all the fun fair food—as Dad liked to call it. Mandy liked all those things, and this year she was planning to ride the Ferris wheel with Brandon. They'd sit close—knees touching—and hold hands.

Would he want to kiss her?

She'd been dreaming about it. When they went to the ballpark, they were always with Mandy's parents, and no way would she do that in front of them. But on the Ferris wheel, they could be alone, and then when they got stuck at the top, no one would even see. It would be perfect, and oh so romantic. Just like a scene in a movie.

On the drive over, Mandy didn't even complain about Dad's music choice that had way too much drumming. All she could think about was Brandon, her Ferris wheel ride, and her (hopefully) first kiss.

Soon Mom parked, and the three of them walked past lines of cars. The sweet scent of sugar and salt of over-buttered popcorn wafted through the air. Screams of joy—or terror—from rides like the Gravitron and the Zipper could be heard blocks away.

"What do you want to do first?" Mom asked.

Mandy and Dad exchanged a look and together they responded, "Corn dogs."

"I don't even know why I asked." Mom started pulling prepaid food tickets from her purse. There wasn't a price of admission, but everything needed tickets. Food, rides, games—and they were all different.

It was already packed as Mandy entered with her parents and snaked through the masses of people. Her art teacher had a stand set up for drawing caricatures, and her PE teacher staffed a booth where you could kick a ball through a board where giant faces with their mouths wide open were painted. The whole kindergarten class was setting up on a stage getting ready to sing a few songs. Mandy had done that when she was their age. But so far, no Brandon.

Excitement bubbled in Mandy's chest as she entered the food tent and got in line with her parents, searching the crowd. Her friend Laura sat at a long table with the rest of her gigantic family. They were easy to spot since almost all of them had the same raven-black hair—some of them had straight hair and some curly, but it all was so black it looked almost blue, which stood out against their mostly cream-colored skin. Clay and José—Brandon's friends—were goofing around near the beverage stand. Mandy's other friend Sara stood waiting for chicken nuggets on the opposite side of the tent with her mom, who wore the most beautiful sari—that's what Sara had told Mandy the dresses her mom always wore were called. There were a bunch of other kids from her class too, but still no Brandon. He should've been with Clay—since they were as tight as Mandy and Isa—so maybe he didn't come? But that didn't make any sense. He had to be around there somewhere.

As soon as Mom handed Mandy her corn dog, Mandy asked, "Can I go look for people?"

Dad glanced at his watch. "Check back here in one hour."

Mandy raced off.

"One hour," Dad called after her.

"One hour," Mandy parroted to let her parents know she was listening.

Surely, she would be able to find Brandon and ride the Ferris wheel with him within the hour. Since he wasn't in the food tent, maybe he was in line to take pictures with his family in front of the school. That was another big draw for this event. The school hired a professional photographer, and most of the pictures taken ended up on Christmas cards that Mom would later put on display until the first weekend of January, when all the decor would be cleaned up and put away for next year—and the cards tossed in the garbage.

Mandy bobbed and wove her way through the crowd, past the kiddie rides where some toddlers screeched as they zoomed along in minicars on a small track, and others rode horses on the merry-go-round. When she came to the front of the school and didn't spot him—only his parents talking in a group of adults—Mandy pivoted and headed for the games. Of course he must be there. Probably trying to win the biggest stuffed bear for Mandy. Why hadn't she thought of that sooner?

People threw darts at balloons and balls at bottles; the crashes and squeals of excitement merged with ringing bells, but Mandy ignored them all. At one point someone—Sara maybe—yelled her name, but Mandy was on a mission. She ducked behind a group of high schoolers and kept hunting.

Her time was running out. She would have to check in with her parents soon, and then she'd have to stand in line for their picture to be taken, and by that time Isa would be there, and they always went on the Scrambler together, then spent the rest of their time alternating between snacking and more rides, always ending on the Tilt-a-Whirl with as many people as they could pack into one carriage without getting in trouble.

It didn't make any sense. Brandon's friends were here, his parents were here, so where the heck was he? Her pace slowed from a frantic rush until her feet stopped her right in front of the Ferris wheel. How close she was and yet so very far.

A rush of wind pushed her hair away from her face as the wheel spun, bringing with it the sound of a familiar voice.

Three baskets up were Brandon's signature Air Jordans, but

those were not the feet of another boy sitting next to him. Mandy's heart started to race. She wanted so badly for it to be his sister, but she was only six, and this girl's legs were way too long. Mandy shifted through the crowd as the wheel came to a stop, her hands starting to shake. And there through the steel bars and flashing lights was Brandon—with Alison Dainton and a giant stuffed bear, forcing them to sit closer together, knees touching and holding hands. Alison was an eighth grader, on the swim team, and class president.

What was he doing with *her*?

Mandy already knew the answer long before her brain asked the question. She knew the moment she spotted those fluorescent-orange-painted toes in sandals.

Everything around Mandy blurred. The lights. The shrieks of joy. The hordes of people. This wasn't supposed to be how it happened. It was supposed to be Mandy in that seat next to Brandon. Mandy's hand he was holding. Mandy's lips he was kissing.

This *was* like a movie. A horrible, terrible, awful movie. Before anyone could notice her, and before anyone could notice her noticing what Brandon and Alison were doing, Mandy sprinted away.

BY THE TIME THE MOON CAME OUT AND STARS FILLED an inky sky that night, Mandy's sadness had morphed into something else. Perhaps it was because of the way Isa responded to the news.

"That's messed up," she had said. "Brandon's a total pendejo."

Of course, Isa was right. Mandy was too good for Brandon—Isa's words—and now as Isa and Mandy walked down a suburban street full of single-family homes, wearing all black and carrying a bag full of rolls of toilet paper, Brandon was about to find out just how wrong he was to cheat on her.

Mandy checked behind them.

"Stop doing that." Isa swatted Mandy's arm.

"Are you sure this is a good idea?"

"He didn't even break up with you first."

Mandy shrugged. "I know, but—"

"But nothing." Isa's voice held more conviction than Mandy's whole body. It had been her idea to raid Mandy's pantry of their mega-sized stash of toilet paper and, under the cover of night, leave Brandon a little message in sidewalk chalk on his driveway. "No one treats you that way. No one."

The crickets seemed to agree with Isa, getting louder the closer they got to Brandon's house. Like their own personal cheering squad. But Mandy's stomach clenched, and the fried Oreos she protested eating earlier threatened to make an appearance.

Sneaking out of Mandy's house would've been impossible, since every time a door or window opened, their alarm system would beep. And sneaking out of Isa's wasn't any easier. There were rosebushes outside her window, so they had to use the front door, and Abuela liked to fall asleep on the couch most nights. But the noise of the TV helped them escape, even though there was still the task of sneaking back inside ahead of them. They would both be in extra-big trouble if they were found out, but Isa had assured Mandy it would be worth it. Isa had never been so fired up before. Usually, she was the cautious one.

As the blocks went on, and the rows of smaller houses that characterized Isa's neighborhood gave way to larger and more spacious lots, with gates and gardens that hid the homes from view, Mandy wasn't so sure they made the right choice. Yes, she was hurt, and angry, but maybe it had been Mandy's fault. Maybe Mandy needed to be a better girlfriend. Maybe there was more Mandy could've done.

Amber streetlights cast an almost ominous glow along their journey. Somewhere in a tree nearby, an owl hooted. Or maybe he was saying, "Go home. Go home."

Mandy glanced back again.

"Stop doing—"

"Car." Mandy pulled Isa out of the road and behind some garbage cans, her heart ricocheting in her chest faster than a rogue pinball. "That was close."

"We aren't going to get caught."

Mandy didn't know how Isa could be so sure, but she also didn't question her when she got like this. When Isa was determined it was best to go along with it.

As soon as the passing car's taillights faded to black, Mandy and Isa emerged from their hiding spot and continued down the road. And before Mandy had the chance to second-guess herself again, they'd arrived.

Brandon's house looked exactly the same as it had the last time Mandy was there—except it was a lot darker out. Her parents had picked him up for an afternoon Dodgers game, so the porch light wasn't on and there had only been one car in the driveway, but the yellow paint looked just as sunshiny, and the bushes under the windows still had a few blooms. The grass was still neatly mowed, and the little sign alerting passersby that a dog was "on duty" still hung from the wooden gate that led to the backyard. Not that Mandy had ever been in the backyard, or inside the house for that matter, but she was pretty sure they didn't have a dog. She had never heard it bark when she came knocking to pick Brandon up, and wasn't that what dogs did?

"Come on." Isa's voice jarred Mandy from her thoughts. "You start over there, and I'll do this side." She shoved a roll into Mandy's hands.

The paper seemed heavier—just as soft, but heavier.

Isa launched her roll into the avocado tree, the paper snagging on a branch and then cascading to the ground. The white strip rippled in a passing breeze like the water in Mandy's backyard fountain when her mother turned it on. Isa mumbled something under her breath ending with "Alison" as she launched the roll back into the tree.

And that was all it took to snap Mandy into action. No, it wasn't Alison's fault. Mandy wasn't mad at her. Brandon probably didn't even tell her about Mandy. About all the games she brought him to because Mandy loved Brandon, and Brandon loved baseball. He loved it so much that it was all he ever talked about.

That was it, wasn't it?

Baseball, not Mandy.

It had never been about Mandy, had it?

Rage burned in Mandy's chest, and she launched her own roll and then another. Sweat dripped down her neck, soaking into the band of her black sweatpants as tentacles of white all fluttered in the wind, making the yard look more like a papier-mâché project gone wrong than a place someone lived. Empty cardboard tubes littered the manicured lawn, and the bags that had been full what felt like moments before were practically empty.

"You know, this feels good." Mandy panted.

"Shhh . . ."

"You're right. He's a pendejo."

"SHHH . . ."

"A really, really—"

The porch light flipped on, and Mandy's heart turned off. Oh no.

Mandy froze mid-throw—arm back, roll clenched in her hand. Locks clicked. The door creaked as it started to open.

"Come on." Isa's fingers wrapped around Mandy's wrist and yanked.

Mandy's brain might not have been working, but her feet got the message as she took off with Isa.

"Hey!" someone yelled, but no way was Mandy checking behind them now. No. They had to get out of there. But what if someone raced after them? Was that the sound of a car door slamming? No way could they outrun Brandon's dad's pickup truck.

This wasn't good. They'd get caught, and they'd get in trouble. They needed to get out of sight and lie low for a while, and quick. Bright lights rounded the corner behind them. Now it was Mandy's turn to grab Isa and pull her off the main road.

Isa didn't resist. She followed Mandy just as Mandy had followed Isa before—without question. Gravel crunched under her feet as she tugged her friend along, through an open gate to an expansive backyard, and ducked under a trampoline.

Mandy lay on her stomach waiting, listening to the nothingness in the night. It was as though the air itself were holding its collective breath for them. Mandy couldn't even hear the rapid beat of her own heart. Then at last a vehicle drove past, and her pulse finally started to slow.

"That was close," Isa whispered as she panted by Mandy's side.

"Too close."

"But so worth it." Isa's wide grin made Mandy smile.

There under the taut material of the trampoline, the cool grass tickled Mandy's chin, and the crushing silence ended as a cacophony of crickets chirped. They had just TP'ed Brandon Martínez's house, turning it into a winter wonderland of sorts. Mandy couldn't help but imagine a toilet sitting on the lawn amid all the streams of toilet paper.

"I'm really sorry that happened to you." Isa's voice broke through the vision swirling in Mandy's head.

"It's not your fault."

"I know, but"—Isa paused—"you didn't deserve that. And one day you'll find someone who likes you for you, not for anything you can give them or do for them. Because you are amazing, Mandy. You are so caring, and loving, and creative, and talented, and loyal, and I . . . I love you for real," Isa said.

Mandy turned to her best friend. The girl who committed a misdemeanor and almost got caught with her and never blinked an eye. "I love you for real back."

Mandy reached over and pulled Isa into a side squeeze—which was an awkward way to hug, but it did the job—then she flopped onto her back. Isa lay next to her. And there in the darkness, in the damp grass with the crickets chirping, Mandy interlaced their fingers and tried to find the stars through the underside of the trampoline.

CHAPTER SEVEN

May 2011

MANDY GOT UP FROM the table, placed her black napkin on her chair, and smoothed down the front of her knee-length red dress. She had felt so powerful when she tried it on. Like stepping into a stronger version of herself.

"Fits like a glove," the saleswoman had said.

"Don't worry about the price." Mom had her hands clasped over her heart.

But wearing it now in this fancy restaurant with chandeliers the size of small cars, surrounded by people wearing equally fancy clothes, all Mandy felt was exposed. Once she was out of her parents' sight, she swerved left toward the bar instead of heading right to the bathroom. She needed a moment alone. The conversation she just had with Isa played in the back of her mind on repeat.

"One shot of tequila," Mandy told the bartender.

"One tequila, two tequila, three tequila, floor." A handsome

man slid up next to Mandy, sipping on his own glass of dark amber liquor. "This is probably going to sound terrible, but that
frown does *not* fit your face."

He was right. It did sound terrible, and if Mandy hadn't been
questioning everything that had just happened with Isa, she
probably would've told him so. But her brain was tired. Her
heart was heavy. And she needed something to make her stop
thinking about it. Thinking about Isa.

"Really," she responded instead. "Whose face would it fit on?"

The man with dark brown skin and light brown eyes chuckled, showing off perfectly straight teeth just past full, luscious
lips. He was well dressed in a suit expertly cut to fit his body—
likely custom made. "Touché."

The bartender slid Mandy's drink toward her. "Should I add
this to your table?" she asked.

"Put it on my tab," the man said.

"Thank you." Mandy raised her drink to him, and he clinked
his glass against hers.

"What are we drinking to?"

That was a great question. Mandy should be celebrating—
that was what today was all about, after all—but in that moment,
there didn't feel like much *to* celebrate. Everything seemed so
daunting, and complicated, and . . . impossible. Was Mandy losing the one person who ever really meant anything to her? No.
She couldn't think about it. "To the unknown," she landed on,
not knowing what else to say.

"To the unknown."

Mandy took the liquor down in one gulp, allowing it to burn
a little before she carefully placed the lime between her lips and

sucked. "Thanks again," she said, and then she walked away from the gorgeous man, who on any other day she might have tried to flirt with. But not today.

The tequila didn't take away the hurt Mandy felt under her ribs, but it was what she needed to plaster on a smile and return to her parents.

"So what are we talking about?" she asked as she slid back into her chair, laying the napkin back over her lap.

"*Bridesmaids*," Dad said as he picked up his champagne flute and took a sip.

Mandy scrunched her brows. "Who's getting married?"

"No, not like that, honey," Mom said. "The movie with Melissa McCarthy and Kristen Wiig."

Mandy nodded. She'd heard about it, but with finals and everything, she hadn't had time to go, though she had wanted to. "Isn't that like the girl version of *The Hangover*?" she asked.

"Yes, exactly." Mom slapped her hand on the table. "Which I went to with your father, and so I think he should go to this movie with me."

"And you don't want to see it?" Mandy asked Dad.

"That's not what I said. I just suggested your mother might have more fun going with some of her girlfriends is all."

Mandy and Mom exchanged a glance. "So exactly what I said then." Usually, Mandy was all about team Dad, but tonight he was being ridiculous. "It looks really funny. Plus, you love popcorn." It was because of Dad that Mandy knew the best way to eat movie theater popcorn—extra butter with M&M's mixed in. Salty and sweet—the perfect combination.

"I'm sure it will be," Dad reasoned.

"Then why won't you take me to see it?" Mom prodded.

"You think you're going to be the only guy there, is that it?" Mandy asked.

"It just seems better suited for a female audience is all." Dad's cheeks got red.

"Why do men think that movies for women aren't as good?" Mom's cheeks were also getting red.

"I think we should all go." Maybe it was the tequila talking but, at the moment, sitting in a dark room stuffing her face with buttery deliciousness didn't sound half-bad.

"That's a great idea." Mom rubbed Mandy's arm. "What do you say? Family movie night?"

Dad glanced back and forth between Mandy and Mom. "Now how can a man say no to going out with his two favorite girls?"

"Good answer, Dad."

Mom winked at Mandy.

"I think you're going to like it," Mandy added.

"I'm sure I will." Dad drained his champagne and gave himself a refill.

"We should wear coordinated outfits too." Oh, it was definitely the tequila, because Mandy was poking the bear. But sometimes teasing Dad was just fun. It wasn't often Mom and Mandy were on the same side, and Dad was being really silly about the whole thing. He'd go and he'd laugh, and he'd have a great time—sometimes he just needed an extra nudge.

"Yes, perfect," Mom chimed in. "We could all wear pink like in the movie poster."

Now Mandy winked at Dad. He smirked back, acknowledging he knew what she was doing.

"Sounds like a great idea, love," he said to Mom.

Mandy laughed. "Can you pass the bread?"

"This bread is so delicious, isn't it?" Mom said.

The two of them each took a slice, and Mandy slid the plate of olive oil with balsamic vinegar between them so they could share. That was another thing Mandy and Mom could agree on—their love of carbohydrates.

"Maybe we can get some loaves to take home," Mandy said.

"Another great idea," Mom replied.

Dad leaned back in his chair like he was glad to be out of the hot seat.

Course after course, the ache from Mandy's call with Isa didn't completely go away, but the food was heavenly, and soon the three were sharing a crème brûlée and sipping port. Mandy always felt so fancy with the tiny glass of sweet red wine.

"Thanks again for all of this," she told them.

"We really are so proud of you." Mom had tears in her eyes.

"Best meal I've had in ages," Dad said as he flagged down the waiter, probably realizing that Mom would be in full-on sobs soon—like she had been earlier at the graduation. "I think we're ready for the check now, but you might have to roll me out of here." He rubbed his stomach with a hearty chuckle.

"It's already been taken care of." The waiter pulled a card from his breast pocket. "This is for you."

Mandy took the card. Written in some of the neatest hand-writing Mandy had ever seen was *No more frowning. If you want to get to know the unknown, call me.* Mandy flipped the card over.

Edmund Prince — International Finance Manager

Mandy couldn't help but smile.

CHAPTER EIGHT

December 2006

WINTER IN SOUTHERN CALIFORNIA was weird. Especially after those winters in Europe that were so blistering cold Mandy thought she would never be warm again. But as her flip-flops slapped the pavement of Main Street, the chill in the air didn't bother her at all.

When Mandy first left for Europe, she had only intended to stay a few months. But three turned to four, which turned to six and then a year and half later Mandy had finally come home.

Being back was surreal in a lot of ways. Everything was basically unchanged, but at the same time everything was different. The trees were taller, and Mandy's favorite art supply store had moved, leaving her padding along the street in search of its new location. Her time overseas changed Mandy, not just as an artist but as a person. She seemed to see life in brighter colors, and even though Mandy wasn't sure what she was going to do next, she felt excited for what could be. She missed her friends, especially Sophie, but it wasn't the ache she'd had when she first got to Europe all alone.

Today, Mandy headed to Grace's Art and Supply in search of a canvas. She enjoyed stretching her own, but there was something in Mandy's head and heart that ached to get out, so she couldn't wait any longer. And she desperately wanted to see Grace too. The middle-aged woman had always been a sort of mentor to Mandy, so coming home would never be complete without seeing one of her favorite people.

Finally, the familiar *ding-ding-dong* greeted Mandy as she walked into Grace's.

"Look what the cat dragged in." Grace Chan herself chuckled from one of the registers. "Your mom said you were coming home, and she showed me pictures, but I want to hear it from you. How was it?" Just like every day Mandy had ever come into the shop, Grace was dressed in paint-splattered overalls and a tie-dyed T-shirt. Grace's had always held a number of art classes, and from the looks of the new larger location, things must've been going well. Mandy still needed to set up her own workspace, but that would happen in time.

"Inspiring," Mandy breathed.

"It is, isn't it?" Grace tied her long black graying hair around her hand and used a pencil to secure it to the top of her head. "I remember my first trip. I didn't want to come home either. I thought for sure we'd lose you to the Louvre or Rijksmuseum or the Palace of Versailles"—Grace sighed longingly—"or the pastries." She winked.

"Oh, Grace, it was so incredible. All of it was." And from there the conversation flowed as smooth as a cappuccino. Grace leaned in and listened with her whole body as Mandy went on about her favorite places and all the secret nooks and crannies that Europe had to offer. Then Grace would respond and share some of her own. She had a way of understanding Mandy that not even Mom did—although she always tried.

"What did you think of her in person?" Grace set her elbows on the counter and propped her head on her hands.

Mandy closed her eyes, taking her back to the moment she stood in front of Berthe Morisot's art for the first time. She was one of the first women to break through into the good old boys' club of Impressionist painters, and she was beyond talented. It was a shame most people still didn't recognize her by name. "Her work isn't the same in person as it is printed in books, you know?" she said, and Grace nodded like she knew exactly what Mandy was talking about. "It's like standing there, you can really see the purpose behind each brushstroke. She wasn't trying to hide anything or cover it up, it was all right there on the canvas. Crisp. Refined. Intentional. Like she knew she was good, and why shouldn't she know?" Mandy sighed, and Grace smiled. "I don't know. I just felt seen. Even if it was for just a moment. Does that make sense?"

"Completely," Grace agreed. "I'm so glad you got to experience that in person."

"Me too." Mandy let out a long breath. "I could talk to you all day about this." Mandy glanced at the clock on the wall of paintbrushes. "Yikes, I kind of already have. But I know you've got other things you need to do, and I have this idea . . ." Mandy launched into excruciating detail about the depth and scope of her next project. "I'm going to need a canvas. A big one." Mandy stretched her arms out as wide as they would go.

A sly grin crept up on Grace's face. "I have just the thing."

Grace led Mandy toward the back of the store, and just as Mandy had expected, right into Grace's workroom. "I had the urge to stretch this the other day, and now I know why."

It wasn't the standard size that canvases generally came in but narrower and longer, just how Mandy's mind had envisioned. She had figured she would've needed to buy multiples or find a way to make it work with what was available, but this . . . this was perfect.

"How much do I owe you?" she asked.

"Oh. I know the owner, so I can get you a good deal." Grace winked. "I'll bring it up front so you can wander around." And with that Grace lifted the canvas and walked out before Mandy could argue with her. Not that Grace would allow it.

If Mandy loved Grace's store before, she was even more in love with it now. There were twice the number of options, which seemed like both a blessing and a curse, but today more of a blessing. She already knew exactly what she needed, but that didn't stop Mandy from checking out the store's new layout.

She had somehow stumbled down an aisle with decor, and paper stock for invitations, and practically any knickknack a bride could need for their wedding. "Laura?" It had been almost two years since Mandy had seen Laura last, and she almost didn't recognize her. Laura's raven-black hair had been bleached to an almost white-blonde, and she had more makeup on than she would wear onstage.

"Mandy!" Laura charged toward Mandy, wrapping her in a tight hug. "When did you get back?"

"Just a couple of—"

"I'm engaged!" Laura thrust her hand into Mandy's face, showing off a sparkling single-carat diamond.

"That's so exciting. Congratulations." Mandy smiled, holding in the giggle that wanted to escape. It may have been a while since she had seen Laura, but she hadn't changed a bit. Still dramatic as ever.

"Steven . . . my fiancé . . . he's getting his master's right now, and already has a job with his dad. They buy and sell buildings, not like flipping houses, but, like, buildings." Laura moved her arms to demonstrate she was talking about something big. "It's so weird he knows exactly how many bathrooms the floor of any building would need just by knowing the square footage." She paused. "Weird, right?"

"Totally." Mandy nodded.

"Exactly. Anyway, his dad is going to retire someday, and so, like, needs Steven to be able to run everything, so he's taking these classes . . ." Laura rambled on and on, and it took Mandy more effort than she wanted to admit to pay attention. It couldn't still be jet lag, but still she felt bad. She must've nodded and um-hummed in all the right places, because it seemed as though Laura's smile never faded.

"How's school going?" Mandy asked when Laura paused for breath.

"What? Oh, fine." Laura shrugged. "I'm probably taking the next semester off though to get ready for the wedding, and then Steven really wants to have kids soon, so. It would be really hard to do both, you know?"

"Yeah," Mandy said, but she didn't actually know. Laura always talked about going to college to study film. While she loved acting, she had wanted to do it all. Produce. Direct. She had even written the musical their school performed their senior year. Did people normally give up their dreams for the person they loved? What did that say about Mandy?

". . . So next summer, plan to be there." Laura kept talking. "OMG are you on Facebook?" Laura whipped out her phone.

Face*what*? "No, I don't think so."

"Do they not have it in Europe?" Laura seemed to ponder. "Well, you need to get an account and then friend me, okay? Oh my god, it was so good running into you." After rambling on for another five minutes about all the errands she had to run, Laura kissed Mandy on both cheeks and was gone.

Thirty minutes later, Mandy hobbled down the street with her oversized canvas and bag of supplies, try as she might not to run into people. A storefront door opened just as Mandy approached, and forced her to sidestep into a couple sitting on a large tree-planter box, sharing a cinnamon roll.

Mandy fumbled with her canvas now that she had been thrown off-balance. "Sorry about—" Her mouth went dry, and her heartbeat went into overdrive.

"Mandy?" Isa said. Her voice was a little colder than Mandy remembered—but not without good reason. Next to Isa sat another girl with gorgeous dark brown skin and hazel eyes. On her lap was a cinnamon roll box—just one—with two forks, like it belonged to both of them. Mandy's stomach rolled over.

"I'm sorry," Mandy mumbled—not just about almost crushing them now, but also for the things that happened between them before Mandy left for Europe. She'd wanted to text or email those words to Isa a million times but never had the courage.

"I like your hair." Isa gestured. Although it had been growing out, it was a lot shorter than the last time Mandy had been home.

"Thanks." *You look amazing. And as beautiful as the last time I saw you. I've missed you so much.* "I like yours too." Isa's hair was pulled up into a messy kind of bun, nothing special at all, but Isa would always be special to Mandy. Even if they never talked anymore, staring at Isa now reminded Mandy how much she still loved her.

Mandy stood there, unsure what to do. Unsure what to say. Her arms shook from the weight of her recent shopping excursion, but she didn't want to leave—not yet. Not when she was this close—and she didn't know when she ever would be again. Like somehow just standing here allowed her a moment inside Isa's orbit, and stepping away would send her careening off into the unknown again.

Next to her, someone cleared their throat.

Isa motioned to the girl sitting there. "Oh, this is my girlfriend, Tally."

Mandy didn't miss the way Isa said *girlfriend*, or it could've been the way Mandy heard it—either way, it stung. It was the confirmation that Isa's life had moved on and that Mandy didn't know anything about it—not that she had a right to know.

Tally gave a curt smile. "I've heard a lot about you, Mandy."

Mandy was sure she had. "Well, I should . . ." She teetered back and forth with the canvas and her bags like it was an acceptable excuse to leave.

"Yeah, sure," Isa said, and that was it. She didn't beg Mandy to stay or try to convince her things didn't have to be this way. Isa didn't grab Mandy's arm or ask her why she had to leave again.

"It was great seeing you." And it was, and at the same time, it wasn't. Mandy missed Isa more than the flowers could miss the rain. More than the stars could miss the moon. And yet seeing

Isa made Mandy's chest ache so hard it felt as though it might cave in on itself. Before Mandy could stop herself, she turned to Tally. "Take care of her. She's one special girl." Mandy didn't wait for a response; she did what she had done a year and a half before, and walked away.

MANDY'S MORNING HAD BEEN A TIDAL WAVE OF HIGHS and lows, but once she got home and settled into the space at the back of the garage, she easily sank into her work and forgot about . . . well, basically everything.

This piece had been playing on her heart ever since she stepped off the plane at LAX a few days before. Europe was amazing and wonderful, but Mandy was home now, and for the first time in a long time, she felt like she could move forward. All the classes and trial and error had brought her to where she was today. Not standing in her childhood home, that's not what she meant, but in this headspace, feeling confident that she was good, but she could be better, and Mandy was okay with that.

She had many flaws and had made so many mistakes, but someone who's never failed never truly learned either. Mandy had studied, and reconciled, and had maybe even forgiven herself a little.

As she allowed the brush to find its place against the canvas, she smoothed and slashed and blended.

At some point her mother had brought her a plate of dinner, but Mandy didn't stop. She couldn't. Completing this project was the first step of many in Mandy's future, and she had to get through it before she could move on.

A cool breeze pushed through the open back door of the garage, sending in the scent of someone's fireplace nearby. It was a lot crisper than earlier in the day, but sweat dripped from Mandy's nose as she moved in unison with her brush—bending and stretching as though it were an extension of her.

A *crack*—the sound of something large moving outside—finally broke Mandy's concentration, and she spun around.

There, in the cascading light from the garage, stood Isa. How long had she been there?

"What are you doing here?" Mandy's voice was more surprised and less accusatory than the question itself seemed to imply.

Isa's dark curls cascaded over her shoulders in loose waves. Mandy's fingers itched to braid her hair like they had so many times before. But that was all in the past now.

Isa took a step forward and aligned herself in the doorway but didn't come inside. "That's incredible." She gestured to Mandy's painting. "I guess your trip was worth it."

Mandy wasn't sure if those words were meant to hurt, but they did. A direct hit. "I learned a lot." Which was true in so many ways, not just artistically. "What about you? How's school?"

"It's good. Hard, but good."

"Hard? Really, for you?" Mandy teased like no time between them had passed, but it had.

Isa laughed—or chuckled, really. "Yes, even for me. But it will be worth it. Eventually." The smile was still there, but it didn't quite reach her eyes the way it used to.

"You're going to make an amazing doctor one day," Mandy said. And Isa would. It had been the thing she dreamed about since they were little. The thing she had been working toward her entire life—the thing that made her mom and abuela so proud.

"I hope so."

Mandy knew so, but she stayed quiet. She wasn't sure if it was quite her place to squelch the doubt that sometimes lingered in Isa's head. Her role in Isa's life at one time had been so defined, but not anymore.

For a moment they both stood there, neither moving. Only six feet of space between them, but they had never been farther apart.

Mandy opened her mouth, to say—what? She didn't know. Isa stopped her.

"Why?" she asked Mandy. "Why did you do it?"

Mandy knew the answer to this question better than she knew her primary colors. Like a movie reel stuck on the same frame, she replayed her last hours in the US before leaving for England at the end of the most magical summer. She'd lived with the heartbreak of after. And part of what Mandy had learned when she was away was just how strong she could be. Because as much as she wanted to tell Isa everything, she couldn't. "How are your mom and abuela?" Mandy asked instead of answering.

"They're fine." Isa squared her shoulders. "Now tell me why."

"Really? Mom mentioned something about an accident."

Isa huffed. "Abuela fell off a stool is all, broke her wrist. But she's fine now—"

"That's great—"

"Why are you avoiding the question?"

"Was there a question? I guess I've never been as smart as you."

"Don't do that," Isa scolded. "Don't talk about my frie—just don't. You know you've always been capable of anything. Look at that." She gestured to the painting again, but Mandy didn't

look at it. The painting would always be there, but Isa wouldn't—
Mandy's heart ached. "So, I will ask again. Why are you avoiding
the question?"

"I'm not." She was.

"Then why?"

Tears threatened at the backs of Mandy's eyes, but she didn't
allow any of them to fall.

"Mandy? Why did you do that to me?" Did Isa's voice break?
Or was that Mandy's heart cracking in two all over again?

Mandy shook her head. "I can't," she said, but she really
wanted to. She had practiced exactly what she would say if this
moment had ever presented itself—memorized every word—
and now the moment was here. Mandy wasn't sure if she could
hold out much longer. The way Isa was looking at her. The hitch
in Isa's voice. The static in the air around them. It was too much,
and the walls that Mandy had so carefully constructed were on
the verge of crumbling.

"Can't or won't?" Isa yelled.

A dog barked. The breeze fluttered Isa's hair, pushing it farther over her shoulders. Goose bumps broke out on Mandy's
arms as the moment stretched on and on.

"Won't." Mandy finally met Isa's eyes. "I'm sorry." And she
was for so many things, but this was all she would allow herself
to say.

Isa nodded like she understood, but she never could. "Well,
maybe one day you will."

It didn't ever seem likely, but Mandy responded, "Maybe."

Isa took a step back. "I guess I'll see you around then." And
like that, she was gone.

CHAPTER NINE

April 2019

MANDY HUNG UP FROM yet another call with yet more bad news and stepped out of the bedroom to the main room of her hotel suite, where Ashley had been waiting patiently for her.

"I'm so sorry," Mandy said.

"Don't worry about it. This isn't my first wedding. I've built in plenty of time to make sure we get you more beautiful than you already are. So *this* isn't something you need to stress about." She gestured around them.

Just hearing those words—that someone else had control— made Mandy want to cry. "Thank you." She sucked in a huge breath. Tears, however, couldn't happen. Not unless she wanted to redo her makeup—which she didn't.

Ashley stood and grabbed a black cape, swishing it like she was a matador. Something about the way the silky fabric rolled like a gentle ocean wave calmed Mandy. Maybe it was that she was finally moving on to the next step—and that was one step closer to marrying the person she loved.

And then her phone chimed.

She should've turned it on silent. She should've left it under a pillow on the bed. But it was in her hand, and before she could stop herself, Mandy checked the screen.

NIKKI: Call me real quick!

Because it was Nikki, and because Mandy knew "real quick" did in fact mean real quick, she clicked on Nikki's contact info and let the phone ring. Mandy held up a finger to Ashley. "Just one more second." Then Mandy walked back into the bedroom.

Nikki answered the phone. "Girl, are you sitting down? You need to sit down."

Mandy could not take any more bad news. She sat on the end of her bed. "What is it. Did someone die? Is the venue on fire? Or wait, I'm dead and this is all just a big, huge nightmare."

"Laura is bringing her in-laws."

"What!" Mandy yelled. No, this wasn't as bad as someone dying, it was worse. "But the tables are all set, and everyone has an assigned seat, and we already confirmed the number with the caterer—"

"I know. I told Laura it was bullshit, and she couldn't just show up with random people you don't even know. Who the fuck invites their in-laws to someone else's wedding?"

"Right?"

"I'm telling you this in case you hear from her, but I told her under no circumstances was she to call and even ask you if this was okay. So if you see her name on your screen, ignore her. Or better yet, just block her number. I also told her if she shows up with them, I will break into her house and shave her head in the middle of the night." Nikki totally would. Thank god for her.

"You're the best."

"Don't you worry. I got your back. See you soon. Ciao." Nikki hung up.

Why would anyone think they could just bring extra people to a wedding at the last minute? And how did boats go missing? And who the heck didn't serve blueberry muffins just because it's past a certain time? What the hell was going on today?

Mandy took a deep breath. And then another. But there was a gremlin inside her stomach crawling, clawing its way up and making her entire body shake. She grabbed the closest pillow and screamed into it as loud as she could. She screamed until her throat was dry and until she had to come up for air.

When she put the pillow down, Ashley stood in the doorway. "Everything okay?"

Nothing was okay. Practically everything had gone wrong, and she hadn't even gotten her hair done yet. The absurdity of that question made Mandy laugh.

And laugh.

And laugh.

Fuck, her stomach hurt from laughing so hard. It was like doing a million crunches all at once. She could barely catch her breath. The entire day was falling apart, and it wasn't even noon yet.

That was it. Why hadn't she thought of that before? Thank god it wasn't noon. There was still time. Candy would fix the fish problem. Nikki was probably sharpening her clippers at that very moment. And Mandy needed to get her hair done, so she could get dressed, take pictures, and then get married.

She could do this.

The universe was testing her. Seeing if she would fall apart. Screw you, Universe! Not today!

Okay, maybe not "screw you," but she got it. And she could do this and the next thing, and she would get through it.

Mandy caught her breath and finally responded to Ashley, "I'm good."

There was a knock on the door.

"That's room service with your muffin." Ashley dipped away to answer it.

See. Her muffin was here. The thing they said they wouldn't be able to get when they delivered the sandwiches, but they did. Things were going to finally fall into place.

Ashley popped her head back in the doorway. "Victory!"

"Victory!" Mandy echoed.

"Now let's get you gorgeous!"

"Let's do it." Mandy's cell rang. Laura's name was on the screen. Not today, satan. Mandy clicked the phone to silent, placed it under her screaming pillow, and walked away.

CHAPTER TEN

September 1999

ISA HAD ISSUES WITH her schedule and needed to see the counselor during lunch, leaving Mandy to sit at their usual table without her. Their group of friends were all nice, and they all got along really well. Isa and Mandy weren't as close with any of them as they were with each other, but they were still their friends. Every sleepover and birthday party and field trip—and every lunch—they all were together.

The cafeteria at the School for the Gifted and Talented wasn't like the ones Mandy saw on TV shows. They were a magnet school, and parents were super involved—meaning they were required to put in a number of volunteer hours each year, which the administration claimed made them care more about the school; and maybe they did, because the cafeteria looked like a giant living room in someone's house, with student artwork on the walls, potted plants, and comfy chairs around round tables that all had napkin dispensers in the middle. The food served was always something multicultural—just like the student body—although lots of kids also brought lunch from home. Another nice thing about GAT was that everyone kind of got along. Although they all had their friend groups, it wasn't cliquey like on *Sabrina the Teenage Witch*.

Laura plopped down at their table with her lunch tray, pulled the scrunchie from her wrist, and threw her raven-black hair up into a high ponytail, making a performance out of it in the process. Then again, everything Laura did was a performance—pulling up her hair, applying her lip gloss, scrunching her pale freckled nose when something annoyed her—everything. "Who else wants to go to the movies this weekend?" She set the contents of her lunch in front of her—a vegan rice bowl, sliced apple, and Oreo cookies.

"I'm in." Sara threw her hand in the air, showing off the henna that was still lingering from her sister's wedding that summer—it was intricate and beautiful, and Mandy was a little jealous of it. "Wait, what are we seeing?" She took a bite of her turkey and lettuce wrap.

"My mom wants to see *Double Jeopardy*." Laura stuck her finger in her mouth and made a gagging noise. "But maybe we can go see something else instead."

Mandy opened her paper bag and pulled out her peanut butter and pickle sandwich. "What else is playing?" Her friends thought it was weird, but they didn't comment about Mandy's favorite sandwich anymore. The few of them brave enough to try it even admitted it wasn't bad. Mandy thought it was much better than plain old PB&J, that was for sure.

"I think *10 Things I Hate About You* is still playing." Sara blinked her dark brown eyes innocently.

Mandy loved that movie. She and Isa went to see it on opening weekend, and then she went back again the weekend after with Mom and Dad for family movie night. Mandy was already planning to buy a copy on DVD whenever it came out and had been searching for a movie poster she could hang in her bedroom. There was something really special about that movie—the way it made Mandy feel. As she took a bite of her sandwich—the sweetness of peanut butter mixing with the salty crunch of pickle—she thought back to her absolute favorite scene. Kat was all annoyed and decided to go to a house party, and she kept throwing back shots of something. At one point she jumped up on a table and started dancing. The song that played in the background thumped through Mandy's seat, and she froze mid-popcorn bite, watching Kat. She was so cool, and her hair was amazing, and the way her ashy violet tank top came up and showed off her belly button—

"We all know you just want to see Heath Ledger again." Nikki threw a tortilla chip from her enchilada lunch at Sara.

It bounced off her arm, leaving a dusting of salt behind. "Yeah, so? He's hot." She picked up the chip and threw it back, hitting Nikki in the forehead.

"Heath Ledger is hot," Laura confirmed.

"Exactly," Sara said.

Nikki's usually pale cheeks quickly turned into bright red apples. "Duh. Everyone knows that though. Right, Mandy?"

"Yeah, but Julia Stiles is amazing too, don't ya think?" Mandy was sure of this, but her voice sounded hesitant even to her own ears.

"Oh, totally," Laura said. "She's a really good actress."

"And she gets to kiss Heath Ledger," Sara said.

The sandwich in Mandy's mouth turned gluey, and it was tough for her to swallow. That wasn't what Mandy had meant. Sure, she got to kiss him, but what had Mandy's heart pounding during that movie was that he got to kiss *her*. Was she the only person to think that?

The conversation quickly shifted to who everyone thought was good-looking at their school. Sara mentioned Parker—he played the drums in band. Laura said Ryan—a soccer player. And Nikki said all the boys at their school were too immature. Mandy agreed with all of them, but another name did pop into her head.

Daphne.

She was new that year, in the same homeroom as Mandy and Isa, and anytime Mandy looked at her, honeybees buzzed in her chest.

Daphne's hair was the color of late autumn leaves—brown with a hint of red—and she had a constellation of freckles across the bridge of her light brown nose and on her cheeks. Every day she wore the same black cardigan with tan leather elbow patches—which was both a little nerdy and a little sweet—and a hemp choker. And anytime Daphne knew the answer, she bit her lip before lifting a hand full of rings into the air.

She was, in other words, completely and utterly adorable.

But until that moment, Mandy didn't realize her thoughts about Julia Stiles or Daphne were an opinion. She assumed they were a fact—like how Heath Ledger was hot. Now it seemed that not everyone thought the same way Mandy did, and she wasn't sure how she was supposed to feel about that. It wasn't that her feelings were completely out there—Nikki unofficially had two dads, and no one ever said anything bad about them or acted like it was a big deal—but still Mandy felt . . . scared.

MANDY AND ISA SAT ON THE COLD TILE FLOOR IN MAN-dy's bathroom painting their toenails and munching on M&M's as Britney Spears sang from the stereo in Mandy's bedroom. School had only been back in session a couple of weeks, and over-all, seventh grade was a major improvement from sixth. Mandy and Isa had lockers near each other and had the same homeroom teacher, and they were no longer at the bottom edge of the social hierarchy of middle school, which felt cooler even if it didn't really mean anything.

That evening, however, Mandy didn't feel cool at all. Her hand wasn't as steady as it normally was when she painted, and her heart beat like it did in PE, which wasn't usual when it was just her and Isa. But there had been something on Mandy's mind—something she really wanted to talk to Isa about, but she wasn't sure how to bring it up.

A cotton ball hit Mandy in the nose, shaking her from her thoughts and bringing her back to her bathroom.

"What's going on with you?" Isa asked. "You're being weird."

That's because Mandy was weird. Wasn't she? She glanced at her mermaid toothbrush holder next to the sink, and then to her shower curtain—the mermaid swimming on it seemed to be looking at Mandy like, *Go ahead, talk to her, she's your best friend*. And Isa was. Mandy told Isa everything, and she always listened and never judged her. So why was Mandy so nervous this time? "Have you ever had a crush on anyone?" Mandy asked even though Isa had never expressed interest in anyone—not even when Mandy talked about that butt-face Brandon all the time— but this question was safe. This question gave Mandy time to think more about what she wanted to say. The scent of acetone burned Mandy's nose.

"Is that what this is about?" Isa went back to her nail polish, a bright yellow that reminded Mandy of a new tennis ball. Maybe Mandy shouldn't have said anything. "It's that new girl, Daphne, isn't it?"

Mandy's breath stopped. And there it was—the truth spoken out in the open and without hesitation. She should've been relieved—she didn't have to say it herself—but instead, her insides trembled. Good thing she was already in the bathroom, because she might need to throw up.

"It's okay. I don't think anyone else knows. I just . . ." Isa shrugged. "Know you, you know?"

"You don't think that makes me weird?" Mandy spoke so softly she wasn't even sure she said the words out loud.

"Oh, you're totally weird, but not in the way you mean." Isa glanced up at Mandy. "And, I mean, I guess Daphne is okay. She's got to be better than butt-face, right?" She smiled. "Hand me the black. I think I want to make smiley faces on these." Isa wiggled her fingers.

Mandy reached into her container full of different nail polishes. "Let me do it." Mandy shook the bottle of black.

Isa set her hands on the floor in front of Mandy. "Oh. Can you go to the mall this weekend?"

Mandy placed the bottle down and pulled out the brush. "Yeah. Of course."

"Good, 'cause Abuela gave me the rest of the money so I could get those new Vans. Oh, and at Waldenbooks . . ." Isa rambled on about all the books she needed to check out, and how she heard about a new ice cream place.

And just like that, Mandy was okay. Isa knew Mandy's secret and didn't ask any questions or make fun of her or leave immediately and never speak to her again. It was like it always was when she was with Isa.

Eventually Mandy would have to tell her other friends and, of course, her parents, but for tonight things in Mandy's world were all right.

CHAPTER ELEVEN

October 2002

AS SOON AS MANDY, V, Isa, and Justin walked in the door to the homecoming dance, they were accosted by their other friends—Nikki, Laura, Sara—and their dates.

"What took you guys so long?" Laura complained as she ran her hands down her silver sequined dress that cut off abruptly at mid-thigh. "Oh my god. You two look adorable." She gestured to V and Mandy.

As predicted, Laura was the picture of perfection with her dark locks swept up, showing off her subtly blushed cheekbones and flawless beige skin.

"Yes, I love the color-coordinating dresses." Nikki pulled Mandy into a hug. "And your hair. It's gorgeous," Nikki said as she hugged Isa. The color of Nikki's dress—a ball gown style—was almost the same shade as Isa's.

Sara looked stunning in purple and gold. "You should've come to dinner with us. There was this guy there who was playing a ukulele, and . . ." Sara launched into a long story about something that happened at the restaurant, while V leaned into Mandy's ear.

"You were right," V whispered. She had been nervous about meeting Mandy's friends. V had met Isa before but not the others. Mandy had tried to assure V there was nothing to worry about. People at Mandy's small magnet school were very accepting—the LGBT club was the second biggest club on campus, after the environmental club. It was vastly different from what V had said her school was like.

"I knew you'd like them." Mandy leaned tighter into V's side.

Homecoming quickly turned into everything Mandy had hoped it would be. Mandy and V danced and danced and avoided the spiked punch—mostly because it tasted disgusting. And then they took more pictures—official ones under a balloon arch.

The event was in the school gym, but they had really done a nice job at making it look fancy even if it still smelled like rubber with a hint of BO. The basketball hoops rained a shower of sparkly streamers, and tables with black tablecloths and folding chairs were set up all over. Thankfully they didn't pull the bleachers out—because how embarrassing would that be?

Between "good" songs, they all would congregate around one table they'd claimed earlier in the night. It was a place the boys left their jackets, and the girls left their purses and shoes while out on the dance floor. V sat next to Mandy and tickled her palm with her finger under the table.

"That's it. I've had enough of these." Laura made a show of unbuckling her four-inch heels and then setting them on the table. They were silver with rhinestones and matched her sequined dress to a T. After all the other girls removed their shoes much earlier in the evening and Laura held firm, Mandy was sure Laura would spend the night in her heels just to prove she could. So Mandy was surprised when Laura finally gave in. Her poor feet were red, and it looked as though two blisters were already forming—one on each foot.

"It's so much better without them." Sara wiggled her nyloned toes, which were propped up on one of the chairs. Her heels weren't as high as Laura's—simple black with lots of straps—but she complained they pinched her feet, and removed them as soon as pictures were over.

Mandy was even happier about her shoe choice. Being barefoot inside the gym sounded like athlete's foot waiting to happen.

"Go request some Christina Aguilera," Nikki ordered her date, Julian, tugging on his pocket.

He nudged Bryan—Laura's date—and jerked his head, and the two were off toward the DJ's tables.

"Where's Isa?" Nikki asked as she began pulling bobby pins from her hair, creating a small pile of them on the table.

"She's still dancing." Mandy motioned with her head toward the dance floor.

Isa had her hands thrown in the air and jumped around with the rest of their classmates—smile stretched wide across her face.

The night had already been a success, and it wasn't over yet. Isa and Justin seemed to be really getting along, and then there were the moments that V or Mandy would pull each other into a hidden corner and kiss and tell the other how beautiful they were. V's fingers danced across Mandy's bare arms and then around to the back of her neck in a way that sent goose bumps down to Mandy's toes.

"Oooh, I like this one." V pulled Mandy back onto the dance floor. Kelly Clarkson sang about a special moment, and V and Mandy swayed together like reeds blowing in a warm summer breeze.

V tucked a stray hair behind Mandy's ear and rested her head on Mandy's shoulder.

This was the moment Mandy should say, *I love you*. Those three little words had felt like a caged bird inside her chest since the night they intertwined their fingers and walked down the pier more than a month ago. But Mandy had kept those words locked inside. Too afraid to say them out loud and scare V off. Things had been going so well for them the way they were, and Mandy didn't want to mess it up with professions of love. But now . . . now she could say them, right? It was the perfect night and the perfect moment. But should she? Would V still think it was too soon since they had only been dating officially since school started?

Mandy opened her mouth to finally let those words fly free, when she spotted Isa storming off the dance floor, so instead she said, "I'll be right back."

If V protested, Mandy didn't hear it, too worried about her best friend.

Mandy caught up to Isa as she pushed outside, a breeze whipping up the hem of her skirt. "What happened?"

The door closed behind them as Isa spun around, tears filling her big brown eyes. "It was awful. I tried but it . . . it was all wrong."

Mandy pulled Isa into her arms. "What was wrong? Whose ass do I need to kick?"

"No. Not like that." Isa's words were muffled by Mandy's shoulder. "He kissed me, Mandy, and it was the most disgusting thing ever."

Mandy smirked. Not big enough for Isa to see even if she was looking, which she wasn't. Sweet, innocent Isa. First kisses were rarely great with anyone. And first-ever first kisses were always doomed to be at least a minor disaster. Mandy's sure was. Instead of teasing Isa about it, which Mandy would do endlessly a few days later—when they could both laugh about it—that night she stroked Isa's hair and said, "It'll be okay. Sometimes kissing a frog is just kissing a frog." And then she said, "Don't worry, one day we'll find your prince."

Isa didn't say anything in response, but she did squeeze Mandy tighter—the rattling in Isa's body seeming to calm down—and Mandy squeezed back. And that is where they stayed; bodies locked together as if they were one. The scent of chlorine from the nearby swimming pool filled the air. The stars that weren't hidden by the passing clouds twinkled in the sky. Crickets played their tune, which was not in sync with the bass now thumping through the wall from inside the gym.

And then that song ended and the next one began. But it didn't matter. When Mandy and Isa were together, nothing else mattered at all. They were each other's shield from anything that could hurt them. When one of them felt weak, the other would give them some of their strength.

"I love you for real," Mandy said.

"I love you for real back," Isa responded.

It never occurred to Mandy to go back inside to find V. Mandy was exactly where she was supposed to be. With her best friend.

CHAPTER TWELVE

December 2006

MANDY LAY ON HER bed under the covers, laptop perched on her chest. She couldn't sleep. When she had finally climbed into bed hours after Isa made her appearance, she'd needed to talk to someone. With the eight-hour time difference, Mandy didn't worry about waking Sophie. It had been only a couple of weeks since Mandy had gotten home, but it felt like an eternity since she had seen her friend.

"You can't do this to yourself again," Sophie said.

"I know." And Mandy did, but at the same time, she couldn't help all the feelings from swirling in her gut like the murky water in her brush-cleaning jar. The image of Isa standing in her garage, there and then not, was etched in her mind. "What if I just—"

"What if you just what? Built a time machine and went back in time, then what? What would you really change?"

Everything. Nothing.

"Would you really not ever have come here?"

Europe was the worst and best thing Mandy had ever done. Sophie wasn't saying these things to be mean; she was saying them because they were what Mandy needed to hear. "You're right." Mandy tugged on a loose thread on her duvet, wrapping it around her finger until the tip turned red. "I just—"

"No." Sophie's voice was firm. "That's all in the past. Now tell me more about this painting project you're working on." Sophie perched her head on her hands and leaned closer to the screen.

Oh, how Mandy wished she could reach out and grab her. Sophie's hugs could bring world peace.

"I'm not trying to be a tosser," Sophie said.

"I know."

"If you really want to talk about it, we can." Sophie's eyes softened.

"No. You're right." Mandy did want to talk about it, but at the same time she didn't. Some scars were just deeper than others and took longer to heal. As much work as Mandy had done, she still needed more time. She sat up a little taller in bed and adjusted her laptop. "How's Finny? Planning his wedding yet?"

Sophie laughed. "Not yet. But soon, I think. Rafe says he's in denial."

"Rafe is good too, then?"

Sophie shrugged. "It's fine. He's fine. Blimey, I didn't tell you. You'll never guess who came into the shop today . . ." Sophie named some celebrity Mandy had never heard of—but seeing how excited Sophie was, Mandy wasn't about to question it. "Remember that scene in *The Devil Wears Prada*—where Nigel kept throwing all those things at Andy and she had to juggle them? It was just like that! Her poor assistant, however, handled it like a pro. It was incredible, and she walked out spending almost ten thousand pounds. My next commission check is going to be cracking."

"That's awesome. And it'll get you one step closer to world domination." Mandy rubbed her hands together and did her best evil laugh.

"Damn right." Sophie had big plans to start her own line, and that required a certain amount of money before she could really launch it, which was why she was working at a "posh" boutique that didn't really match her own aesthetic.

"Have they noticed you're wearing, like, the same three outfits on rotation there?"

Sophie laughed. "Oh, they noticed. And Jacquié even offered to give me an extra ten percent off."

"She did not."

"She did. And you should've seen the look on her face when I told her no."

"Oh my god. You're so bad," Mandy said.

Sophie shrugged, but the smug look on her face said she really didn't care.

And then they were both quiet—but it was in that comforting way when you were with someone you were completely at ease with. There were no expectations of having to entertain the other or fill the space with idle chitchat that didn't really mean anything. It felt like times Mandy spent with Isa. Another wave of grief washed over her.

"Do you . . . do you think she will ever forgive me?" Mandy asked.

Sophie sighed—not in annoyance, more like frustration, and Mandy could understand that; she was frustrated too. "I don't know, babes. But what I do know is that just because you're back where you are doesn't mean you have to go back to feeling the way you did. You're mourning something you don't even know would've existed. Sure, things were good, but that didn't mean it was all going to work out."

Mandy had never thought of it that way before.

"You don't know how it would've played out," Sophie continued. "You have no control over that. But you do have control over your life now. So what are you going to do with it?"

Mandy smiled. "Thank you."

"That's what mates are for."

Mandy kissed her fingers and touched the camera on her laptop, and Sophie did the same.

"Go get some sleep, you look knackered," Sophie said. "Talk soon."

"Talk soon," Mandy confirmed.

CHAPTER THIRTEEN

January 2015

THE DOORS OPENED, WINE was poured, the mingling began, and Mandy's official showing was underway. At first people only trickled in, and Mandy worried her debut as an artist would be a flop. But as the minutes ticked by, the numbers increased, until Beyond the White Wall was buzzing. Aziz really did an amazing job with marketing. People Mandy had never met or seen before attending *her* event. How wild was that?

However, no matter how many new faces Mandy had been introduced to, she couldn't help but wish Isa were there. They had talked about this moment so many times when they were younger, but Mandy hadn't really heard from Isa since the Fourth of July. One year and six months, to be exact—not that Mandy was counting. She imagined what Isa would look like—her dark curls would hang loosely around her shoulders, and she'd probably be in nice slacks and a colorful sweater, and heels of course. Isa loved her heels. Mandy could even imagine Isa's smile.

"Amanda. Could I get you for a second?" Aziz motioned to

Mandy, and she complied with her practiced, polite, yet not-too-excited smile on her face. She couldn't seem too eager to meet artsy people—for some reason this always turned them off.

For the next hour, she was pulled this way and that, wishing everyone at these events wore name tags. She would never in a million years remember all of them. She hadn't had time to say hello to the few people she did know who were there—only exchanging polite glances across the room. Nikki and her parents sipped white wine, and Mandy thought she may have spotted Laura (if she'd changed her hair color again) but wasn't sure. Grace stood in the corner chatting it up with the people around her, completely in her element. Mandy had kissed so many cheeks and talked so much her throat was dry.

She turned, trying to locate a passing waiter with a tray of anything liquid, but stopped cold. Isa was there. Not in slacks but a knee-length pencil skirt. The bright sweater and heels were correct though, and so was that smile. Isa stood talking to someone Mandy didn't know in front of *Between Raindrops*.

Did Isa know what Mandy felt as her brush swept across that canvas? Could she guess the exact number of tears she had shed?

Isa's head swiveled in Mandy's direction like she could feel Mandy's gaze. But Mandy stepped aside and out of view before Isa could see her. Just like this opening, Mandy had dreamed about talking to Isa again for a long time. She had nightmares about it too. But now, on the precipice of it happening, Mandy was scared shitless. If it weren't for the fact that this was her showing, she probably would've left right then and there. But she couldn't. And deep down she didn't want to. Isa was there. Her Isa.

As much as Mandy was drawn to Isa's light like a moth to a flame, she also knew fire burned, and she wasn't ready.

"Amanda, darling," Aziz cooed. "Allow me to introduce you to Ms. Clarissa Belmont-Yang. She absolutely adores your *Shining Darkness* piece, and I was hoping you would indulge her a little about your inspiration." Mandy understood all the words that weren't spoken by Aziz. *This woman is a collector ready to invest some money on up-and-coming talent in hopes it will pay off, so tell her what she wants to hear.*

"It would be my pleasure," Mandy responded to both the spoken and unspoken message. It might've been Mandy's first show, but that didn't mean she didn't know how this worked.

Ms. Clarissa Belmont-Yang was exactly as Mandy expected. She smelled like expensive perfume and money. Lots and lots of money. And she was the kind of person not just Aziz but also Mandy needed. She was the kind of woman who could make an up-and-coming artist's career—or make sure no one ever heard of them again. It was strange to think one person could have that kind of power, but that's how it was in the art world.

Mandy's insides shook. "Thanks so much for coming out this evening. I love your shoes." It was just the right amount of kissing up. Not too strong and a compliment that was both sincere and a little generic. Mandy had to impress, but she couldn't come off as *trying* to impress. Like a martini, Mandy had to be the correct balance of smooth and strong, which was not an easy feat when a herd of rhinos stomped around in her stomach. Oh, why did she eat that granola bar? If it made a reappearance now, her night—her life—would be over.

"These?" Clarissa swiveled her foot like a model to show

them off and glanced around. "They're new," she whispered just loud enough for Mandy to hear—like she was letting Mandy in on a little secret.

"They're fabulous," Mandy responded.

This was the correct answer, Mandy soon realized, as Clarissa began to ramble on like Mandy was her best friend. And for a short moment, Mandy felt like they could be. Their conversation came so easily, like it had when she met Sophie, like it had when it was just Isa and her that first day of kindergarten.

And just like that, there she was again. Mandy had been so wrapped up with Clarissa that she hadn't realized until it was too late that they both stopped in front of the same painting. Out of all the artwork in the show tonight, this one was extra special to Mandy. It was the first piece Mandy painted when she got back from Europe, when Isa had shown up in her garage and it had been like the stars peeking through the clouds on a stormy night. It had been nowhere close to finished then—Mandy had just gotten started. So how was it that Isa chose this one?

Did she know how much this painting was her—was them— what they had, what they lost?

Mandy both loved and hated everything about this painting. It was one she hadn't even thought to bring until she was telling the movers to load it into the truck. Like letting it go would finally let Mandy move on, but here she was with Isa and this painting. The universe could be such a cruel bitch sometimes.

"Tell me about the inspiration for this one," Clarissa said, but Mandy couldn't speak. Anything she said about this piece wasn't for her, it would've been for Isa, and Mandy wasn't sure she was ready to say all those things. To hear what Isa would say—or, worse, wouldn't say—in response.

Mandy's eyes burned. No, she couldn't cry. Not here. Not in front of Ms. Clarissa Belmont-Yang and certainly not in front of Isa. Instead, Mandy grabbed a flute of champagne off a passing waiter's tray and downed it like a penguin stuck in the desert. But really, she was stuck somewhere between her past and her possible future, unable to move in any direction.

Clarissa's lips quirked up on one side. "I understand." And maybe she did—although likely she didn't. "Aziz," she called, and like any good gallery owner, he appeared. "I'll take this one."

Before Aziz could respond, Isa said, "I'm sorry, this one is already spoken for."

The words barely registered as Aziz put the bright red SOLD sign next to the painting's name.

"I should've been quicker. Congratulations," Clarissa said to Isa, although her words sounded more bitter than congratulatory, and then she turned toward Aziz. "I'm going to need your help over here." And just as quickly as Ms. Clarissa Belmont-Yang was there, she was gone, and it was Mandy and Isa standing in front of a painting—their painting—in an impenetrable silence.

CHAPTER FOURTEEN

July 2004

SLEEPOVERS AT ISA'S HOUSE were the best. So far this summer they had already racked up a number of them—alternating whose house they stayed at. And while Mandy loved her giant bed, the trundle that pulled out from under Isa's was pretty comfortable. But the absolute best part of sleepovers at Isa's was that Abuela made breakfast.

Mandy lay in bed staring at the plastic stars she and Isa had put on her ceiling ages ago as the savory smell of what was most likely eggs and chorizo wafted in from the crack under Isa's door.

Abuela always made chorizo when Mandy stayed over, knowing it was her favorite. And the tortillas Abuela made from scratch were better than any other tortillas ever.

Isa was still curled up in bed fast asleep. They had stayed up late the night before watching movies and eating way too many M&M's and Sour Patch Kids. Mandy would normally still be asleep too if it weren't for two things. One being that V was getting back today from her vacation, and it had been almost a month since Mandy had seen her. And two, the delicious smells had her stomach rumbling.

Without waking up Isa, Mandy crept out of the room, down the hall—past the painting of Jesus that Mandy was convinced always watched her anytime she walked by—and then into the dining room, where she avoided stubbing her toe (for once) on the small table full of pictures of Isa's relatives, and finally into the kitchen.

"Morning, Abuela," Mandy said as she walked over to Isa's grandmother and gave her a big side squeeze.

"Good morning, mija. Orange juice is on the table." Abuela motioned with the spatula.

Mandy spun around, and there on the table in the dining room was a glass pitcher full of juice—likely fresh squeezed from the oranges on their tree out back. She poured herself a glass and went back to help Abuela. Mandy's kitchen was huge—designed by Mom not long after Mandy was born so she could watch Mandy from any angle. It had two separate sinks, and two ovens, and even an extra refrigerator so Mom had places to put trays of food for Dad's work parties. Isa's kitchen was much smaller. It was just one long line, with counters and cabinets on one side and a fridge, oven, and small pantry on the other. Pots hung from a rack over their stove, and on the warm golden-painted wall that held their cordless telephone hung a sign that read EN ESTA CASA COCINAMOS CON AMOR. Mandy always liked that sign, and all the food in this house was definitely made with love.

"What can I do?" Mandy asked as she sipped her juice. Yep, fresh squeezed and delicious.

"Get the cotija from the fridge." This time Abuela didn't point. She was too busy making sure her eggs didn't stick, moving them around in the large cast-iron skillet.

"Is this salsa like last time?" Mandy asked as she got the cheese and salsa out of the refrigerator and put them on the table, where a plate was already waiting for them.

"I didn't make it as spicy. I promise. But we will get you there." Abuela liked that Mandy could handle the heat, but last time Abuela went a little too heavy with the fire-roasted habaneros.

All the food at Isa's house had so much more flavor than what Mom made at home—then again, Mom was no cook. Abuela never used a recipe—she measured things with her heart, and even her "oopses" turned out delicious. Mandy liked to watch, hoping a little culinary magic would rub off on her. The times she attempted to make things like chorizo and eggs at home turned out well, but they weren't the same. And since Mandy didn't have grandparents of her own who lived nearby, Abuela was also like her abuela.

"What do you two have planned for today?" Abuela asked as she scooped the chorizo and eggs onto a dish and met Mandy in the dining room.

Mandy shrugged, then wasted no time digging in to the breakfast, adding the egg mixture to a tortilla with a big spoonful of salsa. "Not sure."

Abuela beamed across the table. She loved to feed people just as much as she loved to cook, maybe even more, and Mandy loved to eat, so ever since the first day she had come over way back in kindergarten, the two of them had bonded.

"V is coming back today, so I'll see her later."

Abuela's smile faded. "You're too good for her."

Mandy had been nervous to tell Abuela that she had a girl-friend. Most older people didn't get it; as her own grandmother said at first, "Oh, it's just a phase." But Abuela surprised Mandy, insisting she meet this girl. "You should love whoever you want," she told Mandy, and kissed her cheeks. "You should be happy."

Later Abuela would tell Mandy about a brother she had who liked other boys, and although he never told the rest of the family, Abuela knew—and she knew how sad he was all the time hiding who he really was.

"You two just got off on the wrong foot," Mandy tried to reason. But reasoning with Abuela wasn't easy, and normally should be avoided at all costs.

"She only has two wrong feet," Abuela muttered before ripping off a piece of tortilla and popping it into her mouth.

Abuela's first meeting with V did *not* go well. At all. And it got worse when V accidentally broke a statue of Our Lady of Guadalupe. Mandy hoped Abuela would give V another chance but never pushed the issue.

"She wakes," Abuela said as Isa appeared from the hallway, rubbing her eyes.

Isa greeted Abuela the same way Mandy had before, then took her usual seat next to Mandy. "It's hard to sleep with all the noise out here. What are we talking about?"

Abuela shook her head and gave Isa a look. A long time ago she would have told Isa in Spanish, but over the years, Mandy picked up more and more until she understood enough to be dangerous. So now Abuela used glances to communicate, but Mandy knew what most of those meant too. This look meant that Isa shouldn't ask. "Eat. Eat."

Isa started to make herself a plate, taking the hint to change the conversation. "That movie gave me the weirdest dreams. I still don't get if all those things really happened or not."

The movie was *Big Fish*, and while it was interesting and had some really fascinating characters, Mandy wasn't entirely sure what it was all about either. "Does it matter?"

"I guess not, I just kinda want to know. Because how cool was some of that? The circus and traveling and meeting all those people?"

"Studying is good too." Abuela always liked to remind them of this whenever she could. "You can learn lots from books."

"Too bad the ones they make us read at school are so boring," Mandy said.

"I told you to take AP." Isa shoved a bite of food into her mouth, then mumbled around it, "We don't use the same books you do."

Mandy could've taken AP. It was an option for every student, but she didn't think she could compare to the kids in those classes. They were all so smart, and Mandy was just average. She excelled in art, and that was where it ended for her. Otherwise, school was something she needed to do, not anything she actually enjoyed, or was "good" at. "Well, I'd love to travel." Mandy changed the conversation back to the movie—a topic she was more comfortable with. "I'm thinking I might want to go to Europe after graduation. So many great artists have come from there. And it has so much history and culture."

"You should," Isa said, and Abuela relaxed into her chair just a little—likely because Isa's response wasn't *me too*.

"You still need to go to college," Abuela said.

"I know. I will. I just . . . it would be fun."

"You know what else is fun?" Abuela asked. "Dishes."

"Yes, Abuela," Mandy and Isa responded in unison.

That was one thing Mandy didn't love about Isa's kitchen. It didn't have a dishwasher, but she had gotten used to helping clean up after a meal. Isa and Mandy had a system. They would switch off who would wash and who would dry, and then occasionally toss each other things just to hear Abuela utter, "Ay, Dios mío," while she sat and watched them from the dining room.

After everything was put away, Mandy went home to get ready for V. She needed to wash her hair, shave, and put on makeup and the new dress she bought. She wanted to really impress V since she had been gone for such an extended time. Their calls hadn't been as often or as long as Mandy wished they'd been. But V was busy with all her family things, so Mandy couldn't be mad at her. What she could do was remind V what she had been missing.

Mandy had worked herself up so much she was practically vibrating by the time she got to V's house, and her hand shook when she rang the bell. What she really wanted to do was rush inside, but the door was likely locked, and Mandy tried her best to be patient. The chimes hanging from the porch jingled, and little kids across the street screeched in delight as they ran back and forth in the sprinkler, a set of moms standing close by, watching them with wineglasses in their hands.

A car drove past, and then another. Did she get the time wrong? Mandy took a step back and looked at the empty driveway. Did V go somewhere and forget Mandy was coming? She pulled out her phone, about to give V a call, when the door creaked open.

A groggy-eyed beauty peeked her head out. "Mandy?"

Not able to contain herself anymore, Mandy launched forward, pushing the door open wider and embracing V. "I've missed you so much."

"Yeah, me too." V wrapped her arms around Mandy. "I'm sorry . . . I was sleeping."

"Jet lag is the worst, isn't it?" Mandy had experience with this every time she got back from her family's holidays. She leaned in to kiss V.

V turned away and covered her mouth. "I should brush."

Duh. Even though it was the afternoon, morning breath was the worst no matter what time it was. Not that Mandy really cared about it, but V did, and Mandy respected that. "So can I come in?"

"Oh, yeah." V stepped back to let Mandy inside.

If Mandy had to describe V's house, she would say it was a cross between her own and Isa's. Sizewise it was right in the middle. Like Isa's home, it had lots of family pictures, and like Mandy's it had a design magazine kind of decor. Except for having a room that no one actually sat in; Mandy had one of those that her mom kept pristine. Every room in V's house was used, and in order to keep it pristine, there was plastic that covered the sofa.

Since it seemed like they were alone, Mandy headed toward the back of the house where V's room was, but V stopped her.

"Let's sit in here instead," she said.

Her parents would probably be home soon, so Mandy didn't question it. She was just so excited it didn't matter where they were. Mandy had missed seeing her face, smelling her lavender body lotion. "I want to hear everything. How was it?" She had never been to Mississippi.

Instead of joining Mandy on the couch, V sat in the chair

next to her. She looked adorable with her hair in a bonnet and wearing her PINK sweatpants and tank. "Good. It was good. My nana was so happy to have everyone together." V pulled her knees into her chest and tugged on the bottom of her sweats. Her toenails had been painted a bright pink with little white flowers on her big toes. She glanced down, and then when she glanced back up again her eyes were glassy. Poor thing. She must've been really, really jet-lagged.

Mandy started to move over to hold her in her arms, but as soon as she leaned forward, V raised a hand.

"I can't do this," she said. "I thought I could, but you look so amazing and you're looking at me like that, and I . . . I have to tell you something."

She looked good, but why was that a bad thing? Bad enough to make V cry. What was Mandy missing?

"At first it wasn't anything. My cousin had a friend with her, and she was really cool, and we would all hang out, and it was no big deal."

Mandy fiddled with the hem of her dress; she heard the words coming out of V's mouth, but she did *not* want to process them. She wanted to tell V to stop, but she couldn't—because at the same time she needed to know what V was going to say.

"And, well, you were here and so far away, and I just didn't get to talk to you enough, and one night she kissed me—"

"What was her name?" Mandy didn't know why this was important, but at that moment it was.

"Kaylee." V couldn't meet Mandy's eyes. "I wasn't even into her like that, but I don't know. Kaylee kissed me, and I didn't stop her, and then we—"

"That's enough." It was all more than enough. Mandy might

have been sitting on a plastic-covered couch, but she was also staring up at a Ferris wheel as Brandon Martínez sat there with someone else. Just like that night, Mandy wanted to run, but she also couldn't move.

"I'm so sorry." Tears rolled down V's cheeks, and she brushed them away with the back of her hand. "I love you so much. I would take it all back if I could. I know it was stupid." She sniffled, and then she used her tank top to wipe her nose.

"You weren't going to tell me." Mandy wasn't sure how she kept her voice so level. "You said you can't do this, meaning you were going to just pretend it didn't happen."

"It didn't mean anything," V tried to reassure her. "She doesn't matter to me. You do. It's in the past. I can't change it. And I didn't want to hurt you. But the way you look at me . . ."

"So this is my fault?"

"That's not what I'm saying."

"But I wasn't there. And now I'm looking at you . . . and you didn't want to hurt me, but now you are. This hurts me, Veronica."

"Don't do that. Don't call me that." She wiped her eyes again.

"What am I supposed to call you?" Mandy didn't want to cry. She wanted to scream, or break or hit something, but she did *not* want to cry.

"V. Babe. Your girlfriend."

Mandy steadied her breath. Her insides shook harder than an earthquake. "You're not my girlfriend anymore." She stood up, and somehow, she left. It felt like she was there and not at the same time. Her body went through the motions. Key, ignition, drive, but her mind was blank. An empty void that echoed the sobs of the girl she left behind. Why did this have to happen to her again? What was wrong with her that people needed someone else? Why wasn't Mandy ever good enough?

She gripped the steering wheel so tightly she should've broken a finger or the wheel itself. But it didn't hurt. Not compared to the ache in her chest. Why couldn't anyone love her back?

The sun had started to set, and Mandy was still driving. She knew where she was, but she had no idea where she was going. Her phone rang again. She had lost count of how many times it had done that. It stopped and then started again.

The traffic slowed down, and Mandy was forced to stop. Her idle hands reached for the phone just as it rang again, and she picked it up.

"Where are you?" Isa's frantic voice came from the other end.

Mandy looked around. "The freeway."

"Where are you going?"

"I don't know."

"You sound so calm," she said. "Mandy?"

"Isa."

"Will you please come to my house?"

Mandy nodded even though Isa couldn't see, flipped on her turn signal, and headed home.

CHAPTER FIFTEEN

April 2019

MANDY FINALLY HAD A chance to pause, or at least she finally had time to take a breath. Candy assured Mandy via text that everything was being taken care of and not to worry, but Mandy was so good at worrying. If worrying were an Olympic sport, Mandy would be a gold medalist.

The margarita, though, was helping, and so was Ashley playing with Mandy's hair. What was it about someone playing with your hair that was always so soothing? The *tink-tink-tink* of the curling iron was a welcome sound, as opposed to the buzzing of Mandy's phone—which was still buried under a pillow in the other room.

A cart next to Mandy was in arm's reach so she could alternate between snacking on chips and salsa and her blueberry muffin—which didn't really go together, but since she'd made such a fuss, she was determined to eat it—while drinking her margarita and getting her hair done. The snacks had been a good choice because the margarita was a little strong, and Mandy hadn't eaten enough today. Plus, if Mandy closed her eyes, she could almost picture herself on a beach somewhere instead of in a hotel room waiting for the next catastrophe to take place.

What would it be? And how long did she have until it happened?

Lion escaped from the zoo.

Alien invasion.

Or maybe an unprecedented tornado would rip through the ceremony site. Now that would be something.

No.

Small sip.

And chip—*crunch*.

Ashley released the iron from Mandy's hair and blew on the curl before pinning it to her head. "They wanted twelve hundred dollars for it," she was saying.

"Just to fix the AC?" Mandy asked. She didn't know much about cars—luckily Dad still helped her when she needed to take hers into the shop—but she also knew that sounded ridiculous. "My dad says the dealership is a rip-off. He's been going to the same guy for years." Rafael was his name, but that was pretty much all Mandy knew—that and where the shop was, but she couldn't remember the name of the place, like it was stuck on the tip of her tongue. It would come to her.

"Well, I'm never going back there." Ashley sectioned off some hair and started her *tink-tink-tink* with the curling iron again. "My friend Joe says he knows a place."

"I can send you the info for the guy we use, if you want."

"That would be great. It's always good to have options."

It was nice not talking about marriage or weddings for once. It was nice to have a moment to feel somewhat normal.

Mandy grabbed another chip and popped it into her mouth. "How's the garden going?" she asked to keep the conversation rolling.

"Oh my god, I didn't tell you about my kale, did I?"

"No, you didn't." Mandy hated kale. Well, *hated* was a strong word. She greatly disliked the vegetable and thought it was completely overrated. But for some reason everyone seemed to be obsessed with it. Like it was some new kind of superfood instead of what it was—which was just angry lettuce. The first time Edmund had tried to put it in her smoothie, Mandy immediately knew something wasn't right.

"What's wrong with this?" she had asked him.

They had been sitting at the counter in his apartment one Saturday morning. The plan had been to have a little something before they were to meet friends for brunch later, so Edmund had offered to make smoothies. He wasn't a chef by any stretch of the imagination—they usually lived off takeout and fine dining—but he could make delicious smoothies. He had a knack for them. Mandy liked to tease that if the whole business thing didn't work out for him, he could open a smoothie bar—which Edmund would pretend to ponder like he was seriously contemplating the idea.

"What do you mean, what's wrong? It's a smoothie. Drink it." He casually took a sip of his own, then opened the newspaper to the investment section—also known as the most boring section ever.

"You did something different." Mandy took another drink. It was bitter. How could a smoothie taste bitter? All it had in it was fruit and a little spinach. Wait. "This isn't spinach."

"No, it's kale. How can you tell?"

"Because it's disgusting." Mandy set her drink down and pushed it his way. "Kale is disgusting."

Edmund shook his head. "I can't even taste the difference."

"Then your taste buds are broken." Mandy wiped her tongue on a napkin to try to get the taste out of her mouth.

"Oh, they are, are they?" Edmund set his glass down too. "I think you're broken." He launched himself at her and blew raspberries on her neck. He was funny like that sometimes—and sweet. Sweet enough to make Mandy a new smoothie *without* the kale.

The *tink-tink-tink* of the curling iron brought Mandy back to the moment at hand.

". . . It basically took over everything. I have so much of the stuff I don't know what to do with it all. Damn it. I should've brought some with me. Why didn't I think of that?" Ashley said.

"I think kale is the first anniversary gift." Mandy laughed.

"Shut up." Ashley nudged Mandy's back. "Just for that I'm going to bring you extra next time I see you."

Mandy raised her margarita into the air. "I'd like to cancel my next appointment."

Ashley laughed. "Nope. Sorry. No cancellations or transfers, you're getting extra kale." They both laughed together.

Mandy took a sip of her cocktail, allowing the tart flavor to flood over her tongue. "Whoever looked at kale and thought, 'Yeah, that looks like something I want to put in my mouth'?"

"That's what he said?" And they both laughed again.

Mandy took another drink of her margarita and relaxed deeper into her chair. Maybe this meant things would be all right. Maybe there wouldn't be any catastrophes.

As soon as she thought it, she wanted to take it back, but it was too late.

The lights in the hotel room flashed and the smoke alarm sounded.

"You've got to be kidding me," Mandy said.

"I'm sure it's a false alarm." Ashley put her curling iron down. "I'll call the front desk."

She wouldn't get through. Everyone in the hotel was likely doing the exact same thing. Worst-case scenario, the hotel would burn down—and if they didn't get out, they would burn down with it.

Mandy retrieved her phone and purse from the other room.

When she returned, Ashley was holding her dress. "The line was busy," she said. "But think of all the fabulous stories you'll get to tell about your wedding day." Was that pity in Ashley's eyes?

Mandy didn't want to tell any stories. She would've been fine if her wedding day was boring. She let out a long breath. "Let's just go."

The hall was packed full of people carrying as much as they could—some even with suitcases. Mandy could go back into her room and grab all her stuff too, but then she'd be another person clogging the hallway when a fire could be raging nearby.

"I don't smell any smoke. So that's good," Ashley said.

Mandy was glad Ashley could see a bright side, because Mandy had officially lost all hope.

CHAPTER SIXTEEN

June 2005

THE DAY HAD BLOWN by in such a blur, captured by Mom's camera as soon as Mandy opened her eyes that morning. Hair styled. Cap and gown. Friends. Family. Speeches. Walking across the stage. Diploma. People screaming. Tears . . . so many tears.

As the sun faded, filling the sky with watercolors that ranged from rose to tangerine to periwinkle, Mandy and her fellow graduates loaded buses to head back to campus for Grad Nite, an evening arranged by the parents of all the seniors that year. It was a tradition at their school, and each year tried to outdo the last. Mandy's mom had been on the fundraising committee that started the summer before Mandy's senior year. Mom had been extra secretive about the whole affair—which for her was quite the feat. Keeping secrets was not her strong suit and why Mandy always knew what she was getting for Christmas well before the day arrived. A rush of excitement flooded Mandy's veins. Which felt a little silly since she now stood outside the school gymnasium.

How many times had Mandy been inside there for spirit ral-
lies or gym class? The memory of Steve Gillespie throwing up
after a robust game of chubby bunny, and the time she got floor
burn sliding to save a rough ball during volleyball week in PE
rushed through her head.

"This looks so cool," Ashanta de la Cruz turned and said to
Mandy.

"So cool," Mandy repeated.

A tall set of stairs stood in front of them, and there was a
slide feeding through one of the high windows of the gym.

A parent with a walkie-talkie stood at the top dressed as the
Mad Hatter, directing the graduates one at a time.

Ashanta bounced from one foot to the other. "Where is it
you're going to college again?"

"I'm not. Or not right away. I'm doing this program in Europe
and going to spend a little time there before I commit to anything." Mandy had perfected this answer, having been asked it
so many times over the last few months. "How about you?"

"UCLA. For econ." Economics made sense for Ashanta. She
was the vice president of their school's environmental club, and
she was really good at math.

They continued to chat as they slowly climbed. They may
have gone to school with each other for years, but the pair had
never said more than a dozen words to each other. But that night
it didn't matter. That night every senior spoke to one another as
though they were friends—because that night they were.

"I'm just excited to be going away to school, you know?"
Ashanta said. "Even if it isn't very far."

"For sure." Mandy was excited about her forthcoming adventures as well. "But it's weird too, right? Like all of a sudden we're

going to be on our own, when, I don't know about you, but I've never been on my own before."

"Oh my god. That's so true. And I've thought of that, but not really, you know? I have two younger brothers. It's going to be so weird without them fighting all the time." Ashanta laughed but she had a faraway look in her eye, like she was trying to capture a memory. "Europe will be fun though. I'm kind of jealous actually. I've never been there before."

"Oh, it's amazing." Mandy was lucky to be able to take such a trip, but it didn't make the nerves any less. "If you ever get the chance to go, you totally should."

Before they knew it, they had reached the top of the stairs, and Ashanta disappeared behind a large black cloth, her squeal echoing through the crisp night air, and then it was Mandy's turn. Butterflies filled her chest. She climbed onto the slide; the same black cloth that had made her classmate vanish a moment before hung in front of her, so she couldn't even get a glimpse of what was below.

And just like that, Mandy closed her eyes and let go. The black fabric rushed across her skin, and she was inside. Every inch of the gym—from ceiling to floor—had been transformed. Mandy couldn't help but think she was like Alice sliding into Wonderland. Even the usual smell of rubber and body odor was gone and replaced by the sugary scent of cotton candy. And was that funnel cake?

Her friend Nikki was at the bottom of the slide waiting for her when Mandy finally landed. "Can you believe this?" she asked Mandy as soon as a parent dressed as the White Rabbit ushered her out of the way for the next person to come down the slide.

Mandy shook her head. There was so much to take in.

"There's an artist here doing these caricatures that turn you into a Wonderland character. We so have to do that."

"I promised Isa I'd wait for her," Mandy said.

"Totally. We might have to come back for Sara though since it could be a while until she gets in, and I'm not sure how long I can wait. Laura already took off."

Mandy laughed. Since they all had been separated into the buses by last name, that was how they were released into the event. On one hand it made sure no one was left behind, but it also felt like it took forever for her friends to get inside—although it was probably only about twenty minutes.

"Someone said they were giving tattoos," Nikki said.

"Probably just the temporary kind," Mandy replied.

"Oh, that makes more sense." Nikki laughed.

Mandy shook her head. "I wonder what else there is though."

"I wish they would hurry up and get here." And just as the words left Nikki's lips, Isa slid into Wonderland. Mandy was glad she was there to see her face as she made her way down—head pivoting as though taking it all in. Mandy was sure she had looked similar—wide eyes, open mouth.

Isa stood once she got to the bottom and was ushered to them by the White Rabbit. "This is incredible."

"Right?" Nikki confirmed.

"Where's Laura?" Isa asked.

Nikki rolled her eyes. "She couldn't wait."

"Of course," Isa said.

As soon as Sara dropped in, Mandy looped her arm through Isa's, and then Isa's through Sara's, and then hers through Nikki's, and they all were off into the thick of things.

Their plan of all sticking together didn't last long once they realized how much there was to do—a fortune teller, henna, jugglers on stilts, cotton candy and funnel cakes, corn dogs and street tacos, carnival-style games, an arena where people could put on sumo suits and "wrestle," carnival rides outside, and so much more. Sara and Nikki ran off to get "tattoos"—temporary, of course—and it was just Mandy and Isa. Mandy's head swam with all their options, and she didn't know what she wanted to do first.

"I'm starving," Isa said. "Let's go get one of those sticks with meat."

"We probably should start snacking now, so we have time to try everything by the end of the night," Mandy agreed.

She was about to walk back outside, when Ishan Patel called to her from behind. "Mandy, ride the Ferris wheel with me." Like all the other graduates, he had changed out of his dress clothes into a Grad Nite shirt and jeans—but he filled his shirt out better than most. The sleeves strained against his biceps and across his broad chest, and his dark hair practically sparkled in the lights from all the rides.

If it had been any other night, Mandy would've jumped at the chance. Would've made out with him at the top just because she could—because this was their last night and there would be no questioning if it meant anything more than what it was. But this wasn't just any night. "Maybe later," she called back.

"I'll hold you to that," he responded as Mandy pulled Isa inside.

"Why didn't you go with him?" Isa asked as they headed toward the far corner of their own Wonderland.

"Because I'm hanging out with you. Duh." Mandy shook her

head. "Come on." This had been their plan. They may not have known what would happen at Grad Nite, but Mandy and Isa decided long ago that they were going to spend it together no matter what. Mandy would be leaving for Europe before the summer was over, and by the time she got back, Isa would be off to college all the way across the country—so they planned to spend every minute they could together.

After they shared kebabs, and lumpia, and fries, Isa sat down to get a henna tattoo while Mandy got her fortune told—and after they would switch.

Madame Seer—who was just one of the parents dressed in bright scarves—had a small tent only big enough inside for a table and two chairs. It was draped with colorful fabric, and the potent scent of incense burned Mandy's nose.

"Amanda Dean"—Madame Seer stretched out her name like a long breath—"it's so good to see you tonight." Mandy had given the parent outside the tent her name when she "signed up" to see Madame Seer, which was pretty clever.

"Madame Seer." Mandy played along. "Did you foretell my arrival tonight?"

"That I did. Sit down." She gestured toward the chair opposite her, and Mandy obliged. Madame Seer ran her hands over the crystal ball in front of her. "I see you have a big trip coming up. A very important trip."

"I do." While this wasn't a secret, Mandy wasn't sure how Madame Seer knew about it.

"And you're feeling a little anxious."

Mandy nodded. As excited as she was about going to Europe, it would be the first time she'd be traveling alone. The first time her parents wouldn't be with her; and she'd be staying in a room (similar to a bed-and-breakfast-type thing without the breakfast part) where the woman who owned the place rented to all sorts of other people, although she assured Mandy and her parents it was mostly other students. Still, they would all be practically strangers. And aside from the Spanish she had picked up from school and hanging out with Isa, Mandy didn't speak any other language besides English fluently, and she wanted to see France and Germany and so many other places while she was there.

Madame Seer ran her hands over the glass orb. "You needn't worry. All will be well."

Even though Madame Seer wasn't magical, hearing her say those words lightened the heavy feeling Mandy had been carrying around in her chest. "Do you see anything in there . . . maybe about love?" She couldn't help thinking about Ishan and his proposition about riding the Ferris wheel.

"Oh yes." Madam Seer stared deep into the crystal ball. "It's right here. Love is on the horizon, but don't let it get in the way of your dreams."

Mandy bit back a grin. Such a mom thing to say. "I promise, I won't."

After her time with Madame Seer was over, the hours ticked by quickly as Mandy and Isa explored every inch of their Wonderland. Isa bested Mandy in a round of "sumo wrestling," but Mandy beat Isa to the top of the rock-climbing wall. They got their photos taken at least a dozen times in all the different photo booths set up, and they ate their way around the entire gym. Sometime around one in the morning, they wandered off arm in arm to take a break from the lights and sounds and all the people. Mandy would miss this—her school, her friends—but she needed to get away even just for a little while.

The rapid beat of feet scampering off sounded as Mandy and Isa rounded the corner to the back side of the library—better known as the farthest location away from the gym that had a low likelihood of discovery.

"I guess we aren't the only ones who needed a break," Isa said as she slid her back down the wall and sat with her legs stretched out in front of her. "Guess they thought we were narcs or something."

Mandy sniffed the air. "'Or something' is right." She bent down and picked up a joint.

"Is that—"

"Yep." Mandy plopped down and searched the area, finding a pack of matches not far away. "Their loss, our gain." She wiggled them at Isa.

"Do you really think we should?"

"Not like they can expel us now, and you already got your acceptance letter from Boston University." Mandy raised her eyebrows. "Come on. It'll be fun."

Isa twirled her hair around her finger as a mischievous grin pulled at her lips. "Let's do it."

Mandy scooted closer to Isa, put the joint in her mouth, and struck a match. She had smoked a couple of times at parties, so she knew the basics. The scent filled the air as Mandy held the flame to the end of the paper, taking a deep pull. Then, with the tip still lit, she handed it to Isa.

After about three drags each and a good coughing fit from both of them, they lay back on the cool cement and gazed up at the dark sky. Away from the carnival and without any lights on in the school, the stars seemed to shine brighter where they were.

"Serpens." Isa pointed. "Right there. Oh, and there's Hercules, and Lyra . . ."

Mandy tried to follow Isa's finger, and if she tried really hard, she could picture a centaur in the sky, but she was pretty sure it wasn't what Isa had been pointing to. "Awesome."

And it was.

With the shrieks of excitement muted by the passing breeze and the scent of damp earth swirling around them, time seemed to stand still. The chill in the air prickled Mandy's skin, all of her senses seeming to kick into overdrive.

"This reminds me of that one night under the trampoline," Isa said.

Mandy chuckled, the vibrations of which tickled her chest. "I can't believe we didn't get caught."

"We should've."

"We totally should've." Mandy hadn't thought about Brandon in a long time. What a complete ass he was. A month after she and Isa decorated the front of his house, Brandon was pulled from school and his family moved away. Something about his dad getting a new job, but Mandy wasn't sad to see him go. Actually, she hoped he was miserable wherever he went. The thought didn't make her petty, just committed to her feelings, she rationalized.

Isa reached over and squeezed Mandy's hand. "I wouldn't want to be here with anyone else right now."

"Are you sure that's not the weed talking?"

"I'm sure." Isa turned onto her side. "You're my favorite person."

"You're my favorite person, weirdo."

"I'm being serious."

Mandy turned onto her side too, to face Isa. "So am I."

"Mandy."

"Isa."

"There's something I need to tell you, and I don't know how to say it, or what you'll think, or feel about it, but I know I have to tell you. Because who knows if I'll ever have the courage to say it again . . . Or maybe I shouldn't . . ."

Mandy's brain may have been fuzzy, but the nerves running through Isa's words had Mandy hearing her loud and clear. "What's going on?"

"It's just . . ." Isa seemed to study everything about Mandy's face, her gaze sweeping across it looking for . . . well, Mandy wasn't sure what. "I'm gay."

"Okay."

"That's it?"

Mandy was really high. "Wait. What did I just say?"

"Oh my god, Mandy." Isa pushed Mandy's shoulder—not hard, but it made her roll onto her back anyway.

The world swooshed around Mandy like a wave. "What did you say?"

"I just told you I'm gay. I am so fucking gay, it hurts."

Mandy struggled to get back onto her side. "Yeah. I know. It's cool."

"What? How do you know? Oh my god. Who else knows? What did I—"

"No. Not like that." Mandy finally righted herself and propped her head on her hand. "It's just—I'm your best friend, and bi, and, well, you've never had a real boyfriend, and even though you've talked about boys and there was that time with you-know-who that we will *not* talk about. I don't know. I could tell you didn't really like any of them. I'm sure no one else knows. I just know *you*, is all." It was more than that though. Mandy had been "dragging" Isa to her LGBT and Allies club meetings for years, and in those moments with those people, Isa always seemed her most relaxed—like she could actually take a breath. But Mandy only saw it because she knew Isa like no one else did. Knew she chewed on the caps of her pens during really stressful tests. Knew she liked order in almost everything but rarely matched her socks. Knew that she could never eat just one cookie, because she didn't want it to be lonely in her stomach. Just like how Isa knew everything there was to know about Mandy. She was sure when Isa was ready, she would tell her, like how Mandy told Isa all those years ago in her bathroom. Hearing Mandy say all of this should've made Isa feel better about the whole thing, but Isa still looked like she was ready to puke. "Hold on. Did I say something wrong? I'm really stoned. So if I messed up—"

"No." Isa shook her head. "I'm the one who messed up." She looked as though she was on the verge of tears.

"Whatever it is, it'll be okay." Mandy tried to sound reassuring, but then it hit her. "Oh. You *like* someone."

Isa nodded.

"And we graduated. And everyone is about to go their own way."

Isa nodded again.

Mandy was feeling a little more sober now—or the brain fog wasn't as thick. "Well, let's go tell them."

Isa shook her head. "But what if it ruins everything?"

Mandy stood up. "You're leaving for Boston in a few months. So who cares?" She offered her hands to help Isa up, and Isa accepted. "I'll be right there with you. You can do it."

"I don't know if I can." Isa visibly trembled, so Mandy wrapped her arms around her.

"Come on. You're, like, the toughest girl I know." Mandy rubbed Isa's back. "Who took down Valerie Kellogg as debate team captain? And who stood up to Santiago Dominguez when he was being a total douche?"

"But *this* is different."

Mandy looked straight into Isa's eyes. "You are an amazing person. Any girl would be a fool if they didn't immediately kiss you after you told them you liked them. You can do this."

Isa slowly nodded.

"Good, let's—" Mandy tried to pull Isa forward, but she didn't move.

"It's you," Isa said. "The girl I'm hard-core crushing on is you."

Mandy heard the words coming out of Isa's mouth, but for a moment Mandy thought she had imagined them. She was really high, so it was possible she was hallucinating or daydreaming or something. But Isa—her Isa—stared at Mandy with those amazing dark brown eyes and kept a hold of her hand even though Mandy hadn't said anything yet. Isa's finger stroked Mandy's knuckles, sending tingles up her arm. If Mandy said she had never thought about this moment happening, she'd be a liar. She dreamed about it sometimes when she lay awake at night—a blissful fantasy she never shared with anyone, and now it was coming true.

Isa licked her lips. "Say some—"

Mandy's mouth crashed into Isa's.

Mandy was no fool.

As their lips met, it was like a million sensations all wrapped up in one. Fireworks, and first drops on roller coaster rides, and catching air on a ski jump, or riding your first wave. Mandy's heart beat faster than it ever had before. Or was that Isa's heart Mandy felt as they pressed against each other?

When they finally broke apart, nothing had changed around them, and yet everything was different. The air was more temperate, the stars were blazing, and the crickets practically cheered. Graduation meant the beginning of new things, and this was the best new thing that could ever have happened.

Mandy loved Isa—she always had—but that night it seemed to transform into something brighter, stronger, if that were even possible. "I love you for real."

Isa tucked a stray hair behind Mandy's ear. "I love you for real back."

CHAPTER SEVENTEEN

March 1993

MANDY SWUNG HER FEET back and forth as she sat on a stool at the kitchen island after school, having some juice and a new kind of animal crackers Mom had picked up earlier that day for her—which tasted more like cookies, but Mandy wasn't going to say anything. "During free time we didn't get to play in the dress-up corner because Brandon and his friends hogged it." She rolled her eyes.

"Well, maybe you'll get your chance tomorrow," Mom said before taking a sip from her coffee mug. "Sharing is caring. Isn't that what you always say?"

Mandy frowned. "I guess." Mom didn't understand. She and Isa had a plan today that involved dressing up like princesses, and Brandon and his friends absolutely did not share even though Mandy asked them repeatedly.

Mom set her mug down with a clink against the stone countertop. "I know what you need," she said. "Mommy-daughter date night."

Mandy practically bounced out of her seat. "Tonight?"

"Yep. Daddy had to take a work trip, so that just leaves you and me. And I think we may need to get dressed up for it. What do you say?"

Mandy was already off her stool. "I'm going to wear my pink dress," she called out as she ran out of the kitchen and up the stairs.

Mommy-daughter date night was Mandy's favorite. Not because Daddy wasn't home but because they could do whatever they wanted. Like once they had dessert *before* dinner. Another time they went and had a real tea party with little sandwiches that didn't have any crusts on them. And another time they went to a place with big giant chairs, and someone painted their nails. Mandy watched as the lady put little dots of white paint on her toes and turned them into flowers—it was so cool. Mommy-daughter date night always meant something fun.

Mandy got her favorite pink dress out from her closet—the one she was allowed to wear only for "special occasions"—and slipped it on. Next, she found her ruffliest socks and her shoes with the rainbow glitter. She didn't even move or complain when Mom brushed her knotted hair and pulled it back into a single braid. Then she sat patiently on Mom's bed while she got ready. Mom always took a lot longer than Mandy to get dressed.

Mom stood at the mirror in the bathroom applying her makeup. "Not until you're older," was what she had told Mandy a few months ago when she asked if she could wear some too.

The brushes Mom used weren't like the ones Mandy painted with. Hers were dry and stiff, but Mom's had supersoft bristles that painted on her face. How cool was that? Mom was so precise—her hand so steady as she blended and powdered and used special pencils that Mandy was not allowed to use on paper after that one time she did. When Mom colored with Mandy, she was always good at staying in the lines—probably because she had so much practice doing this. It was like its own kind of art—a kind Mandy couldn't wait to learn herself.

"I think tonight calls for a little eye shadow. What do you think?" Mom had turned around and waved one of those brushes in the air.

Mandy nodded as she climbed off the bed and headed into the bathroom.

Mom picked her up and sat her on the counter, where Mandy held perfectly still and closed her eyes. Then that soft brush swept across Mandy's lids—it tickled a little, but she didn't laugh. "All done," Mom said.

Mandy carefully opened her eyes and spun toward the mirror. Her eyelids shimmered—the color of a peach if it had been dusted with fine glitter.

"Do you want a little lipstick too?"

This was Mandy's lucky day. Mommy-daughter date night. Eye shadow. *And* lipstick. "Yes, please." She carefully turned back while Mom made Mandy's lips a pale pink.

Mandy studied herself in the mirror, turning her head back and forth, watching her eyelids sparkle while Mom put all her makeup away.

Mom stood next to Mandy, looking at her in the mirror. They had the same blonde hair, but Mandy's eyes were brown like Daddy's, not blue like Mom's. "Now, I want you to know that you don't need to wear makeup to make you beautiful. You are already beautiful no matter what. Don't let anyone tell you different. Do you understand?"

Mandy turned, wrapping her arms around Mom's neck in a big hug. "You're beautiful too, Mommy."

Mom hugged Mandy back, picking her up off the counter and spinning her around before setting her back on the floor. "We better hurry, the show starts soon." Mom held out her hand.

Mandy took it. Tonight was going to be so fun.

First, they went to the movies and saw *Aladdin*, where they got the biggest tub of popcorn with extra butter, and Mandy was mesmerized when Jasmine and Aladdin rode a carpet and sang about a Whole New World. Mandy really wanted a flying carpet—or at least to ride one once.

Even though they snacked on popcorn, afterward Mom wanted to get some "real food," she called it, so they walked hand in hand down the busy street.

"I want to be Jasmine for Halloween," she told Mom.

"Oh, okay. I think we still have a little time though, just in case you change your mind."

Mandy wouldn't be changing her mind. "I want silky blue pants and a blue shirt just like hers."

"We will see what we can do." That was Mom code for she would think about it, but Mandy wasn't going to argue. She'd have plenty of time to convince Mom it was a good idea.

There were lots of people out that night, holding hands just like Mom and Mandy. Mostly adults—like how Mom and Dad would hold hands when they all went out together sometimes.

They stopped at the corner to wait for the little green man to tell them it was safe to walk. Mandy's feet were starting to hurt. "How much farther is it?"

"We're almost there," Mom said.

Mandy glanced around. Maybe there was another place they

could eat that was closer. Behind her two men ducked down an alley where they stood toe to toe for a moment—smiles on their faces. One man leaned into the other, and they quickly kissed before spilling back onto the sidewalk with all the people, laughing like one of them had just told a joke, not like they had just done what they did.

"Mommy—"

"It's our turn." Mom tugged on Mandy's hand.

As soon as they crossed the street, Mom told the lady at the little stand that there were two of them, and they were quickly seated.

"What do you think you want to eat?" Mom asked as she studied her menu.

Mandy's menu wasn't as big as Mom's, and there was nowhere for her to color on hers, but Mandy wasn't thinking about the menu or food. "Why were those men kissing?"

Mom peeked over her menu and glanced around. "What men?"

"The ones in the alley. Why were they kissing?"

Mom set her menu down. "People kiss when they love each other. Like Aladdin and Jasmine."

Mandy scrunched her eyebrows. "Like you and Daddy?"

"Yes."

That made sense. Well, kind of. "So, two boys can love each other?"

Mom nodded. "Yes."

"Can two girls love each other?"

"They can." Mom nodded again.

Mandy glanced around at all the people in the restaurant, and then at the people walking outside. "Why don't they hold hands then?"

"They do sometimes," Mom said. "There's no wrong way to love someone. Sometimes that means holding hands and kissing, and sometimes it doesn't."

Mandy kissed Mom and Dad. And her grandparents would kiss her when she saw them, and she would kiss them back. Mandy held hands with Mom on mommy-daughter date night, and sometimes she and Isa held hands when they played at school, but she didn't know about wanting to do that with anyone else. So she was glad she didn't have to if she didn't want to. "Can I have noodles with butter?" she asked.

"You can have whatever you want," Mom said. "I love you."

"I love you too." Mandy picked up her crayon. "Will you help me find the pretzel?" she asked. Mom was really good at finding all the things in the hidden picture puzzles.

"Let me figure out what I'm going to eat first, and then I'll help, okay?"

"I got the baseball bat." Mandy circled the bat and crossed it off from the list of pictures she was supposed to find.

"Nice job," Mom said. "Do you think you'll have room for tiramisu tonight?"

"Uh, yeah." Mandy always had room for tiramisu.

CHAPTER EIGHTEEN

January 2015

MANDY HAD BEEN TO a number of art shows, starting with the one she dragged her mother to when she was just thirteen. That had been at a gallery twice the size of Beyond the White Wall, where the artist was already a household name, so the pieces cost as much as a Los Angeles condo—even more. It was no surprise Mom didn't buy the painting Mandy had loved at that event, although at the time Mandy was extremely disappointed.

Tonight, Mandy's art wasn't priced that high, but the turnout was just as overwhelming, as were the number of SOLD signs popping up on each of her pieces. And now with Isa there, Mandy thought she might've been dreaming, or the champagne was doing funny things to her, but the hint of coconut in the air from Isa's shampoo grounded Mandy in how real this moment was.

Isa had bought Mandy's painting. And from the markup Aziz put on all the pieces, it wasn't cheap. *Thank you* didn't seem like the right words, so Mandy had said nothing at all and walked off, opening an empty space in her chest Isa filled for a brief moment. But Mandy couldn't risk it.

This situation wasn't as unfamiliar as Mandy wished it could've been. She had been here before with Isa, and, well, Mandy was hoping things could be different—better this time. She did *not* want to mess things up again. She'd done that enough already—over and over.

Mandy kept an eye on Isa as she was pulled this way and that to schmooze and rub elbows with just the right people. Maybe there was still a chance she could make things right with Isa—she hadn't left yet after all.

"Oh, honey." Mom spun Mandy into a tight hug just as she had finally gotten a moment of calm. "I'm so proud of you."

Mandy squeezed back.

"It's quite the turnout," Dad agreed, and took his opportunity to get a hug when Mom finally let Mandy go.

"Thanks for coming," Mandy told them. It meant the world to Mandy that her parents were there. They had always been so supportive of her—allowed her time to explore, and learn, and grow, and tonight they finally got to see it wasn't a waste of time (or money). Not that either of them said that or made Mandy feel that way. She had just heard so many stories, seen too many "disappointed" parents over the years of pursuing her own passion.

"Like we would miss it." Dad squeezed Mandy's shoulder. Dad had recently grown his beard out, and if he didn't already look it before, he looked twice as intimidating with the copious amount of facial hair, but to Mandy he was a big old teddy bear.

Mom and Dad had both dressed for the occasion—even a little overdressed, from an artist's standpoint. Dad in his black suit and red power tie. Mom was donning a new black dress with a red belt that matched Dad's tie perfectly. It was like her mother had googled "what to wear to a gallery opening" but then ignored the results and gone along with what matched her extremely particular fashion ideas of what should be worn. Mandy was so lucky. Parents weren't supposed to be so supportive or so adorable, and yet they were. Still in love with each other so much they dressed alike after thirty-five years of marriage. Mandy could only dream of finding a love as strong as theirs one day.

"Speaking of not missing things, I haven't seen Edmund. We didn't miss him, did we?" Mom didn't hide the disdain in her voice. Edmund had not been a particular favorite of her mother's, but Mandy was sure he'd grow on her in time. If Edmund were a painting, he'd be an abstract one—one that you had to study, and learn, and try to get to know intimately before you could really make an assessment about it. He wasn't an open book, or "warm" in the traditional sense. But he loved Mandy, she knew that; he supported her even if he truly didn't understand her, and even if he had meetings, Edmund always made the time to show up for Mandy if she asked him to. He wasn't perfect but neither was she, so they were imperfectly perfect together—or at least that was what Mandy liked to think.

"I'm sure he'll be here soon," Mandy reasoned. "Probably just caught up in a meeting." Edmund was routinely caught up with something work-related that had him showing up late or changing plans at the last minute, but that's why Mandy was good for him. He was all business and schedules, and Mandy was much more go-with-the-flow. Opposites were supposed to attract, right?

"Hmm . . ." Mom said. "I did see Isa though. She looks amazing."

"Sounds like residency is going well for her too," Dad chimed in.

"Yeah." Mandy didn't know what else to say. If it were just her and them, she would've let it spill that she hadn't spoken to Isa yet. But it wasn't, and Mandy couldn't be seen crying at her own opening.

"Obstetrics is a good specialty," Dad continued. He had always been so proud of Isa, as if she were his own daughter— Mom and Dad both, really.

Mandy was proud too. Maybe she should get over herself and just go talk to her.

"Oh, I didn't tell you," Mom said. "I talked to Janice at the gym, and I think I've finally got it right." Janice was one of Mom's new friends that got her into baking—or attempting to bake. Mom had been on a bread kick, trying to make her own sourdough. It seemed so much easier to just buy it at the store.

"Yes. It's crispy on the outside, and the middle is nice and spongy," Dad chimed in.

"You really think?" Mom blushed.

"I told you I could've eaten the whole loaf." Dad chuckled.

"I thought you were just being nice," Mom said.

Was bread supposed to be spongy? That didn't seem like the most flattering word to Mandy, but she'd never really thought about bread that much. She just enjoyed eating it. "That's awesome, Mom."

"The next time you come to paint, I'll make sure to bake a fresh loaf." Mom beamed.

Even though Mandy didn't live with them anymore, she still used the space in the back of the garage for her art. One day she would have a real studio, but for now it worked just fine.

"I was thinking of dropping some off to Sandy and Abuela," Mom said. "Maybe you could help me with that?" Mom was trying to be encouraging—she knew everything there was to know about what happened with Isa, but Mandy wasn't sure she was ready to face Isa, Isa's mom, and Abuela at the same time. Mandy really needed to suck it up and just go talk to her now. As she was about to excuse herself from her parents, someone came up behind her.

"For the lady of the hour." Edmund thrust a large bouquet of red roses at Mandy and pressed his lips to hers. A rush flooded through her like it did every time she was with him. He was the kind of guy Mandy never thought would be into her. Smart, handsome—someone who commanded attention. She had felt so lucky that he had chosen to be with her. Yes, he was late. And yes, he brought her flowers that she could absolutely not carry around all night, but it was the thought that counted. He took the time to stop and get them for her—or had his assistant do it—but either way, Edmund liked to make a show of how much he cared. Sometimes it was too much, and other times it made Mandy feel important. She wasn't sure how she felt about it tonight. There were too many emotions swirling through her gut.

"They're lovely," Mom replied on Mandy's behalf, as though she knew Mandy was struggling with finding all the right words, and took the bouquet from him. "I'll keep these safe for you until later."

"Thanks, Mom, and yes, they are lovely, thank you." Mandy leaned into Edmund, the scent of his cologne subtle but still there from when he applied it that morning. It was a tad too peppery for Mandy's taste, but she wasn't the one wearing it all day, so she didn't complain. Pick your battles. And when it came to love, Mandy always chose love.

Edmund took a moment to survey the room. It was still quite bustling, considering the hour. A couple stood in front of one of the paintings that hadn't been sold, peering around as though looking for Aziz, but he was nowhere to be seen. Mandy didn't like the thought of losing a sale because he took a bathroom break. She'd had to pee for the last hour, and you didn't see her running off to the ladies' room. No. She was going to tough it out.

"I should probably—" Mandy gestured, but Edmund stopped her.

"Before you go, there's something I wanted to ask you."

Just then the lights dimmed except the one Edmund was standing under, and the rumble of idle chatter faded. Performative art was a thing some artists did during their shows, but Mandy wasn't one of them. Sometimes she didn't like people knowing *she* was even the artist at all. What the hell was going on? Music started playing, a song Mandy recognized from Edmund's favorite album.

"Amanda Dean . . ." It was at this moment Mandy realized Edmund had been speaking to her, and now he was on one knee, a little black box in his hand. "Will you marry me?"

Mandy glanced up. The crowd of people all stared at her. Mom and Dad stared at her. Isa was staring at her. Weren't there supposed to be conversations that took place before . . . well . . . this? *What is happening?*

"She's speechless," someone in the crowd said.

"Aww . . . isn't that sweet," said another.

Mandy wasn't sure *sweet* was the word she'd use, but she

plastered on a smile. Why was her heart beating so fast? Wasn't this what she had always wanted? What was wrong with her? Was it the stress of the show?

"Make me the happiest man in the world . . ." Edmund leaned forward. His light brown eyes were wider than Mandy had ever seen them before.

Fuck. Shit. Fuck. What was she supposed to do? She couldn't even think. How could he put her on the spot like this? On this night? In front of all these people? Mandy didn't know what to do. She could picture the headlines—*Artist Shuns Lover at Opening*. Or would they think it was a stunt? *Artist Arranges Proposal to Sell Paintings—Pathetic*. What would the critics say? She would be eaten alive. That's all they'd talk about. Not her work that she poured her heart and soul into but how she crushed some guy's heart in front of a crowd. Her career in the art world would be over before it ever had a chance to start.

She took a moment and gazed at Edmund. He was a good guy. They might've fought sometimes, and they didn't always agree on everything, and sometimes he didn't think things through all the way—like tonight—but his smile was sincere, and he just looked so . . . so . . . vulnerable.

"Yes," she choked out. "Yes, I'll marry you."

CHAPTER NINETEEN

March–April 2009

MANDY HATED THE SMELL of Theo's apartment. It wasn't that it was dirty—although it was always a mess—but whatever his cleaning person used, because yes, he had a cleaning person, the scent seemed to linger. It was sour and floral, and those just did *not* go together.

"I have so much stuff I have to get done today," Theo whispered in Mandy's ear as they snuggled in his bed. As he kissed Mandy's neck and ran his hand up her shirt, she tried not to focus on the smell. But trying not to focus on it made her focus on it even more, which made making out not as enjoyable.

"Yeah, totally, so do I," she said. It wasn't that he was bad at it; it was just that Mandy wasn't even sure she really liked him all that much, which made her feel guilty, but she was pretty sure Theo was using her too. He was Mandy's attempt at a one-night stand that had lasted a month already. She'd only wanted to let off some steam. To do something that wouldn't be as stressful as school or her internship. It was supposed to be a fun fling. But as the days went on, it became more and more work, and Mandy knew less and less how to end it with him. "Maybe we should put this on pause for another time," she encouraged.

"We totally should." But Theo didn't stop, and to be fair, Mandy wasn't sure she wanted him to. Theo was an escape from all the things she didn't want to think about or do.

In most regards, Theo was a catch. He played water polo and came from what her roommate called "a good family"—meaning his parents were rich—which explained why he had his own apartment and a cleaning person. He was good-looking in the traditional sense, with a sharp jaw and greenish-gray eyes that didn't seem natural but were.

But he liked horror movies, and Mandy liked rom-coms. He enjoyed the club, and Mandy preferred dinner and drinks. He liked to work out, and Mandy hated to sweat. Being with Theo was the first time Mandy didn't try the way she had in all her other relationships. She would steal fries from his plate, and poop in his bathroom, because when it all came down to it, she didn't really care. And yet for some reason, it was working. "I could skip washing my hair, though, you know?" she said.

"Mmmmmhhh," he hummed into her hair and softly bit her neck. "Clean hair is overrated."

She seemed to intrigue Theo more and more. He'd often tell her that he loved that she was different from the other girls he dated and that it was rad that she was so confident, and if Mandy were being completely honest, she started to like these compliments. It had been a long time since someone had said things like that to her. Nice things. Things that didn't make her second-guess herself. And despite the smell of the apartment, his sheets were so soft, and his shower had the best water pressure, and he had his own cappuccino machine in the kitchen. And he always tried to satisfy Mandy.

It wasn't that Mandy didn't like him, she just wasn't sure she was *in like* with him—which, yes, were totally different things.

Theo's hand slid down Mandy's stomach and then lower, and she melted into him. She did like how he took the lead. How he always wanted to make sure she felt good. And how he liked to make sure she orgasmed first—and often.

"I really do need to get going," he said, but again he didn't stop.

"Uh-huh." Mandy raked her nails gently across his six-pack. "Don't let me keep you." She leaned in and nibbled on his ear.

"Well, maybe I can be late."

"Sounds good to me."

And he kissed her again.

This was them. It was easy and maybe easy was exactly what Mandy needed right then. Maybe she deserved easy for once.

MANDY STOOD IN THE ART STUDIO, STARING AT ONE of the most important projects in her life, trying to decide why it sucked so bad. The scent of turpentine hung heavy in the air like a humid summer day. She had booked the time weeks ago thinking that if she needed the extra hours to put the final touches together, it would be nice, but she wasn't close to final at this point. She didn't even feel like she was halfway done.

If she'd spent more time working and less time at Theo's, she wouldn't be in this position. Not that he had forced her to be there, and not that she didn't want to be. The last couple of weeks had been great. She got him to ask his cleaning person to use a different brand of disinfectant, so his apartment didn't smell so terrible. He even started introducing her to his friends as his girlfriend, and honestly, it wasn't the worst thing in the world. When other girls gave her the *what-does-he-see-in-her* look, she inwardly celebrated. Because what wouldn't he see in her? Mandy was a great girlfriend. Attentive, loyal, caring. And while she wasn't as tall or as lean, or what society would call "beautiful," Mandy wasn't bad-looking either. She may have been vertically challenged, and her thighs rubbed together when she walked, but she liked herself and wasn't ashamed of her body, even if the beauty magazines told her she should be. She would think back to the thing Isa used to always say to her. "You have to love yourself first." And while Mandy wasn't sure she was there, she felt like she could be on her way, which was a huge leap for her.

But in the art studio now, there was no huge leap to be had. She stood back from the newest piece she was working on to try to get some perspective on it. Even though the room was large, it felt like the walls were closing in on her.

It was the yellow. It was too mustard and not enough canary. Or the green had too much yellow in it, and that was throwing the whole thing off.

She was ready to chuck her brush at the canvas just to see what would happen. Maybe it could help spark some sort of something to make it better. It couldn't possibly make it any worse.

And what's this purple smear down the center? her professor would ask her.

It's the culmination of anger and frustration trying to burst from the canvas, she could explain to him.

No way would that fly. She backed up farther and then walked to the right, then to the left, and back right again.

Thankfully her cell phone stopped her from another trip back and forth. She dropped her brush and picked up the call. "Save me," she muttered into the phone.

"Oh, come on, it can't be that bad," Isa said.

"No. You're right. It's worse," Mandy said. "Take me out of my misery, please."

"Would finalized dates for graduation cheer you up?"

Mandy perked up. "Yes." Isa's actual graduation date had been set for a little while, but the plans around celebrations were still up in the air. "What's going on?"

"So Mom and Abuela are flying in on Thursday the week before, but the party is going to be on Wednesday after the ceremony, not far from the graduation location." She paused. "But really, if you can't make it because of finals or whatever, it's fine."

"You can't get rid of me that easily. I'll be there." Mandy crossed her legs and sank to the floor crisscross-applesauce style. "Are you sure Tally is okay with me staying there? I don't want to—"

"She's totally cool with it. And even if she wasn't, it wouldn't matter. You're staying with us."

It had taken a while for things to get back to "normal" with Isa ever since what happened between the two of them, so hearing that Isa was ready to go to bat for Mandy made her heart swell. For so long she had missed her best friend, and this made Mandy feel like they had finally gotten back to that place they had been before—before Mandy had messed everything up. She could've asked her parents to help pay for a hotel, which they would've done without question, but Mandy was trying harder and harder to be independent. She didn't like going to them unless it was absolutely necessary.

"Well, I'll make dinner one night for us or something—as a way to say thank you."

"Um . . . that's not really—"

"I'm not my mom, promise. I won't poison you. And spaghetti isn't exactly hard, you know?"

Isa laughed—Mandy still loved that sound, and she relaxed back on her hands, cradling the cell with her shoulder. "Fine. I trust you. But after the ceremony, just in case."

"That's fair," Mandy said, then leaned down a little farther. "I gotta go. I think I figured out what I need to do."

"I knew you would. Chat later."

And they hung up.

If things were completely back to normal, they would tell each other *I love you for real*, before disconnecting, but Mandy couldn't dwell on that. They had come a long way even if things weren't exactly the same, and it was okay that things were different now, and it was fine to rush off the phone, since she really did see what she needed to do to make her project absolutely perfect.

THE PLACE WASN'T EXACTLY MANDY'S SCENE, AND IT wasn't exactly Theo's either, but they had kind of met in the middle. Dinner and dancing were what Theo said to expect. The restaurant was nice, and the first course had been delicious, but

Mandy and Theo were the youngest people in the room by at least two decades.

Theo's hand rested casually on Mandy's hip as he glided her around the floor, doing a simple foxtrot. Thank goodness for those dance classes in PE all those years ago, or Mandy would be in big trouble. Everyone in the room could dance circles around them, but no one seemed to mind that they were there—or that they weren't very good. One woman in the bathroom who had been touching up her much-too-pink lipstick had mentioned how it was nice to see young people interested in partner dancing.

Mandy stepped on Theo's foot again. "Sorry."

"You don't need to keep saying that."

"I'll need to buy you new shoes." She'd lost count of the number of times she had stomped on his feet that night. He walked in with shiny black oxfords, and who knew what they would look like when they finished for the evening.

Theo merely laughed. "You could just put your feet on mine and get it over with. I can do the work for the both of us."

Mandy pinched his neck—not too hard. "Very funny."

"Eyes this way, Richard," an adorable woman with gray-blue hair and a sparkling red dress said as she danced past with her partner.

"He's right, you know," Theo said. "You do look stunning to-night."

Heat flooded Mandy's cheeks. She hadn't been sure what to expect, so she played it careful in a simple black dress that showed off some of her better assets. She'd be lying if she said she didn't feel sexy in it, and the way that Theo looked at her made her feel even more so.

Theo had really been growing on Mandy. What they had was

far from perfect, but none of her relationships had been, so what else was new? He had bought her a special pillow to hide behind when they watched scary movies, and he would very carefully describe the scene she was missing. He even started watching more rom-coms with her—admitting openly that they "weren't actually that bad." And then there were things like tonight. He had been trying more and more to find ways they could meet halfway—dinner and dancing was just that, regardless of the crowd that was there.

"There's something I'd been meaning to talk to you about," Theo said as he pressed his cheek against Mandy's, his stubble tickling her jaw. Her skin would turn red in protest, but other parts of her body responded positively to the sensation.

Mandy closed her eyes and leaned into him. "What is it?" It wasn't unusual for Theo to want to talk to Mandy about something. A guy on the water polo team. A big test coming up. A party he really wanted her to go to.

"My mom's coming into town, and I'd really like you to meet her."

She stomped on Theo's foot again. "Sorry."

He just laughed. "It's fine. I kind of threw you a curveball."

A curveball was an understatement.

"So, what do you think?" He tightened his grip on Mandy's lower back, pressing her body closer to his. Why did that always feel so good? "Just for lunch or something. Nothing big. She just wants to meet the girl I keep talking about."

He talked to his mom—about her? Had Mandy even mentioned Theo to Mom? Oh god, she felt like the biggest asshole. He pressed his cheek against hers again.

"Yeah. Sure. Of course," she said.

"Really?" His voice sounded so hopeful.

"Yes. If you want me to meet your mom, then I want to meet her."

Theo leaned back to gaze into Mandy's eyes. "What did I do to find a girl like you?"

"Just lucky, I guess." Did that sound as narcissistic as it did in her head?

"God, I love you."

The needle didn't slide across the record and make that screeching sound, but it did in Mandy's head. Sure, they were good together. Sure, they'd been having fun. And it was easy being with Theo. But love? Was Mandy there? And how could Theo sound so sure?

"I love you, too," Mandy said anyway, because what else was she supposed to do?

CHAPTER TWENTY

September 2005

WOULD IT EVER STOP fucking raining? Mandy had gone to London to soak in the culture, but for approximately seventy-two hours, all she had gotten was soaked. Like the clouds were crying for her since she couldn't cry herself anymore. This trip had been her dream, and then it became their dream—Isa and Mandy's—but she was alone in her room, missing Isa and feeling sorry for herself.

Maybe she should go home.

She could apologize.

She could grovel, even.

But Isa wouldn't be there. She probably would never talk to Mandy ever again. Mom and Dad were home though. And so were her own bed and pillows—ones she didn't feel as bad sobbing into.

At least she had a private room in the house she was staying in. This way she could wallow in her own misery without anyone else there to watch her. It was a quaint house too—just off the beaten path but close enough to cafés and shops. A woman by the name of Beatrice owned the place, and from their correspondence, Mandy had expected an older woman with gray hair who likely enjoyed an evening of knitting and crossword puzzles. Mandy was extraordinarily wrong. Beatrice, as it turned out, was a vibrant woman with fiery ginger hair in her early fifties who loved leather, her motorbike (as she liked to call it), and her two cats, and had visible tattoos along her arms and legs, and a number of not-so-visible ones she had told Mandy about with a smirk. Mandy didn't mind the cats and wished they would visit her room, but that would mean opening the door once in a while, and, well, that wasn't happening.

This would be—more or less—Mandy's home for the next couple of months while she explored and studied at an artists' program in the city. She was lucky to enroll in a couple of classes. Not a full load or anything, but it was enough to bide her time as she tried to figure out what she really wanted. At least that had been the plan. Now Mandy was too sad to do anything. She lay in her four-poster bed staring at the ornate antique furniture and old books lining the shelves of the little bedsit (that's what Beatrice called it) with her suitcase still packed next to the door. At least the bed was comfortable enough.

But Mandy couldn't help thinking back to just weeks ago when Isa had stayed the night and the two of them were still in bed—because it was summer, and that's what summers were for, sleeping in.

Mom had gently knocked and peeked her head in. "I'm going to run out for a bit," she said as Mandy lifted herself onto her elbows—Isa didn't stir. "I'll grab some bagels on my way home. Blueberry, okay?" Blueberry was Isa's favorite.

"With strawberry cream cheese," Mandy said.

Mom nodded like that was a given. "Don't spend the whole day in bed, you lazybones." She closed the door.

Mandy lay back down and stared at her ceiling. She was too awake, too aware of the girl sleeping next to her in nothing but a tank top and sleep shorts. They had stayed up most of the night talking and kissing—and at some point, Mandy must have fallen asleep.

A few moments later, there were the telltale signs of Mom's car pulling out of the driveway.

Isa spun around. "I thought she would never leave."

"Have you been awake this whole time?"

"As soon as she knocked on the door, yeah." Isa did that one-eyebrow-raise thing, and the message was received loud and clear.

Mandy moved closer—so close their thighs touched. "Morning breath be damned; I'm going to kiss you now."

"You better." Isa closed the space between them, locking her lips against Mandy's. Somehow Isa's still tasted sweet from the Sour Patch Kids and M&M's they'd eaten the night before.

Mandy pulled Isa closer as Isa's hand drifted up Mandy's shirt, her warm palms sending tingles throughout Mandy's body. Her heart slammed inside her chest. Isa's soft tongue caressed Mandy's bottom lip, and in that moment, she wanted—no, needed—to be as close to Isa as possible. Mandy yanked her shirt over her head, and Isa did the same. Skin to skin, the smell of Isa's Love Spell lotion, Mandy pressed Isa closer into her. Their legs entwined. Feeling. Rubbing.

Isa pulled away as if needing to catch her breath. "I love you for real."

"I love you for real back." Mandy spoke into Isa's neck, trailing kisses along the way.

"I'm ready," Isa said.

They had talked about this before, when their make-out sessions got intense, but they hadn't gone all the way.

Isa slid off her shorts.

"Are you sure?" Mandy asked. She never wanted to make Isa do anything she didn't want to.

Isa took Mandy's hand. "I'm sure." She led it down—below the covers—between her legs.

Isa sucked in a breath, and Mandy's heart cracked all the way open. Yes, she loved this beautiful, smart, incredible girl. She was in love with her, and she'd never felt as close to Isa, to anyone, as she did right there. Isa knew Mandy in ways no one else did. Knew her secrets, her accomplishments, her fears. Mandy had never been vulnerable with anyone the way she was in this moment with Isa. This was more than just sex. This was unfiltered, unconditional love.

Mandy had never really put any stock into the idea of losing her virginity. There were so many firsts she had in her life. The first time she rode a two-wheeler without training wheels. The first time she jumped from the high-dive platform at the pool. The first time she drove a car without anyone riding with her. But in that moment, Mandy realized all these firsts did in fact make her feel different. They each came with a special kind of freedom she had never had before. Mandy didn't lose anything at all, but her world had in fact changed forever.

But now, as she lay there in that four-poster bed a continent and ocean away, Mandy was on the precipice of another first. A first of being in a world without Isa. The worst part wasn't when it happened or the screaming and crying that took place in that moment, but every moment after. From then on out, there would be no more talking, no more sharing secrets, or holding hands, or soft kisses, or just being together. Mandy had no idea where Isa's life would go. She had given up that right . . . and even though her reasons were valid, that didn't mean it hadn't torn a hole in her soul to do it. Mandy being here without Isa meant that it was the end of the line. Didn't it? Their lives had been so intertwined, and now—nothing. Would there ever be a time Mandy wouldn't want to reach for the phone to try to tell Isa about something that happened to her? Was that a future Mandy wanted to know?

Wanting it or not, it was the life she had now.

Mandy swallowed against the giant lump in the back of her throat. Even though she hadn't left the room for days, she was exhausted. If only she could close her eyes and sleep forever, or go back in time—but that wasn't possible. Whether Mandy liked it, or was ready for it, time ticked on, the world kept spinning, and the future was here staring her in the face. There was no going back, but for Mandy it seemed impossible to go forward.

A knock sounded, and before Mandy could respond, the door swung open. In walked a girl with curly brown and purple hair, dewy brown skin, thick black eyeliner, and black fishnet tights. Even in the mood Mandy was in, she couldn't help but like this girl immediately.

"Bloody hell, you do look like shit," the girl said, with a long *i* making it sound more like *shite*, but Mandy got the idea. Plus, she probably did look like shite or shit or whatever, since she hadn't moved since she had gotten there—she even had on the same clothes she wore on the almost eleven-hour flight. "I'm

Sophie," the girl announced as she grabbed Mandy's suitcase, threw it on the bed, and rifled through it. "Beatrice gave me the rundown, and I'm here to take you out. So put these on so we can go." The clothes Sophie had thrown to Mandy were hers, but she had never worn these particular garments together. And although she heard the words that had come from Sophie's mouth, Mandy's brain couldn't process them. "What the fuck are you waiting for? Come on." Yep. Mandy really liked this girl. If only she could have the same *I-don't-give-a-fuck* attitude.

Instead of responding, Mandy rolled out of bed, changed into the new outfit, and layered on the deodorant and body spray Sophie had also tossed at her. She had to admit it actually all worked well together. Mixing patterns wasn't something Mandy did, but it seemed Sophie had a knack for it.

"Better but . . ." Sophie stepped out of the room and a moment later came back in, throwing something else at Mandy. "Wear this."

The hat was simple and cute, and Mandy felt better having her long, greasy hair tucked underneath it. "Where are we going?" Mandy asked as she threw her cross-body purse over her shoulder.

"Does it fucking matter?"

"Nope." It actually didn't matter at all.

MANDY HAD NEVER BEEN TO A PUB BEFORE. SHE'D never been to any kind of bar besides the ones inside restaurants where she would have to wait sometimes with her parents for a table when they went out to eat. Although she was aware the legal drinking age in London was eighteen, it really wasn't on her must-do list for the trip. But after a quiet walk with Sophie— that somehow wasn't awkward at all—there she sat, pint glass clutched between her hands.

A fire was lit in the fireplace across the room, and the dark wood and heavy oak furniture along with the Elizabethan memorabilia made the room feel cozy and warm. Mandy slouched on her stool and read for the dozenth time the words painted on the wall about how the place was built in the 1500s. There really was so much more history here in this small little space than in any museum back home.

"So you're a painter." Sophie broke the silence and took a long chug of her beer. "Beatrice told me."

Yes, Beatrice and Mandy had many conversations before her trip. What else had Beatrice told Sophie? "I draw too, but painting is more my passion."

"And that's what brings you here?"

Mandy nodded. Sophie was trying, so Mandy should probably try too. "I'm taking a couple workshops. What about you?"

"I'm a fashion designer. One day I'm going to have my own line, but until then, I'm working at your bog-standard shop." Sophie rolled her eyes, and Mandy scrunched her brow. Sophie laughed. "That means, like, common. You'll get the hang of it."

Fashion. That made sense. Especially seeing how effortless it had been for Sophie to create the look Mandy was currently wearing. And then there was Sophie's outfit, which, the more Mandy studied it, it seemed likely that Sophie herself had made it. Mandy wasn't up on London fashion, but it wasn't anything she had ever seen before, and it fit her so perfectly. The fabric seemed to curve with the shape of Sophie's body. "Well, I know

I just met you, and I don't know much about fashion, but I think you're going to be great at it."

"Thanks. Even if that is coming from someone I just met who doesn't know tosh." She fingered the cuff of Mandy's sweater. "This is nice though."

The indigo polka dots were her favorite—a present from Isa's mom a few years ago, and one of the few items in Mandy's wardrobe that wasn't black. Maybe she should get rid of it. "I like what you have on," was what Mandy replied instead of thinking about Isa or bursting into tears.

"Do you? Well, we're going to get along right nice. It's my own design." Sophie seemed to hold her head even higher than it was before, and then she took another drink. "How you liking that?"

Mandy glanced down at her untouched beverage. "I'm not sure I really like beer."

"That's because American beer is rubbish. Go on."

Mandy tentatively raised the glass to her lips and sipped the amber liquid. It was bitter but then tasted a little citrusy.

"So?"

Mandy shrugged. "It's okay."

Sophie laughed again. "Well, get used to it, 'cause that's what we drink here."

Mandy raised her glass. "Cheers then, I guess."

Sophie shook her head. "Oh, you have so much to learn." But then she clicked her glass against Mandy's.

Conversation after that flowed smoothly. Maybe it was the beer or Sophie's whole relaxed attitude, but hanging out with her was easy. Like somehow they always fit together. The downside to this was that the only other person who was like that for

Mandy was Isa. So while she enjoyed hanging out with Sophie, it also deepened the ache in her chest. It was hard to even try to have fun when Mandy felt so terrible. And to make it worse, all she wanted to do was tell Isa about this amazing person she met, and how she had a real beer in a real pub, and . . . she couldn't.

CHAPTER TWENTY-ONE

May 2011

WHILE IT FELT LIKE a much more significant achievement to graduate from college than from high school, only Mandy's parents were there to witness her accomplishment. As much as she said it wasn't a big deal, it kinda was, and now that the day was there staring her in the face, she wished she had pressed the importance of it a little more. At first, she was embarrassed that she graduated a few years after many of the kids she had gone to high school with. Most of them were already knee-deep in their careers of choice, and there Mandy was still trying to figure her shit out. A degree in painting and drawing, another in digital media, with a minor in Spanish seemed like a good idea at the time, but what was she going to do now?

Mandy was an artist. While she of course appreciated the works of so many out there, she wanted to be the one people appreciated. She wanted her paintings to be hanging in museums one day. There were plenty of artists who were idolized with a lot less talent than Mandy. She didn't just paint a bunch of dots on a canvas and call it great art.

She fussed with the tassels around her neck; they kept slipping to one side, and the last thing Mandy wanted was for them to fall off or for her to trip over them as she made her way across the stage. Not that anyone besides her parents was there to see it, and they loved her and were proud of her no matter what. Deep down Mandy really wanted Isa to be there, but she had her own finals she couldn't miss. Mandy understood better than anyone how important school was for Isa, but it didn't make it any easier that she wasn't there on Mandy's special day.

If it hadn't been for Isa, Mandy might never have even gone back to school. It had been spring break, and Isa had come home once again to visit her mom and abuela—this time without Tally. It wasn't that Mandy didn't like Tally, it just always felt like Tally was competing for Isa's attention when Mandy was around, or Tally had to make it clear that Isa was with her. The way she would always find a reason to touch Isa or to interrupt with a story about their life in Boston. Mandy had her chance with Isa and blew it; she knew that and didn't need the constant reminder.

But that week Isa was back without Tally. Isa had finally stopped asking Mandy "Why?" by that point and seemed to be okay with how things were. Maybe she finally accepted Mandy was never going to give her a real answer because she couldn't. In many ways it felt like old times. When they could tell each other anything and could finish each other's sentences.

"You haven't said anything, but I know you have an opinion already, so just tell me." Isa and Mandy had been walking on the beach, heading toward the pier, where Mandy contemplated getting an elephant ear, but she knew immediately what Isa was talking about, and had been avoiding the conversation since Isa showed up at her door. Now, it seemed, there would be nothing preventing them from having this discussion.

"Honest opinion?" Mandy asked to buy her a little time. Things had been going okay between them, and she really wasn't ready to mess that up.

"They're that bad. I knew it." Isa tried to cover her face with her hair, but a gust of wind made her efforts fruitless. "Why didn't you say something before we left the house? I could've cut bangs or something."

Mandy almost laughed, but she held it in. When Isa showed up with extremely manicured eyebrows, the last thing Mandy wanted to do was mention them. "Bangs would just highlight them more."

"Not if they were long enough." Isa pressed her hand on her forehead. "When my regular girl wasn't there, I should've left. Why didn't I leave?"

"Because you're too nice." That was true. Out of the two of them, Isa was definitely the nicer one.

"Too stupid, is more like it." Isa stopped, so Mandy did too. "You can show me how to fix them, right? With like a brow pencil and some of your magic."

Mandy took the opportunity to study her friend. Really study her the way she used to be able to before. The dusting of the faintest freckles were still on Isa's cheeks. Her Cupid's bow was still higher on the right side, and her bottom lip just as full. And her eyes. Her eyes were still a place Mandy wished she could get lost in. "They're different, that's all. They aren't 'bad,' just different."

"Are you sure? You wouldn't lie to me about this, would you?" That question stung deep. Before, she wouldn't have ever asked Mandy such a thing. Before, she would've taken Mandy's word and moved on. But things were different now, not just Isa's brows.

"I wouldn't lie to you." Mandy surprisingly kept her voice steady. "And if you want, I can show you how to fill them in a little more. Not"—Mandy rushed to say—"because they look bad, but if it would make you feel better, I'd be happy to do it."

"It would."

"Then I'll help you."

Isa started walking again. It took Mandy a second to pull her feet out of the soft sand she had been shimmying them down in to—*just as good as a pedicure*, Sophie would say—and caught up with Isa.

They were both quiet then for a little while. Was Isa regretting asking Mandy for help? Should Mandy try to get the conversation rolling again or just be quiet? The cool water lapped against Mandy's toes when Isa turned to her and said, "You should go to college." Just like that. Of course, Isa somehow knew it was an idea that had been playing at the back of Mandy's mind even though she had never mentioned it.

"I don't know," Mandy responded.

"What else are you going to do? Work at Grace's Art and Supply for the rest of your life?" Isa kicked water at Mandy's legs, splashing all the way up to her shorts.

"Hey." Mandy kicked water back, getting Isa equally wet.

"Okay, truce." Isa brushed water from her thighs. "But you know what I mean. You're better than this. You're smart and talented. You can't let that go to waste."

Would they have had the conversation if Tally were around? Mandy would never know for sure, but she was grateful for it no matter what. "I suppose."

Isa gave her a look—one that said Mandy was being too hard on herself, and maybe she was. "UCLA has a great art program. Yale does too."

"You think *I'm* getting into Yale?" Wasn't it on the East Coast somewhere?

Isa shrugged. "I think you can get into anywhere you put your mind to. You're good, Mandy. It's time you started believing that."

Mandy stayed quiet, the wet sand smooshing between her toes. Why was believing in yourself so hard to do?

"I'll help you with applications if you want."

"You want to help me?"

"Why do you sound so surprised? That's what friends do." Isa didn't smile when she said it, more like she was testing out how those words felt on her lips.

"I'd like that," Mandy blurted. She didn't want Isa to think too long about it—have time to take it back.

"Well then. What are we waiting for?"

If it hadn't been for Isa, Mandy would've never gotten to this point in life—graduation—and it felt strange not celebrating it with her.

Mandy did walk across the stage without tripping, and had her picture taken way too many times—thanks, Mom. But it wasn't until she was sitting down at dinner—with fancy white tablecloths and too many pieces of silverware, where the chandeliers were bigger than small cars and sparkled like a million stars—that Mandy felt truly excited that day.

"We're so proud of you, honey," Mom said as she raised her champagne glass.

"To the future." Dad clicked his against Mom's, and then Mandy joined in.

As she brought the glass to her lips, she was hit with the floral notes of the golden liquid sparkling inside. She took a sip— the bubbles dancing on her tongue. Going to dinner with her parents always meant good wine—Mom had a knack for picking just the right bottle. And since today they were celebrating, Dad didn't even complain about the price.

"Speaking of futures," Mom said, "your father and I think it might be a good idea if you move home for a little while. Just until you get your feet under you."

Mandy figured this would be coming. She had been lucky enough that they paid her rent while she was in school, but she wasn't in school anymore, and her lease would be ending soon.

"But what if I get a job? Then I might have to commute," Mandy reasoned.

"Not if you let your father talk to his colleague. Didn't you say Bert's husband's company was looking for someone to help in marketing? You could do that, couldn't you?" Mom's expression was so encouraging, Mandy wasn't sure if she should be appreciative or annoyed. Mom was just trying to be helpful— it's what she did. But Mandy didn't go to school to work in marketing.

"I want to do something with art," she said.

"You would be making ads, I think, isn't that right, dear?" Mom turned to Dad.

"Dale would be happy to share the details of the position, plus it's a great company with an excellent benefits package."

Mandy had officially been an adult since she was eighteen, but here at this table, she was starting to see that real adulting wasn't just being able to vote, join the military, or buy cigarettes. She would have to think about insurance, and 401(k)s, and retirement. All terms she heard about in the business classes Dad insisted she take. Classes she passed, but not ones she thrived in or enjoyed. "I just might want to see what else is out there." That was fair, wasn't it?

"It's a great position, and they won't be able to hold it for you," Dad said. "You really need to think about your future. You got to do your thing in college, but now it's time to be serious."

"We just want what's best for you," Mom said.

It hadn't even been twenty-four hours since Mandy received her diploma. What happened to *Let's celebrate tonight and worry about tomorrow, tomorrow*? Would that have been so hard to say? And Mandy was very serious about her artwork, so what the heck was Dad even talking about?

"You need to think practically," Dad said.

Luckily, before Mandy could answer him, her phone rang.

She flashed the screen to show her parents who it was and picked up.

"Congratulations!" Isa yelled into her ear.

"Tell her we say hi," Mom cut in.

"Thank you. My parents say hi. How were your tests?"

"Hi back," she said, and Mandy waved to her parents like it was Isa waving to them while Isa continued to talk. "Ugh, so brutal. I would've much rather been there." Isa sighed. "Oh, Tally says congratulations too."

Mandy bet Tally was sitting right there, listening in on everything Mandy and Isa talked about. "Tell her thank you."

Isa mumbled, "Thank you," in the background and then much louder said, "Tell me all about it."

The overwhelming chatter that surrounded Mandy, along with the clinking of silverware against plates, faded into the background as she recounted the day's events with Isa. If the noise was a problem on her end, Isa didn't mention it as she said, "Uh-huh," in all the right places. Mom and Dad sipped their wine and had their own conversation, only butting in a few times to point out something Mandy had forgotten to mention. In a way it almost felt like Isa was there with them. Almost.

As the appetizer plates were taken away, followed by the salad course, Mandy's battery was getting low, and Isa had to get back to Tally, so they said their goodbyes.

"Love you for real," Mandy said.

"Back atcha," Isa responded, and a pain slammed into Mandy's chest. Did she not say it because Tally was there? Did Mandy do something wrong? As she slid the phone into her purse, questions spiraled through her head, and she replayed their conversation over again trying to figure out where things had gone off track or if they had at all. This was the first time one of them didn't say, "Love you for real back," and for all the wonderful things that had happened to Mandy that day, this one moment crushed them all.

"So how is she?" Mom asked.

"Good. Isa's good," was all Mandy could say.

"Now that we've got your attention again, we can talk about you moving back home."

"Yeah, sure, Mom, whatever."

"So you agree?" Mom's voice brightened.

"It's for the best, right?" Home was exactly where Mandy

wanted to be right then—curled on the couch, crying on Mom's shoulder—but she couldn't ruin the night for her parents. Mandy slid her napkin from her lap and placed it on the table. "I'll be back in a minute." She plastered on a smile. "Bathroom," she said, but that wasn't where Mandy was headed.

CHAPTER TWENTY-TWO

April 2019

MANDY STOOD IN FRONT of the full-length mirror in her hotel room. After the fire alarm, and the evacuation, and everyone standing out front while the fire trucks arrived, they'd been told that someone had brought a toaster with them and just burned their morning bagel, which set off the alarm, and it wasn't anything more serious. (People were so weird sometimes.) But the timing of it all wasn't accounted for when Mandy had made her schedule, and with everything else, she was very far behind. If it weren't for a nice older woman who insisted Mandy get to be at the front of the line for the elevators, she'd probably still be waiting downstairs.

Ashley, forever the professional, sat Mandy right down to finish the job. Mandy had never seen anyone work so fast. She wasn't on time, but Mandy was back on track. When Ashley had finished, Mandy's hair was beyond amazing. The only direction she had given Ashley was that Mandy wanted it to be elegant, and it was. And despite the amount of hair spray, it still looked soft, but Mandy was sure even gale-force winds wouldn't blow her updo down.

Her makeup was just right too. Simple yet pretty, and both eyes were symmetrical, with little wings on the ends of her eyeliner. She couldn't have looked better.

That was if she weren't standing in her underwear.

Her beloved dress still hung near the window, and no matter how hard Mandy tried, she couldn't force herself over there to put it on.

She looked perfect.

Her dress was perfect.

And *Mandy* and *perfect* didn't go together. Ever.

Something was wrong. Something other than fish or uninvited guests or burnt bagels.

If Mandy put that dress on, would everything blow up? Would the relationship she'd worked so hard—fought so hard—for just magically implode? It seemed more than reasonable considering her track record.

Her light blue panties with *Bride* embroidered across her bottom in white thread seemed to mock her. How many brides got this far and never made it down the aisle? Maybe she should get in her car and drive away. But to where? And how would she ever be able to explain it?

Everything just seemed too right, so I had to destroy it all.

That was ridiculous. She was being ridiculous. But there she stood. Hair done. Lips layered with just the right amount of color, standing in front of a mirror in her underwear about to cry her eyes out.

Nothing seemed to make sense.

Mandy's phone buzzed. Likely Mom reminding her again

about pictures or talking about shoes. Mandy had forgone the "getting ready" photos because she thought they were silly. No one liked the "before" pictures, only the "after" ones anyway, so why bother? But if someone had been there now, maybe she'd be able to put her damn dress on. Why didn't she want bridesmaids again?

Oh, that's right, because having multiple nervous people in one room was what Mandy had been trying to avoid. Which was why she had it all set up so that she could get herself into her dress without any help. She wanted to know that even on this day she was still a person who was capable of doing whatever she wanted. She needed to know that no matter what, she herself could survive. That it was a choice. She didn't *need* anyone. Getting married was a choice. *Her* choice. And it would never change who she was.

Or would it?

After Laura got married, Mandy hardly ever talked to her. Not that she talked to her that much since seeing her at Grace's after Laura had gotten engaged. But Mandy did try to stay in touch; she made that Facebook profile and would see an occasional update, but it wasn't the same. Laura's world became Steven's world, and while it wasn't like Mandy and Laura hung out or talked all the time, there was still something there—until there wasn't.

Was Laura as happy as her online persona made her out to be? Or did she carefully curate what people saw about who she was now that she was Mrs. Olsen? Mandy should've answered that call from her earlier so she could have asked these questions.

Maybe as much as Mandy wanted to be, she just wasn't the marrying type. While she loved, and loved hard, it wasn't enough to get her happily ever after. She'd kissed so many frogs that turned out to be just frogs that there was no way she was the princess in her own story.

Mom's friend Georgia never got married, and she was fine. Better than fine, if you asked her.

Mandy sank to the floor, a memory of Georgia rushing to the front of her mind.

It was one of those summer evenings when the air was crisp but the heat from the afternoon still radiated from the concrete, creating the ideal temperature. Mom and Georgia sat at the patio table, a bottle of white wine—probably Mom's favorite pinot grigio—and two glasses between them. Mandy hadn't wanted to come outside, but Mom insisted she make an appearance and show Miss Georgia "just how big she'd gotten." Mandy was a fourth grader, not a puppy, although when she heard who was there, she wasn't as reluctant to stop the art project she had been working on.

"My Mandy Candy! How are you, sweetheart?" Georgia got up from the table as soon as Mandy stepped outside, and wrapped her in a hug. The fabric from one of Miss Georgia's signature colorful shawls was cool against Mandy's bare arms. It had been a while since Mandy had seen her last. Miss Georgia's red hair was pulled up and away from her face, showing off her rosy cheeks, and she wore a deep shade of red lipstick that looked like a juicy pomegranate. Out of all of Mom's friends, Mandy liked Miss Georgia best.

"I'm fine," Mandy answered. Miss Georgia was the only person allowed to call Mandy that name, because she always brought candy with her when she visited.

"I got you a little something." Miss Georgia reached into her oversized purse and pulled out a cellophane bag filled with sweet treats.

"You didn't have to do that," Mom said.

"Hush now," she said to Mom. "Sweets for my sweet girl." She handed the bag to Mandy.

"Thank you!" Mandy plopped down at the table, glancing from the bag to Mom.

"Go ahead." Mom waved at her before taking a sip of her wine.

Mandy pulled at the silk purple ribbon holding the bag closed and reached in, grabbing a soft orange confection. As soon as she popped it in her mouth, it was like she was drinking fresh OJ with vanilla ice cream.

"Those are some of my favorites. You'll really like the pink ones too. Strawberry." Miss Georgia winked.

Mandy didn't know what Miss Georgia did for work, but she traveled a lot. Sometimes with the candy she would bring other trinkets from afar—and lots of stories. It all sounded exciting, and yet . . . "Are you ever going to get married?"

Mom covered her mouth like she was trying not to spit out her wine, and Miss Georgia threw her head back and laughed.

"Did you put her up to this?" she asked, pointing between Mandy and Mom.

"No, I swear," Mom said.

Mandy shifted in her seat. "I shouldn't have asked that, huh?"

Miss Georgia rested her hand on Mandy's. "It's fine. Maybe one day I will, but for now, I'm living just for me." She squeezed Mandy's hand. "The only person you need to make you happy is you. And I'm perfectly content with that." Miss Georgia raised her glass, and Mom clicked hers against it.

"Being alone doesn't mean being lonely," Miss Georgia said.

"Don't look at me. I didn't say anything." Mom raised her hands in mock surrender.

At the time, Mandy wasn't sure what that had been all about, but now, standing on the precipice of what was going to be either the best or worst day of her life, she realized maybe Georgia was right. Mandy had much more control over her destiny than she gave herself credit for. She could pack up her bags and run . . . run as far and fast as she possibly could. But then what? She would always wonder if she'd made the right choice. But if she put her dress on and took the pictures and went to the venue and it all blew up anyway, she would at least *know* it wasn't because of her. She tried. She put herself out there, and that's really all she could do.

But how many times had she done that just to be crushed? Just to be told she wasn't enough, or good enough, or the right one. As much as Mandy wanted to be, she felt as strong as an overcooked noodle. She didn't know the first thing about being married, and what if she was bad at it? Like exceptionally bad?

Mandy tipped her head back, and she gazed at the ceiling. Crying would ruin her makeup. She'd spent way too much time perfecting it just to let that happen now. But oh, how she wished she could curl into a ball and sob even for a few minutes. Just to let it out. Holding it all in had its own dangerous consequences— like spontaneously bursting into tears later. But then she could likely play it off, or it would be justified.

Another buzz from Mandy's phone gave her a moment to stop thinking and reach for the offending piece of electronics. Yes. She was late. She didn't need the reminder, Mom.

It wasn't a text from Mom though; it was from Isa. And not even a text, simply a video of a cat hanging from the side of a kitty-scratching-post-tree thing, struggling to get back on, and finally making it. Mandy laughed. Isa had done it again. She had come through with exactly what Mandy needed when she needed it. Like a sixth sense.

With a renewed sense of purpose, Mandy jumped to her feet, grabbed her dress, and slipped it on. A special zipper placed strategically in the side under the arm was all she needed to do, but when she tugged, nothing happened. The zipper wouldn't move. No. This wasn't good. She climbed out of the garment and tried again, the zipper easily moving up and down. Okay, it worked. It likely was just caught on something or who knows, but it worked. Mandy carefully slipped back into the dress and tugged on the zipper. And then she tugged a little harder—but nothing. She twisted her body, trying to get a look, and when still nothing happened, she moved over to the floor-length mirror. It didn't seem to matter though. There was no reason why the stupid zipper wouldn't budge.

This was a sign, wasn't it?

Her phone buzzed again, and Mandy stopped. Stopped twisting. Stopped tugging. Stopped thinking.

Every time she'd tried the dress on, there was someone there to help her. As much as she wanted to be the strong, independent woman, today she needed help. It was okay to ask for help, because she still chose to ask for it. Mandy took a deep breath and made eye contact with herself in the mirror. "You can do this. It's going to be okay." No matter what happened today, she was going to be that cat and give it her best try.

CHAPTER TWENTY-THREE

September 2005

NOTHING COULD HAVE PREPARED Mandy for how intense the art program turned out to be. She learned so much, but barely saw any part of England past the four walls of her bedroom and the school she attended daily—even on the weekends. Although she was taking only a couple of classes, they occupied every moment of Mandy's waking hours—and sometimes her not-waking hours. Mandy barely had time to eat, or sleep, or breathe, but it was a good thing because it gave her little time to think either. No time to think about missing home, or her parents, or Isa. No time to think about what she had done.

So instead of doing any of that, Mandy poured herself into her studies. If she could get through this one task, she could move on to the next, and so forth—but she didn't look forward, and she did everything she could to stop herself from looking back. Anytime one of those before thoughts crept in, she would distract herself. Sometimes in small ways, like scrubbing paint that shouldn't be there from her fingernails, or helping Sophie iron fabric—she'd gotten really good at that.

Today though, she was concentrating on her current assignment, which had her re-creating the work of a master with her own unique POV—meaning she had to take a well-known piece and somehow remake it as her own, but not let it be so far from the original that it couldn't be recognized. And if that weren't hard enough, Mandy chose an artist she admired but whose work was nothing like her own—Artemisia Gentileschi. Realism wasn't Mandy's strength, but there was something about Gentileschi's work that spoke to Mandy in a way she couldn't explain. Plus, Mandy was there to challenge herself. She hadn't come all this way to play things safe.

After carefully preparing all of her supplies, Mandy swept her long hair back into a bun and stared at her blank canvas for a moment. It wouldn't stay that way for long, but it was like a ritual at this point, to take a moment and visualize what she was about to do. In her head she watched herself create exactly what she intended—each stroke of the brush held purpose—and when it was completed, it was perfect. She could do this. She hadn't given everything up for nothing. She needed to succeed.

As always, she started with the background. She would get the base to exactly where she needed it and go from there—the plan seemed simple enough, but the blue wasn't mixing correctly, or there was something wrong with the lighting, because it seemed too dark and not at all the tone she had wanted. Plus, there was a little hair that must've escaped her bun tickling her nose. She swiped her hand across her face to get rid of the sensation, but it persisted.

Mandy clenched her jaw and attempted to ignore it. A little

more white would do the trick—everything was still well in hand. She mixed the color and applied it to her canvas, but now it was too light. What the heck? She stepped back and swiped at her face again—to remove the annoying tickle—before she picked up her canvas and shifted it ninety degrees. It had to be the lighting where she was.

From this angle she got a little natural light from a high window. It was what she needed to get the color just right. Everything was going to work out now. She took a deep breath and once again she mixed, this time adding a little purple but also a drop of black. She almost laughed at how much of a genius she was for doing that. The color was perfect, and she proceeded to apply a nice thick coat so none of the natural canvas texture came through. Sometimes it was nice, but not for this project. By the time Mandy finished covering the middle, she realized her error. In her haste to get the ideal color, she hadn't mixed enough to cover the entire canvas.

No. This was not how this was supposed to go. She was not supposed to fail at this assignment like she had her last one. This time it was all going to work out.

Mandy quickly mixed some more—adding a little purple and a drop of black, just like she had done before, but as she swept it across her canvas, it didn't match. No. This could not be happening. And that damn hair was still tickling her nose! She swiped at her face again—forgetting she still had her brush in her hand—and smeared paint across her cheek and into her hair.

Mandy allowed her head to fall back and let out a deep breath, which was much better than the scream she really wanted to let fly from her lungs—but getting kicked out wasn't an option. She really needed to get a good start on this project.

She really needed something to go right in her life since coming to London.

And to make everything worse, that damn hair was still tickling her nose.

Five hours later, Mandy stood at the sink in her bathroom with steam filling the room. She slid her hand across the mirror and stared at herself. Cyan paint was smeared against her right cheek onto her ear and trailed off into her hair. She hadn't even attempted to clean it off, not wanting to break her concentration from her project, but it didn't matter. By the time she gave up, she was covered in paint and had sore feet, and all she had to show for her effort was a multitone blue canvas, which was not at all what she had wanted.

She attempted to drown her sorrows at the local cantina in a large basket of chips and a small bowl of what they called salsa, but was about as flavorful as ketchup. Mexican food in London was a rarity, so she was lucky there was at least something within walking distance of where she was staying. She allowed herself to think it would somehow magically make her feel better like it used to when she was home. She had been in Europe for weeks, and nothing was going right. Every painting she attempted never got to where she wanted. This was supposed to be her time to prove to her parents that she could be a successful artist—it was something she needed to prove to herself too—and she was failing miserably. The constant crunch between her teeth and the delectable salt of the tortilla chips did little to ease her aching soul. She brushed the elusive hair that had been annoying her all day back again with no success.

Today had ended in yet another epic disaster.

Now, as her fingers curled around the edges of the sink so

hard her knuckles turned white, with enough paint speckled in her hair it looked like confetti, she wanted to scream. She yanked the hair band from her hair, and gold locks tumbled down past her shoulders. Her puffy red eyes with bags so dark underneath from too many nights of restless sleep stared back at her.

What the hell was she doing?

Who was she kidding?

She wasn't some great artist. She couldn't even complete an assignment. And now here she was, thousands of miles from home, and she didn't have any friends, and if she ever saw the sun again, it would be some kind of miracle. Why was England so fucking gray? It wasn't even a pretty gray. It was cold, and dreary. She never should have come here. She never should have let herself believe she could actually be good at this. She blew up her life, and for what? She hated it here, in this house, in this country, a gazillion miles from home. But most of all she hated that girl in the mirror. And that damn hair was still tickling her nose!

Without any thought, she grabbed the scissors from the top drawer and started chopping. But with each cut, that annoying little tickle was still there. Still reminding her of what a disaster her life had become. Blonde strands littered the black-and-white-tiled floor. She cut one side, then crumpled into a ball on the floor and let out a guttural sob. Tears splashed down among the clumps of golden hair.

There was a gentle knock on the door followed by, "Are you okay in there?"

With the little strength Mandy had, she unlocked the door because no, she was not okay. She was very *not* okay.

"Bloody hell, what have you done?" Sophie knelt next to Mandy and took the scissors from her.

"It wouldn't stop tickling," was all Mandy could say. She'd fucked up. Just like she'd been fucking everything up lately. She'd destroyed her hair. And she deserved it.

"Get in the shower, and I'll deal with the mess. And then . . . and then we'll figure this out."

Mandy nodded and unclipped the straps of her overalls. She didn't care that Sophie was there. She didn't care about anything anymore.

She didn't need to look in the mirror to understand the mess she had created on her head. As soon as she went to shampoo, her hair was obviously different—at least on one side. Where she once would've had to pull up her hair and pile it on top of her head to reach the ends to wash them properly, she didn't have to do that anymore. There was no need to reach, as there was nothing to reach for.

The water never got quite warm enough, but Mandy didn't bother trying to turn up the heat. She washed and scrubbed until her skin was red and angry, just like she was with herself. When she got out, Sophie had removed the evidence of Mandy's earlier breakdown, scheduled her an appointment at a salon later that day, and made her a cup of tea, sending her to her room for a lie-down before they had to go. Mandy didn't deserve someone being so kind to her. Especially not after all she'd done.

She lay on her bed, wrapped in her down comforter, and picked up the phone. She had to dial so many numbers to make a call, and she didn't even know what time it was in California. But no matter, caller ID would say it was her—or at least someone calling from London—and they'd pick up no matter the hour. And Mandy needed Mom.

"Amanda, sweetheart. How's it going?" Mom's voice echoed

through the receiver, and the dam of Mandy's emotions broke. What was it about hearing your mom's voice that did that? Tears ran down her face so quickly, she couldn't catch them all—and she didn't even try. "Oh, honey."

"I messed up, Mom. I messed up so bad."

"It's going to be okay."

"I miss her so much," Mandy confessed.

"I know you do."

Before Mandy had left, Mom chalked up Mandy's attitude to stress and thought that Isa and she had just had a fight and that was why she wasn't with Mandy when she left. But she didn't know everything, and Mandy didn't even know where to start. And now since she'd been gone, had Mom talked to Sandy? Did Isa even tell her own mom what Mandy had done? How was Isa doing? Was she as miserable as Mandy?

"But you don't know. You don't know what I did," Mandy said.

"I'm sure it's something you two can work out. You've been friends forever," Mom tried to reason.

"I don't think we can this time." Mandy used her blanket to wipe her face. "I should've never come here."

"It's never easy being away from home for the first time."

But it was more than that, so much more. It wasn't just the place that Mandy longed for. "I need to tell you something, and I don't want you to get mad."

"You can tell me anything, but I can't promise I won't be upset."

Mandy nodded to herself. That was fair, she supposed, and she couldn't bear to keep it inside anymore. She cleared her throat and let it all out. As she cried into the phone and used her blanket as a tissue, Mandy told Mom everything—well, almost everything—there was to know about her and Isa, and how Mandy messed everything up.

Mom had been true to her word and just listened, like she always listened. She wasn't happy Mandy had kept their relationship a secret from her, but Mom also didn't yell. Maybe because Mandy was already so upset, or because yelling wouldn't do any good, but either way she was relieved.

"You shouldn't be so hard on yourself," Mom said. But that's what moms were supposed to say.

"I don't know what to do."

"It seems that the only thing you can do is move forward. You made your choices, and now you need to let Isa make hers."

"But I was wrong. I fucked up. What can I do to take it back?"

Mom took a deep breath. "As tough as it is, actions have consequences. Sometimes there's no going back to the way things were. But maybe if you give it a little time, you can make something new."

Mandy didn't want anything new, or different. "But I love her."

"Then give her time."

"How much time?"

"As much as she needs. All you can do is reach out, and then it's up to her."

Reach out. If only it were that simple. Mandy was thousands of miles away. She had already tried to call, but no one answered, even though it was almost impossible that no one was home. And Mandy couldn't leave a message—not without knowing what Isa could've told her family. "What am I supposed to do, email her?" That seemed so impersonal.

"Have you thought about writing her a letter? That way you give her the opportunity to open it when she's ready."

A letter seemed like an even worse idea, but Mandy was out of options.

"I love you, sweetheart. Things will get better. I know it doesn't seem like it now, but they will," Mom said. "Go make some friends. Perhaps your—what did you call her?—flatmate wants to hang out."

Mandy had almost forgotten until Mom mentioned Sophie—even if it wasn't by name. "That's something else. I should tell you what happened with my hair—"

"Amanda Elizabeth Dean. What did you do?"

CHAPTER TWENTY-FOUR

July 2013

FOURTH OF JULY WAS never one of Mandy's favorite holidays. It came in the middle of the summer, it was always too hot, there was really never much to do before fireworks went off, and even after that, it was just over. It seemed like a silly reason for people to get together and barbecue. They could've done that any day.

This year Mandy was stuck at an event with a bunch of Edmund's coworkers. They didn't have to work, and yet they chose to spend the day together talking about work. Yep. Mandy just did not get Fourth of July parties at all.

June gloom had lasted a little longer, and while the sun did its job making Mandy sweat, the haze of the day hadn't completely burned off yet, giving a little protection from the sun's rays. The venue was lovely, near the water with a view of the marina, where they would all board a boat later to watch fireworks. Until then, however, a large fountain sat in the middle of the courtyard and, with an occasional breeze, blew cool droplets in Mandy's direction. If it wouldn't have elicited stares, she considered for a moment taking off her heels and soaking her feet. She couldn't believe she allowed Edmund to talk her into such footwear to begin with.

"They make your legs look amazing," he had said that morning when Mandy was getting dressed. It felt as though she hadn't seen him for weeks, with his late hours at the office and early mornings in the gym, so the compliment hit much harder than it normally might have. "Plus, I need to make a good impression, and you're an extension of me." And then he kissed her neck in that special place that made her knees weak, so she complied with his request.

Now, as she leaned against a high-top table under a billowing blue canopy, she regretted that decision. Where *was* Edmund? He had gone to get them drinks a while ago and hadn't come back yet. She didn't want to leave and miss him, and she didn't really know anyone well enough to feel comfortable wandering around on her own. Even in her summer dress, Mandy felt woefully underdressed. Most of the women donned either linen pantsuits or pencil skirts. It was Fourth of July, and a party, and it was like a million degrees out, but only Mandy seemed to be uncomfortably aware of each of these factors.

"Who schedules a work party on a holiday?" A man who didn't get the *dress-much-too-formally-for-an-outdoor-summer-event* memo sidled up to the high-top Mandy leaned on and set his sweating beer can down. "Oh, sorry. Do you mind?" He gestured to the table.

"No. It's fine." Mandy shifted from one foot to the other.

"You don't work for Hartsfield Baldwin, do you?" the man asked. His tan skin glistened in the summer sun. His khaki shorts and light blue polo looked freshly pressed. And he was tall, taller than Edmund, but just as fit. Likely a swimmer, with the way his body narrowed at his hips, but he was broad across the shoulders.

"I don't," Mandy confirmed.

"Yeah, you look way too normal . . . I mean that in a good way. Like down to earth, not . . ." As if on cue, a trio walked past the table, two men and a woman wearing navy suits. "I'm sweating my balls off in this. Sorry." He pushed his sun-lightened brown hair off his forehead.

Mandy chuckled. "It's fine. I'm sweating my tits off."

"Exactly." The man raised his beer to cheers with Mandy. "No drink?"

"I was waiting—"

"Excuse me." The man raised his arm and a waiter scurried over. "We need some cold drinks over here. Can you help us?"

"Of course. What can I get for you?" the waiter, who looked just as uncomfortable in black slacks and a white button-up, asked. Did Hartsfield Baldwin ask for them to dress so formally, or was that their normal uniform?

The man turned to Mandy, and then so did the waiter. What the hell. It was a party, after all. "Piña colada."

"Make it two," the man said. "Good choice." He nodded at Mandy as the waiter rushed off.

"It sounds refreshing," Mandy said. "And if you can't go on vacation . . ."

"Let the vacation come to you. I like it." He chugged the last of his beer, crushed the can in his hand, and set it down. "I'm Khalan, by the way."

"Amanda." She stuck out a hand. Edmund preferred she used

her full name—said it sounded more professional—and she didn't want to fight about it.

Khalan shook it. "Well, Amanda. What brings a girl like you to an event like this?"

"I'm here with Edmund Prince. Or I came with him, but I have no idea where he went."

Khalan nodded like this made sense. "Making his rounds, I'm sure. But he'll be back soon."

"What makes you say that?"

"Just a hunch." Khalan shrugged, but the way he did it made Mandy sense there was more to it. Like maybe he knew Edmund rather well.

The waiter came back and placed two piña coladas on the table—each a lovely pale yellow with a slice of pineapple perched on the rims of the glasses.

"To sweating our balls and tits off." Khalan raised his glass, and Mandy clicked hers against it. The sweet blended drink immediately seemed to cool her down by ten degrees as soon as it hit her lips. It really was like a vacation in her mouth.

"Oh, that's good," he said.

"So good," Mandy confirmed.

"So besides knowing how to pick the perfect beverage, what is it that you do?"

Mandy took another sip, and before she could answer, Edmund appeared just as Khalan had suggested he would.

"Keeping my girl company, are you?" Edmund clapped a hand on Khalan's shoulder. It was the type of gesture Mandy was never sure the meaning of. Was it friendly or a subtle way for men to try to assert their dominance over each other? Either way, it always seemed rather ridiculous.

Khalan took a relaxed sip of his cocktail. "Well, someone has to since it seems you left her out here to fend for herself."

While it was annoying they were talking like she wasn't there, it was nice that someone stood up for Mandy. She had been lonely, and hot, and thirsty, and Edmund returned without the beverage he had set out for. "Yes, Khalan was nice enough to order me this." Mandy raised her glass in a *remember-you-were-supposed-to-get-me-some-kind-of-refreshment?* way.

Edmund flinched—which momentarily made Mandy think he felt bad for forgetting about her, but then he said, "That was very kind of you, Mr. Jain."

Now that Mandy looked at him, Khalan did seem a little older than Edmund perhaps, but not by much. Why did Edmund address him so formally? What was Mandy missing?

"No reason to thank me. Without Amanda here, this party was seeming rather dull."

Edmund grinned like he was in on a secret. "She does know how to have a good time."

Thankfully neither seemed to glance in Mandy's direction. Her cheeks blazed hotter than the day's rising temperatures. She took a big swallow of her cocktail to cool them down.

"She was just about to tell me what it is she does when she isn't at work functions on a national holiday."

"Right now, I'm consulting for a marketing firm, but really I'm an artist—"

"What Amanda means is that her job allows great artistic freedom. She can do things on the computer I've never seen before. You know that billboard off Thirty-Second? That's her work."

On one hand it felt like Edmund was bragging about Mandy's work, and yet on the other, it felt like he was ashamed of her.

Why mention the billboard but not that she was also a painter—even if it had been a while since she'd picked up a brush—that her passion was on the canvas, not on the computer?

Khalan chuckled heartily. "Oh, that's a good one."

"Thank you," was all Mandy could muster. Her gut twisted tighter than a package of dried ramen. The ad campaign was getting attention, sure, and it wasn't that she looked down on those who did that type of work, but for her it was just a means to an end—a way to support her true passion. And the way people talked about the billboard like it was some great accomplishment, when in reality it was just an ad for shitty yogurt. There weren't many people that could claim "artist" as a profession, and Mandy hadn't given up on the idea completely. Not that she was naive, she was just hopeful, and there was nothing wrong with that.

Edmund then brought the conversation back to work. He constantly talked about work. Why not, just for one day—even with all his coworkers around—talk about something else? Wasn't this event supposed to be fun? Wasn't it about "getting to know each other" or whatever it said on the invitation?

Khalan looked as disappointed as Mandy felt by the shift of conversation. Maybe Edmund didn't realize Khalan didn't want to be talking about work on his day off. Edmund was clearly attempting to make a good impression and failing miserably at it. But this was what Mandy was there for, right? To make sure Edmund looked good to important people. That was why she was in those god-awfully uncomfortable heels, right? Khalan seemed to be looking for his escape, when Mandy touched his arm.

"You know what would go great with these?" She held up her drink. "Hot wings."

Edmund chuckled nervously, but Khalan smiled.

"But, like, really hot ones . . ." he said.

"The kind that make your nose run," Mandy finished.

"Exactly." Khalan took another drink of his cocktail.

"I think there are chicken skewers." Edmund shifted his attention to the hors d'oeuvres table that had a large fountain of cheese with crackers and fruit that sat under glass domes. There had been a few waiters who passed by with trays, but by the time they got to Mandy's table, they were mostly empty.

"It's not the same," Mandy said.

"I'll go see what I can rustle up." Khalan grabbed his cocktail and excused himself.

He had barely gotten out of earshot when Edmund wrapped his hand around Mandy's arm. "You're embarrassing me. Mr. Jain doesn't care about hot wings." He released her arm, but the place he had held her pulsed.

"No, Khalan didn't want to talk about portfolios. I was trying to save you there."

"Well, do me a favor and don't do me any more favors. I have to work with these people. And they don't want to see you shoving your face full of messy chicken wings." Edmund was stressed, that's why he was being a complete ass, but it didn't make it okay.

"Oh, I won't." Mandy grabbed her purse and took off her shoes.

"What are you doing?"

"I'm leaving. God knows I wouldn't want to embarrass you more."

"And you think leaving in the middle of my work party is making a good impression?"

"Tell them I had a graphic design emergency. Tell them whatever you want. I don't care." She slammed the rest of her cocktail and walked away before Edmund could say anything else.

She hadn't wanted to come to this party to begin with, but she had. For Edmund. Because she was always doing things for Edmund. Mandy didn't even know where she was going or how she would get there. She had driven with Edmund because he liked his car more than hers, but she had to get away. She was hot, and hungry, and damn it, she wanted some chicken wings.

Being this close to the water had its perks. First, she stopped in the yacht club's shop and bought a pair of overpriced flip-flops and a bottle of ice-cold water. They were worth every penny if it meant she didn't have to wear her heels anymore, and the water refreshed her in a way even the piña colada couldn't. Part of her still felt a teeny-tiny bit bad for leaving Edmund, but it wasn't enough to make her go back. So Mandy did what she always did in situations like this.

She pulled out her cell.

THE CANTINA WAS SURPRISINGLY BUSY, BUT MANDY found a seat at the bar and ordered a margarita on the rocks with extra salt, and something called Mexican egg rolls. They weren't spicy chicken wings, but they were fried and sounded as ridiculous as Edmund made her feel for wanting them, which was perfect for Mandy.

There was something about crunchy chips and spicy salsa that soothed Mandy's soul. It wasn't the chilaquiles Isa's mom or Abuela would make when she had been feeling down, but it had the same kind of effect with the banda music playing softly over the chatter of other patrons. Chips and salsa had been one of the only Mexican foods Mandy could find in Europe when she'd sought the same kind of consoling she needed today.

Those days seemed so long ago now. Days she had to get through without Isa. Where everything was new and yet it all still seemed to remind Mandy of her.

And just like that, Isa was there.

"What's going on?" she asked as she pulled up a stool next to Mandy and helped herself to some chips. "What are those?"

"They're called Mexican egg rolls."

Isa cocked a brow, just the one, her way of saying *WTF* without having to say it. "Sounds disgusting." She picked one up and took a bite.

The bartender made their way over and placed a napkin down in front of Isa. "What can I get you?"

Isa pointed to Mandy's cocktail. "One of those, and another order of these." She pointed to the egg rolls.

"Coming up." The bartender walked away.

Mandy shook her head and smiled.

"What? I'm going to need to eat like five more to make any kind of decision about them." She popped the rest of the egg roll into her mouth.

"They're weird, right?"

"So weird," Isa said around a mouthful.

The bartender made their way back with Isa's margarita and another basket of chips.

Mandy picked up her glass. "Fuck the Fourth of July."

"Fuck it." Isa clicked her glass against Mandy's.

Thank god Isa was there. She had come home for an impromptu visit before starting her residency back on the East

Coast. If she ended up getting a job out there, Mandy didn't know what she would do. It had taken time, but Isa was back in her life, a part of her world, and she never wanted to be estranged from her best friend again—one out of ten, would not recommend. It was hard enough with her being so far away and their hangouts done over the phone. From time to time, they would both put on their sweats and baseball hats and go out running errands on the phone together—they would call it an "ugly day," and if anyone tried to talk to either of them, the trick was to pretend they didn't know them. But when Isa was in town, things were so much easier. And their "ugly days" could be spent on the couch, or tucked into the corner of some café, or out together—while they ignored everyone else.

Mandy's phone chimed. She already knew who it was but checked it anyway.

EDMUND: I'm sorry. I was a dick. Let me make it up to you.

It was better than the ones he sent before, but Mandy was still upset, so she switched the phone off and shoved it into her purse.

"You want to talk about it, or you want to drink?" Isa asked, nibbling on her second egg roll.

"Drink now, talk later."

And that's what they did. The conversation stayed light and casual as they each sipped their oversized margaritas and ended up sharing an order of fajitas. It was the kind of meal that wasn't anything special, and yet that was what made it perfect.

"All I'm saying is that Sophie would disagree with you."

Mandy popped the last part of her egg roll into her mouth. They had really grown on her, especially after the second margarita.

"What's there to disagree with? I wear them on my legs. They are the definition of pants." Isa held up her leg, showing off her leggings. "Plus, they're more comfortable than jeans, and bonus, if I fall asleep in them, that's okay too."

It was nice that Mandy could bring up Sophie without having it be a thing. Without worrying that it reminded Isa of why they broke up. Plus, Isa would really like Sophie. One day they should all hang out together.

"Feel them." Isa grabbed Mandy's hand and put it on her thigh.

"Oh, that is soft."

"Exactly."

"But . . . if you can sleep in them, doesn't that make them pajamas?"

"I sleep in T-shirts, and that doesn't mean I can't wear them out in public." Isa had a point, and Mandy could admit the pants looked really cute on Isa. (Or was that the margarita talking?) Mandy needed to stop thinking about Isa's body right now—with the alcohol, her mind was slipping into dangerous places.

"You win. Leggings are pants. Next subject." Mandy grabbed her ice water and took a long swig.

Isa narrowed her eyes at Mandy, but then her look morphed into satisfaction. "Organic tampons. Are you using them?"

Mandy almost spit out her water—not at the absurdity but just at how funny the question caught her off guard. "Do you always think about vaginas?"

"Every day." Isa was specializing in obstetrics.

"I just grab whatever's on sale." Mandy shrugged.

"Amanda!"

"Marisa!"

"Have I taught you nothing?"

"You've taught me a lot of things." More things than Mandy ever wanted to know, actually. "I promise to do better."

"I'm going to hold you to that."

"I expect nothing less."

As Mandy sat there atop that barstool, licking salt from her fingers, she realized she didn't need fancy parties at yacht clubs, or canapés or petits fours, and she definitely didn't need parties where she had to wear heels, and get dressed up just to impress a bunch of people who would likely forget her name by tomorrow anyway. She was utterly content with flip-flops and fried appetizers you ate with your fingers, and just being herself.

Had she ever truly been herself with Edmund? Did he even know who she was?

They had dated for so long, Mandy could barely remember a time without him, but were those memories from before better than anything in her present? When was the last time she fell asleep on the couch and stayed there all night, leaving the bowl of ice cream she'd just eaten on the coffee table, where it got all dried and petrified by morning? Or the last time she didn't wash her hair for an entire week because she had spent so much time working on her art?

She needed to do that again. Well, not the *not-washing-her-hair-for-a-week* thing. But paint. Get so wrapped up in her projects that the world around her would fade away. Mandy needed to remember who *she* was.

"Let's get out of here," Mandy announced to Isa, then motioned to the bartender for their check.

One thing about the Fourth of July was that many places were closed, but that didn't matter so much, because art was everywhere if you knew where to look. Mandy and Isa took a drive to one of their favorite beachside locations, where an enormous amount of chalk art could always be found. The holiday did make parking more challenging, but luckily being extra familiar with the area helped. And while the number of people who were out that day was more than usual, the number of artists scratching away on the concrete did not disappoint.

Some guys banged on their drums—or banged on things meant to be drums—but the sound was amazing. They were creating music with everyday items—buckets, cans, even a two-liter bottle full of beans—just like the people on the ground were making art with their hands.

"Dance with me." Isa pulled Mandy aside and threw her hands in the air. Dance like no one was watching—that had been their thing, something they hadn't done in far too long. Hell, Mandy couldn't remember the last time they had danced. And even though there were plenty of people watching, it didn't matter.

She grabbed Isa's hands, and they spun in circles, throwing their heads back and laughing. Mandy hadn't laughed that hard in a really long time. They likely looked ridiculous, but it didn't matter. Their charisma must've been contagious, because soon a nice crowd had joined in on the fun.

Sweat trickled down Mandy's face, but this was exactly what she needed. To let loose and have fun. To refill her creative well. To reignite her passion. She wasn't just the girl who made the pretty ads; Mandy was an artist. She had a point of view. She had something to say. And while maybe her voice had been quieted over the past couple of years, it wasn't gone.

And with Isa by her side, Mandy felt inspired for the first time in a long time.

She almost felt like she could take on the world. Almost.

After pulling Isa off the impromptu dance floor, they wandered down the path next to the beach as skateboarders, rollerbladers, and bicyclists passed by.

"He said that I was embarrassing him." Mandy was finally ready to talk about it. "He left me all alone, and this guy started talking to me. What was I supposed to do, ignore him? How was I supposed to know he was like the boss or something?"

"What did you say?"

"Nothing. That's the thing. It was a perfectly normal conversation. I mentioned chicken wings, and Edmund's head practically exploded."

Isa stifled a laugh. "Sorry. I mean, could you imagine Edmund eating a chicken wing? With his fingers?"

Okay, that image was funny. Edmund would likely try to use a knife and fork if he attempted to eat one at all. "It's just, why does it matter if I eat chicken wings, or talk about eating chicken wings?"

"It doesn't."

"Sometimes I wonder if Edmund even knows me at all." Mandy had never said those words out loud before.

"Well, have you shown him who you are?"

"Are you saying it's my fault?"

"No, that's not it. You just always do this thing where you lose yourself in every relationship you've had. You become a different person." Isa was right, and Mandy hated to admit that. The only time she had ever been 100 percent herself was with Isa—that is, until the very end, and well, look how great that turned out.

Mandy stopped in front of a bench and sat, exhausted from either walking or the conversation, she wasn't sure. "I don't mean to."

"I know you don't," Isa said, but did she really mean it? Mandy never told her about why things went down between them the way they did. Isa had stopped asking, but it was unlikely she forgot—Mandy still thought about it all the time. "It's just, maybe it's time to be the real you. And if he doesn't love that, love you for who you are, then at least you'll know."

It sounded so simple. So why did it feel so impossible? If things didn't work out with Edmund, then what? Where would that leave her? Just a girl with another failed relationship. Mandy was so tired of that. Tired of dating. Tired of trying people on to see if they were the right fit. People weren't shoes. Shouldn't people bend a little for each other? Mandy never meant to change who she was for the person she was with. It always started innocently enough. She just wanted to make them happy. Wasn't that what you were supposed to do? But was she the only one? Were they not trying to make her happy in return? Was that where the problem lay?

Why did it feel like no one would be able to love Mandy just the way she was?

Well, there was one person.

She took Isa's hand. Maybe to ground herself. Maybe to try to get that feeling back that they once had so long ago. When they used to hold hands and tell each other all their secrets and kiss when Abuela wasn't looking. And while Mandy's hand felt so at home in Isa's, it wasn't the same. Mandy had ruined that, and there was no hope she'd ever get it back.

Her gaze shifted from their hands up to Isa's face. Isa stared back. Was she thinking the same thing? Could Isa have been trying to tell Mandy this whole time it was her she should be with? Mandy glanced at Isa's lips and leaned in ever so slightly.

"No," was all Isa said, and she let go of Mandy's hand—but Mandy understood what she was really saying. *No, it will never happen with us again. No, I can't ever trust you with my heart. No, you are ruining everything. No. No. No.*

I'm sorry were the words Mandy wanted to say, but she was tired of saying them, and they wouldn't make a difference. She'd gone and fucked things up again. Just when they were okay. Mandy was surprised Isa didn't get up and leave, but Isa was her ride, and no matter how mad she was at Mandy, Isa would never abandon her—never do what Mandy did.

The air between them shifted—from a comfortable silence to tense and thick. Part of Mandy wanted to leave, but the other had a sick feeling this would be the last time Isa and she would be alone again, so Mandy didn't move even when a hollow emptiness filled her insides and she started to tremble—was it from the breeze coming off the water? Or maybe her trembling was something else entirely.

With the sun now hidden beyond the horizon, fireworks lit up the sky with a distant *boom*.

"Ooooh . . ." Isa cooed next to her. She always did love fireworks.

Mandy settled in. They weren't in the best position to see the show, but it wasn't bad either. Silently they watched as the sky filled with smoke and colors erupted against the dark backdrop.

All too soon after the finale and Isa and Mandy had gone their separate ways, Mandy slid into bed next to Edmund.

"Baby . . ." He rolled over smelling of whatever he had been drinking, and started kissing Mandy's neck. "I'm sorry. I was such an ass. I promise I won't do it again."

She could stop him. She could tell him everything she was feeling. But he was drunk and saying all the right things, and the bed was warm, and Mandy didn't want to be alone, so she let him run his hand under her nightshirt and then much lower.

CHAPTER TWENTY-FIVE

August 2005

SINCE ISA'S ANNOUNCEMENT AT Grad Nite, the pair had been inseparable in a different kind of way. Maybe it was wrong of Mandy not to tell her mother about her and Isa's new relationship status, but then again, if Mandy had, she wouldn't be standing in her kitchen in her underwear and slippers making cookies with Isa at midnight while her parents slept. Isa wore her favorite plaid pajama pants and shirt combo—but for some reason, she looked extra cute in it that night.

"We should crush up pretzels and put them in there too," Isa said.

"Pretzels in chocolate chip cookies?" Mandy was intrigued—she wouldn't knock a food combination without ever trying it herself.

"Salty and sweet." Isa nudged Mandy with her hip. "Like you and me."

"Which one of us is salty?"

Isa quirked that eyebrow of hers, and Mandy just wanted to tackle her right then and there and kiss her all over.

"Very funny." Mandy instead threw an M&M—the thing they were using instead of chocolate chips—at her girlfriend, which hit her in the chest and slid into the pocket of her shirt.

"Nice shot." Isa, with a satisfied grin, plucked the candy out and popped it into her mouth. "Hey, M&M. Mandy and Marisa."

"See? We were always meant to be," Mandy said. "They even named a candy after us."

"Uh-huh." Isa leaned in close to Mandy, so close Mandy got a whiff of Isa's coconut shampoo. Close enough that Isa's hair tickled Mandy's cheek. Close enough that if Mandy just leaned in a little more—

"What's going on in here?" Mom's voice behind Mandy made her jump, spilling a bunch of M&M's on the floor.

"We're making a little midnight snack." How did Isa sound so calm? Mandy's heart was about to pound out of her chest.

"Making a mess is more like it," Mom said. She rubbed her eyes and seemed to contemplate how much energy she wanted to expend on the situation. She sighed. "Just keep it down. Your father has to get up early for work in the morning. Not everyone is on a summer vacation." She pointed to the tile. "Make sure you clean all this up, okay?"

"Sure, Mom, no problem." Mandy almost saluted. What was wrong with her? Why was it so hard to act natural?

"We'll make sure to clean up, Mrs. Dean."

"I know I can count on you. It's that one I'm worried about." Mom gestured toward Mandy. "How is she ever going to be on her own for almost three whole months?" Mom's eyes got glassy.

"Hey. I'm not incompetent," Mandy said.

"That's not what I'm saying," Mom said. "I'm just going to miss you."

"I'll miss you too, Mom." She walked over to her mother and kissed her cheek. "Now go back to bed, and we promise to clean up."

Mom glanced at Isa.

"Cross our hearts." Isa made a crisscross sign over her chest.

"Okay. Don't stay up all night." She kissed Mandy on the forehead and headed back toward her room.

Mandy and Isa quietly finished mixing the cookie dough, measuring it out, and cleaning up, and while the cookies were baking in the oven, Mandy turned out the kitchen light so it wouldn't attract any more attention from Mom. The only light was from inside the oven and the full moon shining in from the skylights. Mandy hopped up on the counter, and Isa stood between her legs.

"I'm going to miss you while you're gone too," Isa said.

Mandy pulled her in. "I won't be gone forever, and when I get back, I'll meet you in Boston."

"I know, but it's just a long time apart, you know?"

"I'm going to miss you too." She rested her chin on the top of Isa's head and hugged her tightly.

"What if I went with you?" Isa's voice was so quiet Mandy wasn't sure she heard her right.

"You want to come with me? To England?"

Isa pushed back just a little and gazed up at Mandy. "Do you think that's weird?"

Mandy shook her head. "No. But it won't be long until you have to be at school, so I'm just not sure it's worth it to go for such a quick trip. Not that I don't want you to go," Mandy quickly added. "I do. I'd love to spend three months in Europe with you, but you have school."

"Yeah, but . . . what if I defer my start? I'd only be behind one semester, and then we can go to England and do what you need to do. And then we can go and be in Boston for me."

The sweet scent of baking cookies mingled with the smell of Isa's shampoo. Could it really all be that easy? Isa coming with Mandy would be a dream come true. "And you could just start late? You wouldn't lose your spot?"

"I'd have to figure out some financing stuff, but yes. I could totally just start later without losing my spot."

Mandy studied Isa's face—her bright eyes, her lifted brows. "So you're going to England with me?"

Isa smiled up at Mandy. "I'm going to England with you."

Instead of squealing for joy and risking waking up her parents, Mandy leaned down and kissed Isa. When she pulled away, the blush on Isa's cheeks made Mandy's heart swell. Yes, she was completely and irrevocably in love with this girl. "This is going to be the best trip ever."

THIS SUMMER HAD TRULY BECOME THE BEST IN MANdy's entire life. Once Isa decided she was coming with Mandy, each day held a new kind of excitement. Late-night sleepovers turned into late-night make-out sessions. Holding hands during movies underneath a giant tub of popcorn. Sitting at the bookstore, knees touching while they perused the new releases section for Isa or the magazine rack for Mandy. Or sometimes they would just drive around, find a secluded place, and sit in the back of Mandy's car so they could be alone to talk about anything and everything—but there they could also tangle themselves up in each other's arms, which also sometimes led to more making out.

The stack of clothes on the chair in the corner of Isa's room got bigger and bigger as the days passed. She kept adding things to pack on their trip, thinking she would need everything. Mandy hadn't started packing even though they'd be leaving in just over a week. She had used a good portion of her "spending money" to help pay for Isa's ticket, but it was worth it. If she had to miss a meal here or there, it was fine as long as Isa was with her. But Mandy had more than enough, with all the "gifts" she had gotten from her parents' friends for graduation—this trip was already well funded.

Isa had a map of Paris sprawled out in front of them, and they both lay on their stomachs on Isa's bed, leaning on their elbows, feet intertwined.

"We have to see the Eiffel Tower," Isa said, pushing aside their open bag of M&M's to grab a gold foil sticker, affixing it to the spot on the map. That was how they marked the places they wanted to go—with stickers that, according to their color, prioritized the location. Gold was the highest level, so this meant it was a nonnegotiable sightseeing spot. They each were allowed one per map, and this one was Isa's.

"We also have to go to Centre Pompidou." Mandy affixed her own gold star on the map.

"You promised we wouldn't just go to museums."

"But this is Centre Pompidou." It wasn't the Louvre, which of course Mandy had to go to too, but still, she needed to see the collection they had there and this building that people either loved or loved to hate. "I can't be that close and not go." She leaned over and kissed Isa on the cheek.

"Mandy," Isa whispered. "What if Abuela walked by?"

"We'd hear her coming first. Don't be so paranoid." Mandy nudged Isa with her shoulder and then fed her an M&M—a green one. "And I promise my next pick won't be a museum. Okay?"

"I'm holding you to that." Isa leaned into Mandy. "And you're sure it's cool I stay at this place with you while you're doing your classes, right? It's not going to be weird?"

"For the hundredth time. It's fine. You can hang there while I'm doing my thing, or come and go as you please. Beatrice doesn't care." Mandy had corresponded endlessly with the woman whose room she would be renting while she was there, and she assured Mandy it wouldn't be an issue. The room had a queen-sized bed and was really meant for two anyway. Mom had insisted on the larger space thinking Mandy would feel more at home that way.

"I can't believe we're really doing this." Isa would say that a lot when they talked about going to Europe—because it would be the farthest she'd ever been from home, the farthest without her mom or Abuela. It was the first time Mandy would be away from her parents too, but she knew Isa was more nervous about it. Isa would go to Mexico to visit family, so it wasn't like she never traveled, but this time neither of them would have any family nearby if anything went wrong. Mandy didn't like to play the *what-bad-things-could-happen* game—there was no reason to worry about things out of their control—while Isa rationalized that planning for the worst would ensure they'd have the best experience.

Regardless, it was going to be an amazing trip.

A floorboard in the hallway squeaked, and Isa and Mandy quickly separated—well, separated enough. Isa hadn't gotten around to telling her mom or Abuela about Mandy and Isa's new arrangement, and it was probably better that way. The sleepovers would stop, for one thing. Mandy and Isa also hadn't gotten around to telling their other friends. Everyone was so busy getting ready for college that they decided to live in their bubble for a while—just the two of them. There would be plenty of time later to tell everyone. For now, they enjoyed this secret little life they were sharing together. Without questions, or prying eyes.

Abuela shuffled past Isa's room and grunted. Mandy and Isa exchanged a glance. Abuela had made it known that she wasn't happy with Isa's choice to defer a semester. But Isa had it all planned out. And being one semester behind wouldn't throw her entire future off track. Plus, the life experiences she was going to gain from a trip like this would be irreplaceable. Mandy even asked Isa a dozen times if she was sure she wanted to do this. That they would only be apart for a short time, and while it would suck, it would be okay. But Isa was adamant. Said if Mandy was going, so was she, and there was nothing Mandy could do to stop her. And it wasn't as if Mandy didn't like the idea of having Isa there. She wasn't as likely to get homesick with Isa next to her. She would always have someone to go sightseeing with her when she didn't have classwork to complete. She'd have a piece of home with her the whole time—the best part of home. It really was the ideal plan.

"Oh crap. Is that really what time it is?" Isa jumped up, scrambling to find her shoes.

The clock on her dresser read 3:52 p.m., and Isa was supposed to babysit for a family down the street at 4:00 p.m.

"I wish you didn't have to go." Mandy meant those words, but she probably shouldn't have said them. Isa had taken on a number of babysitting jobs to make money for their trip. Isa didn't like that Mandy had spent so much on her ticket and didn't want to rely on her the whole time they were there. Mandy had never mentioned the cost, because it didn't matter. To cover her tracks though, she added, "Those kids are kind of a disaster."

Isa laughed. "Teddy isn't always like that." Meaning he didn't always scream so loud or throw his toys all over the house, but Mandy wasn't convinced.

"If you say so," Mandy said. "Need me to get anything for you while I'm at the mall?"

"No, I'm going to get those Nikes before we go myself. Now get out of here so I'm not late." Isa kissed Mandy's nose and handed over her shoes.

Mandy rolled off the bed, slid the shoes on, and kissed Isa's nose back. "Call me when you tuck those monsters into bed."

"I will."

They both headed out the door at the same time, Isa walking down the street even though Mandy offered to drive her over, and Mandy to her car—she still had a little last-minute shopping to do for the trip. Mandy honked as she passed Isa and headed to the mall.

HER QUICK TRIP TO PICK UP A FEW THINGS ENDED with Mandy spending too much time and way too much money. It was as if, once she got started, she didn't know how to stop. Plus, she wanted to look good for Isa. Mandy also couldn't help herself when she saw the Nikes Isa wanted and bought those too.

Isa needed them, and Mandy already had her credit card out. Isa would likely be mad at first, but she would get over it.

Mandy pulled up to the front of her house to dump her bags before circling around to the garage. Lucky for her, Mom and Dad weren't home, so she didn't have to explain her overzealous shopping excursion. What she didn't expect to find was the person sitting on her front porch.

"Abuela?" Mandy's thoughts began to ricochet inside her brain. Was Isa okay? What happened? "Is there something wrong?"

"Sit, mija." Abuela patted the bench next to her—the one that hung from the porch where a scarecrow sat every year the few weeks before Halloween, and then the night of was replaced by Dad jumping to scare unsuspecting teens. "Everyone is fine. There's no need to worry."

Mandy set her bags on the ground, her trunk still open in the driveway, and did what Abuela asked. In the years Mandy and Isa had been friends, Abuela had been to Mandy's often, sometimes showing up to drop off caldo de pollo when one of them was sick, or with "extra" flan knowing Dad loved it more than anything. But there was something about the way Abuela sat there now, hands folded in her lap, that set Mandy's nerves on edge. If there wasn't anything wrong, then why was she here?

"Sandra and I have always wanted what is best for Marisa." It was strange hearing Abuela use Isa's and her mom's formal names. To Mandy they were Sandy and Isa—as they were most of the time for Abuela too. "When Roberto passed, it was hard for Sandra. She had to work two jobs, and she sacrificed so much to make sure Marisa got the best education."

This story wasn't new to Mandy; she knew everything there was to know about Isa and her family. They were practically

Mandy's family, after all. When Mandy and Isa were growing up, there were many nights Mandy slept over at Isa's that her mom wasn't there—just Abuela to look after them—because Sandy worked all night to come home, eat a meal with them, and head off to work again. And although Mandy never met Isa's dad, she saw pictures of him on the table in the dining room, and in Sandy's bedroom, and he was always prominently displayed each year on their ofrenda. "Isa's the smartest girl I know."

"She is. And I know you want what's best for her too, don't you?"

"Yes, of course."

"I know you do. I know you love her. But sometimes loving isn't enough. Sandra and Roberto loved each other and, well . . ." Abuela made the sign of the cross before she turned and held Mandy's gaze. "I know your love for each other is the same."

Did Abuela know about Isa and Mandy? Was she upset that they were together or that no one told her about it? Isa had planned to tell Sandy and Abuela when they got back from Europe, she just didn't want to do it before. Didn't want to ruin their summer of love—plus, the sneaking-around thing was pretty hot. Mandy opened her mouth, but Abuela held up a hand. "I'm not here to discuss that. I am here because I want to ask you, why are you going to Europe?"

Mandy chewed on the inside of her cheek; she didn't know where Abuela was going with this. "It's been a dream of mine, I suppose."

"And what is Isa's dream?"

To be a doctor, both of them knew that. "What are you saying?"

"Why not wait to go to Europe? Isa has scholarships and

plans, but now"—Abuela raised an empty hand—"she wants to go to Europe too. But it will still be there—the scholarships and plans, maybe not."

"Are you saying Isa will lose her college money?" Isa had never mentioned this to Mandy. She had said that she would have to figure out loans and how to pay for things when they got back but never said she was giving anything up. Why wouldn't she tell Mandy something as important as this? "She never said."

"Isa wants to do what will make you happy."

Mandy wasn't sure how she should feel hearing that. She wanted to do what made Isa happy too. They had made plans together, but as the porch swing shifted under her, Mandy realized how much of these plans had been made around Mandy. Plans Mandy had made months before Isa was even a part of them. This trip was Mandy's dream. "I can't not go."

"And Isa can't not be a doctor." Abuela took Mandy's hand. "Ahogado el niño, tapando el pozo." Mandy scrunched her face. What did kids and wells have to do with this? "It's better to do what is right now, before worse things happen," Abuela said. "It won't be easy, for either of you, but it will be what's best."

Mandy understood. Isa needed to be a doctor, she needed her scholarships, and Sandy had worked so hard to help Isa achieve her dream. Having Isa come with Mandy could ruin that dream for Isa forever. And if Mandy didn't go, it would ruin her dream. A knot formed in Mandy's chest. "I don't want to hurt her."

"I know, mija. But it's for the best."

Was it though? How could not being with Isa be the best thing? What would she say if Mandy told her Abuela talked to her? So many questions raced through Mandy's head.

Long after Abuela left, Mandy's stomach was still in knots as she lay on her bed staring at the ceiling. There had to be a way to figure this out. There had to be something Mandy hadn't thought of so they could both get what they wanted.

Maybe Mandy could help pay for Isa's college. Then again, she was already going to be upset Mandy bought her shoes; there was no way Isa would let Mandy do that. Maybe Isa wouldn't lose all her scholarships. Or maybe there was something else she could do to arrange it with the school—like get a job or work on campus. How much could it cost to go to Boston University, anyway? Mandy never looked up colleges or how much they were because she knew she wasn't going to one right away.

Determined that there had to be something she hadn't thought of, Mandy sat at her computer and started to search. Student loans. College tuition. Personal loans. Off-campus housing—it wasn't like Mandy could stay in the dorms with her. Would Isa still be allowed to live there if she were late checking in? Wow, apartments in Boston were expensive. Mandy would definitely need her parents' help if she wanted to move there. They loved Isa, but they weren't going to like this. They'd also want to know what Mandy would plan to do—she hadn't really thought about it beyond just being with Isa.

Then Mandy searched for her art program. Looked at all the pictures of smiling students and of the school's spacious studios to work in. Plus, she'd already paid to watch a guest lecture and demonstration from one of her favorite artists. When would she ever get to do that again?

Isa wanted to experience Europe with Mandy. She wanted them to eat fish and chips, and buy ridiculous hats, and drink espresso from tiny little cups at an outdoor café, and Isa really wanted to see the Eiffel Tower. Mandy wanted to do those things with Isa too. They'd made plans and had maps with special star stickers on them of all the things they wanted to experience together. But none of that was what Isa *needed*.

Abuela was right. Isa had too much to lose—and their dreams of being together in Boston weren't going to be as easy as they'd hoped. Mandy was being selfish thinking Isa could drop everything to be with her. Isa had worked too hard. But just telling Isa no, that she couldn't come along, wasn't that simple. Tears soaked into Mandy's pillow. She was going to have to do the hardest thing she'd ever had to do. She was going to have to break Isa's heart, and in the process, she'd also be breaking her own.

CHAPTER TWENTY-SIX

May 1995

THERE WAS SOMETHING ABOUT being at school when it wasn't school time that felt rebellious or naughty, even if it was for a school event. Everything about being there felt different. The lights were brighter, the carpet in the hallway bluer, and it didn't smell like tomato sauce or whatever was cooking in the cafeteria. Actually, tonight it smelled like fresh-baked cookies—chocolate chip and oatmeal raisin.

This wasn't the first night Mandy's parents had gone to her school, but this was the first time Mandy's art was going to be on display.

It was GAT's first official "A Night for Stars" program, where the theater and music kids would perform, and there would be a gallery showing off every student's artwork. Mom said something about it being because of the school's new director, but Mandy didn't care why. She skipped along through all the kindergarten and first graders' art until she came to the wall full of all the second graders' projects. Mom and Dad lingered behind, carefully inspecting all the drawings and paintings along the way, commenting on this or that, but Mandy didn't pay much attention. She wanted them to see *her* art. Their art teacher had been keeping it all year to display for this very occasion.

"Mandy, nice to see you." Her art teacher, Mr. Wu, held out his hand for a high five, and Mandy jumped into the air before slapping his palm with hers, unable to contain her excited energy anymore.

"My mom and dad are here too." Mandy turned around and pointed at them as they finally came wandering up behind her.

"It's so good to finally meet you, Mr. and Mrs. Dean," Mr. Wu said. "You must be so proud of Mandy. She's one of my best students."

Mom didn't hang Mandy's art on the refrigerator like they did at Isa's house. She had black frames that hung on the walls where she would periodically swap old pieces for new ones. The one exception was the rainbow that hung in Dad's office. As soon as that painting came home, it went up there and never got taken down.

"She's our little Picasso." Mom laughed.

"Hopefully not as tragic, but talentwise she's well on her way." Mr. Wu chuckled. "Have you seen what she's been working on this year?" He led them to the middle of the second-grade display, where one of Mandy's paintings hung right in the center. For this project, they were each supposed to select an animal and paint it as best they could. Mr. Wu had expressed the importance of showing detail and texture, and where most of her classmates decided to use the natural color of the animal they chose, Mandy went the completely opposite way. She picked bright colors in varying shades, and she layered on the paint and used the edge of her pencil to carve grooves into it when it was drying.

Dad put a hand on Mandy's shoulder and squeezed.

"Looks like I'm going to need to buy another frame," Mom said.

"This one is mine too." Mandy walked a little farther down and pointed to another one of her pieces. They had to use charcoal for that one, so it wasn't as bright, but she thought it still turned out pretty good.

"You're going to need a lot of new frames, I think." Mr. Wu gave Mandy another high five. "If you'll excuse me." And he left them to go talk to other parents.

"So tell me about this one," Mom said. That's what she always did. She never told Mandy what she thought, or commented on anything; she would always ask her first.

"We got to pick out different objects from this big box, and I thought these flowers were the prettiest," she told them. "They were kind of an ugly orange color, but since it's black-and-white, you can't really tell."

Dad chuckled.

"I think they're beautiful." Mom beamed at her. "This one here is yours too, isn't it?" Mom walked a few paces down and picked out another one of Mandy's pieces.

"How did you know?" Mandy asked.

Mom leaned down close to Mandy's ear. "Because it's one of the best."

Mandy smiled so big her cheeks hurt.

After she got to tell them about each one of her art pieces, and they listened to music, and they watched a skit from the theater department, they headed out to the car. Mandy skipped along even if the night air still held the heat from the day and sweat built up on her nose. It didn't matter.

"I don't know about you, but I could really go for a dip cone," Dad said.

Mom raised her brows at him. "It's Mandy's night, so I think that should be up to her." She turned to Mandy. "What do you think?"

Dad winked, and she said, "Dip cones for sure." She grabbed his hand, and then she grabbed Mom's in the other.

Pop Rocks danced in her belly. Mom had said her art was the best—even better than some of the older kids. And now they were going out to get ice cream. On a school night. As her arms swung forward and then back, in sync with both her parents, Mandy smiled so big she bet the moon reflected off her teeth—even though she was missing one in the front.

CHAPTER TWENTY-SEVEN

June 2015

THE ENTIRE STORE WAS like a sea of white, and tulle, and sparkles. Literally everything glistened, from the crystal chandeliers to the bubbles floating in Mandy's champagne glass. It was as if Glinda the Good Witch barfed on everything, showering it in a rainbow of glitter. It was so frilly, and girly, and not at all like Mandy. Not that she didn't like pretty, girly things. This was just completely over-the-top.

"Oh, this would look absolutely to die for on you." The salesperson who had been assigned to them, Krystin, sounded way too cheerful. She held up the poofiest dress Mandy had ever laid eyes on. It was strapless and the top looked like a heart, and the bottom looked like an over-frosted cupcake with sparkles, of course. Mandy's gaze connected with Isa's, and it was obvious she thought the same thing. That dress was hideous.

"Well, that is something." Mom poked her head out from behind a rack. That was her nice way of saying she hated it too.

"I'll put it with the others." Krystin strolled off.

"'To die for.'" Isa edged up to Mandy's side.

"I might die if I have to wear that," Mandy whispered.

"You never know unless you try it on," Mom said—always diplomatic. "Now what about this one?" The dress she held was better. Not perfect, but better. It had straps, for one thing, and the sparkle was subtle. But it was princess-style, and even though Dad still liked to call Mandy his princess, that kind of dress just wasn't really her thing. Mom, though, was trying—which was nice, since she picked this boutique out.

The whole shopping excursion had been Mom's idea. She "did the research" and made the appointment. This was supposed to be the best bridal shop in all of Southern California, but Mandy was having her doubts. Maybe it was the best bridal shop for drag queens, or Kardashian wannabes, but for other people? Mandy had so many things she needed to do, like finish the commissions for Aziz, who—thankfully, even though Mandy probably didn't deserve it—still talked about her and her work and continued to sell her pieces. He'd been hinting at another show, but Mandy didn't have the emotional bandwidth. Mandy was lucky she had Aziz, and she was well aware of that, so she didn't want to do anything that could jeopardize their relationship—like blowing off the time she should be painting on looking at overpriced dresses.

"It's not bad," Isa said for Mandy—trying to play the peace-keeper.

"I'll have Krystin put it with the others." Mom followed the path Krystin had gone just moments before.

"No one ever buys a dress from the first place they go to." Isa pushed a cream-colored gown to the side.

"And you know this how?" It wasn't like Isa had ever been

married. Mandy didn't even think she'd been wedding dress shopping before today. Mandy hadn't.

"TLC. Like everyone else." She bumped Mandy with her hip. "Come on. Just try the things on and make your mom happy."

"Easy for you to say. You don't have to squeeze your ass into them and then parade around."

"Fair. But . . . I bet you one hundred dollars I can find the ugliest dress." Isa smiled.

Mandy glanced around. If she had to be here and do this anyway, she might as well make it as fun as possible, right? "Oh, you're on."

Isa took off in one direction and Mandy in the other. This new task almost made sifting through hundreds of dresses mildly enjoyable, and even though Mandy's arms started to ache, she wasn't about to give up. And if she was going to be completely honest, some of these weren't *that* bad. There were actually a few that could be okay, maybe. Mandy pushed a basic sheath dress to the side and hit the jackpot. What hung before her was quite the monstrosity—it even needed two hangers to hold it all up. Off-white, sparkly (of course), and oh god, did it have beaded fringe?

"Krystin," Mandy called. "Could you help me with this one?" Mandy was totally going to win.

"Oh yes, isn't the iridescent overlay simply to die for?" Krystin asked as she attempted to pull the giant gown from the rack. She wrestled with it for a solid two minutes before she was swallowed by a mound of "iridescent overlay," Mandy assumed.

Once it was gone, however, she got the opportunity to see

what was behind that dress, and it was, well . . . kind of perfect. It was white but not bright white, and it was simple—understated. She actually kind of liked it. "Could I try this one too?"

"I'll be right back for it," Krystin said from under the mountain of fabric, and shuffled off.

Mandy stared at the dress a moment longer. It was pretty. And the price wasn't even half of the one that had just been taken to her fitting room. If she tilted her head the right way, she could even picture herself in it. Isa's laughter pulled her out of her thoughts and back to the task at hand.

"You're going to love this one," Isa said from somewhere.

Twenty minutes later, the fitting room Mandy stood in wasn't anything fancy—a square room with a small chair for her to place her clothes on, and just enough room for Mandy, Krystin, and all that tulle. A large mirror was on one wall, and every other available space was full of dresses. Isa had really come through on some "special"-looking choices. Mandy had to give it to Krystin, not once did she giggle or make an uncomplimentary comment. Like when Mandy slipped into a mermaid-style strapless gown with see-through lace around her middle and a train three times as long as she was tall, Krystin's comment was, "While this does nice things for your derriere, I'm not sure this is the one, but let's see what your family thinks."

Isa covered her mouth—likely because she was about to spit out her champagne—when Mandy turned the corner and came into view of the couches where Isa and Mom sat to wait for Mandy. Mom, on the other hand, was not amused.

"Oh no. Just turn around." Mom shook her head.

"I don't know. How does it look with the veil?" Isa somehow held a straight face.

Mom scowled at her. "You're kidding, right?"

Krystin—forever the polite sales associate—said, "Yeah, this wasn't my favorite either, but don't worry, there are lots more options," and ushered Mandy back to the dressing room.

The next dress was somehow worse than the first. The material on top was completely sheer, but strategically placed rhinestones covered Mandy from her shoulders all the way down the front of either side of her torso to her hips, but left the center down to her belly button completely exposed. From there, layers of organza circled her hips and flared out around her legs like wrinkled wrapping paper. And then there was the enormous rhinestone bow right on Mandy's ass.

"Maybe not this one," Krystin suggested, but Mandy knew she couldn't *not* show Isa one of her amazing picks.

"I don't know. Let's see what they say."

Poor Krystin plastered on a smile as she followed Mandy out of the dressing room back to the couches.

Mom, momentarily distracted by her phone, didn't look up until Mandy was standing on the stage in front of them with three mirrors behind her so whoever was seated on the couches could get a full 360-degree view.

Isa's chin quivered; she was trying so hard not to laugh that Mandy couldn't keep a straight face.

"What is going on here?" Mom demanded.

And Isa lost it, so of course Mandy burst out laughing.

Krystin stood there, not sure what was going on. Poor, poor Krystin.

"You two." Mom tried not to smile now that she seemed to

figure out what was happening. "You've had your fun, now go try on that Alfred Angelo one I picked out."

"I win," Isa called after Mandy as she retreated to the dressing room.

Without looking back, Mandy flipped her off before turning the corner.

The Alfred Angelo, as Mom called it, had a halter top, a cinched waist with a rhinestone belt, and a full princess skirt. Krystin paired it with a faux fur wrap, since the wedding was in December, and a tea-length veil.

"You look absolutely stunning," Mom gushed, her eyes filling with tears. Which made Mandy's eyes burn a little too.

Mom reached for the box of tissues, but it was empty. "Excuse me," she said, and headed toward the bathroom.

"I'm so sorry about that. I'll get some more." Krystin hurried off for more tissues. And so, it was just Isa and Mandy.

Mandy stood there staring at herself in all three mirrors. She did look like a bride, but she didn't exactly feel like one.

"I thought you wanted a spring wedding." Isa fidgeted with the faux wrap. It was nice and warm, but it made Mandy's neck itch.

"Edmund thought a winter wedding would be romantic."

"In New England?"

Edmund argued everything went with snow, and that they could order all the flowers Mandy wanted, but she couldn't deny that her heart had been set on a spring wedding.

Mandy had almost forgotten about the time she and Isa sat inside Waldenbooks looking at bridal magazines. How did Isa remember? It had been the summer before freshman year, and with nothing else to do, Mandy and Isa were hanging at the mall.

It was too hot that day for the beach, so any place with air-conditioning was preferable to sweltering in the sun. Isa had dragged Mandy into the store, but it was Mandy who had been hard-core crushing on Justin Timberlake and saw a magazine with his face plastered on the cover and pulled Isa to that section instead of looking at the new releases like Isa wanted. It wasn't like they didn't have plenty of time, so Isa relented, and they settled on the floor next to the overflowing rack with magazines on every topic under the sun. Mandy, however, was the one who got them looking at all the bridal ones.

"I don't know if I want to get married," Isa said as she flipped through the pages of *Martha Stewart Weddings*.

"I do," Mandy said. "It's going to be in a garden somewhere, full of flowers, and instead of throwing rice, we'll release butterflies, and they'll flutter all around me before they fly away."

"I don't think you can train butterflies to do that."

Mandy ignored her. "It will be a perfect spring day, not too hot and not too cold. And we will stand under a shady tree, and Justin will say how he's never loved anyone as much as me, and I'll tell him he's so beautiful, and then we'll kiss." Mandy held the magazine to her chest and let out a long sigh.

"Okay." Isa put the bridal magazine back and picked up one with a fluffy white kitten on the cover. "Do you think my mom will let me get a cat?"

"Litter boxes are gross."

"Yeah, but kittens are cute." Isa flipped the page around for Mandy to see.

"Awwww . . ." Mandy threw her magazine back on the rack and scooted next to Isa so they could look at all the cats together.

Mom *ooh*ed, bringing Mandy back to the present, back to

staring at herself in a mirror with multiple angles. "These heels would match perfectly. Try them on."

"You hate heels," Isa said.

Mandy, however, didn't say anything. She just complied with what her mother wanted—sometimes it was easier—and slid her feet into the uncomfortable shoes. They pinched her toes, and the right one dug into her heel. Even with them on, the dress was too long and pooled around her feet.

"We can do all the alterations in-house," Krystin said.

Mandy stared at herself. The lights in there were extra bright, and the wrap around her shoulders grated against her skin. Mandy's cheeks flushed, and a trickle of sweat ran down her back like a slowly creeping spider. Wasn't she supposed to feel something? A spark. Some magic. She was getting married. Possibly in this very dress, and instead of being excited, Mandy's heart pounded harder.

Was this it? The one? And she didn't just mean the dress.

"I think this could be it, but I know we don't always meet eye to eye, so if you want to try some more on before you decide, I promise I won't say anything. But you do look like the picture-perfect bride in this one." Mom went for the new box of tissues.

Mandy had always wanted to get married. She knew from even before that moment in Waldenbooks that one day she'd be a bride, and wear a white dress, and Dad would walk her down the aisle. Mandy loved love more than the bees loved the flowers.

So why couldn't she breathe?

Isa interlaced her fingers with Mandy's and gave her a squeeze. "I don't think we're ready to make any decisions yet, right, Mandy?"

Mandy just nodded.

"No, of course not. We have so many more to try. But let's keep this one on the list, shall we? It's a solid contender," Krystin said.

"It'll be okay," Isa whispered and gave Mandy's hand another squeeze.

Would it though?

CHAPTER TWENTY-EIGHT

April 2019

MANDY'S PHONE WOULD NOT stop buzzing as she sat half-dressed in the back of the limousine. She had been partly tempted to ask the chauffeur to zip her up but realized how awkward that would be, so she slid inside, waiting to ask Mom to do it when she got to the park where they were meeting the photographer for pictures. But it was taking forever to get there.

The little separator from the front seat to the back had been rolled up by Mandy as soon as she got inside (since half her body could pop out and into view at any moment). But as she gazed out the tinted window at the same car that had been next to them five minutes ago that stood next to the same tree on the same sidewalk next to that, she had to do something.

She hit the button, lowering the screen enough to get a view of the top of the driver's face, and turned the open side of her dress away from him. "Is something wrong?" she asked.

The driver looked into his rearview mirror, making eye contact with Mandy. "The traffic isn't moving. I'm not sure why."

"Can we get off this road?" It was a ridiculous question. They were in a giant limousine with cars that weren't moving on either side of them.

"Yes, miss. I'll see what I can do."

"I'm sorry," Mandy said. "This isn't your fault. I'm just stressed is all."

"Most brides are." The skin around his eyes wrinkled at the corners. "There's champagne chilling back there if you'd like." There wasn't just champagne but a fully loaded bar—crystal decanters filled with all sorts of different kinds of liquors, ranging from clear to a golden, honey brown. Most likely scotch. Edmund enjoyed an occasional scotch after dinner—and sometimes before dinner. Mandy never really developed a taste for it. But she couldn't deny it always did kind of calm her. Or maybe it was the soothing tone of Edmund's voice—*Nothing to get so worked up about*, he'd say.

However, the margarita and blueberry muffin Mandy ate already sat like a brick in her stomach. "I probably shouldn't."

"Very good, miss."

"You can call me Mandy. It seems like we're going to be together for a while."

"Roger," he replied, and it took her a moment to realize it was his name and not him saying, *Okay, sounds good.*

Mandy tugged the fabric on her dress over and attempted to get more comfortable. "So, Roger, are most brides as late as I am?"

His gaze shifted to the dash, then back to her. "The ceremony doesn't start till four thirty. You have plenty of time." Four thirty, because Mandy decided she wanted to start on an upswing instead of the minute hand ticking down. It seemed even sillier now considering how her day had already been. "Might not get to all the pictures you wanted before, but photographers are used to it, and there will be time after the ceremony and before dinner is served. Who's the photographer?"

Well, that was a good question. Mom had picked them out. She had been thumbing through some magazine when she declared she found the best wedding photographer in all of Southern California—those had become Mom's favorite words. Now whether that was what the magazine said or actually had any truth behind it, Mandy never found out for sure, but less than twenty-four hours later, the contracts were signed, and Mandy had a photographer named—Stupendous. Suspicious. "Serendipitous something?"

Roger chuckled. "Sweet Serendipity. Whitney is excellent. Very professional. You're in good hands."

"You've been doing this awhile?" Like the art world or the marketing world, there was probably a wedding world—where everyone knew each other because they likely hung out almost every weekend.

"Twenty years," Roger answered. Mandy didn't really get a good look at him when she got into the car—if he had been a kidnapper and she was required to do a drawing for identification purposes, it would be a blank page—but now that she studied his eyes in the mirror, they did seem to be the kind that said he'd seen a lot of things. Roger had wise eyes.

"You like it then?"

"It keeps me busy."

Mandy nodded. Living in LA where limo sightings were common probably kept him booked year-round. "I bet you've met some interesting people."

Roger's eyes wrinkled again. "That I have."

"Not a name-dropper, are you, Roger?"

"When it's a name worth dropping." He winked.

The car slowly moved forward as Mandy shot off another message to her mother: On my way.

A reply came almost immediately: And where is that exactly?

Mandy locked the phone and sat it next to her. "You got any hobbies?"

"Driving is my hobby. Started the business so I didn't have to work in banking anymore, and when my husband passed, well, this is what I do to occupy my time."

"I'm so sorry."

"Don't be. We had a wonderful life together for thirty-five years. Married for almost six of them."

"That's incredible. Got any advice for a newbie?"

"Don't sweat the small stuff. Money comes and goes, but it's the people you surround yourself with that will keep you happy. So when times get tough, 'cause they always do, remember what brought you to this moment right here."

Mandy had to stop and stare at Roger for a moment. "That's really good advice." She hoped her voice didn't sound as surprised as she was. And why should she be? She didn't know him, or anything about him, but he just dropped probably the best thing Mandy had heard since announcing her engagement.

"It served me well."

Mandy relaxed into the seat. For the first time that day it really felt like maybe everything was going to be okay—not just her attempting to be mostly positive about it.

And then her phone buzzed again.

Roger flipped on his turn signal. "Looks like plans have

changed," he said as Mandy checked the message from her wedding planner.

CANDY: Moving photo location

CANDY: Don't worry

CANDY: Everything is in hand

"What's going on?" Mandy asked, but just then Roger flipped his wipers on. Rain. Nothing ruined an outdoor wedding faster than rain. Oh god, she was cursed. The entire day was cursed.

"This doesn't look like it's going to stick around too long, so don't you worry." Roger tried to sound reassuring. "And they say rain is good luck."

Mandy wanted to believe him. She truly did.

CHAPTER TWENTY-NINE

December 2006

WHAT WAS SUPPOSED TO be a three-month sabbatical—a three-month trip to learn about and experience some amazing art—turned into an experience Mandy would never forget, nor did she want to. Europe had been everything Mandy needed it to be. Not everything she wanted, but those were different things. She had wanted to go to Paris with Isa, wanted to introduce her to art pieces that meant something to Mandy, but that didn't happen.

If it had, Mandy may not have been able to stay as long or learn all the things she did and grow as an artist the way she had. The purpose of the trip had transformed, but so had Mandy. As awful as it had started, Mandy wouldn't change anything about it. She was grateful for everything she had gone through.

Mandy's life had changed for the better, and she had to believe that Isa's had too. But she couldn't think about it, or Isa, or even what tomorrow would be because today was her last day in

England, and Sophie had wanted to take Mandy out one last time.

While Mandy continued staying at the same house in the same room she had when she first got to Europe, Sophie moved out about six months later into her own flat—with roommates—not far away. On days like today, Mandy would walk instead of taking a bus to see her. It wasn't often, but there were occasionally days when the sun would come out, even in December, and despite the chilly air, Mandy took her hat off and let those glorious rays shine down on her face.

Sophie's flat was a three-story walk-up just off a main road. Mandy had no idea what Sophie had in store for her, and Mandy's mind raced with ideas as she climbed those stairs. They'd already done a ton of shopping to "prepare Mandy's wardrobe" for when she made it back to the States. And they'd done their last night at their favorite pub, but she supposed they could always go back for one more pint. Mandy carefully tucked her hair behind her ear—it had finally grown out enough to stay secured there for a decent amount of time—and knocked on the door.

As usual, Sophie called out, "Come in," from the other side. Mandy pushed the door open.

"Surprise!"

Holy shit.

Mandy jumped back, clutching her chest. Packed inside the smallish flat was practically everyone Mandy knew and a few faces she didn't recognize. There were people from her art classes and some from Sophie's design school. Finny and his current boyfriend, Leo, stood near the corner with Rafe and Sophie. On more than one occasion, Mandy had been their fifth wheel but never minded. They had become some of her favorite people and tomorrow she would be leaving them.

Happy tears stung Mandy's eyes. "Bloody hell, you guys," she said in her best British accent, which wasn't terrible (but wasn't great either).

And they all laughed and raised their glasses.

The apartment had been decorated with American flags and red, white, and blue balloons. People wore straw cowboy hats and cheap bandannas around their necks.

"We thought we should help you prepare to reacclimate," Darcy, a girl from her advanced modern art class, said.

Mandy stifled a laugh. "It's incredible," she said.

Her friends had really gone all out and seemed to have raided the "American food" section at their local corner shop, ensuring a spread of Twinkies, Strawberry Sensation Pop-Tarts, marshmallows, and hot dogs in a jar—because for some reason the Brits thought this was how Americans sold their hot dogs. Luckily, Sophie made sure to have Mandy's favorite British foods too—like crumpets and Marmite (yes, she enjoyed the tangy, thick brown spread that looked like dirty motor oil), and Scotch eggs, and some of her favorite cheeses. And of course, Sophie had her favorite gin there as well. (Although Mandy didn't know for sure whether she could get it in America—she would have to see when she got back.) Because they were right, in less than twenty-four hours, she would have no problem getting all the American snack foods her heart could desire, but she wouldn't get the few things that were truly British. She wished she could wrap up all the things and people she loved so much about Europe and bring them home with her. What was she going to do without Sophie? They could Skype, but Mandy couldn't walk over to her flat and watch terrible British telly with her or go to the pub and grab a pint after a really long day. Hell, back home she wasn't even allowed to drink legally. And who was going to tell her what to wear? And that she had horrible taste in shoes? Well, actually, Mom would have the shoe thing covered.

As if Sophie knew Mandy was thinking about her, she was suddenly next to her, pulling Mandy into the tightest hug. "You were surprised, right?"

"I had *no* idea." And it was true. Mandy had been too preoccupied with all the things she needed to do to leave to notice anything suspicious. It was a good thing Mandy didn't want to become a detective. If she were being honest, she still wasn't sure what she wanted to do when she got back, she just knew it was time to go. The same feeling in her gut that had been calling her to Europe started calling her home. She missed the beach and the sun and the warm California weather. And she missed Mom and Dad. She loved Europe—there was something there that fed her soul in a way nothing back home did—but she was also a California girl inside and out, and it was her time to return. Those tears threatened again.

"Oh no. You are *not* going to make me cry. Let's get you a drink." Sophie grabbed two glasses and poured gin with seltzer and a splash of Ribena—a black currant juice—into both, one for each of them. "To Mandy!" she called.

"To Mandy," her friends repeated, and then all drank.

And ate.

And drank.

And drank.

And drank.

A few hours later, the flat was overstuffed with people, but

Mandy was terribly drunk. She sat on Sophie's lap on her emerald-green velvet couch talking to Leo about . . . well, actually, she wasn't exactly sure what they were talking about anymore.

Sophie twirled Mandy's hair between her fingers. "It's not just good music though," she was saying, "there's a message there. Take 'A Certain Romance,' for example. It talks about how boredom breeds violence. That's bloody powerful."

Leo gazed at Sophie pensively. Maybe he didn't know what she was talking about either. "I've never thought about it like that."

"I don't even know what you're saying," Mandy said.

Sophie laughed and tugged Mandy's hair. "That's because you're pissed."

"I'm so fucking pissed," Mandy agreed. She probably shouldn't have had that last shot, but it seemed like a good idea at the time. She'd been drunk before, but never *this* drunk.

Rafe handed Mandy a bag of crisps and slipped onto the couch behind Sophie. "Eat something."

Prawn wasn't her favorite flavor, but she needed to soak up some of the alcohol.

"You've been hogging my girl all night," Rafe said as he reached around and tugged a little of Mandy's hair too. "When do I get a turn?"

"When I leave tomorrow," Mandy mumbled through a mouthful. "Bugger off. She's mine until then."

"She's right, babe." Sophie leaned back and kissed Rafe's scruffy cheek. "I'm hers until tomorrow. That was the deal."

Mandy shoved another handful of crisps in her mouth. "I'm gonna miss you so much."

"I'm gonna miss you more." Sophie kissed Mandy's cheek. Nothing romantic ever happened with them—even that kiss on

New Year's Eve the year before couldn't be defined that way—but Mandy loved Sophie, and Sophie loved Mandy. It was something they told each other often. It was a familial love, a sisterly love, the kind of love where they could sit on each other's laps and twirl each other's hair and kiss on the cheek. It was also the familial love where they farted and could be ugly and were just totally real with each other. The same kind of love Mandy had with Isa—before.

Mandy was going to miss it. Miss Sophie. Miss snuggling on the couch together. "You have to come and visit." A rogue tear slipped down Mandy's cheek. "Promise me."

"Fuck," Sophie said, and then she was crying too. "I promise." She kissed Mandy's cheek again. "I promise, I promise."

"You two are so gross," Finny said, and he took a seat on Leo's lap.

"The same could be said about you two." Mandy threw a couple of crisps at them.

"Yes, we are," Leo said. Out of all of Finny's boyfriends, Leo was the one Mandy liked best. He complemented Finny's exuberant side, never got embarrassed when Finny broke out into song and dance at random occasions, and let Finny win at darts. That's how Mandy knew Leo was the real deal—that even though Finny tried to pretend Leo was just a boy he was dating, there was more there.

Rafe and Sophie were good together, but Mandy wasn't as sure about them. They'd likely be friends forever, but Mandy didn't see Rafe as Sophie's forever. Sophie wasn't the kind of girl you could pin down that easily. She needed space to roam. She had too many adventures she still wanted to take. Only time would truly tell though.

The one thing Mandy knew for sure was that she was so grateful she had met them all. She had been a mess when she first got to London, and Sophie was damn near an angel for putting up with Mandy during those first few months. Sophie brought Mandy back to life and saved her. She had been the lantern Mandy needed in the dark cave she had curled herself into. Sophie was the light that led her out.

Mandy loved all of them so much. "I'm going to miss all of you!"

And the group squeezed together into one giant hug.

That night, Mandy slept in Sophie's bed—too drunk to make it home. In the morning, Sophie helped her collect all her gifts—Crunchie bars, and Hobnobs, and Jaffa Cakes, and boxes of tea—and took Mandy back to the room she'd been staying in. Mandy's head throbbed, and she chugged Lucozade—the British version of Gatorade—that had been left over from the night before like a dehydrated camel. She was never going to drink that much ever again.

Sophie was hungover too—not as badly as Mandy though—so she helped Mandy pack up the last of her things and picked her out the cutest outfit—because even if you didn't feel good, you should look good, Sophie would always say. (She really was like Mom in a lot of ways.) They ate a greasy breakfast to help soak up the alcohol, and before either of them were ready, the taxi had pulled up to the curb.

"Don't forget me," Mandy said into Sophie's hair as she squeezed her tight.

"Never." Sophie squeezed her back. "You're an amazing person, Amanda Dean, don't you forget that."

"I'll miss you."

"I'll miss you more."

And they stayed like that for another minute. Mandy clutching the soft fabric of Sophie's jacket, not ready to let go but at the same time so ready to be home again.

She climbed into the taxi and tried not to cry as she waved a final goodbye to her friend. Or not goodbye as Sophie said, but until next time. But who knew when that would be. Mandy was off on her next adventure. Going back home didn't feel like moving forward considering all the things she hadn't had to face while she was gone. Only time would tell if she had done the right thing then, and if she was doing the right thing by coming home now.

CHAPTER THIRTY

February 2010

DEEP BASS RATTLED THROUGH Mandy's chest as she made her way to the bar. Sweat trickled down her back and settled into the waistband of her jeans. Club Apexx hadn't been this packed the last time Nikki dragged her out to what she called the best club in all of LA. Mandy hadn't been to many clubs, but from her inexperience, she was willing to say that Nikki was correct. Club Apexx always had incredible cocktails and played great music, and while it was loud, it wasn't so piercing that she left with her ears ringing. And she could carry on a conversation and order drinks at the bar without screaming, which was also a bonus.

Nikki stayed on the dance floor, claiming she didn't want to lose their spot while Mandy went to get them much-needed refreshments. Nikki had stuck around town after she graduated—she maintained that she needed to find "the perfect job," but basically, she was just living off her parents for as long as she could, and time was up. It had been nice having her around even if they didn't always get to hang out. Nikki was always good for a last-minute "get dressed, we're going out" and really, without her, Mandy might always be at home eating ramen on her couch in pajama pants and her fuzzy cow slippers. Nikki would be leaving soon too, finally having gotten a "real" job—although perhaps not the perfect one—so when she called earlier that evening, Mandy couldn't say no. Although hanging out with Nikki always equaled an interesting time, clubs weren't necessarily Mandy's thing. There were always way too many people all pressed in and sweating all over each other. The first time she had come, she hadn't expected it, so she was uncomfortable and fighting for personal space the whole time. Now—it being at least the eighth time for her and the millionth for Nikki—she still didn't like it, but it also didn't bother her as much. Especially since she and Nikki had come up with a hand signal that meant *help, get this person away from me.* Guys were always really handsy in clubs— they were handsy everywhere, but especially in clubs. And after a couple of drinks, they could also be super aggressive and didn't take too kindly to a strong no, and being polite didn't always work either. So now when they were uncomfortable with anyone, they'd throw their hands in the air, hold two fingers up— like bunny ears that thumped along to the beat of the music—and keep dancing until one of their group came and carefully removed them from the situation. Mandy had come up with the idea on her second time to the club, and Nikki and her other friends used it from there on out.

Mandy slid past a couple in a major lip-lock and sidled up to the bar. "Two Creamy Unicorns," she told the bartender. Mandy wasn't sure what was in the cocktail, just that Nikki ordered them the first time Mandy had come with her, and they were delicious. Strong—but not overpowering—fruity, and a fun turquoise color with glitter that swirled around inside the clear plastic cup. Mandy also didn't know what that glitter did to the inside of her body, nor did she care after a couple of sips.

The bartender came back a moment later, and Mandy slapped down some cash—including an extremely generous tip, which was how she could always walk right up to the bar and order no matter who else had been waiting—and headed back out to the dance floor.

Nikki was in the same place Mandy had left her, with a white guy with ash-blond hair and a purple polo shirt who was wrapped around her like a scarf. For a second, he reminded Mandy of Theo, the way he would press his nose into Mandy's neck and kiss her collarbone. There were still times she missed him and considered reaching out, but she never did. As soon as Nikki made eye contact with Mandy, her hands went right into the air—two fingers up on each hand, tapping to the beat of the music.

Shit.

There were a lot of people between Mandy and where Nikki was, plus now she had two full drinks in her hands. She took a gulp from each hoping that would be enough for them not to go sloshing over the rim as she fought her way through a mass of gyrating bodies.

The guy laid his head on Nikki's shoulder . . . or wait. Did he just lick her neck? Nikki tried to turn and reposition herself, but Mr. Handsy wasn't getting the message. Just a few more feet and Mandy would be there.

Mandy lifted the plastic cups up above her head and spun, wedging herself around a couple who were much more comfortable with each other than poor Nikki. Just as Mandy spun around them, another white guy seemed to notice Mandy's frantic push to get across the dance floor and where she was headed, and he nudged his friend. They were much closer to Nikki than Mandy, and they also started pushing toward her. The white guy with honey-brown hair and a checkered collared shirt led his white friend with chocolate-brown hair and a yellow shirt toward Nikki. Checkered Shirt Guy tapped Mr. Handsy on the shoulder, and Yellow Shirt Guy carefully spun Nikki out of his grasp. Checkered Shirt and Mr. Handsy carried on some kind of conversation followed by awkward fist bumps before Checkered Shirt led Mr. Handsy away. About two beats later, Mandy finally reached them.

"Are you okay?" She spoke directly into Nikki's ear and handed her a drink.

"OMG." Nikki took a long sip. "I am now. Thank you," she said to Mr. Yellow Shirt.

"It's all good. I'm Evan."

"Nikki." She gestured to herself. "And this is—"

"Hold on," Mandy said. "Do you know that guy?"

Evan put both his hands up. "Oh no. He's not with us. We've seen him around though."

Mandy narrowed her eyes at him. "So why did your friend walk away with him?" She wouldn't have put it past them to have planned the whole thing. One buddy is all touchy-feely and then the white knight swoops in. It seemed too easy.

"Probably to push him out the back door. Seriously though. He's not with us." Evan seemed to spot someone in the crowd and raised his arm in the air. "Justin, over here," he yelled over the music.

It was Checkered Shirt Guy. He slid this way and that between the masses of people and quickly beelined to his friend. "I talked to the bouncer, that guy won't be coming back ever." He looked at Mandy and smiled. Like he was really noticing her for the first time. "They put him in a cab as I was coming back inside."

Nikki, being Nikki, hugged him and then Evan. "Thank you so much! Let me buy you guys a drink."

"You don't have—"

"I want to," Nikki said.

Mandy wasn't so sure about this idea. Yes, these guys helped them, but she wasn't 100 percent sure it wasn't fabricated. It all seemed a little too convenient—like something you would see in a rom-com but not in real life. But Nikki didn't seem to care. Then again, she had been the one in the situation, and maybe Mandy would feel differently if it had been her. Still, she wasn't going to make eye contact with the bartender and use her "superpower" to get them drinks any faster. She contentedly sipped her cocktail, listening in on the conversation Nikki had been holding with the guys. So far, she'd managed to get out of them that they'd both graduated from UCLA and were working for some kind of app startup, which didn't sound anything remotely like a "real" job. But Mandy had to admit they were nice enough. And once she took the giant chip off her shoulder, she joined in on the conversation.

"So, you said you do art or something?" Evan asked Mandy when it seemed as though the conversation between Nikki and Justin became that—between just the two of them.

"'Art or something' sounds about right." Mandy laughed. "This semester it hasn't been as hands-on. It's been mostly computer stuff, which I get that's important and all, and I could probably find a job or something with it, but I miss getting my hands dirty, you know? Like these classes I took in Europe were incredible, and I think I lived under a layer of paint while I was there." Mandy laughed again and took another sip. Yep, these drinks were amazing, and obviously made her really chatty.

"You've been to Europe. Me too. Italy was my favorite. What about you? Let me guess. Paris."

Mandy had been to Paris briefly, and the one museum she got to see was inspiring, but because of the party, it was not her favorite memory. "I actually really just loved London. I had all these plans of traveling, but when I got there, they didn't really happen." She didn't get into why, and how the person she had planned to travel with didn't go. Evan didn't need all her baggage.

"I pegged you as an Eiffel Tower girl."

"Well, you would be wrong."

"You're one intriguing girl, Mandy." And the way he smiled at her made her knees go soft.

Mandy had to admit the rest of the night was actually fun. Evan had turned out to be an interesting guy, and the two of them hit it off much better than Mandy expected—especially seeing how it all started out. Or maybe it was the four Creamy Unicorns Mandy had drunk—two above her usual limit. Either way, last call was announced, and Nikki had left ages before with Justin—which wasn't an unusual thing for her, leaving with someone—and it was time for Mandy to call it a night.

Evan held the door to the club open for her as they both stumbled outside. The air was surprisingly warm for a February evening. They walked down the street a quarter of a block away from the club's entrance so Mandy could get in line for a cab, which—since they came out quickly—luckily wasn't too long. "This can't be where our night ends." He sure was cute, but Mandy knew better than to bring home a guy she'd just met. And even though she was drunk, she also knew better than to go home with him. Mandy had learned her lesson with Theo, and she wasn't a one-night-stand kind of girl.

"We could meet up some other time," Mandy suggested as a compromise. She wouldn't mind seeing him again.

"Come on." He tugged her close and wrapped his arms around her waist. "Let me buy you some pancakes." He nuzzled his nose into Mandy's neck, sending gooseflesh rippling along her skin.

"How'd I know?" someone said, and Evan released Mandy faster than a hot mug just out of the microwave. A gorgeous girl with straight black hair, light brown skin, jeans and a Harvard Law hoodie, and the best *oh-you've-been-caught* look on her face stood on the sidewalk next to a parked car.

"Lilia, I can explain," Evan said.

Mandy may have had one too many, but it didn't take a sober person to figure out what was going on. Evan was a dirty, lying cheater. And to make it all worse, he made Mandy an accomplice. "You've got to be fucking kidding me."

"He didn't tell you, did he?" Lilia asked Mandy.

"No. God. No. I'm so sorry." Mandy was going to throw up, and not from the liquor.

"You have nothing to apologize to me about." Lilia sounded a lot calmer than Mandy expected someone in her position to be. But then again, she had been there once herself—more than once, actually. "He, however, has some serious explaining to do." Lilia perched one perfectly manicured hand on her hip.

"Babe. You were just—"

"You know what? I don't even want to hear it. I just want you out of my apartment and out of my life." She clicked a button on her keys, and the trunk on the car next to her popped open. Lilia then proceeded to throw a bunch of clothes, a couple of books, a lamp, and several other items out onto the sidewalk.

As he tried to gather up all his crap, Evan started with the whole "I'm so sorry. You don't understand. I made a mistake." Blah, blah, blah.

A large group of people who likely were pushed out of the club for closing stood around to watch what was going on. Mandy really needed a cab ASAP. And pancakes. She really still needed some pancakes.

"I don't know what I ever saw in you," Lilia was yelling. Except Mandy knew. Evan, as terrible as he was, had a way of making a person feel special. Hell, he was able to do it to Mandy in just a couple of hours. That didn't make it right, but she totally felt for Lilia. It sucked putting yourself into someone who didn't appreciate you. And even though Evan was good-looking, Mandy was sure it was Lilia who could have anyone she wanted.

The trunk slammed, and Lilia turned to Mandy. "You good? Or do you need a ride?"

The line for a cab was exceedingly long now that the club was officially closed for the night. And for whatever reason, she felt a kind of kinship with Lilia she couldn't explain.

"Do you like pancakes?" Mandy asked.

"I fucking love them," Lilia responded.

So Mandy hopped into the front seat of Lilia's car, and they left Evan on the sidewalk with all of his possessions.

THE DENNY'S WAS BUSY—BUT NOT SO MUCH THAT Lilia and Mandy had to wait for a table. There was the typical late-night crowd, bartenders and shift workers winding down, and people like Mandy who needed to soak up some of the alcohol they'd consumed.

As soon as they sat down, Mandy ordered a short stack and coffee. Lilia opted for a Belgian waffle with a side of bacon and hash browns.

"So, Harvard Law," Mandy said as she shoved a huge bite of pancakes dripping in maple syrup into her mouth. "That's badass."

"Thanks," Lilia said. "You would not believe the number of times I was confused for custodial staff." She rolled her eyes.

"Don't you wear, like, suits and stuff?" Mandy hadn't been to court herself, but from the movies and TV shows she'd seen, lawyers were always in suits.

Lilia raised her brows and just nodded before she broke off a piece of bacon and speared it with a bite of her waffle.

"No!" Mandy almost fell into her pancakes.

"Girl. Sexism is everywhere."

Mandy had just met Lilia but already loved her.

"You said you go to USC?" Lilia asked, and Mandy nodded. "What are you studying? Not prelaw, I hope."

Mandy shook her head. "No. Although I'm sure my dad would've loved that." She laughed. "I'm doing graphic design and stuff." She was still drunk and didn't want to get into it all too deeply.

"That's awesome. I can't draw to save my life. My stick figures are completely unrecognizable."

"Everyone has some artistic ability."

Lilia tipped her head to the side. "I guess I do like to write."

"You're painting with words," Mandy said. "That's what my friend would call it." How did everything make her think about Isa?

"I'd never really thought about it that way. I like it."

"What kind of stuff do you write?"

Lilia took a moment to eat another bite, as if she was debating how much to say. "I'm a lawyer, right? So I kind of like to write thrillers where people get away with crimes. I like to play out scenarios, see what would be possible and how someone could do it without getting prosecuted. It's cooler than it sounds, I swear."

"It sounds supercool, actually. I'd read it." Mandy wasn't a huge reader, but when Isa recommended something, Mandy felt obligated to give it a try. Isa would definitely want to read Lilia's stories.

Lilia took another bite of her waffle, her fork cutting through the crispy outside and right through the soft middle. Ever since the food was delivered, Mandy has had some serious order envy. Not that her pancakes weren't delicious, but she loved waffles just a little bit more.

"You want some?" Lilia asked.

Mandy shouldn't. "Just a little."

Lilia smiled and cut a section of her waffle off. "I'll trade you for some of your pancakes."

"Done." Mandy sliced off a good portion of her short stack,

and then they both exchanged. As soon as the waffle hit her plate, Mandy took a bite. Oh god. Yep, Denny's knew how to make a mean waffle.

Lilia commented on the pancakes. "These are really good."

And then they both were quiet for a bit while they ate. The buzz of other patrons and the heavy scent of bacon and coffee hung in the air. A couple of girls a few tables over drank water with lemon and shared a plate of fries. They didn't look old enough to be in a Denny's so late, but it was totally something Isa and Mandy would've done back in high school, so she wasn't about to judge. The server passed with a tray so full of food she had to balance it on her shoulder.

"I'm sorry Evan did that to you," Lilia said, breaking the silence.

It took a moment for Mandy to realize what Lilia was talking about. "You do *not* need to apologize to me." Mandy wiped her mouth with her napkin, the cloudiness in her head slowly fading. "I'm sorry he did that to *you*. What a total douche move."

"'Douche' is an excellent word to describe Evan. But I'm not any better for putting up with it."

"That wasn't the first time?"

"More like the third. The second was with my old roommate, and they dated three months before I figured it out."

"Ouch." Mandy cringed. "That's the worst. I don't understand why people do that."

"Cheat, you mean?"

Mandy nodded.

"People are selfish." Lilia took a drink of her coffee. "I also think they do it because they either are too worried they're missing something better, or they know something isn't working and instead of admitting it to themselves and being an adult and having an adult conversation, they fuck around." She set her mug down. "That's why I did it."

Mandy's brows shot up. "You cheated?" Lilia seemed so nice, but so had Brandon and V, and they still cheated on Mandy.

"Yep. And the guy I had been with was fine, but it just wasn't working, and instead of talking about it, well . . . I made a bad decision. As soon as it happened, I felt terrible. But you can't take things back. Once things are out there, they're out there. You can't unbake a cake." Lilia cut another slice of her waffle off.

"Do you think that dating Evan is your way of getting back at yourself for what you did?" Mandy fingered her hair. It had grown out considerably, but she'd never forget that moment in the bathroom as long as she lived.

"Holy shit. Yeah. I guess maybe it is." Lilia took a bite of her waffle and chewed slowly. "I'd never really thought about it like that."

"So when do you stop punishing yourself?"

Lilia seemed to study Mandy. "That's a great question."

"We all fuck up sometimes, and like you said, you can't un-bake the cake, so you have to move forward." How was it that Mandy was the one giving this advice? And to someone like Lilia. Smart and beautiful and a fucking Harvard Law School grad. "Are you going to forgive him this time?"

Lilia huffed. "Honestly?" She moved some bacon around in her syrup. "I might've considered it before, but not anymore." She smiled. "You know, I'm glad I met you tonight," Lilia said.

"I'm glad I met you too."

CHAPTER THIRTY-ONE

August 2001

HOW HAD MANDY EVER enjoyed going to the mall? As a teen she would spend hours there with her friends trying on clothes they were never going to buy—the more hideous the better—and sampling things held on trays from food court workers in weird hats. Those days seemed so long ago now—a blur of ugly dresses, and Cinnabon, and McDonald's french fries with sweet and sour sauce—simpler times when homework, who kissed who, or who was caught smoking behind the gym were the only problems in the world.

Today the mall was packed, which was not unexpected with school starting up again for everyone. This year though, that included Mandy. She had finally done it. She applied to a few places and got into the art and design program—with a double major because of course Dad insisted—at USC. When the big envelope arrived in the mail, Mandy could hardly believe it. She had almost given up on the idea of college altogether until that time she and Isa and had spent at the beach. She had said Mandy was capable of anything—words Mom would say to her often—but the way Isa looked at her, the timbre in her voice, something clicked. Or kicked her in the ass. She wanted Isa to be proud of her; she needed to prove to her that she was capable of anything, because maybe just maybe it was the way Mandy could start to make things right between them again. Not like the way things were, but better at least.

They had seen each other—as long as Tally didn't mind—the few occasions Isa was home from college, but Mandy still hoped that they could get back to being *real* friends. She never stopped missing Isa, and if friendship was all she could have, Mandy would be happy about it, ecstatic even. She needed Isa as a friend if nothing more.

So that day she and Isa sat down and applied to schools, Mandy thought it could be the magical thing she needed to get back into Isa's good graces. Maybe Isa would start calling her again, and they could be more than casual friends who just spoke when Isa was back in town. When the acceptance came, Mandy was sure Mom told Isa's mom, who had surely told Isa, but it hadn't worked. They still hadn't really spoken since the last time Isa had been home all those months ago.

The thing was, once USC said yes, Mandy didn't want to say no. Even if it didn't bring Isa back the way Mandy wanted. Even if they could never be real friends again, she wanted to go. A new chance at a new life awaited her, even if she could drive home whenever she wanted. It lit a spark inside Mandy she had thought all but burned out long before.

"We should get you one of those little things so you can carry all your shower necessities with you to the bathroom." Mom's voice brought Mandy back to the task at hand. Buying all the "essentials" for her dorm, as Mom called it.

Mandy was the age of most juniors, but with her time in Europe, and all the time she spent home working at Grace's, she was starting as a freshman and decided even if she was the oldest in the dorm, she should experience all college had to offer—which meant shower shoes and communal living. Sharing a bathroom was not something she was used to, but how bad could it really be?

Mom pulled Mandy into Pottery Barn to pick out new linens for her dorm bed. A twin-sized mattress was also something Mandy wasn't used to, but if it was comfortable Mandy didn't think a smaller size would be an issue. As long as she had a bed, she told herself, she'd be happy. But Mom was all about trying to make Mandy as comfortable as possible, and that included decorating her room—which Mom was possibly more excited about than she was.

"These are cute." Mandy held up a pack of sheets that were mostly white but had a bunch of different-colored hearts all over them.

Mom wrinkled her nose. "What's the thread count?"

Was there a difference? Mandy handed the pack to Mom because she didn't even know where to look for such information.

Mom grunted. "I think we can do better. Plus, aren't the school colors red and gold?"

Mandy was sure that didn't matter, but she wasn't going to get into that either. And she really didn't care what her sheets looked like. She'd be sleeping on them, not wearing them to class. "Yep, you're right, Mom." This answer made Mom smile, and Mandy used it to her advantage. "I think I need some caffeine, and you're so much better at this than me. Why don't I go grab us some Starbucks? I'm sure I'll love whatever you pick out."

Mom huffed, but then glanced around as if weighing whether Mandy would in fact be helpful or just in the way of her design plans. "You know we only have today to do this; tomorrow you have a hair appointment, and your father's colleague is having us over, and—"

"I know. And we'll get it all done. Caffeine will help. Promise."

Mom seemed to consider this more than she considered the sheets Mandy had selected. "I suppose a nonfat sugar-free vanilla latte would be nice."

"You're the best." Mandy kissed Mom's cheek.

"Now you're just trying to butter me up."

"Is it working?"

Mom grinned. "Just go. We still have a lot of shopping to do." Mom picked up a fuzzy white throw pillow and inspected it intently. What Mandy needed throw pillows for she had no idea. She also didn't know why she needed Trojan bookends, but Mom insisted on buying those at their last stop. Now they seemed to weigh a million pounds as Mandy lugged the bags and fought against the flow of people around her. She should've left the bags with Mom.

Just like every other place in the mall, Starbucks was packed, so Mandy got in a line that extended well outside the coffee shop and down a store. Her caffeine addiction started in Europe with all the tea they would drink, and transferred over to the States when she got back. Tea wasn't the same here as it was over there, and while she still enjoyed a cuppa, she also loved her espresso. And right now, a double-shot cappuccino was needed, so she didn't care how long she had to wait, she was getting her fix.

When Mandy finally turned in to Starbucks, however, she froze. Isa, her mom, and Abuela sat at a table just on the other side of the small café space near the counter that held the sugar, creamers, straws, and napkins.

Mandy should leave. That was the first thought that went through her head—which was silly because it wasn't like they were enemies. It wasn't even like they hated each other, or at least Mandy didn't hate Isa at all. But Mandy hadn't seen Isa's mom or Abuela in what felt like ages, at least not since that night on Mandy's front porch.

The line shifted forward again, and Mandy's feet shuffled with it. Isa and her family would probably be gone by the time Mandy ordered. They looked like they were finishing up anyway. As Mandy went to turn to look at the display of coffee mugs, and not at how Isa wore a new shade of lipstick, Mandy caught Abuela's eye, who gave Mandy a sad smile.

Oh yes, she should leave, but now she'd been spotted. Now they would know she left. Mandy fidgeted with a coffee mug she plucked off the shelf to busy her hands. Twenty dollars? For a coffee mug? Were they out of their minds? Focus, Mandy. It was fine. You did what was best. That was what Mandy had told herself over and over since that terrible day more than two years ago now, and she still wasn't 100 percent convinced of it.

"Need a Frappuccino fix, huh?"

Mandy fumbled with the mug still in her hands and spun around to find Isa wearing tight jeans with a flannel over a purple tank top and a smile—and not a sad one. "I haven't had one of those in forever." Mandy forced a chuckle. Oh god, she sounded nervous and anxious—which she was.

And the smile on Isa's face was gone. Already Mandy was blowing this.

"I crossed over to the dark side," Mandy attempted to joke.

"Coffee, huh?"

"Cappuccino. I got hooked on them in . . ." Real smooth, Mandy. She changed the subject. "What are you guys doing here?"

"Shopping," Isa said. Was she nervous too? "Need to get some things before I head back to Boston."

"Yeah. Same. I mean getting things for school, not in Boston of course . . ." Dear god, could she stop rambling?

"You're going then. To college?" Isa's eyebrows lifted.

"Yeah. Someone told me I could do anything, and so I thought what the heck."

"That's great." Isa's smile was back, and it was brighter than it was before. Mandy could stare at it all day, but instead she looked at the menu board.

"Where are you going?" Isa asked.

"Oh. USC."

"That's cool. Far enough to be away, but close enough to come home when you need to do laundry." Isa chuckled.

Laundry. Mandy hadn't thought about laundry. How did she do that?

"Nikki transferred there. NYU wasn't for her." Isa shrugged.

So she still talked to Nikki. Did she talk to anyone else? Did she tell them about what had happened between the two of them? Mandy kind of lost touch with everyone when she went away. And then when she got back, she wasn't sure if they knew or what they knew so she just didn't bother finding out.

"You should call her. Nikki, that is. She's home for the summer."

The number rattled off in Mandy's head. Funny how some things you couldn't forget. Like phone numbers even when you hadn't used them for a while. "Yeah. I'll do that."

Isa did the thing where she lifted just one brow, and while Mandy knew exactly what it meant, it made the ache in her chest deepen.

"I really will. I swear."

The line shifted again, and Mandy ordered her drinks and paid for them. To her surprise, Isa was waiting for her at the other end of the counter where Mandy would pick up her order. But before she could say anything, Mom pushed her way through the crowd with her overstuffed Pottery Barn bags. "I was wondering what was taking so long."

"Hi, Mrs. Dean," Isa said.

Mom dropped the bags and pulled Isa into a tight hug. "You look so beautiful. I bet you're driving all those Boston boys crazy."

"Mom," Mandy snapped.

"Oh, I mean girls."

Mandy shook her head. Could she be more embarrassing?

"It's fine," Isa said. "My girlfriend, Tally, teases me about it all the time. It's like the boys in Boston have never seen a Mexican." She wanted to be happy for Isa, for her and Tally, but Mandy's stomach burned all the way up to her cheeks.

"That's wonderful," Mom said.

"Yeah. Sometimes things happen for a reason," Isa said, but Mandy was pretty sure she wasn't talking about boys on campus and instead about what had happened between Isa and her. Mandy glanced to the table where Isa had been sitting before with her mom and Abuela, but they were gone, and a bunch of rowdy boys had taken their place.

"You should come by before you head back. We're planning a last supper, so to speak, this weekend. Bring your mom and Abuela," Mom said.

"That's sweet, but I'm leaving on Friday. Mamá and Abuela could stop by though."

"Absolutely. Please tell them seven and not to bring anything; I have it all covered." Which meant the caterers had everything under control.

"I will." Her eyes met Mandy's. "If you're not busy, maybe we can get lunch or something tomorrow." Did her voice sound hopeful? Or was that Mandy just wishing it did?

Mom shook her head. "We've got—"

"Totally. Yes. Not busy at all tomorrow."

"Great. I'll call you," Isa said.

"Okay," Mandy said.

"Talk to you then." And Isa walked away.

"Honey, we've got plans tomorrow," Mom complained. "And you cannot miss your hair appointment." She eyed Mandy's messy locks. She hadn't had it cut since the time she decided to go all Edward Scissorhands.

"Mom." Mandy glanced toward where Isa just left. It wasn't like Mom didn't know their history. Didn't listen to Mandy cry over the phone for weeks after she went to Europe. Although Mom didn't know the exact details that brought about the end of Mandy's relationship with Isa, she knew enough to understand how big a step this was. And it had to be a step in the right direction, didn't it?

Mom's jaw clenched, and she let out a long sigh. "Well, we better get a move on then."

CHAPTER THIRTY-TWO

January 2015

THE NEW RING ON Mandy's finger was too big, and she had to bend her hand awkwardly to make sure it didn't fall off. After a round of champagne flutes were passed out and loads of congratulations were patted onto Edmund's shoulders, he had to get back to the office to finish up a few things, and Mandy had to pretend she wasn't completely undone by how the evening transformed. Aziz was beyond excited when the rush of euphoria in the room translated into all her paintings being sold. Admittedly Mandy should've been pleased too. Ecstatic even. And while she wasn't unhappy, something was missing.

"Congratulations."

Mandy didn't need to turn around to know that voice, and a rush of tingles raced up her spine, but she spun around anyway.

Isa.

Things had still been awkward since their last encounter, and that was putting it mildly. Mandy had fucked up—again. She was really good at that when it came to Isa, it seemed.

"Thanks," Mandy said as she tucked a stray hair that had come loose from her chignon behind her ear. "And thank you for coming."

Isa shook her head. "As if I'd miss this." She gestured around. "It's really incredible. I always knew you could do it."

The back of Mandy's throat got thick. She would not cry.

"I feel like I've missed so much." Isa's gaze continued to sweep the room.

Mandy wasn't sure how she was supposed to take that. Did it mean that she missed seeing Mandy working on all these projects? Staying up late, pulling her hair out trying to get them all just right. Or was she trying to say that she missed Mandy? "I mean, it's not like you haven't been busy, Dr. Jiménez."

Isa grinned, but she didn't smile. Mandy knew the difference. "Sometimes I wonder if it's worth it. I mean, I know it is, but the long hours, and no sleep, and Boston is great and all but . . ."

"It's not home."

"Exactly."

Something passed between them. Understanding. Or maybe something else. Mandy wasn't sure, and she wasn't sure she even wanted to try to name it. This was the first time since the last time things felt like they could be okay, but it was all still so fragile—one wrong move and . . . *crack*.

"How's Tally?" Mandy blurted, because breaking things was what she did best.

"We broke up." Isa said it so matter-of-factly, without even the slightest hitch in her voice.

"What? Why?" They had been together forever. Tally had even stayed in Boston with Isa for her residency, leaving behind a job she had gotten in her hometown. She gave up her dream for Isa, something Mandy couldn't do.

Isa shrugged. "It just didn't work."

Mandy wanted to press. She needed to know what happened and why. Didn't Tally do all the things a girlfriend should do? Hadn't Isa told Mandy how much she loved Tally? And if this were another time, and the things between Isa and Mandy never happened, she could've asked all those things, but not now, so all she said was, "I'm sorry."

"I'm not." Isa stood there, shoulders back, head high.

While things between Mandy and Isa had been fraught lately, Mandy was familiar with this look. It was the same one Isa had when she didn't win secretary of their seventh-grade class. The same look she had given to Mandy before she left for Europe years ago. It must've been really bad. All Mandy wanted to do was pull Isa in for a hug, and before Mandy could overthink it to death, that's exactly what she did.

One moment she was in front of Isa and the next, Mandy's arms were around her, her face pressed against Isa's coconut-scented hair. For a second, Isa's body tensed, her arms dangled at her sides, and then a second later they were around Mandy just as tight if not tighter than the way Mandy held her. Isa's chest hitched against Mandy's, and soon tears ran down Mandy's shoulder.

Mandy clenched her jaw tight. She didn't know what Tally had done, but in that instant, if she had been there, Mandy would've probably killed her. Okay, maybe not full-on murder, but Mandy was pissed enough to contemplate it. How dare anyone treat Isa this way. She was brilliant, and caring, and wonderful.

The crowd around them didn't seem to pay any attention; they all seemed to go along with their evening, enjoying the libations and conversations they were involved in. The fact that a woman was sobbing in the middle of an art show didn't seem to matter to any of them, and even if it did, Mandy didn't care. She held on to Isa for as long as she needed. Until the sniffles started, and Isa pulled away.

"I'm sorry about that," Isa said, wiping her eyes and making a mess of her mascara.

"Don't be," Mandy tried to reassure her.

"It's a special night for you. You're supposed to be celebrating. I don't even know what came over me."

A server appeared with a few napkins and handed them to Isa. So maybe someone was paying attention after all.

Isa mumbled her thanks before the server strolled away, and dabbed at her eyes.

"Let me." Mandy held out her hand, and Isa gave her one of the napkins. It was already damp from the tears Isa had mopped up, and Mandy gently cleaned away the streaks of black from under Isa's eyes.

"Oh my god, your arm." Isa started furiously wiping Mandy's shoulder.

"It's fine." Mandy didn't care about the black streaks; if anything, they were proof to remind her later of this moment. Of when she got to hold Isa. And how she would give anything to be able to do it again. "I've missed you." Her words were clear, but her voice was low—tentative. She couldn't mess things up—not again.

"We should talk more often," Isa responded, and Mandy's heart practically jumped for joy. Oh, how she had missed her best friend. How she had dreamed Isa would say these very words. Mandy almost pinched herself to make sure it was real, but when she let her hand fall her new ring slipped, and Mandy's heart slipped too. She was engaged. Isa was here, and Mandy had just gotten engaged.

Mandy hesitated. "Tacos?"

Isa's lips twitched. "Don't you need to, like, stay and mingle?"

All the paintings had been sold. Mandy could strip naked and run through the room, and Aziz wouldn't bat an eye, nor would any of the remaining guests, from the looks of it. And even if none of that were true—if she hadn't sold a single painting, or if her career hinged on her being there until dawn—she'd give it all up for the chance to just be with Isa again. "Nope."

"Tacos then?" Isa asked this time.

"Tacos," Mandy confirmed.

THE PLACE THAT WAS ALWAYS BUSY ANY NIGHT OF the week was especially packed for a Friday. It was a small, order-at-the-counter type of restaurant with an outside patio but no tables inside, so it was wall-to-wall people. And if you didn't know how the system worked—because yes, there was a system—you were shit out of luck.

You approached the counter only when you were ready to order, and they only took cash. As quirky as it was, they had the best tacos, especially late-night tacos—although for LA it wasn't that late yet. The real rush happened when the bars closed at two in the morning, and they were still a little while off from that.

Mandy took the lead on ordering since she had been there a

million times before, and soon she was sitting at a stone table with a mosaic-tiled top waiting for number seventy-three to be called and begging the universe to give her a break. Or at least help her out a little.

Isa licked her lips. "Smells amazing."

"You already said that." Mandy wanted to hide under the table. Why was this so hard? But she knew the answer. She had a habit of fucking things up and saying or doing the wrong thing, especially when it came to Isa. "I'm sorry."

"*You've* already said that."

And Mandy had. A lot. Over and over in fact. "Well. I am. The last time I saw you—"

"We don't have to do this," Isa said. "It's in the past. And now . . ." She glanced at Mandy's hand. "Now you're engaged. That's so exciting."

"Yeah." Mandy looked down at her hand too. The emerald-cut diamond wasn't something she would've picked out for herself, but it was pretty even if she did need to get it resized. Maybe she should take it off and put it in her bag, so she didn't lose it. "I was a little surprised by the whole thing, if I'm being honest."

"I could tell." Because of course she could. Would anyone ever know Mandy the way Isa did?

"But it was sweet, right? And it's not like it's a night I'll ever forget," Mandy said as the stone bench bit into the back of her thighs. "And I guess I sold all of my paintings." Was it obvious she was trying to change the subject?

"That's true." Isa's brows pulled together. Yes, it was obvious.

"You didn't have to buy one, you know." Once it came out of her mouth, Mandy flinched. "That's not what I meant. I just meant—"

"I hadn't planned on it when I came. I debated showing up at all, if we're being honest. But then I got there, and I saw it, and, well. I knew I couldn't leave without it. I couldn't think of that painting hanging in anyone else's house. It just spoke to me." Isa smiled, but she didn't meet Mandy's eyes. Mandy had been the one who painted it—knew exactly all the emotions and thoughts she had been feeling when she had done so—so it was no surprise to her that Isa felt something in it too. Isa was just as much a part of that painting as Mandy was. A chill raced through her, sending gooseflesh rippling over her arms.

Mandy wanted to tell her all of these things, but instead she looked at her ring again. It was just like Edmund to have picked something like this out—something that made a statement. He was predictable like that, which Mandy supposed was a good thing. Not the same kind of solace as a pair of broken-in shoes, or her favorite slippers, but the predictability of being offered champagne while she waited for Edmund to get fitted for a new suit—it wasn't comfortable sitting there while the tailor measured and pinned, but she knew what to expect.

"Are you happy?" Isa asked.

The question caught Mandy off guard, although it shouldn't have. This was Isa, after all, and she knew Mandy better than Mandy knew herself. She lifted her chin and met Isa's eyes. A gust of wind blew Isa's hair over her shoulders. God, she was so beautiful. Maybe if Edmund hadn't gotten on one knee just a few hours ago, she could've reached across the table and held Isa's hand. Or maybe sat next to her, thighs touching, instead of being across from her with a million pieces of shattered tiles artfully plastered between them. Right now, as the wind blew and all the other patrons chatted around them, it felt more like a million miles.

Was she happy?

"Seventy-three," came booming over the intercom.

And instead of trying to answer Isa's question, Mandy said, "I'll get it," stood up, and pushed her way through the crowd.

CHAPTER THIRTY-THREE

April 2019

TIME SEEMED TO CRAWL slower than the traffic outside the limo as raindrops streaked down the glass. It wasn't anything like a downpour, more of a light sprinkling, but it was enough to throw the entire pre-wedding plan into chaos.

Mandy didn't respond to the group messages flying back and forth among her family. Just thinking about it made her want to scream, or cry, maybe both.

Roger had taken a call, likely getting new instructions on where they were supposed to be headed, but Mandy ignored all that too. Now that she had time with nothing else to do and no one else to talk to—with the limo's AC pumping to help control her stress sweats—she reflected on the previous night's festivities. It all should've been a warning of how today was going to go. Because the rehearsal went off without a hitch.

Rehearsals were the time things were meant to go wrong, problems were supposed to reveal themselves so they could be worked out, but none of that happened. Dinner especially had seemingly been error free.

And all of that should've been a red flag to Mandy. Now that she thought about it, it seemed that Sophie had been trying to warn her.

"Are you sure you're ready for this?" Sophie had asked as Mandy stood outside the restaurant, needing some air between dinner and dessert. She had attempted to go to the car to get some last-minute gifts to distribute, but the valet seemed to be off somewhere, so she took the time to enjoy the night air. "Just say the word and I can get you out of here."

Mandy laughed. If she had chosen to have bridesmaids, Sophie would've been one of them for this very reason. She always seemed to know what Mandy needed to hear. Not that she was planning to run away, but because that was something she expected her girls to do for her—have her back and ask. "I'm good."

"Yeah. I know you are." Sophie leaned next to Mandy, shoulders touching. "It's nice to see you so happy."

Mandy hadn't really thought about it, but she was smiling— even there outside where no one else was, she had a smile on her face that when she tried, she couldn't stop. "I never thought this would happen. I guess it all sort of feels surreal."

"I knew," Sophie said. "Not the who, but I knew I'd be here one day with you, eating canapés and drinking expensive champagne. The champagne is excellent by the way."

"I'll let my parents know you approve." Mom had picked it out, and even though Dad had that look, gawking at Mom's expensive taste, it only flashed on his face momentarily, and he didn't say a word as he handed over his credit card. Knowing it got a compliment would make him feel better.

"He's something else. Your dad." Sophie wrapped a stray thread around her finger from the hem of her skirt and tugged. "He doesn't say much, but when he does . . ." She shook her head. "He's funny."

"'Funny' is usually not a word associated with my father," Mandy said.

"Well, I think he's bloody hysterical. He was in there with—who's the woman with the leopard-print top?"

"Aunt Mary."

"Oh my god, Aunt Mary." Sophie bent at the waist and started laughing. "That woman has had like three drinks too many. She's right pissed."

"I don't even know how she's my aunt."

"No way."

Mandy shook her head. "My dad's an only child, and my mom has two brothers—neither of which are married to Mary." Mandy lifted her head away from the wall to see if the valet had made it back yet. "I think she's like a family friend or something. Or like somehow related to one of Dad's business partners, but really no idea."

"That does help explain things." Sophie wrapped and un-wrapped the rogue thread around her finger. "At first, I thought she was a crasher, but she was there nattering with your dad. Anyway, she's like the exact opposite of the stodgiest woman I've ever met."

"Yeah, she's a hot mess." It's funny how certain people had a way of sticking in your life. And it's funny that you never knew which ones those would be. There were times when you couldn't picture your life without someone in it, but then they'd be gone—things happened, you lost touch, you messed everything up. And then there were people like Aunt Mary who were always around even when you didn't expect them to be. Mandy smiled at Sophie.

"You can say that again. She started talking about her vibrator, and the look on your dad's face." Sophie laughed again. "Priceless."

"How did that even come up as a topic of conversation?" Mandy asked. Sure, Aunt Mary was a little out there, and she had the habit of saying inappropriate things at inappropriate times, but still it seemed a little much for her, especially with Dad around.

"No idea."

"Well, she does keep things interesting." Mandy shrugged. It was nice out here with Sophie. Mandy put her arm around Sophie's shoulder and pulled her in closer. "I've missed you."

"Don't get all mushy on me. I'm not making a mess of my mascara until the toasts." Sophie hip checked Mandy, but then rested her head on Mandy's shoulder. "I've missed you too. Finny is sorry he couldn't make it."

"He's about to have a baby. There's really no explanation needed." A few years after Mandy had left Europe, Finny and Leo finally made it official and tied the knot. Mandy had been disappointed they had eloped—she would've loved an excuse to go back out to Europe and see all her friends again—but she also understood why they chose to do it that way. As soon as Mandy had mentioned her engagement, her entire life revolved around the wedding and planning. So many people had come to town for the event—like Sophie—but she barely had time to see any of them.

"Leo is so excited. He's taking bets it comes out with red hair."

The idea of kids was something Mandy had been warming up to. Now that she was finally getting married, it seemed like the right time to think about having a family of her own.

"They're going to make great dads."

Sophie nodded.

A cool breeze ruffled the light fabric of Mandy's skirt, and she shivered slightly. At this rate the valet was never going to reappear, and as she'd been outside for a while, people would start to wonder what happened to her. The gifts weren't that important anyway. She could always give them out later. "Ready to go back inside?" she asked.

"Only if you are," Sophie responded.

Mandy pushed herself off the wall. "Then, shall we?"

"I really am so happy for you."

"I'm happy you're here," Mandy said.

"I wouldn't have missed it." Sophie took Mandy's hand. "I've always got your back." She pulled Mandy in for a hug and squeezed her tight.

But now that Mandy sat in the back of the limo, she couldn't stop thinking of that hug, or what Sophie had said. Did she know something Mandy didn't about today? Was Sophie trying to prepare Mandy for the worst, and let her know she had a shoulder to cry on when it all came crashing down?

Mandy traced the raindrops on the window and gazed up to the gray sky, a sinking feeling in her stomach. Maybe it was time to tell Roger to turn around.

CHAPTER THIRTY-FOUR

December 2005

NEVER IN A MILLION years did Mandy ever think she would be spending New Year's Eve in Paris. Mandy should've been home in California, but the closer and closer her departure date approached, the more apprehensive she was about actually going back. What would she be going back to anyway? Her old room in her parents' house? Back to apply for colleges she wasn't even sure she wanted to go to? Back to a town where everything in it reminded her of Isa?

It had been about four months since Mandy said goodbye to her, and it didn't hurt any less to think about. She poured herself into her studies. Tried and failed at so many pieces, because she was blocked—because she wasn't good enough. And she needed to talk to someone about it but couldn't, since the only person Mandy needed wasn't talking to her. Nor would there be any reason for Isa to ever want to talk to Mandy again.

Mandy couldn't even make it home for Christmas. Her heart

was in the United States, but it wasn't in California. It was somewhere on the East Coast. Breakups had never been this hard
before. But Mandy knew why this one was different. Because Isa
was different. Because their relationship was different. Because
Mandy never wanted to break up with her to begin with. So she
convinced her parents to come out and spend the holidays in
Europe with her, and then she convinced them to allow her to
extend her studies, saying she could apply to colleges from anywhere, and telling them schools wouldn't take her midterm
anyway.

The New Year's party Mandy attended was in the flat of a
friend of a friend of Sophie's. Some guy with shoulder-length
dark hair, deep brown eyes, warm bronze skin, and by the looks
of the flat, lots of money. There were so many people, there was
no place for Mandy to be alone—which was probably a good
thing. Although this not being alone didn't stop her from all the
thoughts swirling in her head. Mandy didn't know why she even
agreed to come to this. Trying to socialize with a bunch of random people was the last thing Mandy wanted to do. Her plans
were to go to the cantina near her flat, gorge herself on chips and
terrible salsa, and then go home to cry in bed alone. So basically,
the thing she had done at least once a week since being in Europe. But Sophie dressed her up and dragged her out, saying she
couldn't keep moping around. But moping was the only thing
Mandy wanted to do.

She casually sipped from her bottle and pretended to be interested in the painting on the wall. A French artist from what
Mandy could tell by the signature, but one Mandy hadn't heard
of before.

"Pretty," someone said on her right. The voice was like

Sophie's—British, not French. A girl with platinum blonde hair and the bluest eyes stood next to Mandy in a sequined minidress.

"The composition is a little too busy for my tastes. But I do appreciate the limited color palette. It shows some restraint and makes you really think about why they placed the gold where they did." Mandy tipped her head to the side, studying the piece a little more.

"I wasn't talking about the painting." The girl was looking straight at Mandy.

Mandy blinked.

"That was bad, wasn't it? My mates told me to come over and talk to you, and now I must look like the biggest wanker. Giles said that Sophie said that you were into girls too and . . . I should piss off, shouldn't I?" It was adorable the way her pale cheeks lit up like two bright neon cherries. Mandy had never really been hit on before like this. She was being hit on, right?

Mandy smiled. "No. You don't have to go."

The girl smiled back. "Cool. I'm Poppy."

"Mandy."

"Yeah, I know."

For a moment they just stared at each other. Mandy swirled the liquid around in her bottle and got a whiff of what had to be Poppy's perfume—lavender and patchouli. "So you were asking about me, huh?"

"You are the only posh American girl in the room. We all just really want to hear your accent. I know I could personally listen to it all night."

Mandy laughed. "The feeling's mutual." And there were those red cheeks again. "Poppy's fitting. At first, I'd say you are more of a sunflower, but I get it now."

As though she knew what Mandy was talking about, Poppy touched her cheeks with both hands. "It's a curse, really. I'm shit at poker."

"There are worse things than not being able to lie."

Poppy shrugged. "When you put it that way."

Mandy wasn't sure what to say. She stood there fidgeting with the bottle in her hands. The liquid inside had already grown warm, so she didn't really want to drink it, but Mandy also didn't know what she was supposed to do, so she took a small swig and tried not to make a face when the yeasty mixture hit her tongue. This whole flirting thing was exhausting.

"Yeah, I hate that stuff too." Poppy lowered her voice. "Come on, let's get you something better."

Mandy didn't really want anything else, but she also didn't really want to talk about it, so she followed Poppy. The crowd of people's faces blurred, their conversations crashed into the music playing somewhere in the background, turning it into the sound of a traffic accident.

In the kitchen it wasn't as loud, but the scent of stale beer lingered like someone had spilled some and didn't properly clean it up. Poppy took her time mixing an amber-colored fruity liquor with something like Sprite, but she called it lemonade. She joked and glanced at Mandy through her eyelashes, until she was finally done and handed Mandy a glass. It tasted significantly better than the warm beer.

In a way, it was strange being with Poppy. She was sweet, and funny, and pretty, and she was definitely flirting with Mandy— which was why Mandy's stomach rolled around with moments of calm that shifted to moments of panic. Because there were things Poppy did that reminded Mandy of Isa. The way Poppy would lightly jab her elbow into Mandy's side, or the way she could raise just one single eyebrow. Mandy alternated between being in the moment and not thinking of Isa at all, to all of her thoughts being consumed with her, which made being with Poppy excruciatingly awkward from time to time.

Poppy took a sip of her drink, blue eyes peering over the top of her glass. "Sophie said you're a painter."

That was what Mandy had come to Europe to learn more about, but she had way more failures than she did successes. And aside from showing in a "student gallery," no one had ever even seen her work, so could she even call herself a painter? "I mean, I paint."

Poppy giggled—that was the only way to describe the way she laughed, all quiet and shy, and she covered her mouth anytime it happened. "Well, that would make you a painter then."

Mandy just shrugged.

"It's like me. I'm studying costume design, but I already make costumes, so doesn't that make me a costume designer? Just because I haven't finished learning doesn't mean I'm not already one. With art there will never be a finished learning moment, so when do we get to claim it?" She took another small sip and quickly brought her glass down. "I say we get to now. It's not like being a solicitor or doctor or anything." Satisfied with that answer, Poppy brought her glass back up to her lips.

But there it was again. The reason Mandy was in Europe alone. The reason her heart still hurt after all these months. Isa had to become a doctor. That was her plan, and Mandy couldn't take that away from her. The air seemed to thicken as Mandy slid her finger across the glass clutched in her hand, removing some of the condensation, and she was immediately thrown back to the time when she and Isa had taken one of their little "trips" to get away from parental eyes.

They'd do that from time to time—make up a reason or a place they had to go so they could be alone and have deep conversations where they could stare into each other's eyes or hold each other, which also sometimes—okay, lots of times—led to making out. It wasn't as if she could help it; Isa was so beautiful, and the physical connection was something Mandy yearned for.

One time in particular though, Mandy parked her car behind the movie theater and slid into the back seat with Isa. That time it wasn't to talk. Electricity had been brewing between them all day, and Mandy felt as though she'd jump out of her skin if she couldn't just touch Isa. The way Isa grabbed Mandy by the collar as soon as Mandy closed the door said Isa felt it too. Isa kissed Mandy with so much force it sent tingles to her toes. She wanted, no, needed, to be closer—for their skin to connect. Mandy's breathing was rapid as she trailed kisses down the front of Isa's body and continued lower. Isa's moans shook Mandy to her core as they took turns satisfying each other. After they were both completely spent, Mandy had to wipe her hand across the window to remove the evidence of their labored breathing before she could drive Isa home.

Now as Mandy stood in that kitchen, the backs of her eyes burned. "I have to go to the bathroom." And before Poppy could say anything, Mandy took off. The air inside the flat was too heavy and warm; it was hard to breathe.

She pushed out onto the terrace and found a corner away from everyone, bracing herself against the railing—the cold metal biting into her palms. Don't cry. Don't cry. Her chest tightened, and a tear slipped down Mandy's cheek. She should never have come to this party.

"Mandy?" Sophie said before she came up next to Mandy.

"I just needed some air," Mandy lied.

Sophie placed her hand on Mandy's arm. "No. You just need to stop punishing yourself."

"I'm not—"

"But you are. Look. I know you miss her, but you can't change the past."

"I should've stayed. I shouldn't have come . . ."

"And why's that? Because her dreams were more important than yours?"

"I could've waited."

Sophie tugged Mandy's arm to get her to face her, and then held Mandy's arms in her hands. "You get to have your dreams too. I obviously don't know Isa, but from what you've told me, she would never have wanted you to give up on your dreams either. You did the right thing. For her *and* for you."

"It doesn't feel that way."

"And it may not for a long time. But you can't keep doing this to yourself. You have to move on. You were meant to be here. You're going to be a famous artist one day. Just like how she's going to be some great doctor."

Cold air nipped at Mandy's damp cheeks and nose. "I miss her."

"I know you do." Sophie squeezed both of Mandy's elbows. "I'm going to kiss you now because I care about you. And it's going to feel awkward and wrong, but it's something you need to do so you can press on, and it needs to be with someone who understands, okay?"

Mandy hadn't even thought about kissing anyone since she left the States. She wouldn't. She couldn't. Isa had been the love of Mandy's life—the person she confided in, the person she could be the most vulnerable with, and being vulnerable wasn't easy for Mandy. She may have loved love, but she was always a little bit scared to let her walls completely down—except with Isa. Maybe it was stupid, but Mandy thought she'd never kiss anyone but Isa for the rest of her life. And now she was here—in Paris—without her.

Sophie stared at Mandy, her hands so warm, so steady on Mandy's arms. Maybe Sophie was right. As much as Mandy hated the thought of a life without Isa, Mandy couldn't stop living; she had to move on. So she didn't say anything, she just nodded.

Sophie pressed her lips to Mandy's. They were soft and kind, but she was right, they were also so awkward and wrong. Tears streamed down Mandy's cheeks, but she didn't push away. She stayed there with her lips pressed against Sophie's until her chest tightened so hard she couldn't breathe, and then she sobbed into Sophie's shoulder.

Sophie tightened her grip around Mandy there on that balcony, holding her up when all she wanted to do was crumble to the ground. "It's going to get better. I promise."

As the crisp air stung Mandy's wet cheeks, and her lungs started to fill once again, Mandy wanted so badly to believe Sophie, and for a fleeting moment she did.

CHAPTER THIRTY-FIVE

December 2009

MANDY STARED AT THE stack of magazines on the table in front of her. Not at the other people waiting their turn, or the receptionist who checked people in, but the outdated *US Weekly*, *Vogue*, and *Better Homes & Gardens* that had likely been donated or brought in by one of the nurses.

The chair next to her was empty. Everyone else had someone with them—their person who was there to hold their hand or support them or who knew who they were, but Mandy had no one, and she'd never felt more alone.

How did she even get here?

Oh, that's right Theo. Fucking Theo and all his . . . well, fucking.

"Aren't you on the pill?" he asked her when she showed him the little stick with the practically glowing pink plus sign.

"It's not one hundred percent effective; that's why you were supposed to use a condom." Mandy's cheeks heated. No way Theo's neighbors couldn't hear them right now.

"Oh, this is all my fault?"

"Actually, it is. If you were more responsible with your semen. I did my part. You were supposed to do yours."

"Well, obviously you weren't that great at your part."

"Which was why you were supposed to do yours!" They were going nowhere. Mandy'd had a feeling Theo would have some strong feelings about this news when she told him, she just wasn't expecting these feelings. She had only found out that morning herself, and she wasn't entirely sure how she felt about it, but this wasn't the kind of information a person could keep to themselves; she had to tell Theo. He had a right to know. But maybe Mandy should've waited until she sat with the news a little longer, because this? This was something she really was not ready for.

"Tina Marie," the nurse called, and Mandy watched the person who must be Tina Marie make her way to the nurse, and the door shut behind them.

This sucked. This whole situation sucked. She grabbed a magazine at random and started to thumb through. She did not need to know how to create her own indoor herb garden, and making smoothies didn't require a recipe. She tossed it back—sending the scent of old paper into the air—and checked the time on her cell phone.

She had gotten there early, which was completely unnecessary, seeing as doctors always ran late. And all this waiting just gave Mandy more time to dwell on things.

Three days after she broke the news to Theo, he finally called her to talk.

"I'm sorry," he said as she walked into his apartment. The cleaning person must have switched back to using the old stuff, because Mandy's stomach churned. It had only been three days, *for fuck's sake, and now she was pregnant, and they had already started acting like she was never coming back.* "She ran out of the other stuff," *he said like he knew what Mandy was thinking.*

Mandy didn't respond, mostly because she thought she might throw up if she opened her mouth, and instead took a seat on the couch. The same couch that was likely the "scene of the crime."

"How are you feeling?" *Theo sat beside her.*

"How do you think I'm feeling? I tell you I'm pregnant and you don't call me for days."

"I was scared," *he admitted.*

"And I wasn't? This thing is inside me." *She gestured to her body.*

"It's not a thing," *he said.*

But it was. To Mandy it was just a thing. According to the research she'd been doing, about 80 percent of miscarriages happened in the first trimester. It was the reason people didn't disclose pregnancies to other people until the second trimester, because there was a chance it would never happen. There was a possibility it would never become a baby, and Mandy wasn't ready to think of it like that just in case. She couldn't. Her anxiety had already felt off the charts lately, and her boobs hurt, and certain smells, like Theo's apartment, made her want to puke. She couldn't think of the thing inside her as anything more than that for her own sanity.

"I was an asshole. I'm sorry," *he said and reached his hand out. Mandy took it and weaved her fingers through his. He had soft hands, and his nails were always manicured—more often than Mandy's were, that was for sure.* "Yes, you were."

"Well, I've done a lot of thinking, and I talked to my mom, and she said after the wedding we could stay in the guesthouse until we find something more permanent. She could go find something for us,* *but she figured you would want a say." He had talked to his mom? Already? Mandy hadn't even talked to hers yet. She didn't know what to say or how to say it. She didn't want to hear the disappointment in her mom's voice—at least she assumed Mom would be disappointed in her. Mandy was disappointed in herself. But wait . . .*

"What wedding?" Mandy's brain really wasn't working the way it used to. If this was what pregnancy was like, she already hated it. How could she live like this for eight more months?

"I mean, you're having my baby. I just thought . . ."

"Do you even want to marry me?" Mandy wasn't sure she wanted to marry him. Theo was sweet and nice, and aside from all the clutter, he had the cleanest apartment out of everyone she'd ever known, and he dressed impeccably, but marriage?

"Maybe we could just live together. I think Mom would still let us use the guesthouse, and if not, we could figure something else out, I suppose."

"In Boston?"

"That's where my parents live. That's where I'm going to be working." He had talked about it before, how his dad had a job for him at his firm as soon as he graduated, but Mandy never really thought about it. Not that she didn't care about Theo, she just never thought much beyond what they were right now. And what they were right now was going to be parents. Oh god.

Mandy's mouth flooded with saliva. "But my parents live here in California." All this talk of moving and weddings was making Mandy sick.

"I want to be in my kid's life, Mandy."

"But what if it doesn't happen? What if something happens and there is no baby? Then what? We'll be married in Boston and then what?"

Theo didn't let go of Mandy's hand, but he did lean back on the couch. Maybe thinking about all the things that could go wrong and not how perfect it could all be if it went right. But what did things going right look like to Mandy? She was sure for Theo it was living near his parents and him working and coming home to his wife and child—but that was a perfect world for him, and Mandy knew those worlds didn't just happen. You had to work for them. Was he ready for that? Was she? And was that really what she wanted? "I just want to do what's right," he said.

"I know." She leaned back on the couch with him, and he pulled her into him.

Mandy couldn't deny it was nice resting there against his chest. "Are you really ready to be a dad?"

"I don't know."

The nurse called another name. "Larissa Jeffries."

Across the room, a girl who couldn't have been any older than sixteen sat with a woman who looked to be her mom—the two had the same nose and chin even if their hair colors were different. And Mandy couldn't help but wish her own mother were there. It had been nearly three weeks since she had found out she was pregnant, and she still hadn't talked to her mother about it. What was Mandy so afraid of?

Mandy had only gotten up the nerve to tell one person.

"How do you feel?" Isa had asked when Mandy broke the news, and that's all it took for Mandy to fall apart. She cried into the phone no less than ten straight minutes, not being able to utter a single word. Isa just listened. She didn't coax or say anything ridiculous like "Don't worry" or "It's all going to be okay," because how could Mandy not worry, and it felt like it would never be okay again.

"I'm not ready to be a mom." It was the first time Mandy uttered those words out loud, even though they had been bouncing around in her head since the moment she found out. They were no more true that day than every moment before and since, but saying them released something inside Mandy she couldn't explain. A heaviness that seemed to lighten just by telling her truth.

"And that's okay. We can talk about your options whenever you're ready." Isa's voice was so reassuring—she never made Mandy feel guilty or ashamed, and Isa never, never questioned Mandy about what she wanted.

It wasn't that day, but they did speak at length about Mandy's options, and today Mandy was seeing it through. As Mandy sat in the small waiting room of that clinic, surrounded by other people—some with full round bellies, some hoping to avoid the situation Mandy was in—she didn't feel judged or regretful. No, she felt supported. They didn't know why Mandy was there, just like Mandy didn't know why they were, but they were all there together. They all had the common bond that they needed help, and they trusted the people at this clinic to give it to them— whether that be prenatal care, or birth control, or an abortion.

Mandy closed her eyes for a moment. Nerves ricocheted through her body, but not because she thought she could be making the wrong decision. She was confident it was the right choice for her. One day she would cry tears of joy, not tears of sorrow. One day she would gleefully give up her body to create another, but that time wasn't now.

A breeze pushed in as the clinic door opened, fluttering the pages of the magazines on the table. Something told Mandy to glance up, but she almost couldn't believe who was there.

Isa pulled the strap of her purse back over her shoulder, it having slipped down when she came in the door, and she scanned the room. A light smile graced her face when her gaze connected with Mandy's, and a new sense of calm flooded over her.

"Don't you have finals or something?" she asked Isa as she got to the seat next to Mandy and pulled her into a side hug. The topic of Isa being there that day had never come up. Mandy knew how stressful Isa's school had been for her, and just being able to talk to Isa about it all was enough. Mandy had Isa's support—even though it was thousands of miles away—and that was enough to buoy her.

"I'm exactly where I need to be." Isa took Mandy's hand and squeezed it.

Mandy nodded, and rested her head on Isa's shoulder, inhaling the scent of Isa's coconut shampoo.

NAUSEA ROLLED AROUND IN MANDY'S STOMACH AS she slipped between the sheets of her own bed. Sick from the medicine she'd just been given, not from the decision she had followed through on. In that respect she felt relieved. Relieved and ready to puke. It was a strange combination.

"Just in case." Isa brought the garbage can from the bathroom and set it next to Mandy's bed like she knew exactly what Mandy was feeling—she always did.

"Thanks."

Isa placed a hand on Mandy's forehead. "You don't have chills or anything, right?"

Mandy shook her head.

"That's good." Isa glanced around. This was the first time she had been in Mandy's apartment. Was she thinking it was the first time Mandy's space didn't look like the inside spread of a home decorating catalog? Or was she noticing that there weren't any pictures of the two of them like there had been in her childhood bedroom? Or maybe she saw the photo of Mandy and Sophie at a pub in London, thinking how that should've been a picture of them. "I'll let you rest." Isa turned to leave, but Mandy grabbed her hand to stop her. Now that she was here, Mandy wasn't ready for her to go.

"Stay with me. Please. I don't want to be alone." It wasn't a lie. Although Mandy didn't regret what she did, she wasn't ready for the storm of emotions brewing inside her.

Isa was quiet, likely debating herself inside her head—weighing the pros and cons.

A cramp pulsated through Mandy's abdomen, and she gritted her teeth, trying not to show the pain on her face. It might've been selfish of her to ask Isa to stay, but she didn't want her to feel guilted into it.

"Just for a little while." Isa's voice was soft, and then she made her way around the footboard. The bed jostled as she lay on top of the covers.

Mandy carefully rolled over. "Thanks for being here today."

"What are friends for?" Why did Isa sound sad saying that?

"You'll have to thank Tally for letting you come for me." Mandy tried to chuckle, but it hurt too much.

"I don't need her permission," Isa retorted.

"I'm sorry. That's not what I—"

"No, I'm sorry. I shouldn't have snapped like that." Isa rolled over and met Mandy's gaze. "She doesn't know I'm here. She thinks I'm visiting Mamá and Abuela."

"Is everything okay?"

"It's fine. I just . . ." Isa let out a long breath. "She wouldn't understand is all. And I didn't want to fight about it."

It was then that Mandy really studied Isa—her cheekbones were more pronounced than Mandy remembered, and Isa looked as tired as Mandy felt. If things were different, Mandy would've asked Isa if she wanted to talk about it. A long time ago, Mandy wouldn't have even had to ask. But so much had happened between them that they each stayed quiet. Isa's thigh was so close to Mandy's that heat penetrated the layers of fabric that separated them. All Mandy wanted to do was reach out and touch Isa. Let their bodies connect in some small way. But the down blanket stopped her. Or it wasn't the blanket at all. How could they be this close and still feel so far apart?

Another cramp seized Mandy's stomach. Isa's fingers brushed against Mandy's head, the sensation lingering as she placed her hand there on Mandy's pillow. "You should rest."

But Mandy didn't want to sleep right then. She wanted to stay in this moment, staring at the turquoise stone in Isa's ring, feeling the tug of the mattress from the weight of Isa being there with her. If she tried, Mandy could forget about everything in the past and talk herself into believing this was just like before. When everything between them was perfect and wonderful. Before Europe, and Tally, and Theo. Because in a lot of ways it was, or it could be. No matter all of those things, she was still Mandy, and this was still her Isa.

Mandy thought about that night under the trampoline, and Grad Nite behind the gym, and all those times in the back of her car, and their first time—together. That seemed so long ago, and so much had changed, but somehow, they'd managed to find their way back here.

———

CHAPTER THIRTY-SIX

November 2015

THE WEDDING WAS ONLY a few months away and while there was still so much to do, Mandy stood in Isa's kitchen stirring a pot of . . . actually, she didn't know what it was exactly. She hadn't been paying attention when the job was turned over to her; she'd been thinking about flowers. But now wasn't the time to complain about the lack of ranunculus.

Now really wasn't the time to even be thinking about getting married. It just didn't seem right. Maybe they should postpone it. Let Abuela get better.

But no one was acting like Abuela *could* get better. The entire family had flown in for Thanksgiving thinking this would be Abuela's last. Mandy couldn't think like that. She had to be strong for Isa, for Sandy, for the whole family. And for herself. A world without Abuela would be like a world without Isa, and, well, she knew what that was like, and Mandy didn't want any part of it.

The Jiménez house had been full the last couple of days, so

it was strange that this morning only Mandy, Sandy, and Abuela were there. Isa had taken the family for a little sightseeing, but really Mandy thought it was to give Isa's mother and abuela a break. The lack of constant chatter seemed deafening—the only sound coming from the buzz of machines in Abuela's room, the rush of water racing through the pipes to the bathroom, and the noises from the coffee maker. They'd already gone through two pots before everyone left, but Mandy figured Sandy would enjoy a cup and some quiet when she got out of the shower. Hopefully there was still hot water for Sandy left in there.

Just as Mandy was making herself a cup of coffee, Sandy entered the kitchen wearing her bathrobe with a towel around her hair.

"It's as though you read my mind." Sandy took the mug Mandy handed her.

Mandy poured herself another. She knew better than to go looking for milk since that had been finished off earlier, so she added a little extra sugar. "I'll head to the store to grab some things whenever you're ready."

Sandy always wanted someone in earshot of Abuela, just in case, she said. But Abuela was still sleeping. Not a single alarm had gone off—unlike the time Abuela removed her heart monitor because it was making her itch, which caused quite the scene. "Oh, mija, I don't know what we would do without you." She pulled Mandy into a tight side hug.

"I have a list there"—Mandy pointed to the counter—"if you want to add anything." When she had talked to Edmund before Sandy got in the shower, there were already over a dozen things they were either out of or running low on. Mandy thought it would be better to get everything now—there was nothing worse than needing to go to the bathroom only to find you were out of toilet paper, an experience she herself had had in college.

Sandy took the list and sat at the dining room table. "We're already out of milk? There was an entire gallon in there."

Mandy shrugged. "I think Little Mateo had a few cupfuls." Little Mateo, not to be confused with Big Mateo (his cousin) or Tío Mateo (their uncle).

"Isn't he lactose intolerant?"

Mandy spun around, thinking of the repercussions that amount of milk could have on his digestive tract, and they were all headed to a place where bathrooms were not easily accessible.

"Wait, no. That's Matías."

There was a *beep, beep, beep*, and they both froze. It took Mandy a second to realize it was just the stove timer.

"You can turn that off and let it set now," Sandy said.

Mandy's heart kicked back on, and she did what Sandy mentioned, turning off the stove and leaving the large spoon across the top of the pot like Abuela used to always do. Mandy swallowed the thickness in her throat before sitting at the table with Sandy. She took a sip of her coffee—bitter but sweet, it would be much better with cream, but she wasn't going to say anything.

"I'm sorry there's no milk," Sandy said.

"It's fine. Really."

And then they were quiet. Mandy needed to call the venue and make sure they were able to get that runner she asked for, and there was still the issue with the flowers. They promised her ranunculus, and now for some reason, they had no idea what she was talking about.

"Everything okay?" Sandy asked. Had she said something, and Mandy missed it?

"I'm sorry?"

"I know what's going on here isn't easy, but you've seemed unsettled, even before all of this. I just wanted to make sure you're okay." Sandy laid a hand on top of Mandy's. "You have always been the strong one. Isa is so lucky to have you in her life."

Mandy wanted to laugh at that. Her, strong?

Sandy's gaze dipped to the table, and it was almost as though Mandy could see the weight of everything she was carrying press her deeper into her chair. "You've always done what was best. And I suppose I had always hoped things would've worked out—" Sandy was cut off by a knock at the door.

Mandy got up to answer it. It seemed a little early for a delivery, but flowers had been coming at semi-regular intervals since Abuela came home from the hospital. When Mandy opened the door, she had not expected to find who she did.

"I didn't know if you needed two percent or whole, so I just got both." Edmund stood on the threshold with arms full of grocery bags, and a few more at his feet. When she had spoken to him earlier, she had never in a million years thought he could be writing down the list she rambled off on the other end of the phone. Mandy would ramble on about a lot of things to him, and most of the time she knew he wasn't really listening because he'd ask her questions later about the very thing she'd already told him about. Tears threatened the backs of her eyes. She hadn't even insinuated needing him, but he just knew she needed help. Mandy wanted to tackle him right then and there and kiss him all over. Sometimes he could just be the sweetest.

"Come in. Come in." Mandy stepped aside instead to give Edmund ample space. He kissed her forehead as he passed—the citrusy scent of his new cologne sending tingles to her toes—and Mandy scooped up the remaining bags and closed the door.

"Right in here. That was so kind of you," Sandy was saying.

Edmund set all the bags on the floor in the kitchen. "I had no idea there were so many laundry soap choices. I hope I got the right one." It was true that Edmund sent his clothes out to be laundered, so Mandy couldn't help smiling at the image of him standing in that aisle—likely reading labels and looking for the most expensive one, because to Edmund, that meant it had to be the best, and he knew only the best would be good enough for Isa and her family.

Mandy never fully explained her relationship with Isa to Edmund, all the ups and downs of it. But when she made it clear that Isa was her person, Edmund didn't argue.

Sandy tightened her robe around her. "Whatever you got is perfect."

"I take it this goes in there?" Edmund held a carton of orange juice and motioned toward the fridge. He was going to help put groceries away too? Could she love this man any more in this moment? He didn't wait for a response; he just took the carton and a bag full of refrigerables that way.

"We've got this," Mandy told Sandy.

Sandy rested a hand on Mandy's arm and quietly said, "We just want you to be happy." She glanced at Edmund, then back, giving Mandy a tight-lipped smile before heading toward her room.

"Babe?" Edmund said, holding a bag of flour in one hand and at least four different bags of dried beans, peppers, and what was likely parsley—he'd probably thought it was cilantro—in the other. Edmund had done nice things for Mandy, but this had to be the nicest.

Mandy directed him to where things went while she emptied bags of her own. When she had finished, she came up behind Edmund and wrapped her arms around him.

"How bad did I mess up?" he asked as he spun around and held her back.

Those tears were there threatening again. "You did great."

THAT YEAR THANKSGIVING DINNER WASN'T SET ON A white tablecloth with her mother's fine china or freshly polished silver in Mom's formal dining room. It wasn't food prepared by some chef somewhere and brought into the house that morning, where a team of people set everything out before scurrying off to their next job, hoping to make it home for dinner themselves. Mandy wasn't wearing an uncomfortable dress and heels, and she didn't have to stand in front of the fireplace for their yearly family picture.

No. Thanksgiving was on picnic tables of varying sizes all spread out in the Jiménezes' backyard with mismatched table-cloths and paper plates. And even though Mom wore pressed slacks and a floral blouse, Mandy was in jeans and flats while cousins raced around pelting each other with roasted pumpkin seeds, and oranges from the tree. In other words, it was won-derful.

The weather was as perfect as anyone could ask for, with fluffy white clouds that sailed by overhead like giant white puffs of cotton candy against an azure backdrop. When Abuela was brought outside, the entire family cheered. She had been feeling much better the last couple of days, and Mandy hoped that meant the worst was behind them. Isa, however, wasn't convinced. She'd been called in to the hospital early that morning, so she didn't see Abuela's rosy cheeks or smiling face. But she would. Just as soon as Isa got there. It had been difficult for her to get any time off, seeing as she was in the middle of her residency. And if she had stayed on the East Coast for it, who knew if she would've been able to come home at all.

"Things happen for a reason," was what Mom told Mandy. Like that was the best explanation for why, after spending years in Boston, Isa decided to come home. But Mandy knew better. It wasn't fate, or some kind of magic that brought Isa back. This was simply where she was always meant to be. It had always been a part of her plan—the one she had written out and kept tucked inside the music box Abuela gave her for her eighth birthday. Deep down Mandy admitted it was why she'd chosen to go to college close by. Mandy had spread her wings and then had come home. A part of her had always expected Isa to find her way home to Mandy too.

"We should probably leave soon." Edmund squeezed Mandy's knee. It wouldn't be fair to say she was surprised he decided to stay with her instead of flying home to be with his family, but Mandy *was* surprised in the best way possible. He had also dressed down for the occasion, matching Mandy in jeans and a complementary colored polo shirt. It was what Abuela requested. "Nothing fussy, just familia," was what she had said.

But Mandy wasn't ready to leave her family for his. It wasn't that she didn't like them. It was just different. Their idea of

Thanksgiving was much more in line with Mom's—and when Edmund insisted on helping Mandy pick out the right dress for the occasion, she did not expect to come home with a $3,200 kelly-green, tea-length skirt made by a designer she still couldn't remember. (Sophie had squealed when Mandy had sent her a photo.) That was the way Edmund usually showed his love, but this, being here, was all she really needed. She placed her hand over his, and he smiled back at her and then glanced at his watch.

"I know," Mandy responded instead of asking for just a little more time. "I'll be right back." Mandy got up to greet her best friend, who had just emerged from the house. "Everything okay?" she asked Isa as Mandy wrapped her in a hug.

"Yeah, it was fine. They didn't really even *need* me but whatever. I'm starving."

"I can help make you a plate."

"Mamá's taking care of it." She hitched a thumb behind her as she scanned the backyard. "Abuela made it out after all." Why did she sound so surprised?

"Doesn't she look great?" Right now, Abuela sat with Tía Elisa, holding her hand and smiling.

"She does, but that doesn't mean she's getting better." Isa threaded her arm through Mandy's, linking them together, and pulled her closer.

"I know that's what you keep saying."

"Well, I *am* a doctor."

"One who delivers babies." Could she really know about what was going on with Abuela? She could be wrong, couldn't she? And Abuela could get better.

Isa nudged Mandy with her hip. "And I'm damn good at it too."

Mandy rested her head on Isa's shoulder. "I believe it." She had never seen Isa deliver a baby and probably never wanted to, but if there was one thing Mandy knew about Dr. Marisa Jiménez, it was that she was always the best at everything she put her mind to.

"Babe?" Edmund stood behind her, checking the time on his watch. "We should probably . . ."

Mandy nodded. She wasn't ready, but even in another five minutes or ten minutes or two hours that wouldn't change. "Call me if you need anything, okay? We're only going to be gone a couple of days, so just leave all of this and I'll help you clean it up when I get back."

"It's fine." The look on Isa's face said it was anything but, the way her brow wrinkled and the tightness in her mouth.

Mandy pulled her into a hug and never wanted to let go.

"The car is waiting." Edmund's voice was gentle. He had been so extra patient and understanding the last few weeks. They had made these plans with his family long before Abuela got sick, and it was so kind of his family to postpone their celebrations so Mandy and Edmund could stay in California for this one. She didn't even have to ask; Edmund just said his mom insisted.

"Let me just . . ." Mandy didn't finish though. She raced over to Abuela and bent down to hug her and give her a kiss on the cheek. Mandy couldn't leave without saying goodbye until next time. "Te amo mucho, Abuela." The backs of Mandy's eyes burned.

"Oh, mija. Te amo mucho también." Abuela took Mandy's hand. While she still understood English, Abuela spoke mostly in Spanish these days.

"Estaré en casa pronto, lo prometo."

Abuela smiled up at Mandy, her gaze shifting to something behind her and back again. "No debí haber metido la pata."

Mandy tipped her head to the side, trying to understand.

"Amanda," Edmund called. The look on his face was sympathetic, but they really needed to go; they had a plane to catch.

"Me tengo que ir. Te quiero, Abuela."

Abuela nodded but didn't let go of Mandy's hand. "Hay veces que incluso las ancianas cometen errores." She squeezed Mandy's hand tightly in hers. "Lo siento, mija. Perdóname." Abuela started to cry.

Mandy didn't know what to do, nor did she know what Abuela was going on about. She'd spoken so quickly; Mandy was still trying to process it. Maybe she wasn't doing as well as Mandy thought she was.

"Ven, Mamá. Vamos a entrar." Tía Elisa took Abuela's hands so Mandy could go.

Mandy's brows pulled together. "Maybe I should . . ."

"I've got her. It's okay. She's had a long day," Tía Elisa said.

Mandy gave her a quick hug and ran off toward Edmund. But as she sat in the back of the black sedan on her way to the airport huddled in Edmund's protective arms, Mandy couldn't get Abuela out of her head. She hadn't put her foot into anything that Mandy knew of. Nor had she ever been wrong. But the way she apologized and the tears, Mandy's chest tightened. She pulled out her phone and texted Isa.

MANDY: Please let me know that Abuela is okay.

A few moments later a response came in.

ISA: She's resting now. Probably all the excitement. Don't worry.

But Mandy couldn't not worry.

"Mom has the guesthouse all set up for us, and it should be nice and toasty when we get there." Edmund hugged her tighter into him. "They got five inches of snow today." He was trying to cheer her up—Mandy loved the snow and how it sparkled in the light.

"Wow. Tell her thank you," Mandy said automatically, unable to pull her thoughts from what had happened in the backyard. Something wasn't right. The last time Abuela was that serious was just before Mandy had left for Europe—alone. Her mouth went dry. Mandy needed to talk to Abuela, but she couldn't ask Edmund to turn around now, not after all he'd done for her. She just hoped Abuela would still be around when Mandy got back in a few days so she could talk to her.

CHAPTER THIRTY-SEVEN

January 2006

HER CLASSES HADN'T STARTED yet, but Mandy scheduled some time in the art lab. It had been three days since New Year's, and since then, Mandy had felt lighter. As though for the first time since being in Europe things might be okay. She hadn't completely forgiven herself for what she had done to Isa, but it was in the past. She couldn't change it. She just had to live with it. And living wasn't really something she had let herself do. Before, she was surviving at best, but Sophie was right, Mandy had been punishing herself, and she likely would for a long time, but for now . . . for now she was going to try.

A blank canvas sat in front of her along with three different paint colors. Black, white, and blue. With them she could make a hundred different shades. She didn't need all the colors of the rainbow to express the thing she had been feeling in her heart. And so today, without judgment, or an assignment, or anyone else's voice in her head, Mandy was going to try to paint what she felt. It seemed simple enough, but that's what made getting the first stroke onto the canvas so hard.

Just like painting, emotions weren't easy—and expressing them, especially recently, had been practically impossible. Mandy sucked in a long breath and then pushed it all out, ignoring the sour smell of paint that lingered. Ignoring the sound of cars that passed on the street outside. Ignoring the pounding of her own heart and absorbing the silence. Not long before now, the silence was what she was most afraid of, but she couldn't be afraid anymore. Being alone wasn't a punishment, it was a gift, and Mandy had been wasting it. She had been so afraid that if she got used to the silence it meant it would always be that way. She didn't want to accept that she would never hear certain things again—like pots and pans in the kitchen and cooking chorizo, or Isa's voice. Mandy feared accepting things meant she would have to be alone forever, but would that be the worst thing?

She had never, not once, stood solidly on her own two feet. There had always been someone to lean on until now. And while that seemed slightly terrifying, it was also empowering. Mandy could do this. She could prove to herself that she alone was good enough.

She picked up her brush and started to paint.

AS COMMON AS PUBS WERE IN LONDON, MANDY wasn't sure she would ever get used to going to them. It still felt so weird being able to walk up to the bar and order a drink with no questions asked. Mandy still had a couple of years before she would be able to do it back home. When she strolled up to the bar this time, she couldn't help feeling like she was doing something naughty.

"Pint of Guinness?" Mandy made it sound like a question even though it wasn't one.

Luckily the bartender, a middle-aged white man—who ironically looked like every bartender in every British movie Mandy had ever seen—didn't even blink an eye before picking up a glass and filling it. He didn't say anything as Mandy paid for the drink. Not tipping was also something that still felt strange, but Mandy had learned her lesson on that and collected all her change before heading back to the tables where her friends were.

That was another thing that was different now. Mandy had friends. Maybe because she was sticking around, or because she no longer scowled at everything and everyone, or maybe because Mandy had gotten attention from a couple of her professors already this semester based on a few of her early projects and her classmates had finally started talking to her—or maybe she was finally listening. Either way, they invited her to join them at the pub, and Mandy said yes.

This pub was one many of the nearby art students went to. Sophie had suggested several times in the past that Mandy meet her there, but she never did. So it was no surprise that Mandy found her there with some of her friends and they all joined together into one large group.

"Mandy," Finny shouted. His name was actually Nigel Montgomery O'Connell, but for some reason, no one ever called him that. "Wanna play?" He wiggled a dart at her.

"Sure, why not?" Mandy shrugged. She'd been saying yes a lot more recently, and so far, it'd been working out for her. "I have to warn you though. I've never played before."

"Like never, ever? Not one single time?" Finny asked.

Mandy shook her head. "Nope."

"You hear that?" Finny called. "I might actually win a game."

The table erupted into cheers.

Finny draped an arm over Mandy's shoulder. "We are going to become great friends." He was much taller than Mandy, with bright red hair he liked to wear in a Mohawk and extremely tight jeans.

"What if I'm a natural at this?" Mandy set her beer down on a high-top table and picked up the second set of darts.

"I'll lock you in my boot and claim victory anyway."

"You're that bad, huh?"

"Total shit."

Mandy took a sip of her drink. Guinness was one of the few beers she enjoyed. It had more flavor than many of the lighter ones. "Am I supposed to aim at any certain number?"

"If you can hit the board, you've already got a leg up on old Finny here." Rafe, another classmate and Finny's best friend, joined them. In looks, Rafe was Finny's opposite. Dark skin and hair—but they dressed similarly, in too-tight pants and the same loafers with no socks. Where Finny completed his look with a T-shirt, Rafe wore button-ups.

"Piss off," Finny said.

"And miss the show? Never," Rafe said. "I'll be chalker."

"He means keep score," Finny said to Mandy, and then turned back to Rafe. "We don't need you. So you can still piss off."

Rafe ignored him, set his beer on the table next to Mandy's, and proceeded to the small chalkboard on the wall not far from the dartboard. He was also shorter than Finny and closer to Mandy's height, forcing him to have to reach up just as she would've had to in order to scrawl both of their names across the board. Well, he wrote *Mandy* and *Knob* across the top—which Mandy had come to learn meant "dick," not the thing you turned to open a door, although they did have those in England too.

Finny went first. He stood at a line that had been marked on the wood floor, shook out his shoulders, and took aim, extending his arm back and forth a few times before he released the dart. "Sod it." The dart missed the board but not by much, anchoring itself into the wall next to the number twenty on the board.

"Brilliant." Rafe clapped and raised his beer before taking a drink.

"Wanker." Finny pretended he was about to throw a dart at Rafe, but of course he didn't. From the short time Mandy had gotten to know them, that was just how they were. They would tease each other and call each other names, but they were fiercely defensive if anyone else tried to do it. Finny took aim twice more, hitting the board—earning him thirty-two points. However that worked out, who knew. Darts was seemingly more complicated than Mandy had anticipated.

It was now her turn, and since she had never thrown a dart in her life, she wasn't sure how hard to throw it. Unfortunately, her first attempt never even hit the board—or the wall for that matter—it almost did though.

"Blimey. There's a chance for you, Finny boy," Rafe said, practically spitting out his beer in the process.

"Beginners get a do-over." Sophie pulled up a stool next to Rafe. "I've read it in the official rule book."

Mandy was pretty sure this was a lie, but Rafe fancied Sophie—Finny's words, not Mandy's—so it was no surprise Rafe responded with, "I think I've read that too." Followed by a wink.

"Whose side are you on?" Finny complained.

"Hers, obviously." Rafe tipped his head toward Sophie.

Finny retrieved the dart and gave it back to Mandy for her do-over. When she tried again, she threw it too hard, and it sank into the wall with a thud.

"I take that back. I'm with her." Rafe pointed to Mandy. "She's terrifying."

They all laughed, and Mandy threw her next two darts, earning her fifteen points.

About twenty minutes later—and with no end to the current match in sight since they were both shit—they abandoned the game to get more drinks.

"You're saying they don't have Jaffa Cakes in America?" Finny said. They had gotten on the discussion of the differences between Britain and the United States, and the conversation of course went straight to food.

"No, but we have Oreos." They were both a chocolaty snack—one a cookie, the other a cake the size of a cookie (or what the Brits called a biscuit). Although there was also some contention about that too, whether a Jaffa Cake was a cake or a cookie—but Mandy wasn't about to get into that. Both were chocolate, except one had fruity jelly and the other had cream in the middle. Mandy thought they were both delicious.

"Never heard of them. Must be tosh." Finny cracked a knowing smile. He was on team Britain Is Better, so even if he did know what Oreos were—which likely he did—he wasn't giving up that easy. "But on a more serious note, what do you miss the most?"

Mandy tapped her fingers on the dark wood bar top. "My family, mostly."

Finny rolled his eyes. "Of course you do. But like what else?"
This one was easy. "Mexican food."

"Now that's what I'm talking about. Tell me more." Finny was a total foodie. He loved to eat, and according to Rafe would drag him to the dodgiest places.

"My friend's grandmother would make the best pozole. It's basically this soup with meat and chilies and hominy, and then you put avocado and lime in it, and OMG, it's so good. And then she makes these tortillas and this salsa. Oh, and her enchiladas are amazing, and when corn is at its peak, she makes elote . . ." Mandy's mouth watered just thinking about it.

"So the ground beef tacos at Jose's don't cut it?" Finny kept a straight face for about two seconds before busting out laughing. It was pretty common knowledge that Britain was not the place for Mexican food, and the place he named was known to be *the* worst.

Mandy shook her head and laughed along with him, but what she didn't want to do for the first time just thinking about Isa or Abuela was cry.

The bartender nodded his head in their direction, and Mandy held up four fingers and called out, "Four pints." He acknowledged her with one sharp up and down of his head.

Mandy smiled to herself. Maybe she would actually be okay.

CHAPTER THIRTY-EIGHT

April 2019

THE PRE-WEDDING PHOTOS WERE a complete wash—no pun intended. The new location was dry, as opposed to the last location Mandy's parents had to retreat from, but when they all finally arrived, they had to immediately leave if they were going to make it in time for the ceremony. Now she was back in the limo—with Mom and Dad—but at least she was fully dressed at last. Well, mostly.

"It's zipped. Stop messing with it." Mandy swatted Mom's hands away. She had been tugging and twisting and fixing Mandy since she got in the car.

"This wouldn't have happened if you didn't have to get dressed alone. I knew it was a bad idea," Mom said.

"It's over, and I'm dressed now, so can we drop it, please?"

"There's still the issue of your shoes," Mom said.

"Honey," Dad cautioned, but Mom was not listening.

"I'm not wearing any shoes but the ones I have on, and that's final." Why couldn't Mom ever listen to Mandy?

"I'm just thinking about the future. When you look back at your pictures, I don't want you to be regretful."

"What pictures?" Mandy huffed. It was a low blow and not her mother's fault that they hadn't been able to take any, and poking the bear was never a good idea, but Mandy was already stressed enough. She didn't need to be thinking about how she would feel about her footwear choices on some hypothetical future date. At this rate, the entire day was doomed, and she wouldn't want any pictures to remember it at all.

"Don't get snippy with me. *I* wasn't late," Mom said.

Mandy bit her tongue. Arguing wouldn't change anything. It wouldn't fix anything either, so Mandy let it go.

"I think it's Amanda's day, and we need to respect her choices," Dad, always the voice of reason, chimed in.

"What's wrong with wanting it to be perfect?" Mom asked. "I'm not the bad guy."

"No one said you were," Dad said.

Mom wasn't the bad guy, but Mandy wanted someone to blame for everything that had gone wrong—because if not her mother, then who? Mandy had wanted this day to be perfect, because then it would mean her marriage would be perfect—or it would, at least, set her out on the right foot. If Mandy tried hard enough, maybe this time things would work out, unlike every other time in her life. Unlike the last time she was supposed to get married.

Mandy glanced down at her empty ring finger. It felt so strange taking it off to be soldered together with her new wedding band. She had gotten into such a habit of fiddling with it when she was anxious, and now, she had nothing to fiddle with. She didn't want to think it was the universe's way of saying to get used to it, but those intrusive thoughts were once again in her head.

"I spy, with my little eye, something blue," Dad said. It was a game they'd played in the car when she was little. The drive to Disneyland always seemed excruciatingly long, so Dad would come up with little games to occupy the time.

Mandy looked out the tinted window of the limo.

"Not that side," Dad said, then tipped his head forward to the windows opposite him—since he was sitting basically sideways along the length of the car.

Mandy leaned over Mom, and there it was. "The sky." While on one side of the limo it was still cloudy and gray, there on the other, it was all cloudless skies—a shade of cerulean that eased Mandy's racing heart.

"Clear skies ahead," Roger confirmed.

Maybe the venue had been spared. Mandy could text Candy and get an update—hell, Candy probably had already texted her twelve times by now—but instead, she decided to take a breath, lay her head in her mother's lap, breathing in the floral scent of Mom's signature perfume, and stare out the window.

Mom gently stroked Mandy's arm like she had done since Mandy was little. Was this the message the universe was sending her? That after darkness there was always light. That without rain there'd be no flowers. The world was full of opposites that balanced everything out. There were no absolutes. *Always* and *never* didn't actually exist; they were just words that people gave way too much power to.

Mandy glanced back to the gray side of the limo.

Nothing lasted forever.

Or was that the message?

If nothing lasted forever, was Mandy just fooling herself for believing it could?

By the time the limo pulled to the front of the venue, Mandy's nerves were all over the place, swinging from one extreme to the other. There would be moments she would convince herself it would all be okay, and then in another, worried her presence alone would burn everything to the ground. If she didn't find stability soon, she would likely get motion sickness. Back and forth. Back and forth.

Roger opened the limo door, and Mom was the first to get out.

"Mrs. Dean, you look fantastic," Candy gushed.

Roger's hand was there, and Mandy took it to help her out of the car—because at that moment she needed all the help she could get. Candy stood next to Mom, looking fantastic as always in a crisp pale-peach pantsuit, cell phone at the ready and her Bluetooth headset peeking out from her perfectly poofed Afro. Her always radiant dark brown skin somehow seemed even more radiant.

"Mandy." Candy put her hand to her chest. "Absolutely stunning." The confidence in Candy's voice gave Mandy the strength she needed to let go of Roger's hand and wrap Candy in a hug.

Candy pulled away, taking Mandy's hand. "Don't worry. Everything's under control." And there it was. The anchor Mandy needed. She almost started to cry right then and there, but instead took a deep breath. "The bridal suite is all set up, and guests should start arriving shortly, so let's get you inside before anyone sees you." She turned to Mom and Dad, who stood at the opened trunk of the limo. "My assistant, Austin, is on his way to help with all of this." Candy reached down and picked up Mandy's train, and just like that, she swept Mandy away.

As soon as they pushed through the doors, Mandy was caressed with the sweet smell of lemon cookies. This venue was Mandy's favorite. As soon they walked inside, she knew she wanted the wedding here. Mom would've called it *rustic* or *farmhouse*, but Mandy called it *homey*. There was something so comforting about its cozy nooks and warm color palette that made Mandy feel as though she were wrapped in a reassuring hug. And then there was the garden with its arched birch walkway and fragrant blooms, drenched in twinkle lights that made it feel like walking into a fairy tale.

Candy nudged Mandy's arm. "Emotion check. Where are we at?" This was something Candy introduced when they first started working together. A quick way to gauge from one to ten—one being completely at ease, to ten, a full-blown stress ball—how her clients were feeling.

Mandy took another deep breath. "I was a twelve, now I'm down to a six."

"She brought you shoes, didn't she?"

Mandy nodded, and Candy immediately started typing on her phone. "Austin will make sure we can't find them until tomorrow, or never, whichever you prefer." Candy had made the comment once that it wasn't the brides that made weddings stressful but their mothers—Mandy knew she'd made the right choice of wedding planner.

"Because I don't think you want to deal with my mother forever, tomorrow would be perfect."

"And that's why you are my favorite bride." Candy probably said that to all of her clients, but Mandy didn't care. "And here we are." Candy pushed open the door to the bridal suite. A chandelier hung in the center of the room, and along the far faux brick wall leaned a massive full-length mirror with a thick gold frame. A gold couch ran along another wall, and soft ivory chairs flanked a table with fresh flowers, fruit-infused water, lemon cookies, and a bottle of champagne. Sunlight filtered in from a large window that overlooked a small private garden.

Tranquil. And just what Mandy needed.

"We have a little time, so can I get you anything?" Candy asked.

Mandy stared out the window. There was a feeder, and hummingbirds swarmed around it—their wings going so fast they were just flashes of light. One would drink, then move aside, and another would take its place. It was like watching a choreographed dance. "I'm okay right now."

Candy checked her phone. "Good, 'cause we have incoming in three, two, one—" The door opened, and Mom, Dad, and Austin came inside juggling boxes and bags. Who knew getting married required so much stuff? There was Mandy's "survival kit," which was extra makeup as well as snacks, a Clorox pen, wet wipes, and whatever else she could possibly need. And a box with her bouquet and Mom and Dad's flowers too—a corsage and boutonniere. And then there was Mandy's outfit for when they exited the venue—because yes, she was doing the whole *leave-in-a-different-outfit-while-everyone-threw-biodegradable-confetti-at-them* thing. Then who knew what Mom brought with her, but it seemed like a lot.

"Oh, isn't this place just charming," Mom said. She also said it the day they toured the location, but Mandy wasn't going to mention that.

"Can I pour anyone a glass of champagne?" Austin offered. He was just as crisp and polished as Candy in a turquoise blazer and white pants—which actually made his fair ivory skin look not so pale, at least around the ankles.

"I shouldn't, but what the heck." Mom set her things down and headed his way.

Austin popped the cork like a professional sommelier, then poured a little in each glass, passing them around. The bubbles sparkled in the golden liquid.

"To a magical wedding day," Austin said and raised his glass.

Just as everyone took a sip, Candy's and Austin's phones buzzed simultaneously. They exchanged a glance, and Austin politely excused himself. Candy shook her head at Mandy in a *don't worry* sort of way. Before Mandy could ask, Dad cleared his throat.

"Candy, darling, can you help me with something out here?" Mom put her champagne glass down and headed to the door.

If Candy was surprised by this seemingly random and vague request, she didn't show it. "Of course."

A moment later they were gone and just Mandy and Dad were left.

"Before the day got away from us, I wanted a minute to talk to you alone." Dad wrung his hands together, and a crease ran across his forehead.

"Sure. What's going on?" Mandy hadn't really seen Dad this worked up before, but the sight didn't make her nervous, more like concerned. Dad was always the steady one. The practical one. So whatever this was, it had to be important.

"This is a big day for you, but it's a big day for me too." Did Dad have tears in his eyes? "I have to admit that my little girl is all grown up, and, well, that isn't an easy thing for a dad to say. To me, you'll always be my little girl who used to slide down the banister and would always try to hide in my luggage anytime I had a business trip. I know I haven't been the perfect dad, and I've been hard on you, and I haven't always been as supportive as I should've. But I wanted you to know how proud I am of the woman you've become." Dad's voice broke and a tear slipped down his cheek, making the backs of Mandy's eyes burn. He reached into the side pocket of one of the bags and handed Mandy a box. "I wanted you to have this. To remind you that no matter what, I love you and I'm always thinking of you." Inside was the most beautiful watch Mandy had ever seen—a gray pearlescent face with enough diamonds to make it sparkle but not so many that it was over-the-top. "Your mother wanted me to tell you, you don't have to wear it today—"

"No. I love it. It's perfect." Mandy clasped it onto her wrist. He had bought her a gift, one she was sure he went and picked out by himself, because it didn't look like anything Mom had ever gotten her. It wasn't the gift itself though, but the gesture that had Mandy's heart feeling so full. "Thank you, Daddy."

He pulled her into him, and her nose flooded with the smell of his cologne mixed with fabric softener. Mandy wanted to bottle up that scent and keep it with her forever. He squeezed her tight, and just like when she was little, she felt safe, and loved, and never wanted him to let go.

He kissed the top of her head. "I love you."

"I love you too."

CHAPTER THIRTY-NINE

January 2016

BLACK WAS MANDY'S FAVORITE color, but today she wished she were wearing anything but. Abuela had made it through Christmas, but before midnight struck on January 1, she was gone.

It seemed Thanksgiving was her last good day. After that, and by the time Mandy returned from her second Thanksgiving, Abuela slept most of the day and was more out of it than not. Mandy felt there was little she could offer in those days. When she wasn't working, she would spend her time at Isa's doing laundry or dishes or whatever needed to be done so that Sandy or Isa, when they had time off, could sit by Abuela's side. That's all Isa ever seemed to do those days, work and come home to be with Abuela. Mandy hardly ever saw her even when they were in the same house together. Family would come and go, and the phone never seemed to stop ringing.

Mandy hadn't been there when it happened. Around 11:30 p.m. on December 31, Abuela's heart stopped. Mandy's phone rang sometime shortly after, and when she saw it was Isa calling,

Mandy knew. She answered the phone, "I love you for real," and was answered by Isa's sobs. And together they cried like that until Sandy took the phone and told Mandy exactly what had happened.

After that, Isa's house felt empty.

Flowers and condolences poured in, and there were so many casseroles.

With all the planning that needed to take place, Mandy still hardly saw Isa. They hadn't had a second to be alone and cry while holding each other, and as selfish as it was, Mandy needed that.

Time itself didn't seem to know what to do with Abuela's absence either. It seemed to completely spin out of control or drag on for an eternity. That morning it was spinning, but Mandy was dragging. She was going through the motions—hair, makeup (waterproof mascara, of course), getting dressed, except she still needed shoes, and that was where Mandy was stuck.

If there was anyone in the world who loved Mandy just how she was, it was Abuela—and if she were still there, she would likely laugh at Mandy's selection of tennis shoes with her dress. But Abuela was gone. And there sat a pair of black heels, staring at Mandy as though saying, *You know you should pick us.* Yet Mandy hesitated.

Even the thought of sliding her feet into them felt wrong. Just as everything else felt wrong without Abuela. Mandy didn't know much about death or how or why things happened, but something told her 2016 was going to be the worst year of her life.

"Are you still not ready?" Edmund appeared at the doorway of the walk-in closet. "If we go now, I can maybe make it back in time for the two o'clock meeting."

A flush of heat raced through Mandy's body. Abuela was practically her own grandmother, and Edmund acted as though her funeral were some kind of inconvenience to him. How many times had she dropped everything for him? Done everything he'd ever asked of her? She had gotten used to the fact that he was phlegmatic, and how he could compartmentalize just about everything in his life, but this? Something inside of Mandy snapped. Although she'd never done anything like it before, she picked up a shoe and threw it at him, hitting him right in the chest before the shoe fell to the ground. "You don't have to go if you're too busy. I mean whatever will they do without you at the two o'clock meeting. That is *so* much more important than anything I'm going through today."

Edmund picked up the shoe—because of course he did. Nothing could be out of place in his perfect apartment. "You're upset."

"Damn right I'm fucking upset."

"Amanda." Edmund hated it when she swore. And like always, he was so damn calm when grief burned so fiercely through Mandy she didn't know what to do with it.

Mandy grabbed another shoe and chucked it at him, but this time he caught it. "Fuck you. Abuela is gone and all you can think about is work." All he could do was think about himself.

"She wasn't even your grandmother."

If those words were meant to sting, they did. "If that's what you think, then I don't even want you to come with me."

"You don't mean that. Plus, how would it look—"

"I don't care how it would fucking look." She grabbed another shoe, but this time she didn't throw it. She twisted it in her hands, and that for some reason seemed to make Edmund more upset, but he didn't say anything, his jaw tightening as he stood there staring at her like she was a child having a temper tantrum.

She glanced at his side of the closet—suit jackets hung from various shades of light to dark, ties on racks in color order. Everything was in place, and there seemed to be a place for everything. And then there was Mandy's side. She was lucky she could find anything the way her clothes pressed in on each other. Most of the time they came off the hanger wrinkled, and then there was a pile on the floor underneath. It was the only place in the entire apartment where she was allowed to do things her way. The only place that said she was there. Was that because Edmund could close the door? Was it because the only time he saw the mess was when he was in the closet himself? She ran her hand down the kelly-green dress she wore weeks ago. She looked amazing in it, but it was one of the most uncomfortable dresses she'd ever worn. What the hell was she doing? Mandy started to laugh—the ridiculousness of it all slamming into her like a bullet train. "What do you even like about me?"

"Let's not do this right now," Edmund tried to reason.

"Then when? When do we do this? After your meeting today? Or maybe we can do this right before the wedding? Or even better, on the honeymoon? Or when we have kids—that would be the perfect time to do this. Because you don't even need to answer. I already know there isn't anything you really like about me—the real me. This." She spread out her arms in front of her tornado-tangled clothes rack.

"Don't be absurd. I love you," Edmund said.

"Do you though? Do you really love *me*? Or do you love the idea of me." She looked back at the heel in her hand: black, plain,

boring, and completely not her. It was something he had selected, and she just went along with it. But she was tired of doing
that. "We both know you could have any girl you want, but you
chose me. Why?" But Mandy knew why. She made things easy.
She hid her mess in the closet and closed the door. She was
agreeable and wore uncomfortable shoes and dresses because it
made him happy. But was Mandy happy?

"That's right, I *chose* you. I. Choose. You." Edmund stepped
forward. Handsome, distinguished, successful Edmund in pressed
black slacks and just-out-of-the-package bright white shirt—
collar starched to perfection. Have him throw a jacket "lazily"
over his shoulder, and he would be on the cover of a magazine.
Mandy did love him—or maybe she was just as guilty of loving
the idea of him. When she looked at him, butterflies didn't
threaten to erupt from her stomach. And today, on arguably one
of the toughest days of her life, he wasn't the one she wanted to
wrap her arms around and hold on to.

She slipped on her tennis shoes and walked toward him, sliding the diamond off her finger. "We both know this was never
going to last." She placed the ring in his hand and left alone.

THE SERVICE WAS SET TO START AT 10:00 A.M., SO
when Mandy rolled in fifteen minutes later than that, she was
exactly on time—actually, she was a little early, but only just. No
Jiménez family event ever started exactly when it was supposed
to. There wasn't a chance to say hello before they were ushered
inside the church. The Jiménez family all sat up front, so Mandy
sat next to her parents.

Mom muttered, "Edmund?"

Mandy shook her head. She would have to explain to them later what happened, and she would have to move back into her room for a while.

Dad didn't say anything. He wrapped his arm around her, and she curled into his side like she did when she was little. Even though Mandy's life felt as if it were falling apart, there was always something comforting about Dad's embrace—it was like coming home no matter how old she was.

Once the service started, so did the tears. As soon as they turned on, there didn't seem to be a way to turn them off. Luckily each seat had been supplied with its own small package of tissues, and Dad shared his with Mandy and Mom.

Even as the pastor carried on about how Abuela was in a better place and how her soul was at peace, it didn't ease the ache in Mandy's heart. She couldn't understand how Abuela could be okay with never seeing any of them again, because Mandy wasn't okay with never seeing her. If anything, Mandy yearned to see her, talk to her, hug her one last time. Was it possible to love someone more now that they were gone?

And what did it say that Mandy didn't have those same feelings about Edmund? She would miss him, but not in the same way that Mandy missed Abuela. Was it because Edmund was still around? Was it because the universe had other plans for them—they weren't done in the way things were final for Abuela? Mandy already knew she would have to see him again to apologize for her earlier outburst. No matter how angry, and sad, and hurt she'd felt, it didn't excuse her behavior.

Tears streamed down Mandy's cheeks, and Dad squeezed her tighter as the lingering scent of frankincense tingled Mandy's nose. One day she would be sitting in the front row, and he would be the one who was gone, and one day it would be Mom. It wasn't fair. Why did anyone have to die at all? It felt like such a cruel joke to put people in your life to love just to take them away. What was the purpose of that?

"Consuela's granddaughter would like to say a few words," the pastor said.

Isa didn't move for a moment before she was nudged into action by Tía Maria. Isa slowly rose, made her way from the pew, and stood at the podium. The black dress she wore was new. Her hair was pulled back except for the little hairs that always framed her face and never did what she wanted. And unlike Mandy, Isa's eyes were not red and puffy—like she had no tears left to shed. Isa clenched the note cards in her hand, then looked out to all the people filling the pews. Her eyes locked with Mandy's, and Mandy gave her a reassuring nod saying, *You can do this*, without any words. But the look Isa returned said, *No, I can't.*

All Mandy wanted to do was race up there and hold Isa in her arms. But Tía Maria shuffled out from the pew and got to Isa before Mandy could even move. Tía Maria took the cards from Isa, who then returned to her seat, where Sandy wrapped her arms around her on one side and another tía slid over and did the same from the other.

"Marisa has prepared a few words that I will share with you," Tía Maria said. "Three months ago . . . Three months ago, my life changed.

"Three months ago, I started thinking about this very moment and what I would say, what I *could* say. I even started writing something down because I knew, when this moment came, I wouldn't be able to find the words.

"I thought, what could I tell you about my abuela that you don't already know? You know she had a giving heart . . . there wasn't anyone she wouldn't go out of her way to help. You know she was an amazing cook . . . if you had her pozole rojo, you can consider yourself family. You know she had a great sense of humor . . . even *she* thought she was hilarious. You know she was kind and caring and loving. You know she was persistent, and that she always thought her way was best. You know that she was stubborn, and that she also loved so fiercely. You know that Abuela was never one to care what other people thought of her.

"That is one thing I will not only remember but that I've always admired most about her.

"I can remember a time . . . I think I was nine or ten, and my best friend Mandy was sleeping over, and we had convinced Abuela we needed to make cookies. And if you knew Abuela, you knew sweets were her weakness. We had the flour, and sugar, and the butter, and everything mixed together when she realized we were out of chocolate chips. So what did she do? We all jumped into the car and went to the grocery store in our pajamas and slippers—even Abuela. People must have thought we looked ridiculous, but she didn't care. She wasn't going to let us down. We started those cookies, and we were going to finish them. And we marched through the store as she led the way.

"Abuela was always leading the way. She came to this country to give her children and her grandchildren a better life. She fought and sacrificed and has always been our biggest cheerleader.

"My first year in college, I called one night, miserable. There was nothing I wanted more than to come home, but Abuela made me realize that giving up wasn't an option. I had come too far to let go of my dreams. And look at me now.

"Well, look at her." Tía Maria gestured to Isa.

"Three months ago, my life changed. But today my world has changed forever.

"I miss you, Abuela. You helped prepare me for this world, but you never prepared me for a world without you." Tía Maria took the note cards and went back to her seat.

There were a lot of sniffles, and Mandy too had to wipe her eyes and nose once again. A few more family members came up, and a choir sang some songs. Everyone completely lost it at the photomontage of Abuela's life. And then it was over, and people started to make their way to the reception hall. Abuela was being flown to Mexico later that day to be buried in their family's plot.

As soon as Mandy walked into the reception hall, Isa grabbed her arm and led her through a side door and out into a small garden, where they were alone. She stopped just behind a tall rosebush where no one could see them and held Mandy's hands—one in each of her own.

"She told me," Isa said. "Abuela told me."

For a moment Mandy wasn't sure what Isa meant, but as her brown eyes that had been so dry before filled with tears, Mandy knew. The day on her porch, before Mandy left for Europe, before she told Isa she didn't want her to go anymore and broke both of their hearts.

"Why didn't you tell me?" A tear slid down Isa's cheek.

"What was I supposed to say? Abuela was right. I was being selfish. I couldn't ask you to give up everything for me."

"It was *my* choice. And I wanted to be with you." Isa squeezed Mandy's hands tighter. "I hated you for leaving me. I wasted years being mad at you. It wasn't fair. I should've known."

"And what would that have changed? Look at you." Mandy took her in, all of her—the sweep of her hair, the curve of her neck, the freckle on her left shoulder. "You are an amazing doctor. Your life, your mom and Abuela's lives, and all your patients' lives are better because of that. Keeping you from this would've only benefited me."

Tears spilled from Isa's eyes, each one racing to be the first to drip from her chin.

Mandy took a wrinkled tissue from her pocket and tried to catch them all. "I *am* sorry, but I don't regret it. You became a better person without me. Yes, it was the hardest thing I've ever had to do in my life, and I was miserable without you, but you would've been miserable if you missed your chance at this. This was who you were always meant to be. I can't regret it. I won't. Because when you really love someone, you don't stand in their way."

"It wasn't fair." Isa sobbed. "It just wasn't fair."

Mandy pulled Isa into her, and together they cried.

CHAPTER FORTY

June 1994

AS SOON AS DAD pulled away from the curb, leaving Mandy at Isa's with her brand-new bicycle, the pair of them were off.

"Be safe," Abuela yelled at them as they rode away.

Mandy had slept over at Isa's before, but this was the first time they both had their bicycles. Normally they would just take turns riding up and down the street, or sometimes one would roller-skate while the other rode the bike around the block, but they both always seemed to want to do one over the other, and agreeing wasn't always easy—neither was sharing. This time Mandy begged Dad to let her bring her bike with her, and since she would be spending a couple of days with Isa—so Mom could go with Dad on one of his business trips—Dad loaded her bike into his trunk and carted it over, along with a bag of stuffed animals and a couple of board games. He did draw the line at Mandy bringing her Game Boy, since that was also something they weren't always great about sharing.

Mandy had gotten the bike a couple of weeks ago at the

beginning of summer. It was a sky-blue beach cruiser with white fenders and white-wall tires, with a basket on the front. She had begged for a dog to go in that basket, just like Dorothy did in one of Mandy's favorite movies, but her parents adamantly said no. She did have a stuffed "Toto" that could ride along with her, however.

But today both Isa and Mandy had a bike, so this meant they would be able to ride a little farther than they had before. The wind whipped through Mandy's hair and the blue-and-white streamers on her handlebars as she picked her feet up off the pedals and hooted into the breeze.

"Mandy," Isa scolded. "Be careful." She echoed Abuela's sentiment.

Mandy had only lifted her feet, she didn't let go of the handlebars, but she had really wanted to learn how to ride like that. She'd see people on their bicycles at the beach, eating a burrito, or with their hands behind their heads instead of gripped onto the handles. It had to be something with balance, but Mandy hadn't figured it out. "Don't be such a worrywart." Mandy had heard the expression somewhere, and it stuck. "Come on. Try it. Just lift your feet."

Isa pressed her lips together—a look that said she was considering it.

"I did it and I'm all right."

Isa's lips shifted to one side, and then she pedaled a little faster and lifted her feet.

"Like this." Mandy raced past her and shot her legs out to each side.

Isa gained a little more speed and did just as Mandy had done. "It's like flying."

"Exactly," Mandy agreed.

At the end of the street, Isa took a left instead of a right back toward the house. They were still technically in the neighborhood, so they weren't breaking any rules.

"Maybe Abuela will let us get Slurpees," Isa called back to Mandy.

She caught up with Isa and rode next to her. "Do you think she would let us go all the way there? My dad left some money we could use."

"Let's go ask," Isa said. "Follow me." She took the lead, making a right at the next corner and taking Mandy down an alleyway.

"Where are you going?" Mandy asked.

"It's a shortcut." Isa slowed down and turned between two houses, onto an even smaller pathway. It wasn't very wide, there was just enough room for two bicycles side by side, but Mandy stayed behind Isa in case anyone else was on the path coming toward them. There were old wooden fences on either side covered in colorful spray paint. Some of the words written there weren't nice, but there were pretty hearts and crowns too. Did the people who lived in the houses on the other side of these fences put them there? Or did they even know it was there at all? If Mandy lived in one of the houses, she reasoned, she would paint a whole picture on the alley side of the fence so people would have something pretty to look at as they passed and not just old wood.

The path crossed another street and continued on the other side. Isa never hesitated, so Mandy was sure she knew where she was going even if Mandy was completely lost. When the path opened again, they were in a park with lots of trees. The ground was much more uneven here, and Mandy had to hold on to her handlebars much tighter. This was not the usual park where Abuela would take them to play. Once the trees started to thin out, the pavement under Mandy's tires got smoother too. Yes, it was a much bigger park than they'd been to before. There was a big sandbox, and volleyball nets, and people running along the path that Isa and Mandy were on. Whether this was any shorter a way back to Isa's, Mandy was beginning to have her doubts, but the ride was lovely, and now that the pavement was even, they could pick up their speed a little more.

The path meandered, and Mandy slowed down to watch a little boy and likely his father flying a kite. Or at least there was an attempt being made. The man held the kite in the air, and the little boy would take off running. The kite would catch air for a moment before crashing into the ground. The man would holler, "Let out some string," but the boy wouldn't listen, and they repeated this a couple of times.

Before Mandy realized, Isa had gotten a good distance ahead of her, so Mandy had to pedal harder. Isa dipped down, following a small hill in the pathway, and by the time Mandy caught up, she had been going much too fast, and then the small hill had her gaining even more speed. Panicking, Mandy tried to slow down but jerked her handlebars to the side, and her front tire made contact with something, stopping the bike but not Mandy. She flew over the handlebars and crashed right into the ground—her chin sliding along the pavement. For a moment she couldn't move—stomach to the ground, the heat coming in through her cotton lilac shirt.

"Are you okay?" Isa had turned around and come back, but Mandy just lay there, hands splayed on both sides of her. Isa grabbed under Mandy's arm and helped lift her off the ground. The buckle of her helmet dug into Mandy's neck, and when she

went to slide it forward, her hand came back slick and red. "Oh
no. Your chin," Isa said, then looked around as though searching
for something.

Mandy lifted the hem of her shirt and wiped her bloody chin
with it, leaving a smear of crimson across the soft fabric. "What
did I hit?" Her voice seemed calm considering her accident.

"I don't know," Isa said. "Let's go get you cleaned up though."

Mandy nodded. Her chin and the palms of her hands burned,
and there were people starting to look at them. She felt so fool-
ish. Thankfully none of the kids from school were around. She
could only imagine them making fun of her for not being able to
ride a bike.

One of the white rubber grips on Mandy's handlebars was
scratched, and the basket on the front was loose, but all Mandy
wanted to do was get out of there.

Isa had been right, they were a lot closer to her house than
Mandy realized, and two turns later they were back on Isa's
street. Blood trickled down Mandy's chin and soaked into the
neck of her shirt. Mandy followed Isa, and when she bumped up
onto the driveway, Abuela stood as though she had been waiting
there for their return. As soon as she made eye contact with
Mandy, the tears that had been missing before flooded Mandy's
eyes. Mandy jumped off her bike, leaving it on the lawn, and ran
up to Abuela, wrapping her arms around her waist.

"Oh, mija. What happened?" Abuela rubbed Mandy's back.

Isa told the story of what had happened while Mandy sobbed.
She had seemingly been fine before, but something about seeing
Abuela tore down Mandy's walls. Abuela held Mandy's hand as
she walked them all inside and sat Mandy down at the dining
room table.

Abuela calmly brushed Mandy's hair behind her ears and carefully cleaned her chin. There was a decent-sized scratch there, but it bled like it was a deep gash. "It's going to be okay," Abuela said, and Mandy believed her. Abuela always had a way of making Mandy feel safe and loved.

Isa got Mandy a new shirt, and once a bandage was affixed to Mandy's chin, Abuela got each of the girls an Otter Pop and went to work getting the stains out of Mandy's blood-soaked top.

Once the washing machine was running, Abuela came into the living room. "I think we are done with bikes for today."

Mandy didn't argue, and neither did Isa.

"We could play a game," Isa suggested, but Mandy wasn't really in the mood.

"Why don't we build a fort and watch a movie." Abuela un-folded the colorful afghan that lay across the back of the couch. This made Mandy smile. She loved to build blanket forts, but Mom hated when she did it at home.

"I'll get the blankets from the hall closet." Isa raced off.

Abuela handed one side of the afghan to Mandy. "You tuck this in over there, and I'll put it up on this side."

The three of them worked in harmony, bringing in chairs from the dining room and setting up a massive blanket fort around the TV. Once the structure was done, Mandy and Isa loaded it with pillows while Abuela made popcorn on the stove.

Soon the three of them were snuggled in while the opening credits of the movie they had picked out started to play.

"Can we sleep in here tonight?" Isa asked.

"I think that is a fine idea," Abuela answered.

Mandy laid her head on Abuela's lap, and Abuela smoothed Mandy's hair as they all watched the movie together.

CHAPTER FORTY-ONE

March 2018

THE PAINT ON MANDY'S canvas blended together like an intricately woven fabric. As soon as the last box had been brought into her new apartment, this was the first room she set up. It wasn't as large as the space in the back of her parents' garage, but the lighting was great—especially in the early morning—and she could come in there whenever her art called to her, which was often those days.

As she mixed the colors on her palette to create the perfect shade, Mandy couldn't help thinking about the first time she painted.

Although she had been eyeing the painting center for days, she hesitated to give it a try. Mandy never painted at home. Mom thought it was too messy. But that day her teacher encouraged her to give it a try, so Mandy carefully put on her apron and stood in front of the ashy white paper. All sorts of colors were lined up under the large blank page, and Mandy immediately knew what she wanted to paint.

She started at the top with red and created a big arch that began at the bottom of the left edge and went all the way to the bottom right. But she used a little too much, so it was now dripping down. Mandy quickly rinsed the brush to put on the orange, but she didn't get all the red out, and then when she smeared the orange paint across the page, the colors melded together, leaving only a little that was just red at the top and a little just orange.

It was awful. She tried to use more orange, but that made it too thick. Mandy was no good at this at all. And when she got to yellow, she just made it all worse. Rainbows were seven perfect colors, but hers all kind of blended from one to the next. Tears began to well up in her eyes.

"Wow, that's beautiful," a small voice said behind her.

Mandy turned to find a girl she hadn't seen before in her class standing there with her teacher.

"Mandy, this is Marisa, she's new to our class."

"Hi," Marisa said, then dipped her chin to her chest, where she had on a rainbow T-shirt with a unicorn.

"I love your shirt," Mandy said. "I have a stuffed unicorn that my dad brought home for me after one of his trips. He works a lot and so he's not always home, and he always gets me a present and once he got me a unicorn that looks just like that." Mandy pointed to Marisa's shirt.

Marisa glanced up and smiled.

"Do you want to paint with me? You could make the unicorn and well . . . I could try to make the rainbow?" Mandy glanced at the empty easel next to her.

"I won't be as good as you are," Marisa said.

"I'll leave you two girls to it." Their teacher walked away.

Mandy's cheeks got hot. It was a really bad rainbow. "I can start over—"

"No!" Marisa's voice got loud. "It's perfect. How did you make the paint do that?"

Mandy glanced at her painting and back to Marisa. "You like it?"

"I think it's the most beautiful painting I've ever seen. It looks like a real rainbow."

Mandy's chest swelled.

"You are a very talented artist," Marisa said.

"I can show you," Mandy said and held out a clean brush.

Marisa grabbed the apron hanging off the empty easel, tied it on, and took the brush from Mandy. "You can call me Isa if you want."

"Are you almost ready?" Isa stuck her head into Mandy's painting room, bringing her back to her current art project.

"Yeah, just let me clean up real quick."

NO ONE EVER MENTIONED HOW MUCH OF ONE'S ADULT life was spent at the grocery store. And there weren't usually many different grocery stores, it was usually just one. The same one that was closest to home, even if it didn't have exactly everything you needed, and there was a much better store just a few miles farther away, but that seemed too far most of the time. Okay, all of the time. So week after week, you've done the same thing, and walked up and down the same aisle, picking out the same items. There was nothing particularly spectacular or glamorous about the grocery store. It was just a necessity.

The only nice thing about being in the grocery store that day was that Isa was there with Mandy. Ever since Isa had opened up her own practice, Mandy hardly got to see her. But it wouldn't be like that forever. Once it was established, and all the kinks worked out, it meant Isa would have more time. It meant Isa could set her own terms and treat her patients the way she wanted. No more answering to a misogynistic boss who thought he knew better. It meant Isa wouldn't be as stressed, which, in turn, meant less stress for Mandy too.

As soon as Isa had gotten back from Mexico, they moved in together. A two-bedroom not far from the hospital Isa had been working at or from Mandy's job at the marketing firm. It wasn't anything fancy, but it suited them fine, with just enough room for Mandy's parents and Sandy to come for dinner every now and then.

Later that evening would be one of those occasions—hence the need to go to the grocery store to pick up a few things.

Isa pushed the cart while Mandy picked items off the shelves from here and there. It was nice not having to be the one to maneuver that thing, even if the store was less crowded than Mandy's usual shopping day. Without fail Mandy always seemed to get the cart with the broken wheel—were they all broken? So instead of turning, she'd have to slide it over and pivot it whichever way she wanted to go. But by some miracle, Isa found what had to be the only cart in the store with four working wheels, and effortlessly steered the thing from place to place. There had to be a way to mark it so Mandy could find it next time she came back on her own.

"You know, this would be easier if you brought the list," Isa said as she stood next to Mandy and studied the cereal options.

Mandy had slowly been working her way through them, from one end of the aisle to the other. Today she selected something called Peeps cereal—it had marshmallows and probably more sugar than a can of soda, but at least if her morning coffee didn't wake her up, the sugar rush would. Isa, on the other hand, liked her usual box of Honey Nut Chex—which was right there on the bottom row, but Mandy liked making Isa search for it.

"I have the list. Right here." Mandy tapped her temple. That was another reason she likely had to go to the store so often. The list she kept on the refrigerator—the one that conveniently had *Shopping List* scrawled at the top in bold, black letters—somehow never seemed to end up in her purse when she went to the store, which inevitably led to her forgetting something and having to make multiple trips.

"Well, it's a good thing I brought this." Isa reached into the pocket of her oversized sweatpants and pulled the slip of paper out. For the last few weeks Isa had been wearing them everywhere when they went out. She said they were comfortable, and Mandy couldn't argue with that. And while they were a far cry from Isa's "work uniform"—slacks, a blouse, and usually some kind of small heel—Mandy also could admit that Isa looked adorable in them. But Isa looked adorable in everything.

"Why do you have to be so reasonable?" Mandy shook her head at Isa.

"For the same reason you're not." Isa leaned in and kissed Mandy.

While Isa was gone, they'd spent every moment on the phone, and then upon her return, it just made sense to try again. But to be fair, there wasn't much trying involved. Mandy and Isa always fit together. She was still the cheese to Mandy's macaroni. Not that things were always perfect. They weren't. And sometimes they fought. Like when Isa would forget to text if she was running late. Or when Mandy would leave painted fingerprints on the soap dispenser in the kitchen. And there was the inevitable argument from time to time about what to eat, but there was nothing they couldn't get over. They always worked things out.

"I don't understand why we can't just make spaghetti," Mandy said as she plucked lasagna noodles from the shelf.

"Because we always make spaghetti." Isa studied the label on a jar of sauce. "Where's your sense of adventure?"

"You do know you're going to be eating this too. So if we mess it up—"

"If we mess it up, we'll run down the street and get tacos from Miquel."

Another good thing about their apartment was it introduced them to Miquel's Taco Cart—arguably the best tacos in Southern California. There was no doubt they reminded both Isa and Mandy of Abuela.

"Or we can get tacos to begin with. Or just make spaghetti," Mandy said.

Isa gave Mandy a look that said, *You're being ridiculous* and *I love you so much*, as she placed three different sauces into the cart. "Now for the garlic bread."

Mandy led the way to the bakery, where once again Isa had to consider all their options before choosing a French loaf and asking the bakery attendant to slice it in half for them. If Mandy had gone to the store herself, it would have taken a quarter the amount of time, but as annoyed as she was about the debate between French baguette or sourdough loaf, she liked being there with Isa. Today she wasn't just another woman alone at the store, she was a part of something more.

"We need bananas for the bananas Foster," Isa said.

"Wait. Since when are we making bananas Foster?" Mandy asked. "I'm not sure we should do anything with fire after the Thanksgiving incident last year." It seemed innocent enough, the package had come with strings to help lift the turkey out of the pan once it came out of the oven, but when Mandy had gone to take the bird out, one of those strings hit the heating coil at the bottom and *whoosh*. She'd never seen anything catch fire so quickly.

"It'll be fine," Isa assured her. "I got a special torch thingy."

"Well, if you have a thingy, I'm sure it'll be great."

Isa gave Mandy the very-funny look, and Mandy laughed at her own joke.

Luckily the produce section was right near the bakery, so there was a chance they could still get out of there before all their refrigerables spoiled.

"How about these?" Mandy held up a bunch of six bananas.

"No, the best ones are underneath." Isa bent down and started pawing through the boxes of bananas that hadn't already been set out. At this rate, they might be there all day.

Mandy put her bunch back.

"Check the list to make sure we got everything." Isa's hand appeared, a slip of paper clenched in it, and Mandy took it from her.

If they were going to remember the list, next time they should also bring a pen to check items off as they went along. As she visually marked off each thing, Mandy did have to admit that bringing the list was a lot more helpful than leaving it stuck to the refrigerator at home. "As soon as you pick out the best bananas the store has to offer, we're done." Mandy turned toward Isa, who still hadn't gotten up from the floor, but she was no longer searching through bananas. Isa was staring up at Mandy on one knee, holding a small box in her hand. Mandy's heart raced.

"I've been thinking a lot about how I was going to do this," Isa started. "I wanted it to be special because you're so special to me. And I wanted it to be memorable. But if I did it somewhere unique, you'd only think about this moment if you were there. And that's why I decided to do it here. So every time you come to the grocery store, you remember just how much I love you, and how even when we aren't together, I'm always thinking about you." Isa's beautiful brown eyes filled with tears. "Amanda Dean, will you marry me?"

CHAPTER FORTY-TWO

April 2019

THIS WAS IT.

Mandy stood staring at herself in the full-length mirror. She shouldn't recognize the girl standing there without black yoga pants—an activity she didn't actually partake in—or paint on her cheek and under her nails, wearing a formal white dress. But for some reason she *did* know that girl. Her hair might have been swept up in elegant curls and her fingernails may have been painted all the same shade of pale pink, but it was still her. She was even a little glad her mother talked her into a veil. It was simple and easy to put on and take off, but it did complete the look. But best of all, it actually made her feel like a bride—not just a girl in a pretty dress.

Everything that had gone wrong that day didn't seem as important right then. Standing there, looking into the eyes of the girl in the mirror, Mandy felt invincible. Today she was going to marry her very best friend in the entire world. The person who made her complete. Mandy had spent the entire day worrying about anything and everything that could go wrong, that she hadn't taken a moment to consider everything that could go right.

Today was just the first day of the rest of her life.

No matter what went right or wrong, in the end, it didn't really matter. All that did matter was that her future was starting, and it was one she was excited for.

Mandy did not wear the heels her mother wanted her to wear. They had somehow mysteriously vanished somewhere between the car and her dressing room. She would have to thank Candy and Austin for that later. Not that she could see the Chucks from under her gown, but she knew they were there. She wouldn't slip and fall in them, and she was comfortable. No pinched toes.

Like Mandy, Isa had kept her attire for the day a secret, so she would likely tower over Mandy in her own high heels, but Mandy couldn't have cared less. Isa could walk down the aisle in a potato sack and Mandy would still think she was the most beautiful girl in the world.

Soft, romantic music from the string quartet they had hired played in the distance as their guests arrived. While it meant that they would be starting any minute now, Mandy breathed easily.

Mom and Dad had gone out to make sure everything was going okay, and to help greet their guests, so Mandy took the moment of quiet to gather her thoughts.

A soft knock on the door, and Candy poked her head in. "Ready?"

Mandy gave herself one final look in the mirror, and then without hesitation replied, "Absolutely."

The guests were already standing at attention when Mandy exited the main building on Dad's arm and headed through the tunnel of twinkling lights hung among the trees. He wasn't giving her away. Because Mandy was her own person, who made her own decisions. She didn't need his permission or even his blessing—though she had both—but she still wanted him to walk her in. It was still the dream leftover from childhood that she didn't want to let go of.

As Mandy and Dad came around the last aisle of chairs, she got her first view of Isa. Mandy's breathing stopped, and everything around her faded, leaving only one person. Isa was stunning! She wore a simple off-white dress that curved with the shape of her body, and a rhinestone belt. Her dark hair was swept up to one side and held back with a rhinestone clip, and like Mandy, she had a simple veil that tucked in under her curls in the back. But really, the one thing that made Mandy's heart pound louder than the thunder that had come with the rain earlier that day was Isa's smile and the way she looked at Mandy. A look Mandy knew with her whole being.

Mandy couldn't focus on any of her guests as she passed them, although she was sure Sophie, Nikki, Grace, and every member of the Jiménez family was there. All she could see was Isa.

This was really it. And Mandy could hardly wait a second longer.

She hadn't been to many weddings, but standing up there listening to their officiant speak of love and faith and commitment, Mandy was sure this was the best wedding of all time. Her hands were steady in Isa's as they stared into each other's eyes ready to finally exchange their vows. When they had decided they were going to each write something, Mandy knew exactly what it would be, and today she would finally get to share those words with the person she loved more than anything.

"Isa, today here in front of our friends and family, I'm ready to say, 'I do.' A sentence of two small words and three simple letters. But there is nothing small or simple about their meaning. 'I do' isn't only about today or taking each other at our best. It's *I do* plan to stick by you when times are hard. *I do* promise to try not to hurt you, and if that happens, I'll do whatever I can to fix it. *I do* want a forever with you even if I don't know what the future holds for us. *I do* love you, and *I do* accept your love in return. I don't want to live in a world without you, so today I say two small words and three simple letters, and that is 'I do' to us doing all the things together forever."

Isa wiped her eyes with a special handkerchief she had attached to her wrist so she couldn't drop it. "How am I supposed to follow that?" she said, and it earned her a hearty chuckle from everyone. She cleared her throat. "Mandy. Amanda. Darling. Sweetheart. Love. Babe. The absolute truest love of my life. I have so many names for you, and after today I get to add wife. I've dreamed of this day since the moment I first confessed my love for you under a trampoline. It's taken us a long time to get here, and for a while I didn't think it was ever going to happen, but love is stronger and more stubborn than even me. Through everything we've been through, all our ups and downs, it's also the one thing I never stopped doing—loving you. So today, here, in front of all our family and friends, there's nothing I want more than for you to be my wife, and to spend the rest of my life with you."

Mandy couldn't resist leaning in and kissing Isa.

"It's not that time yet," their officiant scolded, and everyone laughed, but it was worth it.

They exchanged rings, and one of Isa's cousins sang a love song, and they got to kiss—during the right part—and then they were finally married.

After that, the rest of the night seemed to go by in a blink of an eye. Pictures. Food. Dancing. Cake. And so much kissing. It was Mandy's favorite part when everyone would clink their glasses, and Mandy and Isa got to kiss. Mandy never wanted to stop kissing Isa.

Hours that felt like only moments later, Mandy and Isa sat hand in hand in the back of a limousine on their way to the airport. Everything Mandy had been worried about didn't make any difference in the long run. No one noticed the different fish. All the pictures were taken and then some. No one got too drunk and puked on the dance floor. Mandy got to say hello to every single person there. If anything, it all happened a little too fast.

"I think we can officially say that was the best wedding ever." Mandy squeezed Isa's hand.

"Without a doubt." Isa picked confetti out of Mandy's hair. "You were right about these shoes." Isa crossed one leg over the other, showing off her own pair of Chucks. Mandy had been so surprised when Isa picked up the hem of her dress earlier in the night to reveal them. "I don't think I'm ever wearing heels again."

"Is it too early to start saying, 'I told you so'?"

"Yes."

Mandy kissed Isa on the cheek. "Okay, I won't tell you."

Then it was quiet except for the gentle thrum of the tires.

With Isa pressed into Mandy's side, everything was finally perfect.

MANDY SAT IN AN OVERSTUFFED LEATHER CHAIR, SIP-ping her coffee and staring at the large painting of flamenco dancers that hung over the couch—the skirts on their colorful dresses spread out like wings. Less than twenty-four hours ago Mandy wore a dress that now was likely being cleaned and pre-served along with Isa's, per Mom's request. It was less than twenty-four hours ago that Mandy sat alone in a hotel room with nothing but her thoughts crashing inside her head like a fork stuck in the garbage disposal. But this morning, Mandy's head was clear, and her chest was light. Her coffee was rich and sweet and extra hot like she preferred.

"Awake already?" Isa rubbed the sleep from her eyes as she came out from the bedroom.

"I was just thinking." Mandy set her coffee on the table so Isa could climb onto her lap.

Isa rested her head on Mandy's shoulder. "It was awesome, wasn't it."

"The best day ever," Mandy said. "I'm not sure how we'll ever top it."

Isa kissed Mandy's neck. "We can always try."

Mandy pulled Isa in tighter, her warm breath on Mandy's neck, the smell of Isa's coconut shampoo filling her senses as she continued to stare at the painting. The artist used such precision in the dancers' faces, they almost looked alive. They seemed content in their action—just like Mandy was in that moment.

"I wish Abuela could've been there," Isa said.

Mandy kissed the top of Isa's head. "I think she was."

"Yeah?"

"Yeah, I do. I mean, did anything ever happen that she didn't know about?"

Isa laughed. "No. You're right. She's probably why it didn't rain. She was up there like, 'Oh, no. Not on my granddaughter's special day.'"

"That sounds like her all right."

Isa let out a soft breath and snuggled in tighter next to Mandy.

"I love you for real," Mandy said.

"I love you for real back."

EPILOGUE

———

*Amanda Dean
is still in love.*

ACKNOWLEDGMENTS

First, I'd like to thank you, the reader, for taking the time to read this book. There are many out there and you chose to spend your time with these characters—that in and of itself means more to me than you will ever know. If you would be so inclined, I'd be honored if you would consider leaving a review—that's the best way to help other readers find this book, and it's so helpful to authors. Now I've also heard a rumor that for every review you leave an author, a fairy gets their wings. I don't know if that's true or not but just in case, it's probably a good idea.

When I set out to write this book, I had no intentions of doing anything with it aside from writing it for myself, so I really should thank my agent, Eva Scalzo, who insisted I send it her way, otherwise we wouldn't be here today. I couldn't have asked for a better champion.

And as far as champions go, my editor, Esi Sogah—thank you so much for loving Mandy just as much as I do. I don't know if it was her love for peanut butter and pickles that won you over or her messy life and dislike of kale, but no matter what it was, I'm so glad you saw something in her.

A writer is only as good as the writers they surround themselves with, and I'm lucky to have so many amazing writers in my corner. Maurine Trich, thanks for your early insight on these pages. All the Rosebud Authors and #TeamEva authors, y'all make my heart sing. I will forever be grateful to those of you who checked in and helped me through this process. My girl Kelly Colby—XOXO to you.

I also want to give a special shout-out to Autumn. Your willingness to help and your creative ideas kept me going when things started weighing me down. Your keen eye really came through in the final hour.

To my besties in the group chat—Jenny Caswell, Heidi Arbogast, Beth Shaver, and Jodi Cornell. Thanks for being you and for always loving me unconditionally. Everyone should have women like you in their lives. Enrique, mil gracias, for double- and triple-checking my Spanish for me.

Last and definitely not least, a gigantic thank-you to my family. Jim, Orion, and Cyrus, thanks for being my cheerleaders. I love you all so much.

Many people are a part of the publication process, so I would be remiss if I didn't give a big thank-you to Colleen Reinhart, Susanna Gentili, Lyris Bach, Angelina Krahn, Leah Marsh, Liz Gluck, Sareer Khader, Genni Eccles, Christine Legon, Elisha Katz, and Tina Joell. While many of you work behind the scenes, your efforts do not go unnoticed or unappreciated. I couldn't have asked for a better team of people to get this story into the world.

This "Seemingly Impossible" book is in the world because of all of you.

XOXO
Ann

Keep reading for a preview of Ann Rose's next novel!

PEPPER

70 Days Until the Store Closes

ONE OF THE BEST things about having my soul eternally tethered to a seasonal holiday store was that I could eat anything I wanted, and it didn't matter in the slightest. The bag of Skittles crinkled as I reached deep into my pocket and grabbed a couple before popping an orange one in my mouth.

"Pepper! Why does Molly get to work the prosthetic and mask counter today and I'm on general cleanup?" Caleb, one of the other The Dead of Night employees, whined.

Listening to employee complaints, however, was definitely on the list of cons for this position, but it was better than the complaining I had to endure before I got stuck here—at least these complaints weren't directed toward me—so it also wasn't terrible.

Today would be the first day the store opened to the public, and instead of being excited to share the best holiday ever, the chaos had already begun. Some people would likely argue that Christmas mornings were the best—but I'd disagree. On Christmas once the morning is over, everything kind of settles down.

Whereas with Halloween the anticipation rose from the moment you opened your eyes—waiting for the first glimmer of darkness that lasted well into the night. And today was just the first day to get ready for it. And that meant the first day in a long many I got to exist at all. "Well, what did Dewy say?" I popped a few more Skittles into my mouth—breakfast of champions.

"They said I have to do general cleanup."

"So then—"

"Can't you do something about it?"

This was the common misconception that came with being the Keeper of the store. All the staff instinctively recognized me as upper management, but I really didn't have any say in scheduling—I didn't have much say in anything at all. "Look, I know it seems like you got the short end of the stick, but what if I told you we're getting a huge shipment today and someone is going to have to count and tag every scab, scar, and wart that comes into the place." Being Keeper, however, did mean I knew everything about the store. Everything.

Caleb glanced at Molly—dressed as an angel, wings and all—sitting on a stool behind the glass case of fake blood and vampire teeth. "General cleanup sounds amazing."

"I agree." I winked. "A few for the road?" I offered him some Skittles, and he opened his hand while I poured a pile inside.

"Taste the rainbow," he said as he shoved them all in his face, straightened his giant clown bow tie, and scampered away.

Wearing costumes was highly encouraged, but even pieces of costumes with the signature The Dead of Night polo and khakis were preferred to nothing Halloween-related at all.

Caleb grabbed a broom and started sweeping. He was a good kid. Even if he didn't remember me. He'd been tentative the first day he walked into the Intro to Theater class I'd taught at Clover Creek High School, but that didn't last long. There were those kids whose only knowledge of "theater" was a bucket of popcorn and a reclining chair, but when they got on a real stage—even the small one we had in the classroom—they bloomed right before your eyes. That was Caleb. That was also five years ago. My stomach clenched.

That's the toughest part of this job—remembering people and things about them when you're nothing but a stranger to them. There were always the awkward moments when you "knew" something they didn't think you should. But it's especially hard when you want to celebrate their accomplishments with them.

Like, Dewy—standing there behind the register dressed as a scarecrow—had been the manager of this store for the past three years. They weren't the kind of person who trusted easily, so it took them a couple of weeks to open up. Last year they confided in me that they and their partner were looking to adopt—they hadn't told anyone about it but me. I'd been dying to know what's happened on that front since then—if anything at all— but there's no way I could just straight up ask. How could I possibly know something so personal when we haven't ever "met" before? And from experience they weren't one to share personal things with people they didn't know. So I would have to take my time with them.

Then there were people like Molly who were new to the store, but not new to the town—so while she had no idea who I was, I remembered that last year her hair was blonde, not the fiery red it was today, and that she had the most obnoxious boyfriend— who made quite the scene in the store last year. Did she finally see what the rest of us did in him? There's no ring on her finger so that was a good sign. But did she ever register for cosmetology school like she had wanted?

These were the questions swirling around in my mind as everyone prepared the store for its first customers of the year. A whole year had passed since I'd seen any of them or the sky.

Looking back at how it all went down, I couldn't help but wonder if the woman who duped me into this got the life she wanted or what took place exactly when she passed it on to me. That's one thing they don't mention in the rules—the after. So even if I did break this curse, what would happen to me? To the people who knew me before? How would they reconcile the time I've been away? Did I even want to subject them to that even if it were somehow possible?

Perhaps they were all better off. One less thing to worry themselves about. I was fine before; just as I was fine now. Maybe even better in some ways. I dumped a handful of Skittles into my mouth, the mixture of flavors dancing across my tongue.

"What do you think, boss?" Dewy came up from behind, rubbing their hand over their head. Last year their hair had been in twisted locs; this year it was cut short and colored teal blue.

"Not your boss." I shook my head, and Dewy laughed. "Still waiting on more teen costumes but they never decide until the last minute anyway, so I think we're in pretty good shape."

"Prosthetics are looking a little thin." They gestured toward Molly.

"Shipment should be here before noon."

"Corporate said you were good." They adjusted their nametag with the title Store Manager clearly written across the top. My nametag had no title, just my name—Pepper White—not that it mattered. "I'm glad to have you around this year. It'll be nice to have the extra hands for once. New corporate initiative, is it?"

"Yep." My throat was a little thick—probably from all the Skittles. "So what's your story? Do you have any special Halloween plans this year?" Like taking a little one out for their first Halloween? It took everything in me from not grabbing their arm and jumping to find out if there was any news.

The corner of Dewy's lip tugged upward. Was that a good thing? Were they thinking about that first costume? "That's real kind of you to ask, but I know you have more important things to do than chit-chat with me." They tipped their head toward some boxes that still needed to be unpacked. "We should get back to it."

"Sure," I said, but they were already walking away.

My watch chimed. It was almost opening time for us, which meant the entire town would also be opening up soon.

Everything—as chaotic as it seemed—was running on schedule. Shelves stocked, costumes hung, and the décor this year was excellent if I did say so myself. That was the really cool thing about The Dead of Night. It wasn't just a store; it was like an attraction of its own. People who walked through the doors were always in awe of the decor—even the employees who walked through the door gaped at the design but never asked any questions on how it got there. Plus, it was nice that I didn't have to put in all the manual labor to make it happen, unlike the weeks and weeks of work when I'd been in charge of the town's annual haunted house—magic was cool like that. Too bad I didn't really have any of it of my own.

Everyone was busy as I made my way through the back of the shop, grabbed my sweater from over one of the office chairs, and exited for the first time in 294 days.

The chilly fall breeze pushed my hair into my face as I stepped out the back door of the store. It always took me a moment to orient myself. Clover Creek wasn't a big town, but I never knew exactly where the store had set up shop for the year until leaving for the first time. A line of trees and wooden fence separated me from the back side of the town bank. To my left was Glazed & Confused and to the right across what had to be Apple Street was Queenie's Burgers. Meaning we were in the old pharmacy. Did they relocate? Or did Dr. Fisher finally decide to retire?

Regardless I was on the edge of downtown, so I wouldn't have to take out the "company car." Having the option was great even if I did hate driving it.

Another gust of wind sent the sugary scent from early-morning apple fritters swirling around me, and I raised my arms allowing the breeze to lift my magenta cardigan like wings. People probably thought being cursed was all bad, but one upside was that whenever I did finally get to go outside it was always fall. My favorite season. The time for pumpkin everything, and hayrides around Baker's Farm, and hot apple cider. The time for colorful sweaters and boots and scarfs. There was just something special about fall. Like dormant magic woke this time of year and it felt like anything was possible. Because for me, at least, it was.

Bing.

Bong.

Bing . . .

The clock started to ring. Time for me to get going. I only had seventy days to live my best life and there wasn't anything that was going to stop me.

ANN ROSE is a typical Taurus—loyal but stubborn, which means being an author is perfect. While asking the private group chat for ideas on what to include in this bio, Ann was reminded that some of her greatest qualities are her awesome best friends from high school—a fact she couldn't argue with. She loves dark chocolate, sarcasm, her family, tacos, and her cats—obviously not in that order. Ann also writes young adult novels under the pen name A. M. Rose.

VISIT ANN ROSE ONLINE

AnnRoseAuthor.com

𝕏 AnnMRose

◎ ⑥ ♪ Totally_Anntastic

Ready to find
your next great read?

Let us help.

Visit prh.com/nextread

Penguin
Random
House